MW01008398

Lark and the Loon

September 2021

To my dear friend Kate ~
Life is quite the journey – so glad our friendship is a part of it!

Lots of love,

Rhiannon [illegible]

Lark and the Loon

Rhiannon Gelston

E. L. Marker
Salt Lake City

Published by E. L. Marker, an imprint of WiDo Publishing

WiDo Publishing
Salt Lake City, Utah
widopublishing.com

Copyright © 2020 by Rhiannon Gelston

All rights reserved. No part of this book may be reproduced or transmitted in any form or by any means, electronic or mechanical, including photocopying, recording, or by any information storage and retrieval system without the written consent of the publisher.

This book is a work of fiction. Names, characters, places, organizations and incidents either are products of the author's imagination or are used fictitiously. Any resemblance to actual persons, living or dead, events or organizations is entirely coincidental.

SCARLET BEGONIAS
Words and Music by ROBERT HUNTER and JERRY GARCIA
© 1974 (Renewed) ICE NINE PUBLISHING CO., INC.
All Rights Administered by WC MUSIC CORP
All Rights Reserved
Used By Permission of ALFRED MUSIC

Cover design by Steven Novak
Book design by Marny K. Parkin

ISBN 978-1-947966-25-3

For the loves in my life . . .

and for love.

Author's Note

LARK AND THE LOON IS MOSTLY A MEMOIR, WITH A little whimsicality thrown in for good measure. The result is a coming-of-age story that blends the genre of memoir with elements of transcendental fiction. I used elements of transcendental fiction to allow the reader to travel within this true-life journey of both raw and real moments while also offering the freedom to step in and out of the memoir, reflect on lessons learned, and add energy, imagination, and innocence that only a child can bring to an experience. The vicarious memories and the characters in these memories are based on my family, people we have met, and true events as I remember them.

People always ask me and my husband how we are able to stay calm surrounded by our large and energetic tribe of kiddos. The answer, quite simply, is perspective. We went through a tough time and came out on the other end with an awareness. This awareness allows for a total appreciation for life and the magic of the moment. I would love to share this perspective with others so they are also able to embrace the gift of knowledge it has brought us. Lark has taught me to reach for the stars and hopefully will inspire the reader to do the same.

Chapter 1

Lark

"Free to be you and me."

—Marlo Thomas

BEEP. BEEP. BEEP. LARK SLOWLY OPENED HIS EYES. HE was in completely different surroundings once again. BEEP. BEEP. June was no longer here, and Lark was no longer there. Things were no longer red. They were mostly white with hints of vanilla and yellow, with bright lights and people. He looked quickly around and realized he must be in a hospital room: a small room with babies in metal cribs surrounded by beeping machines. Sitting in a chair right in front of him, yet totally oblivious to his sudden presence, was his mother. She looked so tired. She looked more tired than Lark had ever seen her before. Her hair was wild and unbrushed, and deep blue and purple circles cast a shadow under her big brown eyes.

Mommy was singing "You Are My Sunshine" softly in a choked-up whisper, colorless, salty tears streaming down her face, and somehow, Lark was here to see it. He was here to hear it. He was here to see and to hear but mostly here to feel. That was what the adventure was all about.

Lark didn't start out adventurous. He started out impulsive yet hesitant, imaginative yet rigid. Adventure was something he had learned how to do, over time. It was a choice, and like anything else, it took practice. Sometimes it was hard. Sometimes it was easy. No matter what, he found it always seemed to be the right choice if he managed to get out of his own way.

To do that, Lark needed to let go and just go with the flow, and in doing so, he was able to become his true self. Some people spent their entire lives running from themselves, so afraid they would finally catch up with themselves and be forced to have a good, long, hard look at who they were and where they came from and where they were going. Forced to look at who they were becoming.

Lark had done just that; he caught up with himself. He had that good, long, hard look within, and once he did, he realized he didn't need to look forward and backward so much; he found he needed to look within. With a glance to the side every now and then, he could see all around him. He could become.

Lark learned all this by the time he was ten.

Lark was lucky he learned all of that at such a young age. It wasn't easy. Sometimes life threw crazy, upside-down twists and turns at Lark. Lark learned when it was necessary to throw his hands up and let those twists of fate, on the proverbial roller coaster of life, carry him down the rickety track ahead in a rush of adrenaline and smiles.

Sometimes it was hard to enjoy the ride. Sometimes that roller coaster carried him away in a sea of tears until he folded up in sorrow with a heart so heavy that he felt like it could no longer be contained within his small chest. A heart so heavy he was sure it would make him sink, like an anchor, to the bottom of that sea of sorrow with no hope in sight of rising back up to the surface again. Yet somehow, he would; he would rise. One way or another, he would rise up.

That was choosing adventure. Adventure made him feel.

Chapter 2

Gramps

"Life is a verb."

—Charlotte Perkins Gilman

GRAMPS WAS VERY THIN AND VERY TALL. HE USED TO BE taller, but he stood a little bit hunched over these days. He had white hair that stood straight up out of his head as if he had his finger in an electric socket at all times. He had a long mustache too, but this was always perfectly groomed, not a hair out of place. Sometimes he would put some wax in it and turn the hairs up at the ends so the curls matched the permanent, mischievous smirk on his face. Sometimes he let Lark's little sisters braid it or put glitter in it, and he'd unapologetically wear it like that all day. He had been known to dye it green on St. Patrick's Day or pink for Valentine's Day. Gramps always had some sort of sweets hidden in his pocket; he always had a kind word or bit of good advice for those who needed it; and he always had a twinkle in his eye.

People often said Lark looked like Gramps, but Lark couldn't quite see it. Lark was anything but tall; in fact, he was one of the smallest kids in his class.

He did have unruly hair like Gramps. No matter what he did, it stood up in every direction, and it was white—but a blonde white. He was a towhead, even more so in the summer months. Perhaps they did have the same eyes if he looked really hard at Gramps' eyes.

Sometimes it was hard to find the eyes behind the memories. Gramps had lines of memories all over that smiling face. He had lines like the waves rolling in, notable especially next to his eyes, where the remnants of endless smiles lingered. These wrinkles served an important purpose as permanent reminders of both good and hard times lived. There was the depth of a blue ocean next to those lines, overflowing with memories from somewhere so very far away and yet so close and near.

Yes, that was the comment Lark heard the most: that he had the same smiling, blue eyes with that same twinkle.

There was something else that was also similar between Gramps and Lark, but this other thing wasn't as obvious or tangible. It was a similarity on the inside, not on the outside where people could see it. People recognized this similarity nevertheless, even though they couldn't quite put their finger on it. Gramps and Lark were kindred spirits. There was no denying that.

On the morning of Lark's tenth birthday, Gramps turned to him and pulled him up on his knee. "Boy-o, it's time we had a chat," he said, smiling down at little Lark.

"Okay, Gramps, what do you want to chat about?" said Lark enthusiastically.

"Well, now that you are ten, Lark, it is time I let you in on a little secret." Gramps paused for a second, and as he did, he got a far-off look as if he was trying to locate something faded and fuzzy. Lark sat on his knee, looking up at his grandfather in quiet anticipation.

"This is a secret that was passed on to me from my grandfather when I was ten, and now it is my turn to pass it on to you."

Lark tried to imagine Gramps as a ten-year-old boy. His mind started to wander, as it often did, until Gramps spoke again and brought him back to the present.

"Lark, you are special. I mean, of course you are. Because you are you and you are mine, and I am yours, and we belong to this sweet earth and the heaven above, but you are also another kind of special. Not everyone has this other kind of *special* that you have. In fact, few people have it. It is a gift."

Lark wiggled on Gramps' knee with feelings of both excitement and a bit of apprehension, but he knew, coming from Gramps, this was something he would want to hear.

"You are special because you are one of the Wise Ones, just like me."

"What do you mean, Gramps?" said Lark with skepticism in his voice that couldn't quite be disguised, despite respecting his grandfather probably more than any other person he knew.

"Well, I'll tell you Lark. The Wise Ones are simply that: they are wise. They are born that way. And they keep getting better over time. So, you, your special self, arrived here even more special and wiser than me, if you can believe that is possible."

Gramps gave Lark a wink, and with that Lark didn't know if he was winking at the absurdity of the conversation or his lack of self-deprecating humor.

"You were born with knowledge. Most people are born with a completely blank slate. They learn as they go, and that forms who they are, but you and I, we were born with special information already on the inside. We were born with the ability to discover, or recover, this information through very special and unique connections. When you become connected with others, Lark, you will become connected with yourself. Yes, Lark, you are wise and absolutely special."

Lark tried to comprehend but felt rather confused. He did not feel wise at all.

"Have you ever felt like you were just a little bit different from other kids?"

Lark nodded his head hesitantly. Gramps and his words resonated with him. They touched a part of him deep inside.

"What . . . what exactly is this knowledge? I'm not sure I was born with any special knowledge. I don't know much of anything different from anyone else my age. Are you sure I am *special,* Gramps?"

"Yes, Lark, I am sure of it. When you learn to listen to your heart, you will know it, too. You must choose it, though. You must choose this adventure. You will be given the gift of experiences and with that will come the gift of knowledge. You will become wise. You will *become.*"

Lark gave Gramps another worried look. Gramps looked deep into Lark's eyes with a reassuring smile.

"Don't worry, sweet boy, you will understand and then you will know. You will cherish this and live an extraordinary life. You are going to change the world. The *world,* Lark."

Lark sat there on his grandfather's knee, his head spinning as he tried to process everything.

"What am I supposed to do?"

"You will know when it is time, Lark. It is just the way it has always been, but now you know things are different. So, you are different than before."

Lark felt as if he was having déjà vu, as if some truth he had once known had been revealed to him once again. Gramps was truly just verbalizing what Lark already knew in his heart, and this shifted life in some way. This intangible concept stuffed deep inside his soul became a bit clearer.

"When you know, you know," said Gramps with that infamous smirk. The twinkle in his eye shone so brightly that Lark had to look away for a second, like the reflex one has when accidentally getting a glimpse of the noonday sun. Gramps' crazy words somehow made sense. Everything was the same but different. Lark had knowledge he didn't know he had; knowledge he still couldn't access, but he now knew it was there. Gramps was right; things were suddenly feeling very different.

"Lark, your pancakes are ready! Come and get it, birthday boy!" his mother called out from the distant kitchen.

Time stood still for a second, as it has a way of doing at times. It skipped a beat and then just moved along again. Back to reality. Pancakes. Birthday. Gramps gave Lark a little hug and a little wink. For a moment, Lark wondered if Gramps had been making all of this up, but the second he thought it, Gramps gave him a knowing nod, and Lark knew he meant what he had said.

"Let's go eat some of those flapjacks, boy-o."

Lark gently hopped down from Gramps' knee, and Gramps, looking like an elderly giraffe, graceful and gangly all at the same time, raced Lark down the long hallway.

Chapter 3

The Gift

"Love the life you live. Live the life you love."

—Bob Marley

THE REST OF LARK'S BIRTHDAY WAS WONDERFUL. He almost forgot about his chat with Gramps that morning as he was swept away in the festivities of the day. He did carry this newfound knowledge with him, quietly tucked away deep inside. Somehow things seemed crisper now, more vivid. He couldn't quite explain it beyond that.

He would have a birthday party with his friends tomorrow, but today was for his family: aunts, uncles, and cousins came over to celebrate with Lark. His mom and dad were there, along with his four little sisters, and, of course, Gramps. They grilled hot dogs and hamburgers, played games, and sang "Happy Birthday" in their loud and out-of-tune voices that the whole family had been gifted with, none of them caring how off-key they sounded, perhaps because they were *all* off-key; but it was mostly because nobody had time to worry about things like that, especially on such a happy occasion.

Ten. Ten was a big deal. There were lots of comments about double digits and people slapping him "high tens." He felt grown up in some ways and like such a little kid in other ways; it was a funny feeling. Mostly, he didn't really feel any different than he had the day before. Birthdays are funny like that.

There was a little fear inside of him of taking one step farther away from childhood and one step closer to adulthood; a little fear of letting go of something familiar as he moved toward something else, something unknown. Even if you know in your heart it is going to be great, change is a challenge.

The challenge lay within the unknown, but according to Gramps, therein lay the adventure. Even the past, or at least the perception of the past, could morph and change with different experiences and different insights. So really, it was just the now that was known. Lark was starting to grasp this concept on the heels of Gramps' talk. *Choose adventure.* With this slow-seeping realization, this birthday suddenly felt bigger to Lark than a single day in time.

After cake and ice cream, it was time for gifts. There were brightly colored boxes and bags, and he tore through them one after another with excitement and smiles and reminders of saying thank you before he moved on to the next, even though he was just about to say thank you and didn't need the reminder, *Mommy.* Lark was her little boy, and even though he was the ripe old age of ten, she was going to remind him anyway. In reality, he didn't mind.

With wrapping paper flying in a blur, he opened his gifts. Lark got a remote-controlled truck and a whole bunch of books, including one that said it was book about everything. He got art supplies and a new nerf gun with glow-in-the-dark darts and a flag football set. He got camping supplies and a headlamp. He got new clothes. He got a new lacrosse stick and a kit to build his very own robot and some other cool things a ten-year-old boy would covet. When he had opened all his gifts, surrounded by piles of shredded wrappings and ribbons, he looked around and felt happy. He felt loved. No, he *knew* he was loved, and it felt great. Maybe he was becoming more aware, perhaps even becoming a bit wise, after all.

There were times every now and then, without rhyme or reason, that Lark wouldn't want to let on that he was happy. He would hold in his joy and try not to show his true feelings. It was scary when he didn't know where his emotions would take him, even if they were "good" emotions. Lark liked to be in control. He worried if he showed others his feelings, if he let on that he was bursting with some *wild* emotion like happiness, or fear, or whatever it might be, he would be left vulnerable; he would relinquish control. That was scary to Lark.

It was just a small percentage of time that Lark was afraid to show his emotions, not all of the time. Nevertheless, at this moment Lark was bursting with happiness, and he wasn't hiding it. He had a big smile on his face, and there was no denying his exuding joy.

After the presents, Lark and his sister Sophie played with his remote-controlled truck as his littlest sister, Bliss, tried to catch it while it zoomed by her feet. The twins, Gwynnie and Maisy, clapped in delight, and they all laughed at the impromptu cat-and-mouse chase on the living room rug between Bliss and the truck. Gramps walked over, his glitter-filled mustache catching the light.

"Lark, there is one more gift," he stated with a grin. He pulled a small gold box out of his pocket.

Lark jumped to his feet and ran to Gramps' side, delighted by this unexpected, late addition, as it is always so fun to get one more present after you think you have finished. Lark held out his hand, and Gramps placed the small box delicately into his waiting palm.

Lark looked at it for a moment, admiring the sparkling gold wrapping and trying to soak in this moment because he had been too excited to remember to do that with his gifts earlier. He wanted to make this moment last. He grabbed the side of the wrapping and carefully pried it open from beneath the tape holding it to the box. Lark slowly lifted the lid and peered inside.

It was a stone. He reached in and picked it up to have a good look. It was smooth, almost feeling like velvet in his fingers. It was sort of white, sort of blue, sort of silver, depending on which way he held it and how it caught the light. It was so iridescent in nature that he couldn't help holding it up to his eye, half thinking he'd be able to see through it to something hidden at its center if he looked hard enough. He was right about that, but he didn't know it yet.

"Cool, Gramps!" Lark exclaimed, turning the stone over and over again in his small hand. "What kind of stone is it, Gramps?

Where'd ya get it?" Gramps' eyes sparkled as he looked over at his first grandson, and a tear quickly ran down his face before he had a chance to wipe it away.

"What's wrong, Gramps?" yelled Maisy, never missing a beat, from across the room.

All eyes turned expectantly to Gramps with concern and puzzlement.

"That's my lucky stone, Lark. It's special, just like you."

Silence. Crickets. If Gramps thought he could just leave it at that and not acknowledge the tear, he was wrong.

"Um, how so, Dad?" asked Lark's mom, lightening the mood with her question, the same smirk on her face that Gramps had handed down to her. She also had that same sparkle in her eye, though her eyes were a deep, earthy, chocolate brown.

Lark didn't understand what was going on with Gramps and his tear, but Lark didn't always understand feelings, so he wasn't too worried about it. But why was Gramps crying and Mom smiling? Lark usually got in trouble if he smiled when someone was crying.

Gramps quickly looked over at his daughter, returned the smirk, and gave her a wink before looking back over at Lark. "Well, you see, I have had that stone ever since I was a boy your age, Lark. In fact, I got it from my granddaddy when I turned ten. I kind of believe it had magical powers . . . no, I believe it *has* magical powers . . . when you really need them."

Lark continued to turn the stone over in his fingers, more of a subconscious, nervous movement than a conscious, deliberate one. He was brought back to the conversation with Gramps earlier in the day, and he knew that this stone was probably beyond special.

"But why would that make you cry, Gramps?" Gwynnie blurted out.

The twins never let a moment go by without a comment. Gramps gave her a smile and motioned for her to come sit on his lap. She ran over and jumped up on his waiting knee. Within seconds, Maisy landed on the other knee, and they both looked expectantly up at their grandfather, each twin making a twirl at the ends of his sparkling mustache. Gramps paused a moment before he spoke again.

"Well, my little loves, that's a good question. I'm glad you saw that tear; yes, indeed, people cry, young and old, and it's important to do so sometimes, necessary, even. There are happy tears just as there are sad tears and nostalgic tears and scared tears and mad tears, and all of these can also be tears of love. That one tear may have actually had a little of each of these, but mostly love. I'm not quite sure where it came from, to tell you the truth." Gramps switched his gaze from Gwynnie and Maisy over to Lark as he continued. "It's just that I am so proud of our young man here, Lark. I'm so proud of each and every one of you. Lark turning ten is just one of those monumental occasions that makes me reflect. It reminds me how lucky I am, like that lucky stone reminds me. Seeing Lark holding it brought me back to the day my granddaddy gave it to me, and it feels like yesterday. I still miss my granddaddy, so maybe there was a little of missing him in that tear too, along with everyone else I miss that can't be here."

And they all knew who else he was talking about, but the twins again felt the need to state the obvious and in unison yelled, "Gran!" as if they just won a round of charades, and the mention of her name out loud brought tears to everyone's eyes.

"Yes, sweet girls, I miss Gran, too. We all do, but I know she is smiling down on us, and she is up there with my granddaddy and your old dog Coleman and so many other angels, but let's see, where were we? Oh yes, the day I got that stone on my tenth birthday; the whole world lay before me with its endless possibilities. Life goes on, and knowledge is gained, but innocence can be lost, and when it's lost, we may never get it back. The trick is to learn these lessons and, somehow, hold onto some of the innocence, still believe in the magic. That's the trick." He again had a far-off look on his face as if he had gone somewhere else, even though his body remained there in the room with Gwynnie and Maisy on his knees.

Most people in the room now looked puzzled, but they hung on to each word because everyone knew Gramps was wise.

"I can hardly wait to see all the amazing things you will all do in your lives, and at the same moment, I don't want moments like this to end; they are just so beautiful to an old man like me. I love you all so."

Gwynnie and Maisy both shook their heads up and down. Even though they didn't say a word to each other, the twinnies shrugged their shoulders simultaneously in their unspoken twinnie way, and that was that.

Gwynnie and Maisy hopped off and started a game of keep-the-balloon-up-in-the-air, and everyone joined in with glee. Lark buried the stone deep in his pocket just before he punched the green balloon up toward the ceiling, saving it from touching the floor in the nick of time.

Chapter 4

Time

"Put your hand on a hot stove for a minute, and it seems like an hour. Sit with a pretty girl for an hour, and it seems like a minute. That's relativity."

—Albert Einstein

LARK HAD JUST TURNED TEN. THAT IS VERY YOUNG IN the big picture of life. Lark wouldn't know many of the important lessons he was to learn, and rich insights he would gain, until he was ten years old and a day. Today he hadn't been on his adventures quite yet. Today was still his tenth birthday, and he felt like he had been on this big earth for quite some time, although truthfully there was much life to be lived, patiently waiting ahead.

To his wise old gramps, it felt like Lark had just arrived. Heck, some days it felt as if Gramps himself had just arrived. On most days, Gramps felt twenty-two inside, not seventy-two.

He would be forced to recognize the discrepancy in that fifty-year difference shortly after awakening each morning. He would slowly open his eyes and take a drowsy moment to happily and thankfully realize that he was here for another day. He would awake feeling as light as a feather on the soft mattress, but in a comforting, grounded sort of way as he was nestled under the warm, thick quilt his sweet wife, God bless her soul, had made for their bed many moons ago. Then the reality would set in as he slowly turned his head toward her side of the bed, a crushing reminder that his sweet wife was no longer lying there in the bed next to him.

His movements were slow and deliberate until his eyes came to rest on the empty left side of the bed, and his hope would be laid to rest for another day. Every morning, for a split second, there was hope. It was only allowed to make a short appearance in a hazy mind that was having trouble delineating from reality and the vivid dream that seemed so real just seconds ago.

He, somehow, thought he'd find her there, smiling over at him with the same crinkles around her eyes that he had around his, crinkles reflecting the lifetime of shared smiles, shared worries, and the shared life that had belonged to them. He then wanted to travel back to sleep and peace, back before he was aware of this reality that now crashed in chaotically. In this daily morning moment, his heart was suddenly heavy, but he would not allow it to stay heavy. He would give it its heavy moment, acknowledge it, feel it, and then he would let it go as if watching the clouds roll by, passing through the sky on a breezy summer day.

Gramps would then muster up the courage to go ahead and get up out of that bed every day anyway, *every single day,* even if the day that lay before him had now lost that fresh feeling of potential and excitement and light. He would realize in this moment that he was not twenty-two but seventy-two and everything that comes with age.

With those years behind him, Gramps had the gift of attaining the emotional awareness of one who has lived, and loved, and lost, and ultimately won, because he has done all of these things and was still doing all these things, and unfortunately, not everyone gets that chance. He would continue to do so as long as he had the option and the privilege. He would get up to live this day, even if she couldn't, perhaps *because* she couldn't, and that is what she would want him to do. He would do it for her, and he would do it for himself. He would do it for love.

What a grand thought to have this early in the morning! With that, he would find again the potential and excitement and light in the day ahead. Gramps' awareness made him wise and helped him appreciate each and every precious moment. He would gently kiss the pillow next to him and say a little prayer and then Gramps would rise, his old back injury reminding him that twenty-two was long gone, even if he remained twenty-two in his heart.

Life has a way of speeding up when you get older. Gramps could remember like yesterday when he was ten, back when he was just a boy, back when his days seemed to last forever, despite the early bedtime that his dear mother insisted upon as his father quoted Ben Franklin from across the room: "'Early to bed and early to rise, makes a man healthy, wealthy, and wise,' son." The days weren't going to be slowing down anytime soon. Even if his body was slowing down, time was not. No, it was doing quite the opposite, but he was okay with that because he was *aware.*

Some people think it is all downhill after a certain age. Unlike others he knew, Gramps saw that the downhill part of life could be the fun part. He liked to point out that it was going uphill that was tough. With the right attitude you could enjoy the downhill ride, letting go of some things that don't seem to matter quite so much in one's twilight years. In truth, as one's body may be going downhill, one's heart and soul are likely moving upward and higher, closer to being fully aware, and that is just part of the amazing journey of life.

Gramps tried to live a true life every day. He passed on the importance of this to those that he loved. Lark would eventually add these to his most important life lessons. Be true. Have the right attitude and turn it into fruition. An attitude of gratitude will never steer you wrong. Choose adventure. Be kind. Have courage. Find joy. Feel. Become.

Lark was going to end up with quite a list, especially for a ten-year-old boy; but, then again, Lark was not your average ten-year-old boy. He was soon to embark on great adventures. He would know these life lessons by tomorrow, although he didn't know it yet. He, too, would be *aware.* Yes, to Gramps, sometimes, it felt like just yesterday that Lark was born. Yet here Lark was, the ripe old age of ten. This little boy's life was just about to begin.

Chapter 5

Amazing Adventures

"Tell me, what is it you plan to do with your one precious and wild life?"

—Mary Oliver

WHAT AN AFTERNOON! LARK KNEW TEN WAS GOING TO be a great year. He was inside his fort with some essential supplies he had brought within his backpack. Settled comfortably inside, he planned to take a few moments to explore some of the new treasures he had received for his birthday. His new headlamp on, he opened his *Book about Everything* (although he just got it, so he couldn't be sure if that claim was true quite yet). He had a few of his favorite super fizzy candies, Zotz, strewn around, one of which he was presently sucking on, and he was already starting to make that face one makes when something is challenging to the taste buds in a weird, pleasurable way. Nearby he had his half-consumed bottle of grape soda, his glow-in-the-dark nerf gun that he would test when he turned off the lights; and, of course, safely stowed away in his pocket, the lucky stone that Gramps had given him.

"Knock, knock, can I be granted entry, fine sir?" asked someone with a bit of an accent. And then, not waiting a split second for an answer, Gramps came into Lark's fort on his hands and knees in an uncomfortable-looking, hunched-over position. His old body made pops and cracks that resembled a bowl of Rice Krispies upon first getting doused with milk. Lark looked up at him with a smile, and Gramps instantly covered his face protectively, engulfed in the bright light of Lark's headlamp.

"Oh, whoops—sorry!" said Lark with a giggle as he took it off his head and set it down on the rug underneath them.

"What a birthday it has been so far, boy-o." said Gramps with a big smile. His smile revealed the remnants of blue frosting from Lark's birthday cake, hidden within his mustache hairs that were already sprinkled with glitter, compliments of the twins, so he would "look good" for the party.

"I know; it has been awesome!" exclaimed Lark.

"So, did you like all of your gifts, Lark?"

"Oh yes, Gramps, I love them all."

"Where is that lucky rock of yours?" Gramps inquired with a grin.

"I've got it right here in my pocket," said Lark, reaching in to grab it. As his fingers came to touch the smooth stone, he realized it was extremely warm. He was surprised he hadn't noticed it before now. Perhaps it had heated up for some odd reason? It was getting warmer and warmer. He glanced up at Gramps as he pulled the stone out tentatively to see if anything looked different, since it sure did feel different. "That's weird, Gramps. It's hot. Here, feel it."

Lark held it out toward his grandfather, and Gramps slowly reached out as well, extending his fingers but not yet touching the stone sitting in Lark's palm. Lark stared down intently at the stone, and as he looked, he did see something different; it seemed to be changing right before his eyes. As he looked into its center, he saw what appeared to be a star. The bright, twinkling star had suddenly appeared on it, or in it. He couldn't quite tell. Or had it been there before without him seeing it?

"Exactly," said Gramps in answer to Lark's question, the question that had come to Lark's mind but hadn't been verbalized. Gramps' fingers also touched the smooth, warm surface of the stone, and Lark got a funny feeling, like the feeling of trying to remember a dream.

Lark looked up at his grandfather for a clue about his funny feeling, or their unspoken exchange, or the hot stone they were both touching, because things suddenly seemed very different. The twinkle in Gramps' eye shone brighter than ever before, and the shining star on the stone mimicked it. Gramps wrapped his large hand around Lark's small, quivering one, and there the lucky stone lay within a safe cocoon of this multi-generational grasp. A sense of safety flowed over Lark as his grandfather's hand surrounded his own, and Lark looked up at Gramps with wonder. Suddenly, there was a whirlwind of confusion and light.

"We need your spark, your twinkle, Lark. We have mine; we have the stone's; we need yours. Look right at the stone—see within," Gramps stated in a calm but directive voice, although, again, no actual spoken words were used.

Obeying his grandfather, Lark's gaze shifted back to the stone. He loosened his grip and turned the stone over in his hand. With Gramps' hand still supporting his, Lark gazed deeply into the center of the stone. In that instant Lark felt a spark in his own eye. It wasn't painful; it was powerful.

With the joining of these three "twinkles," as Gramps had called them, the star in the stone burst out of the center, right out of the fort, in a fast, blinding shock of light. Lark closed his eyes tightly, shielding himself from this explosion of light while trying to maintain his steadfast grasp on his lucky stone. Although it was almost too hot to do so, he held on to it for dear life. He could feel Gramps' hand still holding on to his, and this helped Lark hold on.

Lark kept his eyes closed for a minute or two longer, partly because he could tell his surroundings were still too bright to look at, but mostly because he was afraid to open them. With the absence of sight, sounds were amplified. It sounded like many things were falling from the sky outside the walls of his fort.

There was that feeling he would get when it had snowed through the night, and he knew it had snowed, even before he opened his eyes. He could tell the lighting was different, and there was a quiet stillness in the air. Lark felt like that. He continued to squeeze his eyes shut and listen closely. Yes, it was almost like that faint sound of falling snow. Lark tried to figure it all out, still afraid to open his eyes and give validity to this situation as a reality rather than a dream.

Perhaps it was snow after all. That seemed like a logical explanation. It was snowing. Outside of his fort? No, wait, that wouldn't make sense: his fort was inside his house. Maybe he wasn't even in his fort anymore. Or maybe he was in his fort, but his fort wasn't in his house anymore, or maybe . . .

"Go ahead, Lark, choose adventure."

It was Gramps' voice again, soft and encouraging. Lark's wild, tangential thoughts of "what ifs" and "maybes" were halted in their tracks, and Lark felt both of Gramps' big, kind hands surrounding his small hands as he held onto the stone. Lark felt supported. For a brief moment, Lark felt brave, and with that he slowly opened his eyes.

He quickly looked around to see if things looked different. They did, for when he opened his eyes, the first surprising difference was that he was all alone. Gramps was no longer in the fort with him, although Lark swore he still felt his hands cupped around his own. All that was left in the fort was his backpack, his nerf gun, his soda, his book, his headlamp, his candy, and his stone.

The next thing he noticed was a sparkling path of what could only be described as stardust, leading right out of the fort, under the flap that led to the room outside.

Lark looked down at his lucky stone, questioning the term lucky as he contemplated what had just happened. He examined the rock for changes or clues without moving his hands much for fear of losing the sensation of Gramps holding them. The stone was no longer hot. The star in the center had almost faded from view and was more inside the stone now rather than on the surface, so he had to look hard to find it. The stone's iridescence resembled the clear light blue of a sky more than any other color.

"Gramps?" Lark yelled in desperation. He frantically peered around the confines of the fort.

"I am with you, Lark. I am here, even though you can't see me right now. We are here," said Gramps, sounding as if he were right next to Lark, even though he wasn't. "When you venture out of the fort, you may not be able to always hear us either, but that doesn't mean we are not with you."

This was too much for little Lark. "I-I-I don't understand. What is happening, Gramps? Why is this happening? Please, don't leave me alone. I don't want this to be happening. I don't like to be alone. I can't be alone!" cried Lark.

"I know, boy-o, but it's going to be okay. I promise you are going to do okay," stated Gramps encouragingly.

Lark did not feel reassured.

"But then, why, Gramps? Why can't I see you? Wait, am I going to see you again?" screamed Lark.

"Of course, Lark. As I said, we are always with you. You just may need to find us in places you wouldn't usually look. Be open. Notice things. Although you may feel alone right now, you are never alone. When you make a connection, you carry a part of that person, or animal, or place, in your heart always.

"Remember you are wise, and you are special. Trust yourself. And always choose adventure. It awaits you on the other side of this fort. The rest of your life is awaiting on the other side of that flap, so open it up. We'll find each other on the other side. I love you, boy-o."

With that, Lark knew he was now the only one in this fort.

The air suddenly seemed thick. He no longer felt Gramps' hands around his own. He was truly alone, maybe for the first time in his life. He didn't want to open up that flap. Lark was paralyzed with fear. Was there an alternative to leaving the fort? Could he survive on a few Zotz and some grape soda? Maybe there was something in his *Book About Everything* that could help him. Maybe there was a chapter on this, even if it was like nothing he'd ever experienced.

Lark placed his headlamp on his head and was frantically opening up his book when his lucky stone, which he had been holding on to tightly the whole time, fell out of his hand and rolled toward the flap of the fort. Lark dove down to catch it, but it slipped through his fingers. It rolled right under the flap to the outside of the fort.

Lark lay there on the fort floor, dumbfounded. He did not know what to do. Lark then thought about his grandfather's advice.

Shaking and terrified, Lark knew what he had to do. He paused for a moment and then jumped up. He picked up his backpack, and he placed all his essential things back inside. He took a deep breath, and then, without hesitation, he pulled the fort flap aside, and there, right in front of him, he found his lucky stone waiting for him. He mustered up even more courage and fully emerged from the fort.

Lark picked up his stone. Glancing ahead, he saw a path of stardust forming a winding road to somewhere, nowhere, anywhere.

Lark's fort was no longer contained inside his home. All that was familiar was gone, aside from the essential supplies in his backpack and the lucky stone. There were no signs of his family, his house, his furniture, his toys, his dogs, his anything. He felt even more alone. He was scared and confused but, at the same time, in awe and curious; for it was a sight to see. Looking around, he seemed to be caught in a sunrise, or perhaps a sunset, with bright, swirling colors of orange, pink, and purple surrounding him. Yet it was unlike any he had ever seen before. It was stunning. Though he was utterly petrified, the depth of this beauty was not lost on little Lark.

The sound Lark had heard while inside the fort, the sound that resembled falling snow, was actually falling stars. Ahead of him stars fell from the sky, too many to count, too many to wish upon, and as they reached the path, each falling star burst into stardust, paving the path a little bit farther.

In a daze, Lark bent down to touch the ground just outside the stardust path, the place where the colors seemed to start, only to find there was nothing concrete to touch. His hand went straight through like a hand running through a stream. The bright and vivid colors swirled around his hand like a whirlpool. Perhaps they were a cloud or a mirage? Reality blurred. He better stick closely to the path and not fall off, for the sky around him and below him seemed endless and uncertain in its beauty. He took a few nervous steps forward. What was he supposed to do? Lark let out a cry for help, but all he heard was an echo back through the empty, beautiful sky.

Chapter 6

Larkisms

"What if I fall?"
"Oh, but my darling, what if you fly?"

—Erin Hanson

THEY WERE ALL CLOSE IN AGE. WHEN LARK WAS TWO and a half and his sister Sophie was one and a half, the twins, Gwynnie and Maisy, were born. Bliss came two and a half years after that. Five kiddos. "Are they all yours?" "Two sets of twins? Oh, really? Those two could be twins as well." "Wow, that's a lot of kids." "You've got your hands full."

That one, "you've got your hands full," was the most common one. People could not pass by their family on the street without commenting on how their parents' hands were so full. Mommy and Daddy would smile with a knowing nod and pretend that person was truly enlightening them with their unsolicited assessment of their family situation. Unsolicited or not, it was friendly and not at all untrue; they really did have their hands full.

Mommy and Daddy would respond with something like, "You should see our hearts." This would make the other person smile, and all parties involved in the exchange would continue down the street feeling good about connecting with another human being. Sometimes it led to long conversations on sidewalks with elderly strangers sharing their parenting stories, like old veterans trading war stories at the local pub long after they had been to battle. Others could be likened to world travelers, sharing the highlights of their journeys through their own unique, unchartered territory of having kids. Whatever their perspective, they had survived, and were still surviving, this thing called parenthood, and they wanted to impart some advice, share some similarities or differences, and connect. Lark's parents would listen intently because they never knew what they might learn, and they wanted to get this parenthood thing right. It was the most important job they would ever do.

Lark's parents loved hustle and bustle, and they loved a little happy chaos. Lark didn't always love the chaos. Sometimes he really loved quiet, even if he rarely got it. Sometimes his little, spirited body needed quiet. He wanted to be around others, having had constant companionship since before he could even remember, but sometimes it all seemed too loud, too busy, too much. That was when he would escape into his fort and get lost in his books or his drawing. If he didn't get the chance to do that, he'd usually end up tackling a sister for no apparent reason or talking back to his parents, losing his privileges for the rest of the week after being sent to his room to think about it.

He didn't need to think about it. He never meant to do it. He tended to react first and think after. Usually, as soon as he did it, he already wished he could go back in time and change it. Going back in time wasn't possible, not yet.

According to Gramps, Lark had a certain brilliance. It wasn't a consistent brilliance across all settings, and in many instances, this confused people because his emotional maturity was nowhere near his intellectual maturity. He could sound like an educated old man while discussing world politics but burst into tears because he couldn't get his LEGO pieces together. Other children would be confused as to why Lark was trying to discuss a tyrant named Robert Mugabe and his reign in Zimbabwe when they were asking Lark to play tag. Adults who were thrilled that he even knew the name of the country of Zimbabwe and amazed he knew some of its political woes would be taken aback by his strong reaction to something as trivial as a LEGO piece.

Sometimes it was hard for Lark to fit in. He was more book smart than street smart, but he also had instinctual insight into things that he had never read about but somehow understood anyway. Maybe that had something to do with what Gramps had told him. "Brilliant." Behind the scenes, Lark had been called brilliant, or outside-of-the-box, his whole life. Sometimes it was used to explain how schoolwork was so easy for him. It was used as an excuse to explain away social behavior that might be less desirable but inevitable if one was blessed, or cursed, with a brilliant mind.

Subtle social nuances could give him a tough time. If he did pick up on them, he may not know how to respond. Sometimes something stopped him. Lark stopped Lark. He had a tendency to get in his own way, to get in the way of *being* himself. Sometimes he pretended he was too busy to hear or so engaged in looking at the loose thread on his cuff that he certainly couldn't be expected to stop tugging at it to look up and respond. Sometimes he just pretended he was invisible, or the other person was invisible, or that the situation was invisible in some way. He would withdraw into his mind so he wouldn't have to reciprocate a greeting or answer a question. His responses, or lack thereof, could come off as rude, even though it was really shyness. His actions and inactions could hurt the feelings of those who didn't know him well. These behaviors were often reserved for those who Lark did not know well. Ambivalence could sting but so could putting yourself out there. There was a certain amount of vulnerability required in connecting with others, and Lark was not sure vulnerability was worth the risk.

To grow, one must venture out of one's comfort zone. Now Lark knew, and he would take that risk. To get a friend, he needed to be a friend, to be interesting, be interested, to be amazing, be both amazed and do amazing things.

Amazing is relative. Something that may seem like a little thing at first glance could have the capability of morphing into the most amazing *big* thing under the right circumstances. Amazing little things can be likened to a small pebble cast into a still pond, with ripples that carry on well beyond one's awareness or initial intent. You never know where those ripples might take you. Throw that pebble into stillness and embrace the ripples. The day after his tenth birthday, Lark understood that to be who he wanted to be, to be his best authentic self, would take both action and the right attitude.

Lark kept people on their toes. If he was in an environment that he knew, with people he was comfortable with, he thrived, and any lack of confidence in social nuance was forgotten. He could be the life of the party, the center of attention. He would rally people and coordinate games or events, and little people would follow this little leader.

Sometimes he would try too hard to be the leader, or make too many rules, and then his sisters would run off, calling him bossy. Lark would get upset and quit, but then, before you knew it, they would all pull together and play another game, laughing and having fun without a care in the world. He ebbed, he flowed, in a complex stream of self. You never knew what you were going to get with Lark.

His thirst for knowledge was utterly insatiable. He devoured books as if his life depended on it. Lark read all he could get his hands on, and then he would read them again. Information was filed away in that brilliant brain of his in some sort of disorganized, orderly fashion. There was his own alternate Dewey Decimal-like classification system inside his head, in which things were stored in a format he could not verbalize but could retrieve whatever he wanted instantly from the "files," as he called them, inside his brain. Lark could pull up the exact picture of what he had seen, or what he had read, or what he had thought, and reiterate it down to the smallest of details. He technically had a photographic memory, but it was beyond that; it was as if he was hurled back into the moment again, reliving it and reporting it. Yet, when Mommy asked what he did earlier in the day, he could scarcely remember a thing.

Lark leaned toward a preference for organization, although he himself was quite disorganized. He always seemed to be losing things. He needed several reminders to do things, such as put on his shoes, or zip up his fly, his backpack, his jacket. Whether it was a book he was reading, or an art project, or or some other task, if it interested him, he could lose himself in it. He would not respond to his mother's voice across the room with the gentle reminders that they were five minutes late already, and it was time to put down the book and get out the door. He wouldn't respond to his sister as she asked whether he wanted to play a game with her. His father's inquiry of how school was that day was lost in the abyss before it had the chance of reaching Lark's ears. It was almost as if he couldn't hear anyone, or see anything, except the thing in front of him that was all-consuming.

Most of the time, Lark was just a fun-loving kid, but it is important to know about these "Larkisms," as his family dubbed them. These behaviors occurred some of the time, far from all of the time, not even most of the time, but they were definitely there and worth noting if one was ever hoping to truly understand the fascinating complexities of little Lark.

Chapter 7

Echo

"A journey of a thousand miles begins with a single step."

—Lao Tzu

"HELP!" LARK YELLED ACROSS THE ABYSS.

For a few seconds, there was silence and then a faint echo reverberated, bouncing his voice back to his small, shaking body, a faint echo of "Help . . . help . . . help . . ."

He tried again. "HELP!" Lark yelled desperately, and again brief silence before the echo bounced back across the vastness.

"Hello . . . hello . . . hello."

Lark contemplated his delayed and not-quite-accurate echo. The reverberations weren't evenly timed. His intonation was preserved, but the words coming back were salutations rather than his pleading outcries. Curious now, Lark cried out loudly once more, "HELP?"

Again, the echo, apparently having a mind of its own, sounded back, even more delayed in its response and a little bit louder this time, but in Lark's distinctive voice. "HELLO? . . . HELLO? . . . HELLO?"

Lark pondered this some more. Was this reflection of his voice somehow playing tricks on his ears, or was someone else perhaps playing a joke on him? He felt annoyed at his echo for not following proper echo etiquette, although there probably wasn't a manual or anything to refer to on echo etiquette. Were there echo rules? Lark's brain started to wander, as it often did. Maybe he should look echoes up in his *Book about Everything*. Lark liked rules, and he liked to follow them.

"Help, help, help?" the echo blurted out, unsolicited, the sound fading into the distance. This snapped Lark out of his thoughts and back to the present situation at hand.

"NO! *I'M* SAYING HELP!" Lark screamed.

"NO! *I'M* SAYING HELLO!" the echo screamed back, so loud it felt as if there was someone screaming right next to him.

Focused on this discourteous echo disobeying the rules of echo etiquette, Lark tried to trace the origin of the echo from somewhere deep within the setting, stumbling sky. Lark found this inquiry to be a welcomed distraction from the loneliness and confusion in this unfamiliar and unreal place. Lark was so distracted, in fact, that he was left utterly oblivious to the figure suddenly standing right behind him.

When the echo belted out an enthusiastic "Hi" over Lark's shoulder, the *hi* turned into a *high* as a startled Lark jumped higher than he had ever jumped before.

"Oh my gosh, Echo, you nearly scared me half to death!" Lark screamed without even turning around. It suddenly felt to Lark as if they were old friends with a history that warranted random nicknames such as "Echo," as if it had been established between the two of them long ago over some inside joke that they shared. Lark used the name Echo freely without asking, or feeling like he needed to, for somehow, Lark did know that Echo was his proper name.

By speaking to his own echo like a friend, there came an acceptance on Lark's part for his odd situation. If he was talking out loud to his own echo, then he had probably officially lost his mind. Losing his mind might be the only reasonable and logical explanation for any of this. Lark liked reason and logic. If he had lost his mind, so be it because it was the only sane thought right now that made sense to him. He was having a conversation with his own echo, after all.

"Nope," answered the voice behind him.

"Excuse me?" asked Lark, wondering if he had asked a question without realizing it.

"Nope, you aren't losing your mind. You are finding it."

Lark realized he wasn't hearing Echo's words with his ears right now. Just like communicating with Gramps earlier in the fort, words were being exchanged telepathically as if these thoughts did not want to be harnessed to the senses as he knew them. Things were getting weirder by the moment. Lark slowly turned around.

"I'm Echo!" yelled the figure standing behind him.

"I know. Somehow, I know," said Lark in a snarky, Larky way.

Echo nodded gleefully. Lark had to admit, he was relieved to have company. Even if he had a feeling Echo might be a bit of a jokester, based on the copycat tendencies that are inherent to the nature of an echo. It had only been a short time since Gramps left, but it was so nice to not be alone anymore.

Upon examining Echo, he didn't seem to have any concrete shape or form. Echo was a swirling cloud, kind of like Pig Pen in the Snoopy comics, no definite outline, but definitely there. Lark could just make out the image of a little boy, but the lines were blurred. Echo was a glittering being of stardust and sparkles and light. He contained some of the colors of the sky, but he was composed of other colors too—colors that Lark had never seen before. These colors were beyond words. They could almost be best described as feelings, but blended feelings that can't quite be placed, deep inside the soul. Words for these colors couldn't be limited to the preconceived constraints of colors as Lark knew them before.

Echo was similar to Lark in size and shape, but again, nothing was concrete or tangible. "So, who exactly are you? What are you? I feel like I have met you somewhere before," said Lark. Usually quiet around new people, he felt comfortable with Echo, and Lark's curiosity was leading the charge.

"Of course, you have met me. I am part of you. I am your echo, Lark."

"But that doesn't make sense to me. I mean, first of all, you weren't echoing what I had to say," said Lark with an accusatory eyebrow raised.

"No, that's what's so great about this place. I don't have to say exactly what you say anymore. I can say what's really on my mind.

I feel so free," proclaimed Echo with a hint of a smile behind that twirling mess of stardust.

"So, then, you aren't really a part of me. You are actually your own self," stated Lark matter-of-factly.

"Well, no, I am still part of you. You just don't know that part very well yet. I am that part you squash down and often won't let out. I am the part of you that sometimes wants to say something, but you won't give it a chance . . . the part of you that *should* say something sometimes, but you just don't give it a chance. If you do get the courage to speak up, I am that part of you, too. And every now and then, I am that part of you that shouldn't say something but does anyway," Echo said with a laugh.

Lark looked at Echo with half-understanding, half-confusion as he half-accepted and half-rejected the possibility of any of this.

Echo gave Lark another smile. "The quintessential half-committed Lark—even when it comes to our emotions—especially with emotions," stated Echo.

Echo sensed what Lark was feeling, and Lark, in turn, sensed Echo's feelings. They were one in the same, at least in this parallel universe outside Lark's safe little fort in his safe little world.

"To put it simply, you can get in the way of yourself. Whether it is shyness or fear or lack of confidence or some other factor, you let opportunities pass you by. We need to work on that. It's holding us back, and we are missing things. If we keep on hanging in the limbo of indecision, we are going to miss big things."

Lark noticed Echo moved freely between the pronouns "you" and "we" as he discussed Lark's quirks and hang-ups. He started to feel defensive, but if they were really a "we," then perhaps he was just being insightful, and this information was valid. He kept listening.

"It may be the choice of an ice cream flavor, or it may be what you want to do with our life. Big or small, decisions of all kinds stop you in your tracks. I am here now to help you be strong, to recognize when opportunities arrive and decisions are required. You need to find confidence. I can help to take away the fear and the shyness and anything else getting in your way. It is time to own who you are and who you are meant to be, Lark, because that person is one and the same."

This was a lot for Lark to take in.

"You will do great things, but you've gotta believe in yourself. You have so many people that believe in you already—Gramps, Mommy, Daddy, Sophie, Gwynnie, Maisy, Bliss, even our dogs, and that's just immediate family. Our aunts, uncles, cousins, I won't even begin to name our teachers, friends, coaches; the list goes on, Lark. We have lots of great things to say. People will believe in you. Don't get in the way of yourself. I am your echo, yours alone, and it is my job to find your true voice on this journey. Let our true voice be heard!"

With that, Echo quickly swirled past Lark, covering him with stardust from the cloud that surrounded him as he ventured down the path in front of them.

"This way," Echo shouted. "We need to find June!"

With that, he plunged ahead with great determination and speed. Heeding Echo's advice, or maybe it was his survival instinct kicking in, Lark made an instant decision to move forward as well. Already on the run, Lark quickly threw his backpack on his back, stuffed his lucky stone back into his pocket, and followed Echo in search of some girl named June.

They ran for what seemed like miles. Echo continued to forge ahead at lightning speed. Lark ran faster and farther than he had ever run before, desperately trying not to lose his newfound companion. "Slow down, Echo, please! I can't run this fast forever!" Lark cried desperately in between huffs and puffs.

Apparently, his voice was lost in the wind, or perhaps it was heard and ignored, because Echo started to run even faster.

The falling stars continued to pave the path ahead in the distance, but Lark saw that there were splits in the path coming up. If he lost Echo, he could accidentally take a different route from him and lose him forever. Plus, not once had Echo shot the tiniest of glances back to see if Lark had followed him. Maybe he was trying to lose Lark, but Lark wasn't about to let that happen. Lark had found his echo, found his voice, and he wasn't about to lose it now.

Without hint or warning, Echo came to a screeching, abrupt, movement-defying stop. Mid-stride, the brakes suddenly applied, he immediately halted without even a tiny lurch forward. This probably defied all laws of motion, or laws of matter, or some sort of law that was no longer matter-of-fact in this outer-fort world where things like that just didn't seem to matter anyway. Lark, not possessing these motion-defying stopping skills or the foresight to even know he'd be coming to a stop, did not have time to stop. He only had time to mentally brace himself to crash into Echo. At full speed, Lark ran right into Echo, and then he ran right *through* Echo. In no way halted by the collision, but finally implementing his own tardy and inferior brakes, Lark tumbled head over heels into a dazed pile on the stardust path in front of Echo.

As Lark lay there stunned, Echo, pointing and smiling down at him from behind, let out a loud "Ba-Haaa!" chortle. Echo found great humor in Lark's erratic tumbleweed impression, a reaction which Lark found to be rather rude, especially before checking to see if Lark was in fact okay from the big tumble caused by Echo himself.

"Remember, we are one and the same, Lark. I already know you're okay. I know you are more than okay." Still giggling and smiling, Echo reached out his colorful, sparkling, blurry hand to help Lark up.

Lark could make out more of what Echo looked like now. The cloud around Echo had thinned, and the little boy behind the cloud sounded like Lark and looked like Lark, just in different colors. Lark felt even more of a connection than he had before to his echo, Echo. Even so, Lark wasn't sure if he should trust this hand that Echo was extending. He wasn't even sure if there was anything concrete to hold on to in Echo's swirling, colorful stardust self. He also wasn't sure if Echo would in fact help him up or pull his hand away and laugh at Lark all over again.

Lark decided to take the chance. He reached toward Echo. It was a small moment, but it was also a big moment. It was a revelation in the beauty of vulnerability and being humble and accepting help and choosing adventure and all the other things that Lark didn't know he was searching for. When their hands met, Lark realized he himself was now shimmering with the same stardust that encompassed Echo. In addition, Lark had also taken on the same inexplicable, stunning, swirling, unnamed colors that Echo possessed.

Echo pulled him up with ease, and Lark stood there, wide-eyed, staring at his hand as if he had just grown a new appendage. Echo chuckled without a care in the world. Lark stood mesmerized. He felt different. Lark felt the same, but different.

He and Echo were one and the same.

Chapter 8

The Loon

"it takes courage to grow up and become who you really are"

—e. e. cummings

"HOW CAN YOU BE LAUGHING AT A TIME LIKE THIS?" cried Lark. "You just made me fall and hurt myself and—"

"You're not hurt; we're not hurt," said Echo in a matter-of-fact tone, maintaining the smile on his face, which Lark now saw as taunting and insensitive.

"You were trying to lose me, and I just found you, and don't call us a *we*," yelled Lark, exasperated. The craziness of the overall situation, not just the moment at hand, was finally crashing over him, crashing into him, much like he had done to Echo. Crashing into this reality he didn't even ask for, with no clue or warning, and it was still his birthday, for crying out loud. He missed his parents; he missed his sisters; he missed Gramps and his dogs and his home and everything that was familiar and safe.

Lark was feeling completely out of control of the swirling emotions, which he typically held deep inside, kept safely tucked away as his own. These sacred emotions that were no longer able to be squashed or downplayed or hidden were now also swirling wildly outside of Lark, too. They were there for all to see, contained within the beautiful colors that now covered his body. His thoughts were also all there to be heard, even when he wasn't speaking. Lark wasn't used to showing his thoughts and emotions on the outside like this.

"*We* are not a *we*. There is *no* way that we are the same. I am not smiling right now, Echo. Stop smiling at me." The big salty tears streaming down Lark's face sprinkled his newly acquired colors all about as they accumulated in a small colorful puddle surrounding his feet.

Echo downshifted to a subtle grin, although his eyes, hard to see amongst the swirling stardust and colors, continued to smile and sparkle. He looked over at Lark for a second and then he looked right past Lark. "Oh good, here comes June. Oh, this is really good. Pru is with her, too!"

June was not on the path. She was swimming smoothly, seamlessly through the beautiful sunset or sunrise, although maybe it was sunrise *and* sunset all the time here. There she was, swimming through the colorful air as if on a wave of the sea, washing effortlessly toward Lark and his echo.

June was a loon, not in the "crazy like a loon" type (although she had been known to get a little wild in her day), but in the feathered variety of a loon. She was a spotted, glorious, black and white bird. Lark had never seen a real loon, only pictures, but he recognized her as a loon immediately, for this was another one of those things he, somehow, knew without an identifiable source of which to attribute this knowledge. He also knew June was different from other loons, for June the Loon was huge. Perched on her back was a small girl with wild, red curls who was missing her two front teeth and waving enthusiastically at the two boys. Lark and Echo stood next to each other, waiting for June and Pru's arrival on the stardust path.

"HELLLLLLOOOOOO, ECHOOOOOOOOO!" swooned June the Loon.

"Hi June, was hoping to see you soon. And you too, Pru."

"Ha! Well done, Echo, well done," said Pru, her eyes dancing back and forth between Lark and Echo. June the Loon opened her large beak and began to speak.

Welcome, Lark, to this world outside your fort.
We are very pleased you chose to follow your cohort.
Not to worry, sweet boy, although you are far from home,
Your adventures await as you explore and roam.

Pru clapped with glee as if listening to the closing number of a hit Broadway show. She and June were next to the path now, and Pru hopped off the back of June with such ease that it seemed for a second that she herself might be floating, too. Lark stood there silently, drained from the emotions that continued to gather at his feet in a growing puddle of colors from his spilled, salty tears.

Pru was slightly shorter than Lark and slightly slighter. She was a tiny waif of a girl with porcelain skin and exactly nine freckles sprinkled on and around her nose. She had green eyes the color of pastures in some land where it rains all the time, like Ireland or Oregon. Not that Lark had been to those places, but he had read about them and seen pictures.

Pru bounded over to Lark. Without hesitation she looked him right in the eyes, put her small hands on his small shoulders, and pulled him in for a big, strong hug. Lark's shoulders tensed up, and he started to pull back out of habit, but she held on with a startling strength for such a small thing. Just when he thought he couldn't handle being hugged, or fighting a hug, for a second longer, he surrendered, almost melting, and accepted the comforting embrace. She held him up as he cried quiet sobs that spilled more colorful tears into her shoulder. He cried over the unknown and the uncertainty that surrounded him. He cried for what felt like an eternity, and when he couldn't cry anymore, he kept his eyes buried in her small shoulder a bit longer. Lark was suddenly painfully aware that he had expressed extreme emotions in front of others he didn't know very well. Lark wasn't used to being so transparent.

Lark finally lifted his head from Pru's flowing white shirt, now stained with a batik of beautiful, swirling colors left from his tears. Pru nodded and smiled a sweet, understanding smile, unlike Echo's glaring, gloating smile from before.

"Mine was a smile of understanding too, Lark," Echo stated, defending himself against Lark's miffed thought, which Lark hadn't realized he was having. Lark suddenly felt exposed and vulnerable with his thoughts and his feelings being displayed like a book for all to read. He turned his eyes to Echo, expecting to see some obnoxious smile. Instead, Echo was now crying, too. Colorful, empathetic tears were streaming down Echo's face. He was less blurry than before. The stardust that had encircled him like a cloud since they met back at the fort seemed to be settling down. His features were clearer, more distinct.

Lark was in awe once again. He had known they looked similar, but it was as if Lark was looking in a mirror. He felt the way he imagined his twin sisters, Gwynnie and Maisy, must feel when strangers first met them, unable to distinguish one from another. Even with the twins, though, they started to look different once you got to know them. Lark knew what he looked like, but he couldn't distinguish any differences between his physical self and Echo's. It was like a reflection of himself crying big, fat, colorful tears. From the outside, they looked the same, but Lark still didn't understand how they could be so different on the inside and still be "one and the same," as Echo had put it.

Pru nodded knowingly. "Hi, Lark. I'm Pru," she said with the slightest hint of a lisp, no doubt due to her missing teeth. Pru smiled at him unapologetically, her grin reaching from ear to ear, highlighting those two missing front teeth and the connection they had just shared. "I hear you," said Pru, a statement which Lark found rather interesting since he hadn't said anything.

"One and the same . . . I'll tell you what." She spoke with the confidence of someone offering advice who had already lived a long life with a commensurate wealth of wisdom. "Every now and then on an airplane, they offer in-flight entertainment. We may find half of the passengers are watching some heart-wrenching movie, although, being ten, you probably haven't seen any of those, but trust me, they are out there. Perhaps the other half of the passengers are watching some obscure comedy. Now, there usually comes a time, near the end of a heart-wrenching film, when you are super-engrossed in the characters and their well-being, you know, where it is the most pinnacle part of the movie, and tears are flowing down passenger's faces as they try and muffle their sobs, only slightly aware that they are in public, but not allowing enough of an awareness to take away from their moment. When people watch movies, they understand the necessary suspension of knowing what is real and what may not be real but feels real. They are feeling, and sometimes that is enough. They know sometimes it is better to live that moment, even if it is heart wrenching, even if it is just a movie. Maybe there is some little hope that if they live this moment fully and vicariously through some movie character while flying in this aircraft stuffed with people, then perhaps, just perhaps, the lesson will be learned, the insight gained. Perhaps they hope that maybe, just maybe, the Powers that Be may decide that they won't have to live through a heart-wrenching experience themselves because they have already lived it vicariously on this airplane. The box has been checked. The lesson learned. The insight gained."

Pru pauses and smiles that toothless smile again. She nods her head slightly, looking for agreement from Lark and Echo. Lark looks back at Pru, unsure if she is full of knowledge or nonsense. He had been trying to follow Pru's complex, rambling analogies that were flying quickly through the air, like the airplane she was describing, but Lark couldn't help it. His mind wandered, as it often did. With Pru's pause in speech, Lark realizes he has drifted and snaps back from his run-on thoughts and tries to refocus on Pru's run-on sentences.

"So, you back, Lark?" Pru asks.

Lark feels his cheeks flush, as there is no hiding the fact that he stopped listening for a moment in this outer-fort world . . . there was simply no hiding anything.

"Okay, good," Pru continued, not missing a beat. "At that exact moment that half of the plane is watching this pinnacle moment and letting out audible gasps and sobs, the comedy then delivers its most hilarious scene, and the other half of the plane erupts in laughter. For a brief moment, the plane appears as though everyone has lost his or her mind to some bi-polar affliction because there is no congruency to emotions.

"Sometimes we worry if we cry too hard, or we laugh too hard, or we feel too hard, what would become of that, if everyone walked around like that, feeling so much? Maybe, just maybe, that might be absolutely wonderful. Anyway, those on the plane laughing hysterically have little awareness of those feeling heart-wrenching pain in the seat next to them because they also might lose the moment if they suspend their unreality and become aware. Plus, they all have on headphones, and it is an escape, or an avoidance, and we really don't need to acknowledge other's feelings, or sometimes our own, if we have on this complex armor shielding us from feeling and communicating and relating, such as headphones, right? Nope, not right."

Echo and Lark look at each other and Pru continues on, barely pausing for a breath. "So, they are in the moment but are afraid to look sideways at the people next to them because this would let the self-consciousness sink in that comes with wearing one's heart on one's sleeve. They would be stuck in this little flying box, vulnerable and exposed (although I think there can be a certain beauty found in a certain level of vulnerability or openness—but I digress)."

Lark raises an eyebrow and gets a chuckle as she seems to be doing nothing but digress, as far as he can tell.

Pru smiles and continues. "They have expressed extreme emotions, in close proximity, to complete strangers, or maybe they aren't strangers and they are next to family or friends; regardless, they have expressed extreme emotions, and if they look sideways and smile and acknowledge it in the middle of the moment, that might make the moment less because they would step away from this escape of the movie and are now aware of the reality around them. Although perhaps it could make the moment more, it would, in fact, I think, usually make it much, much more, especially with those we love, but they will never know because they never glance sideways, and they never remove their headphones. So, unabashedly the passengers laugh, and they cry, and sometimes that is just what you need to do, but you really shouldn't forget to look sideways and connect because then it makes it deeper." Pru paused again, nodding as if she had just revealed some great truth, and Lark nodded back because it seemed like the polite thing to do.

"You see, Lark, you can all be in the same place and all be having different experiences. You can even be one and the same and have this happen, like with you two, Echo and Lark. You can also have happiness and heartache all in the same moment. Maybe you have an amazing moment, and then you are sad because it is over, or maybe you are happy but then also sad because someone amazing is no longer around to share it with you. So, you can have that duality within yourself in a single moment. A moment can be both magical and uncomfortable, challenging and elating. It is also interesting to think, when one is going through the roughest moments in life, somewhere else a baby is born; a child is doing his homework; someone is laughing with their spouse; someone is throwing a stick for their dog; someone is arguing with a meter maid; someone is ordering a cheeseburger; and the list goes on, but to that person, it might be the most heart-wrenching moment in their life—and the same would be true for the most joyful moment in somebody else's life—but they could all be the same moment in time. That's just that, don't you see?"

Lark tried to dissect what in the world Pru was saying. He and Echo could be the same but different; he got that now. It was important to connect with others and okay to show emotions in front of others and also . . . to glance sideways? Lark tried to come up with something smart to say in response, but all he could muster up was, "How old are you, anyway?"

To this, Pru let out a laugh with her gapped-tooth grin, putting Lark at ease, but she didn't answer the question. Lark smiled back. His mind wandered, as it had a tendency to do, while he tried again to figure things out. The gap-toothed smile led Lark to the conclusion that Pru had to be something like seven since that was when those teeth normally fell out, not that much was normal right now. She could be one hundred and seven, for all he knew in this outerfort world.

There is no sense to it. It is non-sense,
Non-sensical, and hence,
Don't think too hard and just try to feel.
When you think with your heart, it all becomes real.

June looked at Lark and splashed a little splash of the sunset/sunrise at him with her wing, soaking him from head to toe with the colors, which felt like a warm bath engulfing him without making him wet. He suddenly felt safe for the first time in a long time. He looked over at the loon. A logical loon. Absurd bird.

"Well done, Lark," Pru squealed, clapping enthusiastically.

Lark looked over at her, confused at first but then realizing her appreciation of the accidental rhyme that he had merely thought in his head.

"So, you read minds too, Pru?" he asked, this time saying out loud just what was on his mind because he might as well if she was going to hear it anyway.

"Too . . . Pru? Well done, Lark!" Pru yelled, spinning into an impromptu cartwheel in celebration.

Another unintentional rhyme. Was he going to start talking like Dr. Seuss or something? Lark decided to ignore Pru for now. Even though she was nice and smart, he was trying to find some real answers.

"Do you always talk in rhyme, June?" asked Lark.

"Yes, I rhyme . . . all of the time. I'm a poet, and I didn't even know it," June said with a wink. Lark gave a small giggle. "I talk in prose as everyone knows. I could talk without rhyme some of the time, but I like the way the words sound when a poetic connection is found."

"And Pru, Pru—what is your deal? What kid actually talks like you?" inquired Lark curtly but not meaning any offense.

Pru raised one eyebrow and shrugged her shoulders with a smile.

It was at that moment he noticed the sparkle in Pru's eyes. June had it, too. They both had the same undeniable sparkle in their eyes that Lark had, that Mommy had, that Gramps had; this must be some connection to this outer fort world in the sunset/sunrise.

"June and Pru will carry us closer to the all-knowing truths on your amazing adventures, Lark," said Echo.

"My amazing adventures?" asked Lark.

"You are on them, your amazing adventures in the outer-fort world. You are Wise. You need to gather your wisdom so that you know what you know."

"I feel like everyone is talking in circles in this place," said Lark, unintentionally rolling his eyes. They looked at him and smiled, beamed, really, and Lark surrendered a bit more to the adventure of the unknown. With that, Lark mimicked Pru's earlier gesture, raising his eyebrow, shrugging his shoulders, and looking at them with smiling, shining eyes.

"The glint and the grin," Echo stated. Lark typically preferred logical, concrete conversations, but he had to admit, he was gaining a fondness for the ridiculousness of it all.

"Let's go, guys," yelled Pru, jumping atop of June's back. "Nothing with feelings is black and white. Don't try and figure it all out now, Lark. Embrace the in-between colors. Let's choose adventure. Come on, hop up here." She patted the feathers next to her.

Choose adventure. There it was once again.

Lark shook his head and muttered, "Larkisms and Pruisms."

They chuckled at this comment, understanding from his thoughts what a Larkism was and appreciating what a Pruism might be. Lark looked over at Echo and then, surprising himself, he grabbed Echo's hand, giving it a tug. Together, they jumped up on top of June's lovely, smooth, spotted back.

With the three children all nestled on her back like little loon chicks, June swam quickly through the colors alongside the stardust path at a speed ten times faster than Lark and Echo had been traveling by foot. When the path split, June spread her wings wide and took flight. This startled Lark, and he quickly wrapped his arms around the shimmering blue circle of feathers around June's neck and held on for dear life, even though he knew somewhere deep inside of himself that his dear life was perfectly safe here on the back of this loon. The path twisted, and it turned, and it went up, and it went down, and after a while, Lark loosened his grip around her neck. He looked over at Pru and Echo and their huge smiles and realized if he let himself enjoy it, this ride could be extremely fun. He slowly put both hands in the air to wave wildly in the wind, and Pru and Echo followed his lead.

"We swoop, we swirl, we spin, we twirl. Choosing adventure, two boys and a girl." June sang out as she flapped her wings harder. The three of them were all holding hands now, clasping them high in the air, laughing so hard they cried colorful, happy tears that flew in the wind behind them. Their faces beamed.

"Ahhhh! The delight in flight," June yelled back with glee. "The wonder of it all; it's time to fall," she sang to the trio on her back. With that, June tucked her wings back and dove straight down toward the sparkling path below and what appeared to be a beautiful pond.

The kids on June's back held tightly onto her neck to brace themselves, but despite the drastic change in elevation, they continued to squeal with delight in between uncontrollable laughter that made their bellies hurt, and they never wanted it to stop because it was that much fun.

Chapter 9

Willow

> "i thank You God for this most amazing day; for the leaping greenly spirits of trees and a blue true dream of sky; and for everything which is natural which is infinite which is yes"
>
> —e.e. cummings

JUNE THREW HER WINGS OUT SUDDENLY, AND THE DRASTIC perpendicular line in which she had been falling smoothed out into a parallel line over the blue pond below. She skimmed across the top of the water, landing next to a green bank of grass and colorful flowers cupping the edge of the pond's crystal-clear water. The children screamed, "Again, again June—please!"

June gave a quiet giggle and a wink and slowly bent her head down so her beak rested on the grass of the shore.

Pru climbed quickly up June's neck. Sitting atop of June's slick black neck, Pru threw her arms back up in the air and let out a loud, "Wheeee!" as she slid down June's beak, landing on her bottom in the green grass below with more gleeful giggles. She motioned to the boys to come join her. Echo went next and then Lark, and they, too, landed on their bums on the green riverbank. This put them into a giggle fit again, rolling around on the soft, velvety grass. June gave them another playful splash, this time from the pond, and this time actually getting them wet with the warm and delicious water as it sprinkled their skin.

Lark's cheeks hurt from smiling so big, and his tummy hurt from laughing so hard. Lark felt truly happy. The children grabbed hands and stood up together, smiling their bright feelings, which literally formed into a warm and bright light that shone from the inside and out of each of them, uniting into a soft and beautiful beam of light. They felt connected to each other, not just by their hands, but by their hearts.

"Explore, take a tour. There is more. It lies before. To find it, though, you must knock on the door," said June as she motioned her wing for them to explore their surroundings.

They wiped away the wet from their faces, the wet from the splash from June, the wet from the happy tears of laughter. After curiously looking at June and then each other, they started to search for some sort of a door, as June had instructed. There were beautiful flowers and beautiful bugs and beautiful plants, and the sunset/sunrise beamed beautiful sunbeams full of color all around them. The air felt thick like a hug and light like a breeze. The moment felt adventurous and perfect. There was a smell to the air that was a mix of everything good, like honeysuckle and cotton candy and summertime. It smelled like a mix of memories that bring back emotions, like when Lark smelled Mommy baking mince pies and Christmas cookies, and the memories of all the joy of Christmases past flooded in at once from a simple smell. Somehow, Lark was smelling memories and seeing emotions. Perhaps that ability was always there; he just hadn't been able to sense it before, but like Gramps talked about, he was becoming aware.

As Lark was lost in his dream-like train of thought, his eyes skimmed over his surroundings. There was a large weeping willow, green tendrils reaching down, dipping into the pond as if searching for something at the bottom of its shallow waters. At the base of the willow, camouflaged within the twisted bark, was a small, rounded door. Lark glanced sideways at his friends. It appeared they had all spotted it simultaneously, which, of course, made sense, since they were all so connected. The three children looked at each other and over to June, who nodded, and then back at the door, but not one of them made a movement toward it.

"You go, Pru," said Echo, giving her a playful nudge.

Pru nudged him back and said, "No, you go, Echo."

Echo returned the nudge, and she gave it back, keeping things playful, but Lark could sense that they were nervous for some reason. Lark lamented that he didn't have access to what they were thinking right now. He was getting used to the idea of knowing each other's thoughts, and he was getting used to the idea of others knowing his thoughts.

Lark and June sat by silently as they watched the nudge exchange between Pru and Echo for another couple of seconds, and then Lark spoke up.

"Why don't we all go together?"

"Well, that's a grand idea," exclaimed Pru, giving Lark a big nudge toward the door that didn't feel at all playful, but when Lark looked into her green eyes and saw the sparkle, he knew she didn't mean anything by it.

"You knock, Lark," said Echo. "You can do it. Be brave."

"Um, well, okay, but we all go up together, right?"

"Right," said Echo and Pru, shaking their heads in convincing agreement.

"Are you coming, June?" asked Lark.

"No, sweet Lark, I am unable to embark. Although I am a loon that can talk, no loon anywhere is able to walk."

Pru shook her head up and down again. "It's true. Loons have feet positioned too far back to walk, but it makes them excellent swimmers."

"Oh, I had no idea. I'm sorry you can't walk, June," said Lark with a twinge of sadness.

"Don't you worry, it's quite okay. I can swim, and I can fly. I like it that way. I wouldn't be me, you see, if I were different, I dare say," said June, and with that she smiled and took off in flight out of the pond, disappearing over the treetops.

"Where is she going?" cried Lark.

"Where is anyone going?" replied Echo.

Lark looked anxiously over at Echo, but he flashed that mischievous grin, and Lark knew his question was another one that would go unanswered. Lark looked hopefully over at Pru for an answer, but she gave her signature shoulder shrug.

"Is she coming back?" Lark asked, concerned.

"Oh, yes, June is always with us, even if we can't hear her or see her."

Lark was starting to understand this nuance of the outer-fort world. He remembered how Gramps had told him back in the fort that he would never *really* be alone if he carried the connections he made with him in his heart. When Lark thought about it, that fact probably held true back home, too. He would have to remember that if he ever had the chance to get back home. Rather than feeling scared or sad, Lark suddenly had an unexpected feeling of confidence and courage. He could feel these qualities becoming a more constant part of him with each step forged ahead.

Lark came to the conclusion that he was right where he was supposed to be with the knowledge he was supposed to have, up until this point.

"Choose adventure. Be courageous," he stated under his breath, enlightening himself with his own convincing pep-talk. Ha! Now he wondered to himself, how old was he? What ten-year-old talked like that, or rather, thought like that? Lark chuckled to himself as he flipped his question to Pru back onto himself. Pru gave him another impatient nudge from behind, hurling him back to the moment.

"Lark, if you want to get philosophical, the answer is that we are all as old as the sun and the moon and as young as the dew and the wind. Now, knock on that door, for goodness sake!"

It was a tiny, little door in a tree. What could be scary about that? Lark tread forward, his little chest thrust out in an attempt at confidence and self-assurance. He bent down and, without hesitation, knocked with authority on the little, round door. Pru and Echo had edged up beside him as promised, and they all stood there, waiting.

Nothing happened. They gave each other nervous glances, wondering if this was the door they were supposed to explore, or were there more? Pru clapped at that rhyming thought, and they all started to giggle again, providing a welcomed distraction from the present situation. As soon as they forgot to be nervous, the tree shook. The hanging green branches whipped around and blew in a breeze that nobody could feel.

"Who"—yelled a deep, angry voice from inside of the tree—"dares"—the voice bellowed, stinging through the air, closer now but slightly muffled from behind the wooden door—"to knock?" the voice screamed as the little door flew open, banging into Lark, who was standing a little closer than his two companions.

The door slammed right into Lark's shins, causing him to wince and bend over in pain. As he instinctively grabbed his bruised shins, Lark now found himself bent over and face to face with what only could be described as some sort of distorted old man, small in stature and big in anger. The little man peered back with a piercing stare, eye to eye, nose to nose with poor, shivering, little Lark, who suddenly felt very small, although he was three times the height of this scary little creature. Lark couldn't help noticing, being in such close proximity, that the little man smelled like strawberries. He also thought he saw, for a split second, a playful hint of a twinkle behind the man's accusatory grey eyes.

"Sorry, sir . . . um, I didn't mean to . . . um . . . we are here for . . . do you know June? I am so sorry if we disturbed you in some way, sir, but I think, according to June the Loon—do you know her? Big, pretty, black and white bird . . . talks in rhyme?"

The little man glared at little Lark, and Lark could feel his hot breath breathing down Lark's hunched-over neck.

"I know—I mean, I know it sounds a little odd, but anyway, she thought you could help us explore, or . . ." Lark looked anxiously sideways to see where Pru and Echo might be and to see if they could help. At that moment, the man grabbed Lark's cheeks in his pudgy, little gnome-like hands and held Lark's head in a steadfast grip, with fire reflecting in his eyes. Lark feared he was about to be the recipient of a swift and painful head-butt or some other interaction that was sure to hurt.

The little man's face burst into a sudden and unexpected smile. "Good job, Lark. Glance sideways. That's what you are supposed to do, right? Share the moments, share the feelings, good and bad." He patted Lark's left cheek as if he was an adoring grandparent showing affection, and he released his grip on Lark's cheeks and looked around, smiling enthusiastically at the three shaking children. Pru and Echo and Lark returned three of the most nervous, unsure, doubting smiles anyone had ever mustered up.

"Come in, come in, my three young explorers." The small being disappeared into the trunk of the tree.

"Pru, did you know about this? I was scared to death. Did you know he would be like that? I was so scared," an exasperated Lark inquired.

Pru shook her head back and forth.

"Oh no, no. I know a lot, Lark, but I'm still a kid, just like you. Even though I'm Wise, I still have a lot to learn. Knowing there is more to know helps make me Wiser."

"Are you coming?" the impatient little man screamed from deep within the trunk.

It was Lark, once again, who decided to lead the charge. He got down on his hands and knees and crawled through the rounded door. Behind him followed Echo and then Pru.

Inside, the tree trunk was completely dark. They weren't sure if there was enough room to stand up, so they continued on their hands and knees, crawling in blind faith through the blackness. Lark tried to shake the looming thought that there could be unseen dangers ahead. Judging from the outside of the willow tree, one would not expect that this little man and three children would ever fit inside. Like time, size can also be relative. Crawling forward on their hands and knees, they traveled through some kind of tunnel.

The little man, or whatever he was, kept yelling back, "This way" or "That way." They followed the sound of his voice. "Ah, yes, hurry up, you poky little things," he said, sounding rather annoyed. They kept crawling on and on. "Ah-ha, don't you see? We are here," exclaimed the small man in excitement from somewhere ahead of them.

"We are where?" asked Lark, stopping his crawling so suddenly that this time it was Echo that ran into Lark, right into Lark's rear-end. The two boys started to laugh at the fact that it was Echo running into Lark this time, and it was all the funnier that he ran into his *rear-end.* That was funny in and of itself. They laughed at the irony of the question "don't you see" in the pitch black and because, as far as they could see (which was not far at all), they were still nowhere at all, and, well, they laughed because it seemed like time to lighten the mood, once again.

"What is so *funny?* Why do you laugh? Do you think it is funny? Well, maybe you will and maybe you won't. So, now, you see—or maybe you don't . . . *ta-da* . . . to the *chakra* . . . and now I must go . . . *ta-ta!*" The man gave a taunting and somewhat eerie laugh, which made Lark and Echo stop laughing immediately, and Pru let out a little whimper.

"Wait? Ta-da and ta-ta?" shouted Echo. "What do you mean, '*ta-da*' and '*ta-ta*'?"

"And what the heck is a chakra? We still can't see anything. It's pitch black in here," Lark chimed in.

No answer. There was no great thing that warranted a "ta-da," and Lark had no clue what that other word was, but how could he dare say "ta-ta"? Was he going somewhere and leaving them there alone in the dark? This moment sure did feel lonely, even with his two companions still behind him. Everything looked the same—dark, black, and indistinguishable. Even so, they could tell, even though they hadn't been able to see him in the first place, that the angry, little man was now gone. Lark felt his heart sink.

Luckily, the three children remained together, and that was certainly better than being completely alone, but they were scared, nonetheless. The only thing that could be heard now was Pru trying to stifle her whimper, which elevated into a full-blown sob. Lark was surprised and worried by this. Firstly, he had considered Pru to be wise beyond her years. To hear her cry like the child she actually was reminded him that they were *all* kids in this situation, a reminder which was slightly disheartening. Secondly, he had hoped that Pru somehow already knew where they were going or maybe had some answer as to what to do now. Maybe she did know, and that was why she was crying. Either way, Lark was worried.

Echo and Lark tried to find words to console Pru, who was shaking and sobbing behind them. There they were, on their hands and knees, feeling quite helpless. Lark explored his surroundings, searching with blind hands for clues. He had touched the walls and ceiling of the tunnel earlier. It had felt like a narrow path carved inside of a tree trunk. He had felt wet, pulpy wood on all sides, all around and above. He still felt the pulpy wood that surrounded them, but when he felt up over his head, he felt nothing but space. The ceiling was no longer hanging as low over his head. With this discovery, he carefully extended his arms high overhead. Lark then went upright on his knees, still not having any contact with the surface of the tree up above. Lark began to stand up, not saying a word to his friends quite yet, as if he were afraid to jinx it. He was standing. His arms were still extended above his head, but he didn't feel a ceiling.

"Guys, stand up! We can stand!" Lark exclaimed. He quickly felt Echo's presence standing next to him, but Pru remained sobbing on her hands and knees below. "Pru, come on—stand up, you can totally stand up in here," Lark told her.

"I-I-I just can't seem to do it. You see, I'm afraid of the dark. Not just a little afraid but really, *really* afraid," she stated between sobs and sniffles. "It was already bad enough not being able to see and being down, close to the ground, but I don't know if I could handle standing and not seeing."

"That doesn't sound like the rational little Pru that we know," said Echo in a coaxing way that bordered on patronizing. Pru was too consumed by the dark situation to remark on it beyond responding with a quiet "humph" between her sniffles and sobs.

"No, really, Pru," Lark said, "how can you be afraid of the dark? The dark is the same thing as light, without the light part."

Geez, look who is talking in circles now, thought Pru. Lark heard her thought and gave her an encouraging smile.

"You told me earlier that nothing is black and white. Think about it. Things may seem black right now, but somewhere in here is also some white hiding away, and there is probably some grey blending that black and white and meeting things halfway with a compromise. And of course, there are probably colors hiding somewhere in here, too. All of the colors on the spectrum live somewhere between black and white. I know we all have some color swirling somewhere on us, and I know these colors aren't gone. Just because it is dark right now and we can't see them with our eyes, it doesn't mean they aren't there."

Pru continued to sniffle, but the sobs had subsided as she listened to Lark. She was still down on the floor of the tree, but his words seemed to be helping. This was just her kind of philosophical conversation.

"Did you know that stars are out, up in the sky, all of the time? The sky is filled with stars all day, just as it is filled with stars all night. We can't see them during the day because the sun is brighter, and their little glow gets drowned out by the great glare of the sun. Yet they are there, patiently waiting until nightfall when they get their chance to shine again. The more we are in the dark and away from light, the better view of the stars we get. Sometimes you need to believe beyond your senses. You need to trust things are okay—have faith. Sometimes you just have to have faith, Pru."

Pru had stopped crying, and everything was quiet for a moment as she let Lark's words soak in.

"Thank you, Lark," said Pru.

Lark could tell from where her voice projected that she had found the courage to stand up into the darkness, and Lark had helped her do so.

Pru sniffled a bit more through the remnants of tears, but Lark could feel her feelings now, her very being becoming calmer and more collected. "I was too scared to move and to try and see beyond sight. I forgot about the importance of faith and seeing with my heart. I felt so alone, even though I knew we were together. I forgot to let you guys in. I forgot how to listen. I forgot how to see. Thank you for helping me find my way out of the darkness."

"You were still in our hearts, Pru, and we were still in yours," replied Echo.

"Always were, always will be," Echo and Lark stated in unison. With that, they all smiled, and even though they couldn't see each other's smiles, they all knew it to be so. They had a connection that was beyond an earthly connection, and not just because the outer-fort world was beyond earth as Lark knew it. It was a connection of all the little moments, too, for Lark would learn those were also just as important. With their connectedness, here within the black, dark trunk, they found a calm within themselves through one another. Things didn't feel quite so dark and lonely anymore.

"Can I give you guys a hug?" Pru asked.

Without another word, they fumbled about, reaching through the darkness for a comforting group hug. The dimmest bit of light began to shine, like when they held hands on the riverbank. Within this tiny ray of light, Lark, with one arm over Echo's shoulder, the other over Pru's, suddenly felt Echo patting his back fervently.

"Lark, your backpack, your backpack," cried Echo. Lark reached back over his shoulder, and there it was, still on his back. He had completely forgotten he had it.

"My headlamp!" Lark and Echo screamed in unison as Lark ripped the bag off his back and started digging around, desperately searching for something that felt like his headlamp, and then, there it was. He grabbed it and twisted it to the right, turning on a beam of light so bright that it was almost blinding to them after their time in utter and complete darkness.

Their eyes adjusted, and Pru's tearstained cheeks rose to the top of an enormous toothless smile as she clapped excitedly. They immediately began to explore their surroundings. Even though they had been crawling through the inside of the tree for quite some time, it appeared that they were still inside the same tree. The opening had a circumference that was just big enough to fit them all, without too much room to spare. There were no signs of tunnels leading into this space and no signs of tunnels leading out of this space. The walls of the willow went way, way up, reaching toward the sky, so high that Lark's headlamp didn't shine that far. They were layered with stripes of colors with the color red surrounding them down here at the burly roots. Their intricate patterns cast wild shadows everywhere that Lark shone his headlamp.

The colored stripes ascended in the colors of the rainbow, although they could only really see up to the yellow stripe, or maybe even a bit of green. The transition between colors was not a harsh line but rather a muted ombre effect, like one might see on a dip-dyed fabric. All the way up the side of the tree, nailed to the inside of the trunk, starting here at the roots, were slats of wood hammered in to form a shoddy-looking ladder.

"I may be afraid of the dark, but I am not afraid of heights," shouted Pru as she scrambled up the first rung of the ladder.

"Okay, let's do this; let's explore full speed ahead," yelled Echo, following in her footsteps.

Lark was glad his companions were no longer apprehensive. Their courage was contagious.

"Okay," cried Lark, soaking up their zest for adventure. "I'll be the caboose, shining the light up. Can you see okay, guys?" He decided not to mention his own apprehension about the sturdiness of the rungs of the ladder and his fear of extreme heights. But then again, he probably didn't have to because if he was thinking it, there was a good chance they already knew it.

Chapter 10

Bliss

"Though she be but little, she is fierce!"

—William Shakespeare

LARK WAS THE OLDEST KID IN HIS FAMILY, EVEN THOUGH he wasn't very old. There were five children, and Lark was the only boy. He and his sisters were all close in age. They looked out for each other, and even if they had the occasional squabble, they truly enjoyed each other's company. If they weren't already his sisters, Lark would've picked them out as best friends.

Sometimes being the only boy was hard. Sometimes it drove him crazy, like when the girls were all dressing their American Girl dolls in their fancy outfits, and Lark would come in with his official police badge that he got from his sixth birthday "policeman" party. He would try and arrest all of the dolls for being naked in public, enforced with his lightsaber and nerf gun, an action which always made the girls so mad. When he did things like that, they yelled at him and told him he was ruining their game while he sat there wondering what he had done wrong. Sometimes he would be wrestling with one of his sisters, rolling around on the ground having fun, when all of a sudden she would burst into tears, saying he was playing too hard, or hurting her, even though he wasn't doing anything different from the way he had been playing five minutes before, when she was laughing so hard she said she might pee her pants. Lark did know that girls could be confusing. He had learned that life lesson even before his amazing adventures.

His mom always said that he was going to be a good husband for some lucky girl one day because he was going to understand women, whether he liked it or not. Sometimes Lark relished the fact that he was the only boy. The king of the castle. Not a bad gig, really. People often joked about how he was going to be so busy watching out for all those little sisters of his, but he didn't mind. It made him feel all the more important. Being a big brother was a big deal. Plus, when his parents thought he was feeling outnumbered, his dad would take him to an Orioles game or something like that, where they got to be dudes, just the two of them, and they'd eat junk food and stay up late, and none of the girls ever got to do that with just him. If anything, sometimes they'd split time doing girlie stuff with Mommy amongst the four of them, so not only were they doing something lame like getting their nails painted, they still only got twenty-five percent parent-time if it was split fair and square.

Now don't get it wrong. The five of them, for the most part, received all the attention and love that they needed. Mommy and Daddy always had enough love to spread around. They found time to play with them and snuggle and read and color and create play-doh masterpieces, amongst cooking dinner and cleaning up the kid clutter that they complained about but didn't worry about in any obsessive, neat-freak way. Usually their parents found a way to help everyone with their homework and keep them bathed and looking somewhat put together with food in their tummies and love in their hearts. They found the time to tuck each one of them in at night, even if they could barely keep their own eyes open as they wondered how their four-year-old was still so full of energy while their own grown-up energy was so depleted.

Even with the best intentions of getting out of the door on time, it rarely happened. Lark often had a role in their delayed departure with a last minute search for a shoe he should have had on fifteen minutes earlier, or the completion of a detail on a project that he "had to finish" before they left, or a need to run back in the house after they were all buckled up and pulling out of the driveway to go grab some necessity that he must "absolutely" have in that moment. Upon completion of any event, when it was time to pack back up and go home, they unknowingly often left one of their belongings behind. It was usually a sippy cup or a mitten or a Barbie accessory, not a kid—their parents never left them behind. The really important things were always accounted for, and those five really important things all knew they were accounted for and cared for and loved. Shoes might be on the wrong feet and hair might not always be brushed, but they were loved, and they knew it.

The hair not being brushed part couldn't be truer than when it came to Lark's littlest sister Bliss. Bliss screamed and hid in protest when the hairbrush came out. Bliss usually fought it long enough that Mommy would warn them all that if they didn't leave the house right that moment, they'd all get late slips at school, and even though it didn't really mean much of anything at their little Catholic school, a late slip would start their day off on the wrong foot, and they didn't like that. So, off they would eventually go, piling into their gigantic car, Bliss's tangles and all.

Bliss was super stubborn but also super cute and super sweet. She was the quintessential youngest child, maintaining perpetual baby status even though she was now four and a half. She insisted on girlie, twirly, sleeveless sundresses in the dead of winter and rarely seemed to feel the cold. She would take off her shoes, the shoes that took Mommy half an hour of debating and wrestling to eventually get on her feet, tossing them aside the second she got into the car. Bliss also refused to wear a jacket. As a result, in the chilly months, more loving wrestling would ensue. Mommy would often resort to pinning Bliss down and zipping her into her pink, puffy winter coat backward so that Bliss couldn't reach the zipper to escape. Through big dramatic tears, Bliss would protest the situation, and Mommy would try and sell her on the idea of how cool it is to have a hood hanging in the front of your neck instead of behind your head so you can store treasures in it and use it for carrying your baby dolls. She would tell Bliss that anytime someone makes a daring fashion statement like that, it makes them unique, like Fancy Nancy or someone cool like that, and all of a sudden, people would all want to wear their coats backward, too, and Bliss would start something called a "trend." According to Mommy, Bliss was going to start a major fashion trend that would be all the rage, this fantastic meld of the dickie meets the fanny pack and had a baby in front of Bliss's neck in the form of a backward-hood fashion statement. Mommy would then encourage all of the kids in the family to wear their jackets the same way to prove to Bliss how cool it was, and with the same fashion prowess that Dickie and Fanny hold today, their ridiculous family would head out with their ridiculous jackets on backward, praising Fancy Nancy in all her glory, happy to be finally getting out the door, ridiculous or not.

Bliss was a surprise to Lark's parents. Her arrival into an already busy home was one that the family hadn't anticipated and didn't realize they needed until she was theirs. Five children. That was a lot of kids. Bliss somehow did not push them over the tipping point, though.

Lark's father was afraid of the tipping point. He was consumed by the fact that there would be financial repercussions from another mouth to feed, to dress, to send to school, to . . . *everything*. There was the possibility of plunging further into financial insecurity. Four kids were already a lot. The cost of childcare meant it didn't make sense for his wife to go back to work, so she was a stay-at-home mom, and that was their preference right now anyway, but supporting a family of seven on one salary was difficult.

Sometimes his wife seemed oblivious to the financial stress. It wasn't that she didn't care about it, she just didn't dwell in it. As Mommy pointed out, this baby was coming one way or another, regardless of whether they worried about how they would afford it. Very few people would have kids if they waited until they were *really* ready to afford it. Children are expensive, but then again, they are priceless. Mommy reminded him that these things had a way of working out; they always did. She was right, of course, and he knew it, so he put that worry on the back burner. The more time and energy you gave a worry, the more it fed the fire. Likewise, blissful ignorance had a certain power, too.

They had the power of blissful ignorance when they were having Lark, their first baby, and there was something enlightening about embracing that again with their last baby, even if they knew so much more now. What they had learned was that, no matter what they thought they knew, when it came to kids, they might as well embrace knowing that they didn't know because things can change in an instant. With that, Daddy was able to blissfully embrace Bliss and the wonderful, beautiful unknown that lay ahead.

Bliss somehow brought with her this magical balance they didn't even know they were missing until they found it through Bliss. Perhaps it took the fifth child for Lark's parents to realize they needed to loosen the reins, relinquish control, and, as Lark learned on his amazing adventures, throw their hands up in the air, put their best foot forward, a smile on their face, and enjoy the ride. Being out of control allowed them to be back in control because they no longer expected to be in control.

Expectations.

That is another concept that Lark encountered on his adventures. Another complex concept. That fine balance between *accept* and *expect.* It is a delicate dance, a dance in which the steps are forever changing just when you think you have it figured out. Another one for Lark's list, this notion of accept and expect.

Chapter 11

Red-Roots & Courage

"Love many, trust few, and always paddle your own canoe."

—Anonymous

WITHIN THE WILLOW TREE, LARK, PRU, AND ECHO began their slow and deliberate climb up the vast red interior. Lark held on for dear life, grasping desperately to each rung of the ladder, as the small children ascended higher and higher into the unknown. At this point in the adventure, Lark was focusing on survival. He wasn't *too* afraid of heights, not usually, but he was a little afraid of heights, especially of heights as great as these. He had a good view of where his hands were to go, but his feet fumbled often, and he had to rely on simple faith that his foot would somehow end up successfully planted on the next rung above. Self-reliance and simple faith. With each solid placement of his foot, Lark felt more and more grounded. It was almost symbolic of him finding his footing in his life and assurance of where he belonged. He whistled softly to himself as he climbed slowly upward amongst the red roots. With each successful step, Lark felt more and more confident and supported, not just by the rung of the ladder, but by something bigger. It was like the whole universe was supporting little Lark in this climb. This was scary, but it was also exciting. It was adventurous.

Lark was a good climber. He loved to climb trees and hang from limbs, almost giving Mommy a heart attack as she peered up from below yelling, "Be careful, Lark!" He had always chosen adventure when he was climbing, with little thought to consequences. He loved to scramble up steep challenges such as trees or rock faces and tended to throw all caution to the wind in these circumstances while Mommy preached the importance of safety, respecting Mother Nature, and respecting our own limits. She didn't discourage him to climb; she just wanted him to be smart about it. She had personal stories of people plunging off the sides of cliffs and plummeting to the ground when they weren't careful. She had a story of how, as a kid, she once climbed to the tippy top of a tall tree when suddenly the sturdy-looking branch she was perched upon snapped in half, and she started to fall. Thankfully, she happened to have a good grip on another branch, and after hanging for a few seconds, she was able to pull herself up, saving herself from a potentially devastating fall. She had a story about admiring the view of the early summer raging rapids on the bank of a Colorado river while hiking alone. Standing at the edge, staring at the water rushing by, she suddenly lost her balance for no reason at all. It was as if the river was trying to pull her in with some trance-like, magnetic force. She almost plunged right into those raging rapids, from which she most certainly would not have emerged.

She had a lot of stories of close calls that all contained the words "suddenly" and "almost." She had a few stories that didn't get the luxury of an "almost" at the end, although she didn't tell Lark any of these stories. He was still so young and sensitive and didn't really need to know about the stories out there without happy endings. Besides, world news provided enough of those stories on a day-to-day basis without Mommy adding to the heap. So, she told Lark stories of close calls to encourage him to be smart and careful, but unlike his mom, he mostly focused on what *didn't* happen versus what *could have happened* or *almost* happened and, therefore, still tended to throw caution to the wind.

Lark was always somewhat surprised to hear stories from back when he was still waiting to be born, back in a time that Mommy and her friends liked to refer to as B.C. (Before Children). Mommy wanted Lark to be adventurous but to think things through first. She wanted him to make sure he had some of the skills needed to tackle something risky before attempting it because things could suddenly go wrong. Test those branches before you solely rely on them to hold you up. Leave an extra step between yourself and a raging river. She went on and on—blow on your hot soup before having a bite, look both ways, don't stick a metal fork in a toaster, jump into the bay feet first because you can't see the bottom and the tide could have changed and brought in the shallows, even if it was safe and deep an hour earlier—on and on and on. Her message was always jump in, climb that mountain, take that leap of faith, choose that adventure, but be smart and aware of the *suddenlys* and the *almosts.* Although, she added, sometimes the *suddenlys* can be a good thing, and sometimes the *almosts* can also be a good thing, too.

Lark listened to her advice as he half wondered how Mommy could have ever truly been a kid like he was while the other half of him was stuffing the information away for later, just in case it ever actually proved relevant.

Right now, Lark was realizing that maybe Mommy knew a bit of what she was talking about after all. Pru's recent outburst resonated with him. He may also be Wise, but he was still a kid and had a lot of learning ahead of him. Mommy had many more experiences than Lark had so far. She was pretty wise too, now that Lark thought about it. Lark's mind continued to wander on and on and on as Lark climbed up and up and up, following in the footsteps of Echo and Pru. They had all grown quiet, even Lark's whistling subsiding, as they concentrated on the ascent that, with every rising rung, took up more of their breath and energy.

Lark heard the sound of a song breeze by that sounded just like June, even though she was obviously not here with them inside the trunk of this narrow willow tree. The far-off song grew into a faint whisper, and then there were distinguishable words:

The roots, they are planted, and oh, they are strong.
When you feel grounded, you can't go wrong.
This is your strongest connection with our earth
And the physical body you acquired at birth.
Here, you may find the soul's foundation and stability.
If you are grounded, it will support you and guide your ability.
You can harness courage, gain answers, and learn to survive.
With spiritual energy, you will begin to revive.
It is the root chakra, this powerful energy.
It provides the basis for personal synergy.
Don't resist the physical world in which you occupy space.
Know you are meant to be here and that this is your place.
For if you let go of your insecurities, your fatigue, and your fear,
Your primal instincts will guide you here.

Lark wasn't quite sure what the poem meant, but it seemed like it might be important. He looked down for a second in the direction the words seemed to have risen from. He was taken aback at how high they seemed to be on this long, endless ladder, and his knees shook a bit with this newfound awareness. They were still in the red and had a long way to go, but they were swiftly making headway.

"Oh my gosh, did y'all hear that?" Lark yelled up, his headlamp bobbing from side to side as he resumed climbing onward and upward, a little faster now as he tried to catch up to his comrades.

Lark waited for an answer. His question was met with total silence. "Pru . . . Echo?"

Nothing. Lark suddenly felt insecure, and anxiety flooded over him, washing away the confidence he had been feeling just a moment ago. "Are you able to hear me still . . . Echo . . . Pru?"

More silence. Then there was a sound, but it wasn't Echo or Pru answering back. It was the sound of something cracking, a cracking slat of wood, and it was the slat of wood that was making up the step that Lark was presently standing on, or more accurately, the step that Lark had previously been standing on, because the next sound that could be heard was Lark screaming as he plunged toward the tree's floor.

Down, down, down he fell. He seemed to be falling much farther than he had climbed up. He fell for so long that it almost felt as if he were floating, but the light cast from his headlamp on the whizzing red roots of the trees let him know he was still catapulting down. He yelled and prayed and squeezed his eyes shut, bracing for the impact that would surely be the end of him.

Still he fell. He opened his eyes and glanced down but immediately wished he hadn't because as soon as he looked down, the light showed the floor within plain sight, approaching with great speed. He squeezed his eyes again as he fell this last bit, and then, he was not. He was no longer falling. He was suddenly stopped and supported by something soft underneath.

"Lark, why hellooo. Why the journey down? Where are you trying to go?"

"June," cried Lark, shaking uncontrollably with fear. He knew he was no longer falling, and he knew he was now safe in this downy haven, but his little body continued to tremor until it could catch up to his mind that was wrapping itself around the fact that he was going to be okay. Lark knew better than to try and make sense of anything here. He was learning there was often a hidden message to be found if he searched for it, but for now, he was simply glad to be alive. Lark threw his shaky arms around June's neck and gave her a big kiss on her beak through fat, colorful, salty tears. June the Loon smiled as she flew through the air.

"I thought that was you. I asked Pru and Echo, but they didn't hear me. Or at least, they didn't answer. Shocker here but, June, I'm confused."

"I know; just go with the flow," said June with her signature wink and smiling beak.

Somehow June had saved Lark from his tragic fall. She had intercepted him on his way down, even though there was no way she could have physically fit into that space, yet here she was. Lark decided to heed her advice. He was going to accept things as they were and trust the process. He was going to enjoy that he was still here, that he was still alive, riding through the air atop June's spotted loveliness. Lark told himself he was going to focus on the now because there was no point in worrying about the future in the outer-fort world. Mommy always said worrying was like praying for something to go wrong, and Lark didn't want anything to go wrong. So, he made his mind up not to worry, as best as he could.

When Lark looked around, he realized they were still surrounded by red, but they were no longer inside the weeping willow. They were soaring through the surreal sky, which swirled now in colors of ruby, crimson, and burgundy. Everywhere had taken on beautiful shades of red.

"Where are Pru and Echo?" asked Lark, wondering why his sidekicks were not flying with them, as worry kicked in unannounced once again.

"They are fine in the tree. You will see," said June.

"But you don't understand—they won't see. I have the flashlight. They are climbing that awful ladder in total blackness, and Pru is really afraid of the dark," cried Lark. "We need to go help. We need to go back and get them," Lark screamed out through the wind.

"They can see. They are in the tree. Now trust you must and fly with me." June started circling down in a descending pattern until she softly landed on top of a building that had somehow appeared amidst the scarlet surroundings.

June bent her beak down, an indication for Lark to slide down and away from the safety between her wings. Lark hesitated.

"Have courage, my dear boy. You are strong. Have courage, Lark, and move along."

Lark crawled up her slick black neck and slid down slowly, this time landing on his feet. "Where are we? Where do we go?" he asked June.

"I'll wait here for you. This is one of the lessons, something you alone must do. Close your eyes, close them tight. You will find yourself in quite the fight."

"But, I-I-I don't like to fight. I'm kinda little. I can't get in a fight. I am not a fighter, and I don't want to be. What kind of lesson is that? I'm not supposed to fight," babbled Lark, scared and confused about what the future held.

"When it is right, you must fight. Sometimes there is strife, and you must fight for your life," encouraged June. "Have courage, my boy. It will lead to joy."

With reluctant acceptance, Lark slowly nodded his head.

"Okay, June. Okay."

June gave him a knowing nod. Lark mustered up all the courage he could find within his little body and closed his eyes tightly.

BEEP. BEEP. BEEP. Lark slowly opened his eyes. He was in completely different surroundings once again, but it felt weirdly familiar. BEEP. BEEP. June was no longer here, and Lark was no longer there. Things were no longer red. They were mostly white with hints of vanilla and yellow. There were bright lights and plenty of people. He was in a small room with babies in metal cribs and beeping machines. He must be in a hospital.

Sitting in a chair right in front of him, yet totally oblivious to his sudden presence, was his mother. She looked tired, more tired than Lark had ever seen her. Her hair was wild and un-brushed, and deep blue and purple circles cast a shadow under her big brown eyes. There, in the crib next to her, was a baby. A baby with tubes in her nose and stickers and wires on her chest. She wore only a diaper and a small, knit, pink hat. She was awake but not making much sound, except the strained hum of her breath going in and going out, laboring over each one with such effort that it brought tears to Lark's eyes. Her little chest was heaving up and down, and with each exhaled breath, the area in the middle of her chest under her ribs caved in as if it may collapse in desperation.

Mommy was singing "You Are My Sunshine" softly in a choked-up whisper, colorless tears streaming down her face. She tucked her head down and started to pray in silence, and Lark found he could hear her prayers inside her head. He could hear Mommy's thoughts, but it went even beyond that. Not only was he privy to her thoughts, he could also feel everything she felt. He shared her worries, her knowledge, and her fears in the *unknowing* of the dire situation at hand. It was Maisy in the crib. Maisy was a baby again, and she was sick.

Lark remembered stories of this time. He maybe had a faint memory of it, but he was very little. He remembered making snowmen and missing Mommy and Daddy and Maisy. He remembered everything had been different for a while. Right now, it was as if he was one and the same with his mother, experiencing the moment through her, with her, while still remaining a spectator.

"Mommy?" he said softly. She did not look up. "Mommy, can you hear me?" he asked hopefully. No response. He thought her eyes flickered with a knowing sparkle for a fleeting moment, but then, it faded as quickly as it came.

It was heartbreaking to see her like this, this woman who was usually so strong, so positive, so comforting, looking so sad. She watched helplessly as her small baby desperately tried to catch each breath, each breath that seemed to be closer and closer to eluding her. Lark reached out to touch his beloved mother, to give her a hug. Oh, he had missed her so. Lark was hoping for her to feel his hug, feel his presence and acknowledge him, but as he reached his arms around her for the embrace, he passed right through her, into her; he was now fully a part of her. It was almost like when he ran into Echo.

His physical-self mingled with a part of her physical-self, and his emotional-self mingled with her emotional-self. When this happened, he did not know any more whether Maisy was going to be okay, even though his self away from the outer-fort world knew that she was alive and thriving, but the feeling he had now, that feeling of the unknown, was the most frightening feeling he had ever felt. He was feeling the uncertainty, the fear, the grief, the exhaustion, the unknown with every ounce that Mommy was at this moment. He was totally unaware of the outcome and no longer had the knowledge, or the insight, of what the future held.

Lark closed his eyes for a moment as this was all so hard to see and so hard to feel, and when he opened them up, he and Mommy were somewhere else. There was a moment of confusion, and then, like a tsunami crashing in, he knew where he was as he again became a part of Mommy and her present thoughts. His awareness kept shifting in and out, jumping back and forth between a separate observer and an immersed experiencer with no real will of his own. Lark knew, somehow, he had to suspend his own thoughts to be back into hers, but he wasn't sure how to efficiently harness the control of doing so or if he would ever truly be able to influence that control. For now, he knew he had traveled back with Mommy, and it was a few days earlier from what he had just witnessed in the hospital.

"She can't seem to catch her breath. She feels miserable, and she has had a fever for days. She is throwing up, and she hasn't been sleeping. Me either. I lie in bed with my hand on her little chest as it heaves rapidly up and down, and I stay awake to make sure it continues to heave because I am so scared that it will suddenly stop altogether. Her twin is also sick. Did I tell you that? I was going to take the heart monitor off Gwynnie and put it on Maisy so that if I accidentally fell asleep, it would beep if she stopped breathing. If I took the monitor off Gwynnie, though, then what if she stops breathing? What if her heart does something that we need to know about? Gwynnie is sick, too, but Maisy can't breathe." Mommy was crying now as she rocked her baby close to her, nebulizer mask in hand, sitting in desperation in the doctor's office.

Lark was a part of her, feeling with her, along for the journey that lay ahead. It was a journey they had already been through but not like this for Lark. He had only just turned three at the time that Maisy became sick. He didn't really remember the details. Right now, Lark was privy to Mommy's thoughts and fears and hopes, as he was now completely a part of her.

"This is my sixth day in here in a row. Each time we have seen someone different. Each day you send us home. If you would give us the same doctor from one day to the next and saw the constant decline as we have, you would not send us home again," Mommy cried to the nurse.

"Okay, Mom, we will see what we can do for your baby," said the nurse, nodding as she glanced nervously at Mommy and then anxiously gazed down at Maisy.

Mommy felt a pang of anger at another stranger calling her "Mom" so casually in this moment of despair. "Mom" was a precious and sacred title. It drove home Mommy's anonymity to the nurse because, once again, they were seeing someone they hadn't seen before. The nurse hadn't even bothered to look at the chart to try and fake some faint name recognition. Mommy knew it was an easy, generic way for doctors and nurses to address her, but right now she wanted more of a connection.

"I understand it must be hard," the nurse said in a rehearsed tone. "She will be okay. The doctor will be in here in just a moment, Mom." And with that, the nurse rushed out of the room rather too quickly, either to express the urgency of the situation or to tell someone else on staff about the crazy mother in room number four. Perhaps the nurse was just trying to escape the tension, the thick desperation, that overtook the air and made it hard for everyone to breathe, not just Maisy.

Several moments later, the door opened. In walked the doctor, a new one, once again. "Good morning. So, tell me what's going on?" he asked in an accent from an island very south of there.

Mommy's mind wandered as she thought about how it would be so nice to be sitting there on that island right now, her healthy family all together on a blanket under a palm tree on a beach rather than stuck in this purple and blue painted box of a room, pictures of smiling teddy bears on the wall, with her sick baby whimpering in her arms. So, once again Mommy told her story, of when it started and what was happening, this story that kept adding unwanted pages, further and further from the unknown ending, with her sick baby whimpering in her arms.

They once again placed a pulse-ox on Maisy's tiny little appendage. It was getting to be too much for Mommy. It was beyond her mommy abilities to help her baby get better with kisses and a nebulizer, songs and sleepless nights, love and prayers. She was ready to share the load she and Daddy had been carrying, to share it with those that could help Maisy get better because if Mommy was feeling like she couldn't handle going on like this much longer, what about poor, sweet little Maisy? She needed to start getting better now.

"I'm sorry, Mom. She is having trouble getting enough oxygen. The numbers, um, I'm sorry—we are going to have to admit her into the hospital," the doctor said with sympathy in his voice.

Mommy certainly didn't want Maisy to be sick enough to need admittance to the hospital, but if she was sick enough to need the hospital, and even before coming to the doctor's office that day, Mommy knew she was indeed that sick, then the hospital was where she wanted Maisy to be. The predominant feeling Mommy felt upon hearing these words was relief.

Finally, Mommy thought, we can get her some real help, we can get her better, we can have someone else help us so that we know she is breathing, so that we know she can catch her breath, so that she can stop getting sick and get rid of her fever and this awful RSV.

"Thank you, doctor. I think that is a good idea." And with that, Mommy/Lark felt hopeful.

Chapter 12

Uncertainty

"be gentle and kind. be fragile and soft. I know the world tells you otherwise, but deep down inside you are not what they want you to be. you are all things that change . . . all leaves that fall, all rain that meets the ground and all petals that the flower can no longer hold. so, if you are meant to shatter, then go ahead, break beautifully, for the more you fall, the more you rise and the more you do both, the easier it will be to find yourself again."

—r.m. drake

GWYNNIE AND MAISY SPENT A FEW WEEKS IN THE HOSpital NICU when they were first born. The twins were born on a Friday with a planned C-section. They had something called twin-to-twin transfusion in utero, so Mommy had to go to the special baby doctor to see how they were doing three times a week. Her regular specialist was kind and knowledgeable, and even when things seemed questionable with the pregnancy, he somehow managed to give her peace of mind.

He was out of town the day she found out about the twin-to-twin transfusion. She was a little over the halfway point of her pregnancy if these two little babies went full term, which was not likely with twins. The doctor working that day delivered the findings to Mommy with a rather bleak outlook. His approach was to prepare her for the worst, to inform her fully of all that could go wrong because it was a possibility. Mommy lay there on the table, her belly still exposed and wet from the ultrasound gel, as she listened to the doctor say things like, "We will need to monitor closely" and "sometimes people need to pick a twin, if the body can't support both, and sometimes they end up without either." Twin-to-twin transfusion could only happen with identical twins because they shared a placenta. The goodies that the placenta delivered, the nutrients and the fluids and all that was needed for these little beings to grow, were not getting divvied up evenly. The doctor's words formed a surreal, dark cloud overhead.

Mommy went home and immediately made a horrible mistake. She got on the computer, and she Googled. She searched the world wide web for all and any information on twin-to-twin transfusion. She Googled information about what exactly it was, and she Googled stories of people that had gone through it and experienced the many possible outcomes. Unfortunately, much of what was being written was not promising and did not have happy endings.

After hours of searching, she slowly closed the computer. She put her hand on her belly and prayed with tears streaming down her face.

That was a Friday. She opened the computer several times over the weekend, searching for any and all information to keep her informed, to make her feel better, but of course, she didn't know the outcome of the stories until they were already read, so many of the stories did just the opposite. She often stumbled across scary anecdotes and daunting medical scenarios related to twin-to-twin transfusion. She couldn't un-read them once they were already read, so her search to make herself feel better did not work out well.

Mommy walked into the doctor's office on Monday morning for her next appointment, literally shaking from nerves and lack of sleep. Her regular doctor was back. Mommy again cried as she discussed the situation with him. Always a comforting presence, he let her know some of the more common challenging scenarios of twin-to-twin transfusion but followed each up with hope and a plan of how to tackle it. There was an excellent hospital in Philadelphia that specialized in a surgery while the babies were still in utero if needed, cutting edge, with good results thus far. Once she was far enough along for them to be viable, they would see if they would need to deliver, but they'd keep them in as long as possible, as long as the benefits of being in her outweighed the risks of being born early. They were aiming for that, and they'd take each day as it came.

The resounding message on Monday versus Friday was that there were things that could be done, but there was also a good chance that those may not be needed. There was hope. Her doctor was an angel here on earth, and he helped her find that hope again. He told Mommy there was no reason, at this point, not to think that this could be a best-case scenario of the condition ending with two very healthy babies in her arms. Then he gave her a prescription with strict medical guidelines that she was to heed, no matter what. She was no longer allowed to get on the computer and Google *anything* about twin-to-twin transfusion. He gave her his cell phone number and said she must give him a call at any time if she was ever feeling scared like that again, or had a question, or if she ever felt the urge to Google anything related to her pregnancy. It was time to embrace blissful ignorance once again.

The babies would do cool things like sit on each other's heads or reach out to touch hands when they were photographed floating around during ultrasounds, but behind the cuteness, there were some serious issues. Gwynnie, Baby B, was the one stealing all of the goodies in utero, and Maisy, Baby A, was giving them up. Gwynnie was receiving extra blood, and as a result, a significant amount of extra amniotic fluid was on Gwynnie's side, surrounding her body so her little heart had to work twice as hard, endangering her and her hard-working heart. Mommy was noticeably more gigantic on Gwynnie's side of her belly. This also carried the risk of pre-term labor, which would occur if the amniotic sac ruptured as a result of its extra-large size. Maisy, Baby A, was the one donating from the placenta. She was small and weak, and there was just barely enough amniotic fluid on her side. This was also dangerous. Death and brain damage were possibilities.

There were endless appointments and tests and waiting and hoping and constant debate about what would be best for them.

Mommy and Daddy tried to carry on, focusing on the end result that they envisioned: two healthy babies in their arms in a very short time. But, every now and then, that was hard.

"It is time. You need to have those babies today," said Mommy's regular OB/GYN over the phone. She had said the same thing five days earlier but then had called Mommy back saying she had changed her mind: they could wait a little bit longer. Mommy trusted her doctor and didn't question it. This time, she knew, there would be no follow up phone call, no changing her mind. Today, they would meet their twins.

Mommy needed a C-section because Gwynnie was transverse in Mommy's belly; she was sideways. This, along with the extra fluid, also contributed to the enormous state of Mommy's tummy on Gwynnie's side. It was Mommy's first surgery aside from her wisdom teeth, and she was nervous and excited and sick and terrified and curious. Mommy's platelets were off, and her numbers were low. There was talk of needing to put Mommy under general anesthesia and have her asleep for the birth. Ultimately it was decided that they would let her be awake. Although the numbers were under the cut-off, they were going to let her slide because this was something that Mommy didn't want to miss. Mommy was glad, but it added another layer of nerves, another potential complication. The babies needed to be here and fine and healthy, and Mommy also needed to be here and fine and healthy. Lark, being a part of her, felt her fear.

When Mommy and Daddy arrived at the hospital, there was some pre-op prep, and then they started on a long walk down a long hallway with a green-scrub-clad parade of people, a parade that took on a feeling of excitement with each step toward the operating room. Once they arrived, they all filed in and started the process. The room was filled with doctors and nurses—NICU specialists, the OB/GYN, her nurses, anesthesiologists, interns, and other people with unique roles unknown to Mommy and Daddy—but they all had a purpose. Mommy and Daddy were there, of course, and soon, very soon, so were two beautiful, wonderful, miraculous baby girls.

Every baby is a miracle, but with the difficult pregnancy, Mommy and Daddy knew this even more than they ever had before.

"Here she is! She's beautiful!" shouted their doctor, the apples of her cheeks high on her face, revealing the hidden existence of the big smile concealed behind her green mask. There was blood spattered across her gown as she held the baby up, as if in a scene from *The Lion King*, holding her up high for all to see. Mommy and Daddy hadn't known if the twins were going to be girls or boys before they were born, but they had the perfect first names picked out for either outcome.

"It's a girl! They are girls!" Daddy said, his voice cracking under the pressure of the joy that consumed him. "It's Maisy," he told Mommy.

The color of Mommy's face matched the green mask covering Daddy's mouth. Mommy emotionally was bursting with happiness, but physically she felt like she was going to pass out. She heard the doctor, and she heard Daddy, but her thoughts were fuzzy as her mind jumped from silent prayers of thanks and hope to "it's a girl," to the fact that she felt like she was having some out of body experience, which she kind of was, for there were bodies coming out of her body, and she was lying there, feeling like a passive observer.

"Congratulations Daddy!" the doctor said to the proud papa, his big smile detectable behind the mask. He did not mind being called "Daddy" by the doctor in this moment at all. Maisy cried out, and Mommy started to cry tears of joy and relief. She still felt as though she might faint or throw up or have a panic attack, but a minute later they were holding up Gwynnie, and just like that, they went from a family of four to a family of six. They brought the small new babies over to Mommy so she could have a quick glance at her twin girls.

"We're going to take them to the room next door. Dad, you can come with us."

They all disappeared in a green parade out the double doors. Mommy laid there as the doctor sewed her back together. She felt sick and dizzy from the anesthesia and slightly disoriented but still aware that she had just given birth to twins. Identical baby girls—it didn't get much better than that.

She still felt scared and panicky and wished Daddy was there holding her clammy hand. Her hands and arms had been archaically strapped down to long boards to ensure she would not interfere in the procedure, in case she panicked. This was a notion she understood much more now post-delivery than she had pre-delivery. Strapped down and unable to move as these babies were removed from her womb, without so much as a contraction or a push, she didn't feel like the active player she had been in her deliveries of Lark and Sophie. The babies were out, though, and they were safe.

Still, she had a strange feeling she couldn't put her finger on. It was probably the anesthesia messing with her mind and the swirl of emotions of the past several months forming a colorful cyclone in her head. It was a cyclone of joy and pain swirling around together, without the ability to delineate one from the other, as they were one in the same. She would feel better once she saw Daddy and Maisy and Gwyneth again.

Finally, they wheeled Mommy's bed to the room next door. It was bustling with motion as nurses and doctors buzzed around with numbers and stats and coos and congratulations. The nurses efficiently and quickly worked on the babies at a table a few feet from Mommy. They were sucking things out and measuring things and checking things. They put both twins in a little plastic bassinet next to each other, and they instinctively held hands, and Daddy took pictures, and Mommy strained her neck to see from the table she was lying on as the doctors continued poking and prodding at her, too. Gwyneth was markedly bigger than Maisy, by a couple of pounds, even though Maisy was the "big sister" because she was born an entire minute prior to her. Her doctor made a comment that they should have done it a week earlier when she saw the size discrepancy between the two babies, but they were here now, and you can't spend your life looking in the rear-view mirror.

An older nurse brought Maisy over to Mommy and held her down next to Mommy's head. "Meet your daughter," the nurse said through her mask. "Baby A."

Mommy let the moment sink in.

"Her name is Maisy," Mommy said softly. She explored her small features, that tiny head beneath the striped blue and pink hat. She didn't know if she had ever seen something so small, so fragile, so beautiful. She looked like a baby bird that had fallen from her nest but landed softly into the hands of this kind nurse. "Maisy. It is so nice to finally meet you . . . my sweet little Maisy," Mommy swooned softly as she reached out to stroke her little cheek. The entire introduction lasted all of thirty seconds.

"She is having a little trouble catching her breath, very common with twins and babies born a bit early. We're going to take her over to the NICU to be on the safe side."

The NICU was the Neonatal Intensive Care Unit, and Mommy nervously looked up at the nurse who continued to hover Maisy next to Mommy's head. Mommy planted a quick kiss on Maisy's cheek. Mommy was about to ask the nurse a question, but before she had the chance, Maisy and the nurse were disappearing around the corner. Maisy had looked helpless but also strangely strong. There was immeasurable strength in her spirit, deep inside that little body. She had already endured quite a fight to get here, and little did she know at the time, she would have to endure a fight to stay here in the days, weeks, and months to come.

Daddy was holding Mommy's hand again, and he gave her an encouraging squeeze. They locked gazes and spoke silently with their eyes, each reassuring the other that Maisy would be fine. They held on to the joy of the moment that remained, for they had just doubled their number of children in the span of a minute. They had made it this far, and things had a way of working out for them. The journey wasn't always easy, but together they got through the tough times they had been dealt. They learned from them, and then they moved on, focusing on the positive.

Seconds later, Mommy was properly meeting Gwynnie for the first time, and four minutes after that, Gwynnie was also disappearing around the corner to meet up with her twin in the NICU. Gwynnie, too, was having respiratory problems.

Soon, Daddy was also on the second floor in the NICU with their new babies. Mommy wasn't allowed to go down there yet. She was still recovering from surgery and suddenly found herself alone in a room on the third floor of the maternity ward. She felt very alone indeed.

Lark, having observed all of this, felt himself traveling again. They were in a different room now. Mommy and Daddy were there. There were two plastic boxes with tubes and circles on the side and one little baby in each. Lark jumped from one moment to the next rather quickly, as if watching an old film, where the frame of the scene hovers just a second before moving on to the next. It creates a rather choppy effect, effective nonetheless, despite the lack of modern fluidity. That was Lark's journey right now, effective but choppy, as he tried to piece together these old clips of life into something congruent.

Maisy was about to get a spinal tap. "Risk factors such as paralysis and possible death, though uncommon, come with the spinal tap. As meningitis has complications such as brain damage and death, we really need to figure this out."

Mommy and Daddy were handed a paper by the doctor to give permission and were told that time was of the essence, and they needed to sign it right now. They did because what other choice did they have? The medical staff whisked Maisy off to plunge a needle bigger than she was into her tiny spinal cord. This poor little baby bird.

Swoosh. Fast forward. Lark looked around. Still in the NICU.

"Two-week course of heavy-duty antibiotics. Not meningitis but she is septic. She has contracted an infection, and it is in her blood. She is still having breathing problems. Gwyneth also continues to have trouble breathing. The infection was either contracted in utero or during birth. They shared a placenta, they shared a birth, so we are going to treat her for it as well—to be on the safe side."

Mommy and Daddy nodded their heads in understanding, holding hands, nervous glances bouncing back and forth between each other and the two plastic boxes holding their precious babies.

Antibiotics and breast milk dripped into the little plastic boxes and into their little, precious babies, within their room at the NICU. Lark had traveled there with them. There was a doctor yelling at Mommy for breastfeeding for the first time in the week and a half since Maisy was born. The doctor's accusatory voice ricocheted through the room, even though the lactation specialist, along with another doctor, had instructed Mommy to do so and helped her to do so with guiding words and encouragement. This bellowing doctor, who had just arrived to her shift, held a lot of authority in the NICU and was the doctor who had performed Maisy's spinal tap. She yelled that Mommy had put her baby's life at risk as tears streamed down Mommy's face. Mommy quietly tried to defend herself, but the dismissive doctor would not listen. When she was finished reprimanding Mommy, she stormed out of the room, shutting the door a little too hard.

Moments earlier, Mommy had cuddled this four-pound little love in her arms and used tubes and tapes and contraptions to help Maisy have a sip of her mama's milk, the first time coming directly from Mommy rather than from a bag dripping through a tube above her. Mommy had soaked in this milestone moment, blocking out the people prodding her parts that were once private and hidden. Her parts were now feeding machines as any sense of modesty was a sacrificial rite of passage into motherhood. Pregnancy, birth, motherhood—there was no more privacy and no room for modesty, and that was okay because it was no longer about her.

Mommy had this magical moment of finally feeding this baby girl. Gwynnie was doing well and had been able to eat a few days earlier. Gwynnie would be able to come home soon, but Maisy was still very sick. At last, to be able to hold her tiny baby close to her and feed her gave Mommy and Maisy a connection they both desperately needed. Breast milk had healing qualities, and Mommy felt lucky that she was able to produce this milk and have it go inside her weak little baby. Feeding her brought hope and gave Mommy a sense of purpose. With this connection, she started to feel like an active player in all of this again, able to make a difference beyond prayers and lullabies.

Lark zoomed into another flash forward: the angry doctor, tail between her legs, cheeks flushed, apologizing profusely for being misinformed in telling Mommy she was not supposed to feed Maisy. Mommy and Daddy, still hurt and slighted but also not wanting to dwell in the negative, forgave her and moved on. Lark felt all of this.

Lark watched Mommy as she placed Gwynnie into the waiting car seat sitting on the NICU floor. Even though Gwynnie had a couple of pounds on Maisy, she looked tiny in the red infant car seat that surrounded her now. Size can be relative. Mommy had changed Gwynnie out of the preemie clothes the hospital had given them, and she was now wearing a soft, little, pink, going-home outfit Mommy had purchased with a matching little pink hat that said "happy girl" on it. Another matching outfit was tucked away in the corner of the room, patiently waiting to be used. The outfit was tiny, but not preemie, so it was quite large on Gwynnie, although it was still perfect. Mommy had imagined the moment she would put these outfits on her babies, visions of two healthy girls wearing them, with the sentiment of "happy girl" displayed in bold defiance of the past couple of weeks they would soon be putting behind them.

Gwynnie was coming home. The hospital was sending Mommy and Daddy home with some preemie onesies, and Gran had already gone out and scoured the stores for any fuzzy onesie pajamas that had preemie on the tag. Gwynnie had a tube coming out of her pant leg, the wire to the heart monitor that she would wear for the next six months. Lark watched as Mommy and Daddy learned how to work the monitor, administer CPR on an infant, and utilize the car seat properly, although they were already quite adept at that one. Once they demonstrated all skills proficiently, they were finally allowed to take the first of their two twin daughters home. It had already been so hard, since Mommy was previously discharged, to leave the babies at the hospital.

Mommy had been discharged from the hospital five days after delivery, but of course, the babies were not. It was a painful transition. Mommy's hurt was compounded when they ran into a pregnant friend in front of the hospital as they were about to pull away in their car after Mommy was discharged. Having heard of the twins' arrival, she asked excitedly to see the babies, smiling as she peered expectantly into the back seat to then find it empty. She quickly looked back at Mommy, confused as her smile faded. Guilt overwhelmed Mommy. Choking back tears, she explained that they couldn't bring the babies home yet. It was like the feeling Mommy had on the day of delivery when she found herself alone in her room on the third floor of the maternity ward. It was a surreal distance, an unwanted space that tried to force itself in despite all efforts to defy it. There are two other babies at home, Mommy thought. *Lark and Sophie also need to see their parents.* After all, they were two and one years old, just babies as well.

In the days ahead, no matter where they were, hospital or home, Mommy and Daddy's hearts were tugging them back to wherever they had just left. Lark, as part of his adventures, felt this difficult and distraught dichotomy through Mommy's tugging heart, and consequently his own heart also felt heavy.

Once little Lark and Sophie were tucked in tight, Gramps and Gran would come over each night so that Mommy and Daddy could venture over to the NICU on floor two of the hospital to tend to their newborns. They would stay there until they couldn't stay up anymore, falling asleep in the upright chairs in the small room as their arms also fell asleep under their poorly propped, bobbing, sleepy heads. During the day, they took shifts, but once Mommy could nurse the twins, it was mostly her at the NICU while Daddy took care of things at home and tried to fit a bit of work in to help pay for this ever-growing brood.

Finally, the day came when they were able to take Maisy home, too. It was Maisy's turn to wear her little pink outfit and her own "happy girl" hat, and Mommy dressed her in it deliberately and ceremoniously, soaking it all in, as simple moments become big moments after those simple moments are threatened.

The NICU nurse gave Maisy a loving hug and a post-NICU pep talk. "You had me so worried, little one," she said, nose to nose with Maisy. Then, with Maisy still dangling in front of her, she glanced up at Mommy and Daddy with a look of relief. "She was just so sick when I first met her. Yes, this little one's a fighter. She'll be just fine."

The ten-year-old Lark bounced around haphazardly in these visceral experiences. Sometimes he was an observer. Sometimes he was transported inside Mommy's thoughts, feelings, and emotions. When Lark was a part of her, he experienced moments in which he was completely in her thoughts, experiencing things for the first time as they happened, without knowing the outcome and how things might turn out. Even if the ten-year-old Lark knew things might be okay, this wasn't information available to him in these adventures through Mommy's vantage point. When he popped back to being an observer, he found a new appreciation of Mommy's perspective on things. It was a perspective gained from experiences, from living one's life and being open to the lessons along the way. Lark made a mental note to really listen to her advice if he ever got the chance to return home.

Lark wasn't sure how he was transported. Sometimes it happened when he closed his eyes; sometimes he thought he was on June's back; sometimes he wondered if he was reading minds; and sometimes he had no idea where he was or what was going on. He continued to travel erratically, learning the lessons presented in each new experience. He had to make these lessons a part of him too, just like they were a part of Mommy. These experiences and lessons were the essence of his adventure.

Chapter 13

Sisters

"You don't choose your family. They are God's gift to you, as you are to them."

—Desmond Tutu

THEY ALL HAD BLONDE HAIR. EVERY SINGLE KID IN Lark's family was blonde, yet they were all unique. Lark's eyes were a steel blue that changed color based on random factors like the color he was wearing that day or the weather or even his mood. He had an unruly mop of blonde hair that was stuck in a never-ending showdown between cowlicks and static. Sophie had light blue eyes with a dark blue ring around the iris for extra emphasis, and her hair was long, thick, wavy, and white. The twins, Gwynnie and Maisy, both had deep chestnut-brown eyes, big and doe-like with long lashes. Their hair was silky and straight and golden blonde. And then there was Bliss with her almond-shaped green eyes and dirty blonde hair that curled into ringlets at the end, hair that would try its best to remain un-brushed and tangled if Bliss had her way. They had their own looks but were undeniably siblings.

The twins were identical, but they had their own unique looks once you got to know them. Maisy and Gwynnie were loud and silly and brought such energy wherever they went. When they were small babies, an older woman approached Mommy and looked back and forth between the two little babies in matching clothes, looking so similar at this point that Mommy could almost get them mixed up.

"What's the difference, what's the difference?" this elderly stranger said out loud with a hint of an accent as she bobbed her head back and forth, comparing the identical, cooing, little bundles. "Ah-ha, I've got it!" she exclaimed victoriously. "That one's a young soul," she said, pointing to Gwynnie, "and that one's an old soul," she said as she motioned to Maisy. She smiled at Mommy with a look of contentment and accomplishment.

Mommy glanced down at the twins, and this suddenly made so much sense.

"I do believe you're right," Mommy agreed, smiling back. The woman gave a pleased nod and quickly disappeared around the corner, leaving Mommy contemplating this thought of old soul versus young soul and the wonder of life's interesting little encounters with random people.

Sophie, with her white-blonde hair and her big, blue eyes, was almost a year and a half older than the twins, and she made sure it was known she was the *big* sister. The twins and Bliss looked up to Sophie and Lark. Sophie and Lark were almost Irish twins; they were so close in age. They were also so close in size that people often asked if they, too, were twins.

Sophie was a total sweetheart. She was easy going but a hard worker, and when she set her mind to learning something new, whether it was hula hooping or Irish dancing or playing the ukulele or diving or playing lacrosse, she was all in, working hard to perfect it.

Lark was more tentative about trying new things. He often claimed he didn't need to practice because he already knew how to do something, even things in which he was a complete novice. In sports, when he was very little, he often wanted to be the coach or the referee instead of engaging in the actual playing of the game. Lark liked to be in charge; it was fun telling other people what to do. Mommy and Daddy wanted him to try, to give his best, to not be so worried about the outcome, and to have fun in the process.

As time went on, when it came to things he was not skilled in yet, Lark's periphery preferences persisted. Mommy and Daddy had a sinking suspicion that it was due to a fear of failure. He'd rather give half-effort and retain full self-preservation of self-concept while his true abilities remained a mystery. Whether he had created delusions of grandeur as a defense mechanism or a paralyzing fear of truly trying his best and not succeeding, Lark could get in the way of himself.

Sophie helped Lark be himself. Sophie and Lark were very different, but they had a special relationship; they adored one another. They had such a mutual understanding, respect, and love for each other that their differences melted away.

When Sophie was three, she went to preschool two mornings a week. Lark was in a classroom down the hall. He loved being in school with Sophie and even brought her in for "show and tell" when the students were to bring in something that was *extra* special and meaningful to them. Lark was so proud to show off his little sister, beaming in the middle of the circle of children as he explained how special Sophie was to him. Mommy watched, and her heart beamed as well. Lark and Sophie had quite the connection.

In her early school years, everyone they came across commented on how cute and funny it was that Sophie spoke her own little language. That comment stung a little bit when Mommy and Daddy heard it. That little language was English with severe speech articulation issues. At the end of the school year when Sophie had turned four, the teacher sat down and told Mommy that, even after an entire year together, she still couldn't understand one word Sophie was saying. Mommy's heart sank. Mommy asked if Sophie's friends understood her, and the teacher said that she didn't really have friends in the classroom because *no one* could understand her. She said Sophie was becoming silent in school because of this. Mommy's heart sank even more as she fought back tears, sitting in this tiny preschooler chair taking in this big news.

As Mommy saw it, it sounded like no one was properly helping Sophie be understood in school. Sophie needed extra support with communication in the classroom, and the entire year had slipped by without it. Mommy couldn't help wondering why this teacher had waited until mid-May to tell her this update. She had never indicated any of this when Mommy checked in to see how things were going during drop off, pick up, volunteering, or class events and parties. Sophie had been in speech therapy since she was two. Mommy had been in communication with the teacher on the different things Sophie was working on, hoping the teacher would carry them into the classroom and help Sophie communicate. Mommy was disheartened that Sophie's spirit was suffering. Her heart felt heavy.

Sophie was boisterous and talkative and loud and happy at home. It did indeed take a lot of effort to concentrate on what she was trying to say. Sometimes it was exhausting for both Sophie and the listener. Sophie had a great vocabulary already, so she could often re-phrase things, or use different synonyms, to get her point across. Sometimes she tried to give up, to dismiss her idea in defeat if it was taking a long time for others to understand. Connections can take effort. Connections can take time. Sophie's family encouraged her, and eventually they figured it out together. They wanted Sophie to know what she had to say was important. It was effort for the whole family, but they were willing to put in the effort because Sophie was worth it.

Out of the classroom, Lark had become her pint-sized translator. He understood her and helped others understand her, too. Mommy wouldn't sign them up for any drop-off activities without each other because she needed Lark there to translate for Sophie, in case Sophie needed something and couldn't get her needs understood on her own. Mommy realized this was a high expectation to put on someone only fifteen months Sophie's senior, but Lark always seemed glad to be there to help Sophie if she needed it.

With hard work and determination, over the years Sophie was able to progress with her speech. She was able to do things like sing in choir and give oral reports and say whatever was on her mind. She spoke, and people listened.

Lark had helped her get there. Lark became her voice when she couldn't find her own. Lark brought out the best in her so others could see her best, too. Sophie also helped bring out the best in Lark. She also helped him find his true voice, too.

Lark, Sophie, Maisy, Gwynnie, and Bliss were siblings and the best of friends. Lark had no brother. He had boy cousins, and they had a close relationship but didn't live close by. He had good friends he'd known his whole life that were kind of like brothers, but not quite.

Now there was Echo. Lark understood that Echo was, somehow, a part of his own make-up, a part of himself, but it also felt like he was a brother. He and Echo had established a brotherly connection. With that connection, Echo would also help Lark find his voice.

Chapter 14
Snow

"The future lies before you,
Like a field of fallen snow,
Be careful how you tread it,
For every step will show."

—Anonymous

LARK, ON HIS ADVENTURES, HAD AGAIN TRAVELED TO A new spot. This spot was not in any kind of medical setting, nor in the magical world. No, he was in the real world, somewhere that he couldn't place, although the scenery was quite magical. He glanced to his right, and there, sitting next to him with a big goofy smile, was Echo. Lark had missed seeing that goofy smile, and he smiled back at him immediately as if this was all totally normal. They leaned into each other, shoulders touching, and Lark instantly felt supported and comforted.

There they sat for a quiet moment in a big bundle of connectivity and contentment. Lark suddenly choked up as colorful tears streamed down his face. They were those complicated tears, like the ones Gramps had at Lark's birthday party; tears that held a world of emotions in each tiny drop. Lark looked over at Echo as Echo also started to cry big, colorful tears. For some reason, maybe being overcome with emotion, maybe Echo's goofy expression, Lark suddenly laughed out loud, which made Echo laugh too, and there they were, back to giggling together uncontrollably for no reason and every reason.

After their laughter subsided, they were so connected that, without a word or a tangible thought, in unison they both looked around, searching for some clues indicating where on earth they were. They could see they were sitting on the edge of a cliff, legs dangling freely over the edge of the abyss, but Lark wasn't scared; he knew he was safe. On the distant horizon, a large red sun was setting. There was a vastness to this space that Lark hadn't experienced before on earth. He had experienced something similar while gazing out at the deep ocean or up at the sea of stars in the sky. It was liberating, humbling, soul-freeing, jaw-dropping, mind-expanding vastness. There was a long howl in the distance. Lark and Echo looked at each other, alarmed.

"Ahhhh, the jackal's call." June's voice drifted by in a soft whisper. "This is it, boys. See, hear, feel it all."

Lark and Echo gazed around, searching for June, for the jackal, for answers.

"When you stop the search and truly see, that is when you will finally be. For it is here many answers lie. Tranquility under an African sky."

June's voice trailed off and left Lark and Echo in quiet contemplation. Then all of a sudden, they consciously stopped contemplating. Heeding June's wise words, Lark and Echo simultaneously stopped searching their surroundings. Subsequently the stunning surroundings washed over them, into them, filled them up, just as June had promised. It was everything. Everything found in the simplicity of the African sky.

The red sun was now spilling into the rest of the sky, lighting it up in glorious colors from the bottom of the spectrum with its brush strokes of red and orange and yellow. Baobab trees stood in majestic magnificence, and acacia trees dotted the landscape, providing an umbrella-like silhouette contrasted against this tie-dyed sky. The sound of distant drums carried across the great vastness from somewhere far away, or maybe somewhere nearby, it was too hard to tell as space can be relative. The sun dipped below the earth, below the horizon, greeting the night. The bright sky gave way to a beautiful twilight from the other end of the spectrum in deep blues and indigos and purples. Then there was black. As darkness surrounded them, stars poured into the sky. The moon was a sliver of a smile, hanging low, just above the earth like a hook, ready to catch anything that came its way. The stars overtook the southern atmosphere with reckless abandon. The Milky Way carved a distinct path through this darkness as shooting stars flew unpredictably across the black sky toward some unseen destination. It was simply stunning.

Again, June's voice sounded. "South of the equator is the Southern Cross; let the stars guide you, should you ever feel lost."

Lark and Echo sat there on that cliff, gazing up at the sky, legs dangling freely, hearts connected and warm in the heart of Africa. Lark and Echo found the Southern Cross together, though neither had been to the southern hemisphere before; they found it through an unspoken knowing. Everything felt right; it felt just as it should.

"Would you like to have African adventures someday, boys?" June asked them, although they still couldn't see her. They both nodded their heads excitedly. "That's a good choice. Not now, but soon, you will find yourself again under the African moon."

Lark and Echo gave confused looks to each other, and before they could say a word, *swoosh*.

Lark was home. He was home! Though Echo wasn't with him like he had been on the cliff, Lark could still feel his presence. The traveling Lark was back home but not in an out-of-the-outer-fort-world way of being home. He was still an invisible observer.

It was nice to be home, nonetheless, even if he knew he wasn't going to stay for long. Lark had traveled back to when he was quite small. Back then, he attended a little preschool close to home on Friday mornings from nine to twelve because Mommy and Daddy thought it would be good for him to have stimulation and social interaction outside of the house, especially since things would be pretty crazy once the twins were born. Lark saw himself now as a very little boy; he was watching himself from outside of himself.

Little Lark was in their living room, holding tiny Maisy in the orange-flowered rocking chair, singing a song to her that he had just learned in preschool that day. Maisy was still healthy. She had turned three months old, and Lark had turned three years old. Mommy stood supervising above, singing praise of what a good big brother he was and how Maisy loved him so much and how he was being so sweet and gentle with his little baby sister. Lark sniffled and smiled as his nose started to run, and before Mommy could do anything, he was diving his runny, little nose down to nuzzle Maisy's little nose while enthusiastically giving one of his new baby twinnies a big kiss on her tiny pink face.

"So sweet, Lark," said Mommy as she quickly scooped them both up. She carefully placed Maisy back in her Moses basket, and after wiping them both down, she propped Lark on her hip and strolled into the kitchen to wash his hands and give him a snack.

Respiratory Syncytial Virus (RSV), a common and very contagious virus, infected the respiratory tract of children. For most, it appeared to be the common cold. Infants that were born early, were multiples, or had siblings in daycare or preschool, were considered high-risk, especially during the cold winter months known as "RSV season."

Gwynnie and Maisy had every one of those risk factors, though Mommy and Daddy didn't know it. The twins would have been candidates for a vaccine against RSV, but they didn't know that either. Lark watched as he was suddenly flooded with the knowledge of this awful illness from some outside source, and he watched his three-year-old self share germs with his three-month-old sister while Mommy unknowingly watched and encouraged them to love on each other in that rocking chair. In hindsight, Mommy would've tried to keep some distance between runny little noses. Maybe Lark gave RSV to her, maybe he didn't. None of that mattered at the end of the day.

Every time Lark was transported, the lucky stone in his pocket heated up. It started to heat up again. He didn't want to leave the safe surroundings of home, but Lark knew he had no say in it. He already knew he was in for quite the journey. *Swoosh.*

Lark skipped along through time, jumping into random but significant moments. Whenever he arrived in a moment, he had the insight gained from earlier experiences, even if he hadn't experienced them himself. He was channeling the experiences of his mother and the knowledge gained in each experience. Lark was experiencing things through Mommy's eyes again, through Mommy's unedited heart.

Maisy was three months old. She left the NICU a few weeks after being born and had been home now for a couple of months. Life had taken on its new normal, whatever that was in a household with four children two and under, two of whom were newborn twins. Now, a few months later, they were back in the same hospital. They had gone straight from the doctor's office to the hospital, and Daddy, anxiously awaiting updates, was home with Lark, Sophie, and Gwynnie.

It was the same day as the doctor visit Lark saw, when they were in the red realm, when Mommy was pleading with the nurse, and the doctor said they needed to be admitted to the hospital. Not much time had gone by. As they checked them into the pediatric ward of the hospital, the doctors had told them not to worry, that Maisy would be fine. She would be "home in a day or two," and they were just keeping her here to watch her, "to be on the safe side."

It was January. It had started snowing earlier that day. Mommy could already see the white blanket being laid upon the earth outside the window of Maisy's hospital room. Things felt almost peaceful for a moment, slightly serene. Finally, Maisy was going to get better, and they were in the right spot to make that happen.

After making phone calls to Daddy and other family members to fill them in, Mommy let her eyes close for what felt like the first time in days. She closed her overly exhausted eyes while their baby slept, and the quiet snow fell outside. Things felt hopeful.

Within a moment, there was a jarring knock on the door. It was the news about a transfer.

"I'm sorry, Mom. I think it's time we transferred her to a hospital with a higher level of care, to be on the safe side," said the doctor.

Lark observed Mommy, watching her expression and feeling her thoughts as she listened intently to this slender woman with long hair and a slight middle eastern accent solemnly deliver this update.

"We aren't going to use the helicopter because of the snow; it's coming down too hard, but the ambulance can take her. You can ride in that, and they'll get you there quickly. Do you have a preference between DC and Baltimore? They are both excellent and both comparable. It's just a precaution, but we'd rather have you at a tertiary hospital in case she needs extra care that we don't have here. Especially with the weather, well, we need to get you there, to be on the safe side. Where do you want to go?"

This was a lot for Mommy to take in. She had questions, but no time to ask them. At the end of the conversation and after a phone call to Daddy, they decided on the hospital closest to Daddy's office in Baltimore because it was only going to be a short stay, and he could easily pop over while at work. He was still trying to make up for lost work time from when the babies were in the NICU.

The doctor assured Mommy again that Maisy was going to be fine, and they were just being overly cautious. They were quick to transfer patients out if there was even a question.

Mommy nodded in understanding and agreement. Of course, she wished the transfer wasn't needed, but she was thankful that they were keeping a close eye on Maisy and giving her everything she needed. Overly cautious sounded like a good approach.

They loaded Maisy into the ambulance, Mommy climbed in next to her, and off they went. The snow was coming down hard now, and everything was completely white. It was hard to see the road, but the ambulance driver didn't seem concerned. After a while, he said he was going to turn off the siren because, besides some snowplows, they were the only ones on the road in this blizzard. With flashing red lights ricocheting off a sheet of snowflakes, they headed north, up the road to Baltimore for the next stop on their journey. Lark felt the worry weighing heavily in Mommy's heart.

They flew out of the ambulance doors through a set of double doors and down a long, almost empty hallway scattered with hospital employees with compassionate, worried looks on their faces, peering down at the tiny creature strapped to the stretcher as Maisy whimpered softly. They then caught eyes with her distraught mama, holding her little hand with tears streaming down her face. Empathetic tears would sting their eyes as the stretcher wheeled past them in a blur.

Lark was now a witness to this surreal scene. At the end of the long hallway, they flew through another set of double doors and found themselves in the middle of the Pediatric Intensive Care Unit (PICU). The unit was one big, open, and overwhelming room, with a busy nurse's station at one end. Hospital beds lined the walls with a couple of somewhat private rooms in the corners. Everywhere there were bright lights, beeping machines, sick babies and children, doctors doctoring, nurses nursing, and parents parenting, chatting, crying, or laughing, depending on how their child was doing at that particular moment.

It was complete and total sensory overload.

They then continued through the double doors at the other end of the PICU. They were in the step-down unit now, and that was where Maisy was heading. The step-down unit was for very sick children not quite needing the level of care that they had just wheeled through, and for that, Mommy was extremely thankful.

They hooked Maisy up to the necessary monitors. It took a while, but they were able to get Mommy a breast pump from the maternity ward so she could make extra milk for her sick baby here in the hospital as well as for her sick baby at home. The nurse in the room told Mommy about the unit and where to find the bathroom and the parent's lounge with a TV and recliners for parents to sleep in because there were no beds for parents in the rooms. The nurse also told Mommy it looked like she had been through a lot and she should try and get some rest because they monitored Maisy around the clock, so she would be just fine. In the morning, if Mommy wanted coffee, there was a Ronald McDonald parent's room with a coffee maker down the hall in the other direction or a Starbucks in the lobby, but it may not be open because of all of the snow. Mommy thanked the nurse, and the nurse left the room, closing the door behind her. With that, their time in Baltimore was under way.

Maisy's chest continued to heave up and down, up and down. Lark recognized this as being the first room he had visited for a few moments when he started his time-traveling adventures. The room when he first saw Maisy lying in that bed as Mommy sang "You Are My Sunshine" to her, choking back tears. As Lark was lost in thought, trying to piece together this puzzle of time and experiences and memories that were no longer his own, someone entered the room. It was the respiratory therapist, a gregarious man named John, with light brown skin and a big smile that lightened the mood. He chatted casually for a moment about the weather and gave a brief synopsis of his background. He'd been "doing this for twenty years now, and this baby girl was going to be just fine."

John then explained things he was doing as he put Maisy on a breathing apparatus. Mommy tried to keep track of everything John was saying and commit it to memory so she could fill Daddy in later on what was happening to their darling daughter. John left, and Maisy seemed a bit more comfortable, although her little chest still plunged up and down, and her eyes still showed a telling fear. She and Mommy were both breathing a little easier. After a while, Maisy fell asleep.

The nurse peeked in to see how things were going. It was about two in the morning, and again, she encouraged Mommy to steal away for a bit to sleep so she would have energy for the next day. The concept was kind of funny in some ways because the time of day is completely and utterly irrelevant in sections of a hospital where the lights are on around the clock, and people are always bustling. Hospitals are like Vegas casinos in that way but not nearly as fun. Emergencies don't save themselves to be neatly packed in between seven a.m. and seven p.m. of a given day. The awareness of what time it was, and eventually what day it was, would all start to blur together into one long nightmare.

Mommy knew that it was essential to follow the nurse's advice and get some sleep. It had been days since she had done so, with the sleepless nights at home prior to their admittance to the hospital. The doctors were going to keep a good eye on Maisy and help her get better. Maisy was hooked up to machines that people were monitoring closely, as well. Mommy had people to share in the worry now and help watch over Maisy with their medical expertise. After careful contemplation and acknowledging that she was beyond exhausted, Mommy let the nurse know she was going down the hall to the parent's lounge to try and grab some sleep. The nurse said she wasn't too busy right now and would sit in with Maisy for a little bit and then check in on her often. Mommy thanked the nurse and shuffled down the hall to find the parent's lounge.

The lights were off, so she entered tentatively and quietly. The lounge had six leather recliners scattered around the room. The TV was on, projecting a dim light, but the volume was low. There were two loungers directly in front of the television with an assortment of potato chips and Cheetos and Doritos bags, and Coca-Cola cans strewn all around them. A skinny man slept in one, a skinny woman in the other. They were both snoring rather loudly, catching flies in their wide-open mouths, revealing a dentist's nightmare of missing and decaying teeth within. There was a large man snoring in another recliner, and yet another recliner occupant was completely hidden under a blanket pulled up over his or her head. Someone else was in the far corner, but Mommy couldn't distinguish anything about that person as it was quite dark back there, away from the TV.

There was one lounger that was not being used. It was worn and cracked with white stuffing coming out in several places. Still, right now it looked rather inviting. Mommy sat down, worried about waking people up as the noisy pleather, adjusting to this newfound occupant, echoed across the lounge. Nobody seemed to hear or care. She settled in and reached for the handle to put it into the reclining position but found it had been ripped out, leaving just a big hole with more stuffing leaking out. Mommy did not give up hope. Mimicking an awkward flounder trying to perform a complicated yoga pose, she slowly thrust her head back and arched her lower back up while pushing her legs down in an effort to extend the lounger without the handle. The chair squeaked, pleather reverberating across the room with every slight movement.

Eventually Mommy was able to successfully wrestle it into a reclined position. She stretched out long, elated by her small victory here in the parent's lounge. After a few moments, Mommy rolled to her side, her preferred sleeping position, keeping pressure on the important parts of the seat to keep her in a horizontal position. She quickly fell asleep and entered the world of much-needed slumber.

Her dreams took her to somewhere far away from the hospital, and her sleep dared to border on the pleasant and calm. Amidst this dreamy sleep, Mommy suddenly found herself flying up in the air through a dark, strange place with alarming force. Lark felt it, too. Was he traveling again? Was Mommy traveling with him? For a moment, Mommy's reality and her dream were blended, but when she landed, she realized she was no longer dreaming.

It took her a confused moment to figure out where she was or what was happening. She must have rolled over in her sleep or adjusted her position in some way so that the recliner jolted upright so powerfully that it propelled Mommy upright, ejecting her into a standing position directly in front of the recliner. She smiled to herself as she looked around the room to see if anyone had woken up from her noisy La-Z-Boy acrobatics. They all snored on. The person under the blanket rustled slightly, but everyone was still asleep.

She sat down and stretched out again, but this time she decided to sleep on her back, hopefully distributing the weight more efficiently to better maintain her position. Again, she drifted off to sleep, and again she was catapulted into an awakened state, quite literally catching air as she was thrown up out of the chair.

The second dismount ended with her in a heap in front of the angry chair and did not feel quite so amusing to her. She was exhausted enough to try again. After the third sit-stretch-sleep for just a few seconds before the ejection from the shredded pleather recliner, it was no longer comical; it was taunting. Mommy retreated back to her room, understanding why no one had claimed that recliner, and decided that the little upright chair in Maisy's room offered a more comfortable option, and really, she hadn't wanted to leave her side in the first place.

Maisy was still sleeping when Mommy entered the room, and her little chest still plunged up and down like a trampoline. It was a trampoline that seemed worthy of holding someone with the same gymnastic skills Mommy had just demonstrated in the parent's lounge. Her tiny chest haphazardly bounced up and down without any control or grace.

They were in a teaching hospital, and many people came in and out, some of the staff seeming knowledgeable, some of them obviously just learning. They gathered around Maisy's bed on their early morning rounds and discussed Maisy and the history of how she came to be lying in this bed. The doctor in charge asked questions, and the interns answered—sometimes correctly, sometime incorrectly, sometimes not at all. Mommy, an occupational therapist before she became a stay-at-home mom, couldn't help but answer one of the questions which was painstakingly stumping the group during the round that first morning. She hadn't slept much, and she was now in this little room, surrounded by strangers that couldn't come up with an answer that was more common sense than anything. When Mommy answered, they looked over at her with surprise, some with a glint of admiration, some with a glint of contempt, some with confusion. When the doctor acknowledged she was correct, they concluded their round, and the interns left the room grumbling while Mommy's confidence in the medical staff was shaken. She was trusting Maisy to them, and there would be a lot of questions that needed answers. She reminded herself that it was a teaching hospital, and everyone started somewhere, but she didn't want their starting point to be on Maisy. She had already learned she had to speak up for Maisy because Maisy couldn't speak for herself. It is important to advocate fiercely in this setting because things could get lost in the shuffle. It was necessary to trust but at the same time speak up with questions, follow up with tests and results, and let one's voice be heard.

Later in the morning, an intern, a young Indian gentleman who wouldn't make eye contact and did not at all attempt to be pleasant or communicative, came in. Mommy remembered him from the crowd of students surrounding Maisy's bed during rounds early that morning. The intern had answered a question, and the answer had been so off that Mommy had caught the attending doctor rolling his eyes with a subtle shake of the head.

The intern was skinny and tall, with glasses covering those eyes that would not make a connection. He gave off an air of arrogance. Even if she hadn't witnessed the attending's reaction, Mommy would have been able to tell that this doctor was relatively new to the doctoring scene. He examined Maisy's chart without so much as a "hello" to Mommy. He barely glanced at Maisy. He walked over to the oxygen machine and turned the dials up with authority and promptly left the room.

It was like when Daddy, feeling manly, decided to tackle a household plumbing project. Eventually, his well-intended amateur efforts would cost them more money to undo the damage ensued from Daddy's efforts than it would have cost to fix the initial problem with a paid professional in the first place. Plumbing was out of Daddy's element, but he didn't always admit it to himself or others. He did successfully replace a garbage disposal once, his big plumbing claim to fame. This successful one-time feat inflated Daddy's plumbing self-confidence, and ever since, Daddy felt that most plumbing issues were within his repertoire of skills. Bless his heart for trying, but sometimes it is important to know one's limits and when it might be a better choice to pass the torch.

This intern was tinkering with things that he shouldn't be tinkering with, and Maisy's little systems suffered. Maisy's oxygen pump was now alarmingly audible. It sounded like the noise a helium tank makes as you pull the balloon away right before you tie it. It was forcefully shoving air into her tiny, fragile lungs. Maisy's eyes were wide and alarmed, and with each powerful pump, her small arms were thrown straight out from the side of her body as if she was on a crucifix. Mommy knew this wasn't right. She put her hand on

Maisy's chest and looked into her petrified brown eyes. Mommy ran out in the hallway to see who could help.

In an instant, John was back in the room, adjusting the dials, turning things down. Mommy knew that the Indian intern had made a mistake, and luckily John was close by to fix it. Even more than before, Mommy noted to herself that she needed to be a mama bear, looking out for her baby in her time of need. Mommy reached up to put her finger within Maisy's tiny palm. Her baby looked desperately into Mommy's eyes, her little eyes pleading, "Help me, Mommy. Please, help me." She gave Mommy's finger a small squeeze, a tiny tear trickling down her face as her chest plunged up and down.

Lark remembered snippets of stories from when Maisy was sick. He remembered Gran and Auntie taking care of them and making snowmen and missing Mommy and Daddy. He remembered worrying about his baby sister because he knew she was sick, but he was too little to know what that meant. He just knew their world had been turned upside down. Now, he was a part of Mommy experiencing it, and he felt Maisy's little squeeze on Mommy's finger, and he saw her pleading eyes and knew things were going to be hard. Helpless. Lark and Mommy felt utterly helpless. *Swoosh.*

Chapter 15

Orange—Find Joy & Feel Deeply

> "It is said an Eastern monarch once charged his wise men to invent him a sentence, to be ever in view, and which should be true and appropriate in all times and situations. They presented him the words: 'And this, too, shall pass away.' How much it expresses! How chastening in the hour of pride! How consoling in the depths of affliction!"
>
> —Abraham Lincoln

ECHO AND LARK WERE BACK IN AFRICA. THEY WERE ON June's back, swiftly and silently soaring through the sky. Lark was glad to have Echo with him again, glad to have the company.

"Were you there for that experience I just had, Echo? Being part of me, were you there just now in the hospital?" Lark asked, hoping Echo would know what the heck he was talking about.

"Yes, remember I am you, too, Lark, so I know, I know."

Lark nodded, relieved to have someone else to talk to and share in the experience. He started to speak more of the experience and all that had just happened, but just as he began, June turned her head back toward them.

"Don't forget your experiences; the lessons are important and true; you can refer to them later, and you'll know what to do. However, for the time being, boys, you must find a way, somehow, to tuck them away in your heart, for you mustn't miss the now."

The loon had intuitively intercepted Lark before his mind wandered wildly back through the recent events. Lark paused to contemplate the thought June presented. He understood what she was saying, but he had seen so much. He wanted to talk it over with Echo and process it. He also would love to hear this wise loon's insight on the matter. Wasn't that the other lesson on the adventure, to let people (or birds) in and to share and connect? They would talk about it later; for now, he realized June was right, and he better get himself back to the now before he missed it. He wouldn't want to miss important parts of his adventures because his meandering mind was lingering too long in something that already happened. Lark did, however, want to ask about Pru and if she was okay, but once again June looked back at him, and before the words left his mouth, he knew she was okay.

Lark gazed back at June and then gazed down below her, past her, for something caught his eye. Lark noticed a herd of buffalo taking over the landscape. It was also dotted with wildebeest and a few giraffes and birds flying in unison, all of the animals in a connected pattern that they all somehow understood, all thundering forward in an elegant sea over the African plains. Lark only noticed this when he was back in the present, and with this acknowledgement it helped June's words resonate even more deeply with him. He had been so in his head he would have missed this stupendous sight.

June smiled a knowing smile.

"Well, I wonder what we are going to learn here in Africa," Lark stated softly to himself.

Lark knew Mommy had spent time in Africa and knew she loved it very much. Gramps was originally from Africa, and they still had quite a bit of family there. At the end of graduate school, Mommy had decided to do her final occupational therapy internship in Cape Town, South Africa. Afterward, she traveled around for several months, and as she liked to say, she "soaked up the moments," learning as many lessons about life as possible. Lark was soaking up her moments now, becoming wiser as this wild awareness flowed through him the moment he opened his eyes and first truly saw Africa.

The lessons in Africa were clear and simple. The people didn't need much to find joy. Food to eat, drink to drink, a roof over their heads, and a song of love in their hearts. In fact, in having less, they were able to have more. More meaning. More quality. More connectedness. More. Things could get cloudy when one started gathering superfluous things. Africans understood it was the simple things that mattered and celebrated this. Even though things were hard, they were also good, and maybe, because they were hard, that made them better because simple things were appreciated and noticed. Their souls were shining; their eyes clear; and their hearts full.

Echo and Lark were here to gain these lessons. Perched on June's back, they were now flying over the tip of Africa, where the Atlantic and Indian Oceans collided at the Cape of Good Hope. Kite boarders zipped across the water as Lark and Echo and June dipped down next to them, feeling a similar thrill as they navigated through the wind and splashing waves. They flew by Robben Island, where Mandela served many years of unjust imprisonment. Apartheid had ended in South Africa, but there were still tangible divisions amongst various races. They flew up past Table Mountain, its flat top covered by what many called the "tablecloth" of narrow cloud formations resting right on top. Hang gliders thrust themselves from cliffs. Turquoise waters met white, sugary sand with stunning rock formations, and mountains jutted right out of the sea. It was so beautiful. Mommy always said Cape Town was the answer to her dilemma since she loved the water and the mountains both equally.

Lark and Echo were awestruck. June swooped down and landed at the water's edge near a beautiful beach and bent her head toward the glistening, blue water. Lark and Echo couldn't resist, and holding hands, they slid down her neck together, flying off her beak in a great splash into the freezing, cold water. Lark had thought it would be warm, but he and Echo screeched in unison at the abrupt chill. They grabbed hands once again and roared with laughter as they splashed together toward the beach, causing quite the scene, though no one actually saw them or heard them.

The other people on the beach were all very chic. There were many different people, of all shapes and colors, dotted along this sandy, white beach, enjoying this warm day. Lark and Echo ran out of the blue water toward shore, dripping with happiness in the moment. They walked along the hot sand, which squeaked as they walked, it was so fine and powdery. They looked back at June, and she nodded her head and gave a little smirk.

Lark was in one of the prettiest spots he had ever seen. Even now that he knew the beauty of the outer-fort world of the sunset/sunrise and all its splendor, this beauty was comparable. He felt lucky to be in this moment and even luckier to be able to notice this moment. He and Echo were two little boys on a beach. They played in the sand; they played in the water; they got their clothes soaking wet as they splashed around, but they didn't worry about it because, well, why worry? Clothes eventually dry, and moments move quickly, so they weren't going to miss it because they weren't wearing their bathing suits. They laughed and splashed and frolicked.

They were in the midst of planning an elaborate sandcastle when June motioned with her wing for the boys to climb back on.

Leaving before constructing this sandcastle would have been something that the nine-year-old Lark wouldn't have been able to handle gracefully. It would have been met with great protest, perhaps even escalating to a tantrum. Historically, Lark's elaborate plans, if they did reach the point of execution, led to more tantrums once they were underway because they were often too complex for any nine-year-old to pull off. Lark liked grand plans. He wasn't a "let's quickly make a pile of sand and put a feather in it" kind of kid.

Building sandcastles is one of the more Zen experiences out there. They are a beautiful and joyful thing but aren't meant to last. Even with the best plans, sand has a way of sifting down and collapsing into tunnels dug with care.

Sometimes a big wave wipes it all away. It is these sudden waves, the ones that cause everyone to run around in a panic as children chase floating flip flops and shovels and parents move sopping wet towels and beach chairs, that someone's true colors are revealed. The situation is beyond anyone's control; it is only reactions that one can control. When that wave does finally crash in, the trick is to be able to roll with it as quickly as it rolled in, switching to a new joy as one laughs at the absurdity of it all.

If one is forced to watch their sandcastle suddenly drift out to sea, depending how one chooses to view the moment, one, too, may be washed away in a sea of smiles or a sea of tears. Hopefully the creator can quickly shift into finding new joy in the drenched sand left behind as they now create "drippy castles" or dig for sand crabs as they desperately try tunneling back into the trenches below. Hopefully they make the choice of smiles and giggles over tears because there is a certain joy in letting go and wallowing in the ridiculousness of it all. Tears will not bring the castle back, but the wave crashed in, so what to do now?

Lark was learning things on these adventures. When June called the boys back to her, Lark knew what he needed to do, and he didn't protest or argue. He was able to leave those sandcastle dreams for another time. Yes, sandcastles are quite Zen, indeed.

Lark and Echo ran back out in the water and hopped onto June's glistening black feathers. She began silently swimming out to sea. June was quiet for some reason, but it felt just as it should, so Lark and Echo didn't push conversation on her, nor even with one another. Lark supposed they were there in that moment to enjoy that moment, and as he was learning the importance of communication, he was also learning that sometimes words weren't necessary.

With that thought, June took flight.

They arrived at what appeared to be another hospital, and Lark suddenly found himself inside. This hospital was not in America; he was still in South Africa. Mommy was working there in occupational therapy. Lark didn't see Echo anymore, although he felt his presence since they were one and the same right now. Lark was in Mommy's head, hearing her thoughts, experiencing right along with her.

AIDS was spreading like wildfire throughout Africa. There was so much misinformation on how it was acquired and how to treat it. There was such a great stigma attached to it in South Africa that sometimes if a person found out they were HIV positive, they kept the diagnosis hidden until it could be hidden no longer. When the secret was finally revealed, the infected person was often ostracized from their village to die, alone. People lived in fear and did not understand this awful disease. In some African cultures, it was accepted that romantic partners in villages were not always monogamous. Men may have multiple partners or multiple wives. If a man found out he was HIV positive, he often continued to take on many partners, from either a lack of understanding the risks or not wanting to raise the suspicion that he was sick. For if he suddenly changed his lifestyle, he ran the risk of being discovered and forced out of the village.

Suggestions of contraceptive use amongst monogamous partners could lead to judgement or suspicion or questions between them. As a result, contraceptives for prevention of HIV/AIDS was often not discussed or looked upon as an option, even if they were available.

Horrific theories of how to cure AIDS led to even more devastation. False rumors with false cures attached to horrid acts traveled amongst villages, and as a result, some infected men would rape young virgins of all ages in an attempt to cure themselves. The lack of facts and the hesitation to discuss the disease, which was pretty devastating all by itself, led to more devastation than the disease alone.

Swoosh. Mommy had come back from teatime in the middle of her morning shift at the hospital in Cape Town. Mommy always found it somewhat amusing that the entire hospital—doctors, nurses, patients, and visitors alike—stopped everything they were doing at ten-thirty a.m. sharp for tea. Mommy was sure a surgeon might even pause mid-surgery, if he was at all able, for a quick sip of some Rooibos tea and sliver of milk tart.

It had been a busy and hard morning in the hand clinic that day, and Mommy had welcomed the pause and the chance to catch up with some of her new friends in the OT department over tea. Lark, being a part of her, tasted the warm liquid and the delicious shortbread cookie she was eating, and they all felt cozy and happy. After tea, it was time for Mommy to go up to the Pediatric Outpatient HIV clinic.

As Mommy walked into the HIV clinic, with Lark still a part of her, she saw a young and beautiful mother who had come in with her baby. This mother had short black hair and smooth, mocha-brown skin. She held her head high and her baby close. There was something striking about this woman. When Mommy entered the clinic, this mother was already speaking to the head of the pediatric ward, a tall, soft-spoken white man with kind eyes. Moments earlier this mother had received the diagnosis that she was HIV positive. She was, of course, distraught. She was presently receiving the news that the beautiful baby in her arms was also HIV positive. Distraught couldn't begin to touch on the way this woman was feeling. Mommy had no experiences of her own to compare it to. Mommy felt a deep sadness for her and her child. Mommy felt so sad for the continent of Africa, and then she felt an extreme sadness for herself, for the next emotion that washed over her was shame. Mommy felt so sad and ashamed of herself. Lark was surprised by the shame that flooded in recklessly.

Shame. A word that can mean "cute" in South Africa. This shame was anything but cute. Mommy suddenly realized she had made assumptions in the clinic that day, and those assumptions had just imploded. Before now, Mommy had heard about people in war-torn countries, or people that existed in tormented times, and how they existed in such tough conditions. She heard somewhere that these people somehow became used to death and destruction, that they found ways to protect themselves emotionally and somehow acclimated to these situations.

In this moment, Mommy realized she didn't have the faintest idea what it was like to live in a war-torn country or what it meant to exist and survive amidst this chaos. Mommy had naively taken on this acclimation assumption, which she now doubted completely, and had transferred this assumption to the war against AIDS in Africa. She had heard of desensitization and had assumed it was true. Maybe it was, maybe it wasn't. Maybe it was something made up. Maybe everyone was an individual and dealt with situations in their own individual way.

What Mommy, and consequently Lark, did realize in this moment was that, in some underlying emotions stuffed into her subconscious, perhaps created out of a need to help her deal with the massive amounts of sick babies that she was seeing every day or in an effort of self-preservation or denial or some other warped emotion, Mommy had fabricated some underlying assumption that since HIV and AIDS were so rampant in Africa right now, someone may be desensitized upon hearing the news that they, or a loved one, was HIV positive, and perhaps, the blow would be less. Mommy felt ashamed at her thought that hadn't been on a conscious level until now, the thought that she now knew to be so far from the truth. She felt deep shame in her ignorance.

Witnessing this mother in the clinic brought Mommy's greatly misinformed defense mechanism to the surface of her thoughts, and it throbbed through Mommy's heart and connected her to this woman with total empathy. The connection taught Mommy to feel the truth—even if it was hard. It taught her to see the truth, feel the truth, hear the truth, reach out and touch the truth, taste the truth and lean into it all. All her emotions and senses tied into this validation of what really *was*. When you can see yourself in another, in everybody, *really see*, then, and only then, you can truly start to see yourself. It taught Mommy to see differently, and now Lark was learning to see differently as well.

Love doesn't discriminate between healthy and sick. It doesn't discriminate between an epidemic or an isolated incident. This mother was just as devastated as any mother would be, anywhere in the world, upon learning her baby had HIV. She was just as distraught as an American mother would be hearing this news. In fact, this mother was probably more distraught, if that were possible, because the situation was grim and the chances slim for a baby with HIV/AIDS in Africa. Anti-retroviral drugs were just starting to make it to Africa and were scarce and pricy and not accessible for most. Mommy learned that this diagnosis wasn't any less impactful, any less devastating, any less scary, sad, awful, earth-shattering, or daunting because they were sitting in the middle of the AIDS epidemic. Even in the midst of an epidemic, everyone would like to hold on to the sliver of hope that they will be the one who defies the odds.

This mother and her baby were regulars at the HIV clinic after that day. This mother was invested, interacting with her baby, connecting, and as a result, her baby was thriving, developing, and responding, HIV and all. This mother and her child were the quintessential example of what it means to be the opposite of someone who is desensitized. Mommy felt honored to play a role in helping her and her child and humbled by the presence of this great mother and her child, who taught Mommy so much. Mommy hoped one day she would be a great mother like her. Mommy's maternal instinct was kicking in, even before she had any clear vision of a baby of her own in her arms. She was connecting with that side of her. Lark felt this, but he felt it initially for someone other than him, someone before him. This didn't make sense based on what Lark knew now, but he was learning new things by the moment. In the meantime, he would add "don't make assumptions" to his list of important lessons he was learning.

In an instant, Lark was transported back to the willow tree. Lark was climbing up, steady again on the rungs of the ladder. Echo somehow remained well above him and was a step or two below Pru, although Lark knew Echo had shared in that experience in the hospital in Africa. They had all progressed into the orange level now, and everywhere Lark shone his headlamp, a lovely tangerine engulfed them. Lark was relieved to see that Pru had been doing okay without him and his light. Lark called out to them up above, but they didn't seem to hear. He still felt the connection to Pru and Echo, even though they didn't respond.

Lark continued to climb. Somehow his headlamp wasn't quite as necessary at this level, as the orange gave off its own shine, its own light. Lark didn't trust the rung of the ladder anymore, but he did trust that he would be safe. He felt the loon's presence as well, even though he couldn't see her. All logic told him there was no way June would fit in this narrow space, but she fit anyway. Lark had learned to leave logic behind.

Up he climbed, rung after rung, trying to move quickly in hopes of being within earshot of Pru and Echo. For now, Lark was alone, and he was okay with that. It gave Lark time to think and process what had happened up until this point. He climbed hand over hand, foot over foot, working his way up. As he climbed, his mind methodically worked its way through some of the events he had experienced. Lark thought back on both the experiences before his outer-fort world and his adventures since he had entered it.

He and Mommy hadn't been seeing eye to eye lately, for some reason. Sometimes Lark felt like she wanted him to be too grown up. Sometimes he felt like she wouldn't let him grow up. She was always pushing him to share his feelings more than he wanted to and giving him a hard time about not talking to her. She nudged him to play with other kids if they were at a playground or somewhere with kids, even though he was perfectly happy digging in the dirt by himself at her feet. She was right, though. He did have more fun once he started playing with other kids.

Mommy said, "If you have feelings that don't feel good—like sadness or anger or fear—if you keep these feelings stuffed inside and don't share them with the people you love, then they keep getting bigger and bigger and bigger until eventually they seem too big to handle. If you do share them with people you love, then these feelings will magically get smaller and less daunting. It lightens your load because you no longer have to carry them by yourself."

On the flip side (there was always a flip side), she would say, "If you have feelings that feel good, like joy or accomplishment or excitement, well, these good feelings tend to get smaller when you don't share them with others that matter to you. They lose their spark, their wonder. Of course, if you do share them with others, they get bigger. You can fill up other people's hearts when your heart is full. Feelings and positivity are contagious."

Lark was lost in his thoughts, contemplating Mommy's words, when he heard the loon's whisper travel by, again on a breeze:

Like the navel of the fruit, closer to center you climb;
A soul creatively expressed, such as with painting or rhyme,
Passion is what feeds our soul to create;
Transformation and connections will open that gate.
So, feel good about yourself, and all that you are,
And if you believe in yourself, that will carry you far.
It is sacred, the sacral, the center of desire,
Senses and feelings, it awakens this fire.
Joy and pleasure are found in this orange realm of the tree;
Intimate connections allow you clearly to see.
In orange, we must live in the moment that we are in,
Filling our hearts with that which is akin,
For if the orange realm starts to go askew,
You will see the havoc which that can do.
You'd see jealousy and the imbalance of doing too much of one thing;
You'd see what would happen if you weren't able to feel, to sing;
The results can be tragic if we lose the connection from our emotions to our soul;
We may hide away our emotions, afraid of losing control.
Beware not to disconnect, for they are closely intertwined,
And always remember the balance between body and mind.
Climb with me, for if you can find these joys,
Well, then, you can do anything, my sweet girl and boys."

The loon was back. Did Pru and Echo hear her too? If they were listening, it didn't seem to break their climbing stride from what Lark could tell. Lark continued to ascend quickly in hopes of reaching his friends.

Suddenly, mid-climb, Lark was stopped in his tracks as he felt June's profound presence. As he peered downward, his headlamp cast a light on a black and white image quickly rising. Before he knew it, Lark was suddenly perched on June's back as she floated straight up through the tangerine-tinted air. How she fit in this narrow space was not apparent. Lark couldn't tell if she was smaller, if the space had become larger, or if his perception had been altered. Size, like time, was relative.

They rose to the level of the ladder where Echo was climbing, and Lark called out to him. This time, Echo did hear him, and he smiled at Lark. Without a word, he let go of the ladder, flinging himself through the air in a leap of faith toward Lark and June the Loon. As he did, he seemed to be heading straight for Lark. Echo and Lark were about to recklessly crash into one another once again. Lark grasped on to June's feathers for fear of being knocked off her back and back down the colorful, dark abyss.

Lark did not fall off. Echo did not fall off either. Echo did crash right into Lark and then through him and finally within him, although Lark didn't realize this at first. Lark searched the loon's feathers frantically, looking everywhere, but Echo was nowhere to be found. Lark did not yet realize he only needed to look within. It was only when Lark stopped searching and acknowledged what he was feeling that he gained clarity. Echo was now in Lark, forever a part of him. Lark's colors sparkled and swirled even brighter, and he now shone so much that he almost gave off his own light.

"Echo is you. You know what to do. Echo is your voice. You have made the right choice. He will help carry your load. Continue on the road," June said reassuringly.

"Wait, so Echo is gone? I mean, I know he's not here, but I can't talk to him or hear him anymore?" Lark said softly.

June shook her head. "Not like before, not in a separate way, anymore."

Lark felt confused again for a second but then transformed as he was fully flooded with understanding and acceptance. "I'm going to miss him," Lark lamented, and the loon smiled her smile and winked her wink as she peered back at Lark.

"Echo is you. You may hear him whenever you listen, and as long as you are you and true, forever within you his colors will glisten. Lark, you are Echo. Your voice, Echo, is you. You both made the choice, and you are no longer two."

Lark tried to process it all.

"You are one and the same. You must let go—the idea of being separate from our dear Echo."

Lark understood, and when he closed his eyes, he could feel this new, but familiar, part of him. It was a newfound confidence. An understanding. A love. It was a love for his friend that was part of him, and it was a love for himself. After all, they were one and the same. He had found his voice and made it truly part of him, and he would carry his Echo with him always. He realized he had a certain courage now. He felt brave. He felt like Lark. For maybe the first time in his life, he felt like himself; his true self.

Pru continued to climb up the ladder above, unaware of what the boys had been doing below, and June the Loon continued to rise up with Lark perched on her back. When they had almost reached Pru, suddenly, *swoosh,* they were not in the tree. Lark was transported in thoughts and experiences, and he left this orange realm in the tree as quickly as he came. Again, he was feeling colors. His senses were being used in new and different ways, but this was all starting to feel normal. The color of tangerine was tangible as he traveled to his next stop.

"Three-month-old Caucasian female presenting with RSV."

There were doctors surrounding the bed. They were doing their rounds, and Mommy and Maisy were now in the Pediatric Intensive Care Unit, in bed number seven, right next to the nurse's station. Maisy only had one night in the little room of the step-down unit down the hall. Maisy's condition had deteriorated, and they transferred them into the PICU the next day, the section that Mommy was glad they were only wheeling through the night before.

It was half past seven in the morning, and Daddy, now at the hospital too, was leaving to do a little work at his office a few streets away. Mommy didn't want him to leave, but he promised her he'd be back soon. He was going to take time off while Maisy was in the PICU and had a few loose ends to tie up at the office. He thought he'd get through them quickly since nobody was in the office that day anyway, due to the snow.

It had been snowing all night, and several feet of snow had already accumulated. Baltimore had all but shut down.

Daddy had driven up slowly and carefully in their SUV, and Gran was at home watching the other kids. Daddy brought up some essentials, as instructed by Mommy. She had scored a toothbrush from the hospital and toothpaste and a little plastic comb, which did nothing for the unruly mane on top of her head. They were going to be there for a few days, so Daddy was bringing up a hairbrush, comfy clothes, a jacket and some mittens and hat for the snow, a familiar and comfortable pillow from their bed, a copy of the cute picture of Maisy and Gwynnie laughing that Mommy had taken three days before Maisy got sick, a picture of Lark, a picture of Sophie, clean underwear and socks, some fun hats for Maisy—the ones with the big flowers on them—and their portable speaker and laptop so they could play music. Music always soothed Mommy's soul.

There had been a few scary moments after arriving in the PICU. Maisy's oxygen levels kept dropping. Doctors and nurses hurried over, placed a mask over her face, and pumped the bag that brought the needed air to her lungs, brain, and heart. It was intense, and each time it happened, Mommy could do nothing but stand aside and pray as they worked feverishly on her baby daughter.

Mommy didn't want Daddy to leave that morning, but she knew he'd be back in a few hours. He hurried through the double doors so he could hurry through his work and hurry back. Mommy watched him go, and although she was surrounded by many other people in the big, wide PICU, she felt very alone.

About an hour after Daddy left, a gentleman that seemed like he was wandering the PICU for kicks came by bed number seven to chat with Maisy's nurse, who was obviously someone he knew well. He wasn't wearing anything medical-looking, but he had medical knowledge. He didn't state his role, although he introduced himself as Tom, and he was friendly and chatty, and it was a welcome distraction. Tom pulled up a chair, talking to the nurse and Mommy as if he were catching up with old friends at a coffee shop. After many moments of chatting, Maisy's machines beeped. Tom and the nurse gave each other an unspoken look that made the hair on the back of Mommy's neck stand up.

It was apparent that Maisy was having some issues. Mommy knew it wasn't good. Tom picked up the mask and bag. The apparatus started to pump Maisy with air. Time stood still.

Tom and the nurse worked in unison, in a beautiful, scary, synchronized dance, and after what seemed like forever, they finally smoothed out the situation and led Maisy back. Mommy had no idea how much time had passed. Time is relative, especially in hospitals. Things seemed calm again for the moment. Moment to moment, that was how things were in the PICU.

Tom came over to Mommy and looked her in the eye with the familiarity of an old friend, and although they had just met, it did feel like they had known each other for a long time. Experiences in the hospital can bring people together quickly because time isn't something to be wasted there. Lessons of time taught whether one is ready to learn them or not. Tom took Mommy's hand in his and placed a yellow sticky note in her palm that had something scribbled in black ink.

Mommy glanced down at the sticky note. "This too shall pass."

Tom gave Mommy's hand a comforting squeeze and told her quietly, "Remember this because it is true."

There was a mutual, deep understanding. They had shared a frightening moment together, and a connection had been made. Tom then turned around and headed out the double doors of the PICU. Mommy stood there, thinking about the meaning of the quote. She was glad to have met Tom and glad he had been there for that moment to help pull Maisy through.

Mommy took the yellow sticky note and placed it on the headboard of Maisy's bed, right next to the picture they had stuck up of Maisy and Gwynnie smiling. This too shall pass. It was a needed reminder that things weren't always going to be like this. Mommy had to believe things were going to get better.

Mommy had taped up all the pictures Daddy brought from home on Maisy's hospital bed earlier that morning. She wanted the doctors and nurses to see Maisy's smile in that picture so they could help her find it again. She wanted to remind them that Maisy had an identical twin at home who was missing her constant companion. She wanted them to see that she also had a brother and another sister that loved her dearly, and she also wanted Maisy to feel their love emanating from their smiling faces taped upon her bed. Mommy wanted the doctors and nurses to see this darling baby as the person she was before she got here because she was the same person smiling in that picture, but she couldn't show them yet.

They needed to find that smiling baby again. She was this family's little light. She already had so much personality. That was also why Mommy had Daddy bring the fun, vibrant caps for Maisy's head, with big flowers and bright colors. Mommy wanted Maisy to stand out so the doctors could truly see Maisy, to look beyond the charts and tubes and machines. She was Maisy, and she was loved. Lark experienced all of this through Mommy.

Mommy sat down next to Maisy, stroking her head and singing "You Are My Sunshine" over and over again.

It was mid-morning in the PICU, and Daddy was still at work. Mommy's phone rang. It was Maisy's uncle, Mommy's big brother, and he was calling to check on her. Mommy filled him in on the details as she moved near the double doors, the doors through which they had first entered from the ambulance just a night ago; in some ways that felt like a lifetime ago. She moved farther over in search of better reception and to downplay that she was talking on her phone because that was against the rules. She was filling her brother in on all that had happened when suddenly Mommy noticed a commotion.

"Hold on a second. I'm just . . . there's something going on. Everybody in here is running . . . sprinting. Oh my God, it's Maisy—"

The entire PICU, every single one of the doctors and nurses, was sprinting as fast as they could to Maisy's bed. There was yelling. The beeps and noises from the machines surrounding her were deafening. People were grabbing medical devices and screaming, "I can't get her back up. It's falling, it's falling . . . no, it's going too low. We can't—"

They squeezed the oxygen bag desperately; they worked, and they worked. Mommy's heart was in her throat. Lark felt as if he might faint. Mommy could do nothing but watch and pray with the forgotten phone dangling in her hand.

They didn't lose her. Her oxygen levels came back up. They saved her. Maisy's nurse, who was excellent but clearly flustered, commented on how that was a scary one. She said Maisy was stable. The crowd slowly dissipated, and things seemed calm again. Mommy felt like she herself needed air, perhaps internalizing her daughter's own battle for air. Mommy felt sick and faint, like things were closing in around her.

The nurse, probably sensing Mommy's fragility, thought getting air was a good idea. Mommy was going to lose it, and for some reason, she didn't want to do it in front of everybody, or in front of Maisy, and the PICU offered absolutely no privacy. "I'll be back," she told the nurse, and after planting a kiss on Maisy, Mommy walked quickly, almost running, down the hall. The origin of the expression, "scared the ____ out of me" was validated as she ran into the bathroom, knowing that her insides were now scared to the outside. Emotions surrounded her, engulfing her with a desperate, strangling vengeance.

Mommy was learning more than ever that parenthood was not for the faint of heart. She needed to call Daddy. Daddy would have wanted to be there for Maisy and for Mommy, and he needed to know what happened so he could be there for both of them in case, God forbid, it happened again. Barely able to speak and battling terrible reception and the beginning of many sobs, Mommy got through to him on the phone that had been dangling in her hand since it all started. Mommy told him plainly, "Please, you need to come now."

He could barely hear her. The connection was bad due to the thick hospital walls inside and the thick blanket of snow outside. The situation wasn't good, and Mommy was scared. She tried to tell Daddy more, but just like that, the connection was lost.

With this lost connection, Mommy never felt more alone. Mommy was hesitant to go too far. Was it simply coincidence that

Maisy had this episode when Mommy had moved away from her bed? Mommy couldn't help fearing that Maisy had sensed Mommy wasn't at her bedside and was starting to give up the fight, trying to slip away while Mommy wasn't looking. Mommy shook this thought from her head and decided she needed to head down to the lobby to get reception so she could be sure Daddy knew to come. Mommy needed Daddy there. She needed to make a connection with Daddy. Maisy needed Daddy there, too. She also needed a connection with him.

As Mommy hurried down the hallway to the elevators, her dear Kerri called to check in on Maisy. Mommy was still crying from Maisy's scary episode and crying from the lost phone call to Daddy and crying from everything that had just happened and crying from the fear of not knowing what would happen next. She was completely amazed that her friend's call had come through when she couldn't get through to her husband five blocks away. Mommy, sobbing, answered her phone to talk to her friend on her way to the lobby.

"She's not doing well. No, Maisy is not doing well at all . . . no, me either . . . my sweet baby, I just feel like we are both literally . . . hanging on by a thread." Mommy sobbed uncontrollably into the phone as she entered the elevator, not even aware she had stepped inside. The doors shut. She cried into the phone to her friend and then realized it was strangely silent on the other end. "Hello—are you there?"

Another lost connection. Surreal sobbing followed that Mommy tried desperately but unsuccessfully to stuff back inside her as this elevator full of people stood by, silently watching. Mommy was suddenly painfully aware that she was crying hysterically in an elevator full of strangers who all knew now that she and her baby were hanging on by a tiny, fraying thread, with a phone next to her ear and nobody on the other side. Mommy slowly lowered the phone and looked around through salty tears. Some people were looking at her with expressions of sadness and concern. Others were uncomfortably exploring the elevator buttons or the walls or anywhere else that would help them avoid eye-contact, avoid a connection. Maybe they were trying give her privacy in this public place because this moment was one they were forced to experience, and they didn't feel like they belonged because it seemed private, even if it was in public. These people probably didn't want to belong in this moment, for it was a pretty miserable moment. Mommy did not want to belong in this moment. It was a crowded elevator, and there was Mommy quickly unraveling on her ride down to the lobby. Her shoulders shook as she looked down at the floor.

Once again, time seemed to be suspended, this time in what seemed like an endless elevator ride. Then, out of the blue, the older woman next to her with light brown skin and warm brown eyes, without saying a word, reached out with both arms and gave Mommy a big hug. Not just a sympathetic pat on the back, and not just a brief embrace, but she hugged her, really hugged her, trying to pass along comfort and compassion and support and understanding within the embrace. It was a hug that said, "I feel your pain, and it is too much for you to carry alone, so I am going to hug you and connect with you and share it with you." Mommy didn't know until now how much she needed that hug. Mommy accepted the kind gesture, and with this acceptance she crumbled into this woman's shoulder as she succumbed to her emotions, letting this stranger support her as she cried unforgivingly. The stranger held on tight without hesitation and compassionately rubbed Mommy's back and told her it would be okay. Even though she knew nothing behind the dire "hanging by a thread" situation, she knew Mommy needed that hug and needed to hear it would be okay, even if they both knew that was still to be determined. She held Mommy up, right when she was no longer able to stand alone.

Mommy believed her words because she needed to; she needed to believe and hope it would be okay.

The elevator stopped, the doors opened, and they looked at each other with the power of the shared moment.

"I'll be praying for you," the woman said.

"Thank you," whispered Mommy, and a second later, this kind stranger vanished into the vast, busy lobby. A lost connection when Mommy entered the elevator, a found connection before she got off.

Most people are kind. Mommy realized it was okay to show her emotions, even around people she didn't know. Lark was learning this, too. It was important to share your emotions with people you know but letting people you don't know see your feelings might change them from someone you don't know to someone you want to know, and then maybe someone you do know. The woman on the elevator wasn't afraid to risk giving Mommy the hug. The moment called for action, and this woman rose to the occasion, not letting the opportunity for kindness pass her by, and courageously acted upon it. Mommy would never forget that angel in the elevator. Mommy picked up her phone and called Daddy again. He answered, and he was already on his way. He would be there in a couple of minutes.

Chapter 16

Yellow—Choose Adventure

"Making the decision to have a child—it is momentous. It is to decide forever to have your heart go walking around outside your body."

—Elizabeth Stone

THEY WERE SUDDENLY BACK IN THE TREE, SURROUNDED by shades of warm, bright, buttery, sunshiny, lemony shades of yellow, and June the Loon was speaking.

The warmth of the yellow solar center beams down upon me, within me, through me.
It is me.
I am powerful like the sun; I am capable, reliable, and can make the changes I want to see.
I become me.
I explore this concept, this concept of me; I am in control of myself; I am able to see.
I find me.
I can move mountains. I can cross a great ocean.
I will do great things. I can move what is still into motion.
Mountains and sea.
I trust me.
I meet the challenges ahead and look them in the eye.
I move forward with the lesson learned, reaching for the sky.
Stay true to myself; I make a pact.
I act.

There is always a choice. Even when it might feel like I can't.
I won't let life pass me by; I just won't; no, I shan't.
Inspiration from within and above.
I love.
I love myself, for I am me, and I am great.
My life is mine to live; and now is now; I shall not wait.
I choose how to act, how to respond, how to be,
Living a life full of love, and all that is me.
I am.

This time Lark wasn't back on the ladder. He was perched on June's back, and they once again fit neatly in the hollow willow, despite June's size. Her wings were out to the side, but she wasn't flapping them. She was soaring upward, almost levitating, and Lark was once again safely nestled within her spotted feathers. His lucky stone was hot in his pocket. He saw the slightest glimpse of Pru, at least he thought it might be her, way up near the green, beyond the yellow realm. There was no sign of Echo anymore as a separate entity. He was officially integrated into a part of Lark.

Lark listened to his rhyming friend, the loon, and her words and tried to make some sense of them. He knew she was Wise, so he wanted to figure it out. Part of the rhyme was the same adage Gramps, Echo, and everyone had told him. Lark thought it was essentially telling him to choose adventure, and in doing so, he might discover himself along the way. He could create his own destiny. Was that right? It seemed that was the gist of it, but was Lark choosing this adventure he was on, or was it choosing him? Lark was trying to choose adventure and get the lessons along the way, but this choice to make a choice was all new to him.

The yellow part of the tree shone even brighter than the orange part had below. Combined with the warm glow cast from Lark's own colorful self, Lark didn't see any more need for extra light. He took off his headlamp and put it into his backpack. There he spotted his fizzy candy Zotz and decided it would be a fine time to eat one. He hadn't eaten a thing since his adventures had started. He hadn't been hungry.

Lark offered a Zotz to June, who politely declined. He told himself he would check and see if Pru wanted one the next time he got to talk to her, and he bet she never had one before. He popped the candy in his mouth and enjoyed the fizzy, powerful flavor and had a moment of completely loving the moment he was in. He felt fully alive, floating through the air on a loon's back, with newfound courage inside, a favorite candy in his mouth, and a beautiful, shining yellow surrounding him. He felt this simple joy, and then, as quickly as it came, the moment was gone. His mind had suddenly wandered. Lark had a scary thought: what if Maisy didn't pull through after all?

He had been distraught while experiencing things through Mommy's vantage point a few minutes ago, but now, he had the knowledge that Maisy would pull through. Maisy was okay when he had left her before his adventures started on the day of his tenth birthday, but everything in the outer-fort world was different. What if history was changing? What if she wasn't okay anymore? If that was the case, he wondered if maybe he could go back and make it so she never got sick in the first place. Maybe they could avoid going through this altogether. Not that he had any control over where he was or where he was going. He shook the scary thoughts out of his head. He certainly wasn't changing history; he couldn't be seen or heard by others when he was on his adventures. If he stopped her from getting sick in the first place, would important lessons be lost?

June nodded her head and began to speak.

There is the story of a man watching a butterfly.

Oh my, how hard does this butterfly try,

Trying to emerge from its safe chrysalis.

The man, watching, fears this is something it will miss.

The butterfly stops for a moment; this is hard; it needs a rest.

The man wants to help, to do what he thinks best;

The man cuts a hole in the chrysalis, thinking it would help it to fly.

Instead, unfortunately, the beautiful butterfly is destined to die.

Alas, the butterfly will not be able to fly without this struggle to emerge;

Sometimes, to grow to the next step, things must be taken to the verge.

The man thought he was helping, but sadly, he was wrong,

For it was this necessary struggle that would make its wings strong.

Lark held up a finger and was about to respond to June's tale. *Swoosh.*

Lark was suddenly back in the hospital, a part of Mommy. He was there within her soul and her heart, the future unknown. The world outside was turning into a blank, white slate. Snow came down in a fury, and with every snowflake that fell, it became harder and harder to see through, to see beyond. White was being draped over the world like a shroud, with no knowledge as to when it might be lifted. Everything that lay ahead felt uncertain. *Swoosh.*

This would be an interesting slice of a social experiment if one were a sociologist or an anthropologist or some field interested in the human species. This would be a great experiment on how the people here differed and how they were the same and how they survived in the wild (the wild being the PICU in Baltimore). The couple in the parents' lounge of the PICU, the ones with the ever-growing pile of castaway, empty chip bags and soda cans gathering at their feet, who hardly ever left those recliners, would be interesting to observe. If they did leave their adopted habitat and ventured outside of their claimed lair of La-Z-Boys, they were not venturing out to see their young. It was to go for a smoke or relieve themselves or forage for more soda or chips. The one left behind would guard their space without apology, draping their legs over the arm of the newly unoccupied chair, staking their territory, in case someone else was looking to cozy up in that open recliner next to them. These two creatures were very territorial.

That was where this couple lived, next to an ever-growing pile of trash, dominating the TV at full volume, laughing their toothless smiles, cursing, living in squalor within the parents' lounge of the PICU while their baby fought for his life a few feet away. Not once did the baby in bed number four get a visit from them. Just through the double doors, a few feet away, a few beds down from Maisy. If the doctors needed to talk to them, they had to talk to them in the parents' lounge because they weren't about to risk giving up those recliners.

It was hard not to judge sometimes. Mommy fought this tendency. It wasn't her place, but sometimes it was harder than others. Mommy was sure this couple's life had been hard. She tried to view the situation from one of empathy, but Mommy was frustrated that these parents seemed more concerned about who was the mother's baby daddy on the latest Jerry Springer show than actually being a mommy and daddy to their own baby in the PICU. It gave her sorrow and made her appreciate that she had good parents. She wondered if this couple ever had a good role model. Maybe substance abuse played a role. She had a sneaking suspicion it might.

Mommy's mind wandered, as it often did. She would try not to judge, try not to make assumptions. She didn't know their story. Expectations must be shifted when dealing with substance abuse if that was a factor here. In addition, pain and grief and fright are all dealt with in unique ways and vary between individuals. Maybe their avoidance was their way of dealing with it.

Nevertheless, it broke Mommy's heart to see that infant alone. Expect and accept again dancing around together. Mommy's mind continued to wander.

There was another baby in the PICU that rarely had a visitor. That was a different situation. This baby had a single working mom who had six other kids. She didn't have a Gran or a great auntie to come in and help at home while she stayed in the hospital with her sick baby. She didn't have a car, and the snow outside was unbelievable, piled several feet high. This mother came in twice to visit before her baby was discharged, and when she came, she came straight to her sick baby. Anyone could tell she was a good mother, and she made up for lost time in the way she held him. Both babies without visitors were looked after well by the hospital staff, but there was nothing quite like a mother or a father to emit love to their child and to advocate for them and be there for them. Mommy and Daddy felt lucky, relatively speaking. Everything is relative in the hospital.

The toothless couple and their baby from bed number four were moved from the PICU a few days later. Lark said a prayer for that little soul. As soon as he started praying, he heard Mommy also praying. She prayed this baby would be happy and he would be loved. Lark joined in this prayer, too. Maybe later, if anyone ever heard Lark's story, they might say a prayer for him, too.

Two free recliners in the parent's lounge were soon occupied by two other people. Mommy and Daddy never really ventured in there. Maisy needed them at her bedside. They never knew what was going to happen. They couldn't be far.

In the hospital, people's lives were shared, experiences shared, living quarters shared. There were moments of crisis and moments of nothing. On the other side of the PICU was a baby boy that looked to be about Maisy's age. His name was Jason, and his parents looked like they were teenagers. The grandmother, the mother of the mother, looked fairly young as well. She cried with big howls that rang across the PICU much of the time that they were there, and her daughter argued with her howling mother a lot.

Swoosh. There were flashes now, bits and pieces of time strung together loosely. Lark wasn't sure if they were in chronological order because the days started to blend together as if in some churning, choppy blender, spinning out of control. There was an image of Mommy in a small room, sitting on a table because the room had no chair. The sound of a machine pumping, like the hee-haw of a sick donkey, attached to her chest, hee-haw, hee-haw . . . tears streamed down her face. Lark plunged into her thoughts, an inner dialogue of despair.

I'm not making enough for two babies right now. I need to nurse Gwynnie. I need to go home soon and see her and Sophie and Lark. I miss all my babies. I miss holding my babies. I need to make more milk. Maisy needs it, and Gwynnie does, too. This is the only thing I can do right now to help Maisy.

Lark heard her silent prayer and saw her milk drip slowly through a tube and into a storage bag so it could ultimately get to Maisy.

Breast milk has magical healing powers. I feel so helpless, but that makes me feel like I am doing something. I need to make more. I'm not making enough. Mommy's mind continued to spin out of control as the pump rhythmically pumped in desperation.

Swoosh. Mommy and Daddy were talking to another parent in the PICU. The little girl in the corner room right next to Maisy belonged to another couple from Annapolis. RSV was rampant that year, and the whole PICU was full of babies and children with RSV. This couple's daughter was doing better now, and they would be moving to the step-down unit soon. Mommy knew this little girl's daddy back in high school, and it was crazy seeing him here in this setting years later. What a small world. A re-connection made. The couples swapped notes on their unwanted RSV journeys. It turned out the little girl was in the same preschool as Lark; they hadn't known that before now. The father told Mommy he was more worried about Maisy now after witnessing her most recent episode. He told them about the little baby that died two days before Maisy got there. The baby died from RSV. The baby had also been in bed number seven. He said he and his wife had absolutely lost it when that happened.

The couple moved to the step-down unit a few days later. Mommy asked the doctor if they could move from bed number seven into the private-ish room in the corner, the one that her high school friend and his wife and his daughter had occupied, the room with the little couch to sleep on. The doctor said no, they needed Maisy right there next to the nurse's station in the open unit so they could all keep their eyes on her. Mommy nodded in unwanted understanding.

Another couple came in a few days later. They also had twins, but both of their babies were in the hospital. One was in the PICU, and the other baby was across the hallway in the pediatric ward. It turned out that Daddy knew this father from his high school. Another re-connection was made. Again, empathetic hugs were given and war stories traded of the unwanted journey to this point, where they were all standing over their sick babies in that PICU in Baltimore. Their twins were newborns, just a couple of weeks old. The mommy had been breastfeeding one of her twins, and the baby turned blue in her arms. The father had to resuscitate the baby to get him breathing again while they were on the phone with 911. Both babies had RSV. Now they were here. After chatting for a while, they said they had to be on their way to try and find some new underwear for the father. After the experience of resuscitating his blue newborn baby back to life, he needed a new pair of underwear. Enough said.

Even though they didn't know each other well, this was not a comment that was shocking or unfit for Mommy and Daddy's ears, nor was it one that should not have been shared. It was the reality of the hell that they had all been thrown into. It was scary as crap. They were now aware of the terrors of the PICU, and when you know you know, even when you don't want to know. They were all members of this PICU club that nobody wanted to belong to. That couple took their babies home a few days later, surely never quite the same again.

Mommy and Daddy had a friend come to visit, and she brought them a folding Baltimore Ravens papasan chair. Mommy and Daddy alternated between sleeping on that and sleeping in a rolling desk chair, one on each side of Maisy's bed. They weren't officially allowed to sleep in the PICU, but if they happened to doze off, most nurses would let them stay. Maisy was having too many ups and downs for them to go anywhere else.

Lark could not be seen or heard. The stone was cool in his pocket. He understood what was happening, though it was beyond the grasp of his ten-year-old self.

They had intubated Maisy shortly after the incident that happened when Daddy was at work. Somehow, Lark knew what it meant to be intubated, even though it was a term he hadn't heard before. Maisy was on a ventilator to help her breathe. Daddy was no longer working and was vigilantly beside Maisy and Mommy in the PICU. When they first put her on the ventilator, the doctors said, Maisy could breathe on her own, but her little body was working so hard to do so. At some point soon, she would no longer be able to, and then she would stop. She would stop breathing. They wanted to give her a break so she could rest and get strong. To ensure the machine did all the work and not her sick little lungs, they were going to intubate Maisy and temporarily paralyze her. They gave her medicine to paralyze her from head to toe so her lungs wouldn't try and do any of their own work.

"Will she be able to feel me if I touch her? Will she know if I am holding her hand or giving her a kiss?" inquired Mommy, her voice cracking a bit at the end of the questions she already knew the answer to.

The doctor looked down at Maisy. "No, she won't be able to feel any touch. I'm sorry. While she's paralyzed, she won't be able to move or feel touch to the skin. She is in a medically induced coma to get her better, so her eyes will remain closed as long as she's in it."

"Can she hear me?" asked Mommy, grasping for a connection.

"Yes, perhaps, she may be able to hear you. We will pay close attention to the monitors, and they will tell us if she is in too much pain, and we can then give her the medicine she needs to manage it."

Mommy was no longer facing the doctor; she had moved over to Maisy.

"I'm still going to give you kisses, my darling. I'm still going to hold your sweet little hand and stroke your sweet little head, my sweet darling baby girl." She kissed Maisy on her cheek while holding her hand with one hand, the other smoothing Maisy's hair to one side. Mommy began to sing "You Are My Sunshine" in Maisy's small waiting ear.

Chapter 17

Lark and the Bark

"Love is not a matter of counting the years—it's making the years count."

—Wolfman Jack Smith

LARK AND JUNE FOLLOWED THE STARDUST PATH through the warm yellow sky. The bright yellow light surrounded Lark. With the hot stone in his pocket, they flew through the outer-fort world. The sunset/sunrise had taken on the lemony and buttery yellow shades found within the willow.

The breeze through Lark's blonde hair felt soothing and refreshing, and warmth shone upon his back as if the sun were beaming in this wild, wonderful world. The feelings of insecurity and uncertainty he had had a second ago faded away. Lark was learning to be in the moment a bit more. That was an important lesson these adventures were trying to teach him, and he was aware of this. Lark knew he wouldn't return home unless he learned the lesson from each event that came his way, or Mommy's way, or any which way that they may be going.

So, here he was in the solar sky, taking it all in. That was what June's words had emphasized back in the orange level, wasn't it? It was about feeling. How did that relate to what June had recited in the yellow realm? He thought about June's words. They had instilled strength and empowerment in Lark, a quiet confidence in his ability to influence his own destiny.

Lark had never been very good at making decisions. These experiences that his mom, dad, and Maisy had gone through were full of necessary decisions. Lark was learning that when life calls for one, the ability to make a smart and swift decision is invaluable.

"Lark, do you hear the bark? Let's go see—down near that tree."

Suddenly a tree came into focus on the sparking path, and Lark heard something barking. Before, he would have assumed it was a dog, but he was learning not to make assumptions here in the outer-fort world.

June descended in a big loop, landing next to the tree in the sea of the swirling colors of the sunset/sunrise.

There, looking up at them, with a wagging tail and big, golden brown eyes was Lark's old dog, Coleman. Lark recognized him immediately. He couldn't clearly remember Coleman on his own, but he had seen so many photos and heard so many stories about Coleman that he had no trouble distinguishing him now. Even if the memories had faded, the connection had not, and the two greeted each other happily, with Coleman planting a wet, slobbery kiss on Lark's cheek. Lark let out a loud laugh and rubbed Coleman behind his ears, and Coleman's tail wagged even harder. Soon they were rolling around together on the stardust path under the big tree in a big bundle of snorts and giggles and tail wags and wet kisses and love.

"Hi, boy! How are you, boy? You are such a good boy. Yes, I love you, too," Lark sang out.

Coleman licked him more, and finally, with a satisfied grunt, he rolled over in hopes of getting a proper belly rub. Lark rubbed his furry tummy, and they both settled down, lying on their backs, looking lovingly at each other and then up to the yellow, curving sky behind the canopy of the big flowering tree.

"Can you understand me, boy?" asked Lark hopefully. "Can you talk here, Coleman?" Lark's cheeks flushed. He felt silly for asking a dog if he could talk.

June the Loon cleared her throat, and Lark glanced over at her; he swore she was raising an eyebrow at him. She didn't actually have eyebrows, but that was the sort of look she was giving Lark, who instantly realized it was no more of a ridiculous thought than this talking loon next to them.

Coleman wagged his tail and gave another lick, which Lark took as confirmation that he was being understood by his canine companion. The question was, would Lark be able to understand him? There was another lick, and with that, Lark was sure he would, for with that adoring lick Lark was reminded that words aren't always necessary for understanding.

A child with autism, a cooing baby, a veteran with PTSD, or a person simply in need of companionship but unable to voice why will often be found with their dog curled up next to them. Without a word exchanged, a dog knows that sometimes being there for someone is the greatest connection of all. Some say that dogs have a special sixth sense connection, knowing beforehand if there will be a fire or if someone is going to have a seizure or if some other safety need calls for attention. Even if it is something simple like sensing that their person needs a lick, a cuddle, or encouragement to get up and get some fresh air with a walk, dogs are tuned in with these special capabilities.

Perhaps dogs are more evolved than humans on some levels. They put another's needs before their own and don't expect anything in return. A friendly dog greets other dogs or people, with a simple and unassuming comfort, often going nose to nose with wagging tails right out of the gates. When a dog meets someone new, with their wagging telltale tail, there is no hiding their happiness in the potential of a new friend. Lark felt he had his own proverbial tail here in the outer-fort world, with his thoughts and feelings exposed for all to see. Whether his tail was wagging or his tail was between his legs, Lark was an open book for all to read. For Lark, that was a good thing.

A dog can help us rise up to be our best self. Rise and shine. Lark and Coleman were giving each other what they needed in this moment. Coleman got up slowly and peered down at Lark, shimmering drool hanging from his jowls over Lark's smiling face. Alarmed, Lark hopped up quickly in an effort to avoid the shimmering drool but also wanting to explore his new surroundings. Coleman followed at his heels.

This tree was different than the willow tree Lark had left a short while ago. This tree was covered in blooming flowers of all different types, the likes of which he had never seen before. There were some that resembled roses, lotus, daisies, and ranunculus, all bundled into one bloom with surreal colors. Lark was lost in their beauty, petting sweet Coleman at his feet.

Lark's family loved a certain amount of chaos. They thrived in it and felt a bit uncomfortable if things were too calm or quiet. That is probably why, in addition to the five children, they also had dogs. They used to have three, before Coleman passed away, but now they had two: one black Labrador named Finn and one yellow lab named Digger. When the kids were having a quiet moment, the dogs saw to it that the quiet moment didn't last.

Finn was such a good boy, so sweet and lovable. He was Mommy's first baby. Finn followed Mommy around wherever she went. She encouraged him to stay put if she was ducking into the other room for a minute, especially when he was older, his muzzle white, his joints creaking. He couldn't hear in his later years, so despite the encouragement to stay put, this obedient boy would give all his effort to get up and stick to her heels, to be near her, to show his constant devotion, love, and companionship. He was a very special dog.

Finn was sensitive and loved things to be surrounded by joy. He took a long time to adjust to Lark when he first came home as a baby. Lark screamed around the clock. Finn loved Lark, but he also wanted him to be happy; he was confused as to why he wasn't happy. Finn glanced worriedly at Mommy, wondering why she couldn't fix it, why she couldn't stop Lark's crying, and in turn, Mommy would give worried glances at Lark and then back at Finn, wondering the same thing. Mommy would say things like, "I know, I know . . . shhhh . . . it's okay, it's going to be okay," saying these words of encouragement as much to herself as to Lark and Finn.

Coleman was still alive when Lark was born. Coleman didn't seem to mind the noise of Lark's constant crying. He was attentive and sweet. Whenever Lark finally settled, Coleman would curl up under Lark's Moses basket, guarding him diligently. The family nicknamed this big dog "Nana," like the sweet and watchful dog from Peter Pan. Coleman was a fox-red lab, and his fur was a dark golden-red color. He had the most expressive eyes, lined in black as though he wore eyeliner, their teardrop shape dipping down at the bottom for extra expressive emphasis. Those golden eyes were a window into that big heart of his, giving away every thought or emotion he may be having.

Then there was Digger. Digger was a maniac. Total. Complete. Maniac. He was a light, almost white lab. Digger was obsessed with fetching tennis balls. He would have been a good hunting dog, but since their family didn't hunt, his retriever skills were displayed in his passion for fetching tennis balls. He gave it the intense focus of a professional athlete battling obsessive compulsive disorder and addiction issues who just drank a case of Red Bull, mixed with a frat boy mentality. The slimy yellow ball was brought back and dropped relentlessly toward anyone who even gave him a glance.

Digger had a mind of his own and hardly ever listened or did what he was told. He was an escape artist, and the neighbors came to know him well. He took enthusiastic visits to the marsh, where he rolled in mud and played with a dead fish or two, eventually morphing into a stinky chocolate lab. Digger went through life without a care in the world. Extremely friendly, he would take a pet, nuzzle, or scratch behind the ears from anyone who was willing. If he was naughty (which he often was), he showed absolutely no remorse but made up for it with his joviality. Though Digger loved people, he had an aversion to people on wheels. Wheels were Digger's nemesis. Skateboards, baby strollers, and wheelchairs brought about wild, ballistic barks and massive pulling on his leash as he lunged and lurched toward the perceived threat. It was mortifying for Mommy and Daddy. Digger was lovable, nonetheless, and Mommy liked to joke that she was ready to handle five teenagers after raising Digger.

Lark caught his wandering mind and stopped running over memories for the moment. Here he was under this beautiful tree with Coleman and June. Was he in heaven? Coleman was surely in heaven, so did that mean Lark was there? If Lark was there, was he alive? He began to worry that maybe he had died and didn't know it, but just then, Coleman gave him a big reassuring lick. With that lick, Lark *knew* that he was alive. In fact, he was feeling more and more alive with every moment that passed on this crazy adventure. Lark smiled at Coleman and thanked him for his unspoken yet powerful perspective, contained in a simple lick.

June waved her wing for Lark to come over to her. "Lark, if you worry so much about where you are going or where you have been, you will miss the moment you are *in*. So, no, Lark, this is not heaven. Come, let's go check in with bed number seven."

Lark looked longingly down at his dog and wondered to himself if he could come. June understood his desire and slowly shook her head. Coleman wagged his tail in reassurance with his own sparkle in those expressive golden eyes, letting Lark know it was okay. Coleman was to stay here. Or maybe Coleman would be going elsewhere. Lark didn't know, but what they all knew was that Lark did have to go, on his own, right now.

He gave Coleman one last nuzzle behind the ears. Coleman wagged his tail with a thump, gave him one last lick goodbye, and with that, he turned around and sauntered off toward the tree. He looked back at Lark, and his golden eye gave Lark a little wink.

As he did, a great wind picked up out of nowhere. All the flowers started to blow off the tree, surrounding Lark in a cyclone of petals so that he could see nothing else. His stone was hot in his pocket.

When the petals settled, Lark was a part of Mommy, inside of her, hearing her thoughts and feeling her feelings.

Right now, Mommy's mind was wandering on an uncertain journey, as it often did, just like Lark's. The random reflection of the moment was on the cleaning lady that used to clean her sister's apartment, or more precisely, on the cleaning lady's little girl that she would often bring along. This little girl literally bounced off the walls. She was a bright spirit, full of energy at all times. When she laughed, she laughed as hard as she could. When she cried, she cried as hard as she could. There was never an apparent middle ground. Lark could be like that too sometimes. He felt deeply: when things were good, he beamed, and when they were bad, he shattered. Mommy and Lark felt the correlation and connection.

After people met the cleaning lady's daughter and her extreme energy and emotions, this little girl's mom would tell them in a serious and matter-of-fact manner that her daughter had ADOS. People would raise an eyebrow and rack their mind to place the diagnosis neatly in some category they had filed away in their brains for later use. As they stood there confused, trying to demonstrate some understanding with this woman's plight in life, the mom would smile and explain, "ADOS: Attention Deficit—Ooohh, Sparkly!" as her little girl fluttered about the room like a butterfly with newly sprouted wings, touching anything and everything that caught her eye.

Whomever the mother was telling this to would then join in her smile of acceptance and appreciation, and they were no longer trying to put this little girl in a box of preconceived ideas of who she was, or how she was, or who or how she will be. The concept of a *plight in life* metamorphized into a *gift in life* in one magical moment with one slight shift in perspective and perceptions. They now all saw the little girl for who she was in this beautiful moment, and with that, a hope would be shared. A connection made. It is all in how you look at it. Mommy looked at Lark like that. She saw him for who he was simply because he was who he was, and she truly cherished who he was, and Lark was feeling that now and appreciating that now.

Perspective is such a powerful thing. Mommy hummed a song in her head by one of her favorite bands, the Grateful Dead. "Once in a while you get shown the light, in the strangest of places if you look at it right." This one line resonated with her so much right now. How true that simple line was; how poignant. She reflected on the lyrics and the power of perspective. It really is all in how you look at it. Music always spoke to Mommy's heart; it spoke to her soul. It brought hope and light where it was most needed.

Mommy and Lark were spirited individuals easily fitting into the ADOS category. Although sometimes it was a challenge, it opened a door to creativity. They noticed things around them others might miss while, at the same time, they missed things around them others might be noticing. Mommy often stated, "Differences are something that needs to be nurtured, cherished, and celebrated." She wouldn't let them be stuffed in a box. Being out of the box could be a good thing.

Medication was discussed for Lark for a brief time. He never had any official diagnosis, but sometimes it seemed his emotions could be too much for him. They wanted to make sure Lark had good coping skills when things didn't work out, and that required maintaining a balance. A life with ADOS could feel overwhelming. Sometimes Lark had a hard time transitioning, making decisions, and dealing with the sensory environment around him. He was passionate about his ideas and walked to the beat of his own drum. He functioned within his own beat and within his own time frame, and sometimes that made it hard to get out the door in a timely manner. He was disorganized with his belongings and getting himself together, which didn't help with timeliness.

Mommy often likened Lark to a mad scientist if he was working on one of his many projects. With his hair sticking straight up, his supplies spilled around him, and his thoughts fully consumed in the project of the moment, he would be oblivious to anything else, or anyone else, around him. Lark had ideas, and he wanted to turn these ideas into a reality. He woke Mommy up at four in the morning to discuss his upcoming carnival "fun-raiser" for the poor that he was planning at the ripe old age of six. He needed to know which station she would be in charge of. At four in the morning, Lark needed to know. He needed her help brainstorming gifts for everyone he knew a week before Christmas. With six days ahead of him, he wanted to craft and create individual presents for all fifty relatives. Aspirations such as these led to tears and frustration for anyone involved in these endeavors. The unrealistic time constraints, likened to those you might find on some random creative competition on reality TV, would crash in on them at an alarming rate, crushing and suffocating Mommy and Lark and taking the joy of Christmas out right along with it. Lark became frustrated if Mommy and Daddy tried to reign in his vision. It was hard as a parent to enthusiastically support these dreams and also help him realize what was possible within the constraints, especially since they knew a meltdown would follow if his vision didn't come to fruition.

Mommy smiled to herself as she thought about his current project of the blue raspberry he was trying to grow. With all the blue raspberry candies and slushies and such, Lark thought there really should be a bright blue raspberry.

Lark was always reaching for the stars, and Mommy and Daddy wanted him to continue to do so. They truly appreciated this side of him. They wouldn't be surprised in the slightest if one day Lark actually captured one of those stars and held it in his hand, beaming with pride. Lark could do anything he set his mind to as long as he didn't get in his own way

Mommy felt lucky that she and Lark were coping with their ADOS together. She cherished their absolute uniqueness. Her attention wasn't great. She had found ways to cope. In school, she had to study longer and harder than most, often reading the same page over and over, trying to get her thinking back on track, but she did just that, and she excelled, going on to get her masters with a perfect grade point average. She worked hard for it.

Sometimes, though, things just flowed, just like for Lark. If it was something either of them was really interested in, they were fully immersed, fully submerged, and it could be hard to come out of it. Stopping something when you are in the middle can be hard. Transitions can be hard. For Mommy, parenthood had been the greatest lesson in how to learn to stop things mid-stride—constantly. Parents need to be flexible. It is hard to complete a sentence at times, let alone a project. Things like going to the bathroom, taking a shower, reading a book all eluded Mommy when she became a mother. In the mornings, she often had to reheat her coffee in the microwave three times before ever getting a sip. Sometimes she found it sitting there in the microwave without a sip ever taken when she went to heat up some frozen vegetables for dinner that night.

For a while, the creative side of her called out desperately, like a flower in a vase with no water on the verge of wilting. At times, she thought she might be wilting. Mommy's creative side needed to be allowed to bloom.

Finally, Mommy was given the gift of a shift in perspective. She realized the creative side of her *was* blooming right now. It was blooming through her greatest creations, through her greatest works of art: her children. There would be time for other creative endeavors down the road, but for now, her focus was her five children. They were her masterpieces. They were her canvas of beautiful colors, layer after layer, developing into the stunning pieces of art that mattered most in the world. She used her creativity in games, songs, Play-Doh and glitter and sidewalk chalk and dance parties. She used her creativity in the way she viewed her children and how she viewed the world. For now, she used her creativity in hope.

Hope. In the hospital, hope was a window that kept shifting between open and shut. Maisy was in the PICU, and there was a window of hope over which they had no control. Sometimes it felt as if this window was haphazardly left ajar on a bleak and rainy night, letting bitter cold, wet air seep in, chilling them to the bone. If only they could shut it. An open window is a symbol for opportunity and growth. This window was not letting any of that through. Mommy got a chill just thinking about it. She needed the window of hope to remain open, but it was time for it to bring fresh air and comfort and sunshine.

They were back in the PICU in Baltimore. "Is she going to be okay?" Mommy asked as the doctor examined Maisy once again. She was not sure why she asked since she had already noticed that, somewhere between when they first arrived until now, the canned response had shifted from "she'll be fine," to "we are hoping . . ."

Mommy was hoping, looking toward the future.

Flashes of x-ray after x-ray.

"She must have had over fifty x-rays already. Is that dangerous?" Mommy asked.

"We protect her as much as we can, but there is always a risk with radiation," replied the doctor. "She *will* be at an increased risk for respiratory problems down the road like asthma, but we have to wait and see."

"With her oxygen levels dropping so low, so frequently, will that have an effect on her brain?" asked Mommy.

"We don't know. It might. It could affect attention or cognition or other things. If she ends up with attention issues, we'll never know whether it was caused by this situation or if she would have had difficulty anyway. Being so young, we don't have a definitive before and after. We need to get her through this," replied the doctor.

"This is not the typical course of RSV," the doctors kept saying, over and over, perhaps more to themselves than to Mommy and Daddy.

They came by Maisy's bed and looked at the machines and the baby in the purple hat with the big flower and scratched their heads. All the doctors could say was, "We are hoping . . ."

The desperate confusion, the unknown of what was going on or how to make it better, was apparent in their eyes. "We are hoping . . ."

The snow kept falling down.

The doctors would give their updates of Maisy's condition, which seemed to change with the wind in a chaotic downward spiral:

"Her lungs have collapsed, but we are hoping . . ."

"She has pneumothoraxes, holes in her lungs, and there is air leaking out, making them collapse, but we are hoping . . ."

"We need to do a small surgery and put in a chest tube, but we are hoping . . ."

"Yes, I'm not sure why the chest tube is not working, Mom. We are going to do another surgery to put in a second chest tube, and we are hoping . . ."

"Not what is typical of RSV, but we are hoping . . ."

"We think something might be wrong with the way her lungs were formed. The cells might not have been formed correctly in utero, but we are hoping . . ."

That last doctor update was not one that sounded hopeful to Mommy and Daddy.

"What do we do if that's the case, if the cells in the lungs aren't formed correctly?" Mommy asked hesitantly.

The doctor shook her head ever so slightly. There was no denying the doctor's loss for words and the tears behind her eyes. She didn't answer the question. She didn't mention hope, and Mommy could feel it being threatened. Mommy would not let her hope wane.

"We need to take her to floor three to get a special CT scan and have a look, as soon as possible," said the doctor. "Unfortunately, she is not stable enough to move. She seems to go into extreme distress if we make the slightest movement, even something as simple as a diaper change. So, we can't move her yet. It is too dangerous."

"But if we need this information to get her better because she is in danger, how will we get her out of danger without it?" inquired Mommy.

"We have to wait. She can't be moved. She can't handle it right now, but we are hoping . . ." And with that the doctor walked away, probably trying to escape any other questions she didn't know the answer to, as the empty "we are hoping" hung in the air. The empty words hovered a second and then fell to the ground like a deflating balloon.

Mommy went down the hall and out the double doors. She had a brilliant idea and was calling the specialist she had seen throughout her pregnancy.

"Hi, how are those sweet twins of yours?" exclaimed the doctor on the other line of the phone.

"Doc, I need help. It's Maisy," she cried into the phone.

"Are you there?" Doc said into the phone. He continued. "I can barely hear you. I don't have a good connection. I'm out shoveling snow; I can't even believe my phone rang because I thought it was dead. So, quickly, my house has no power, and I won't be able to call you back if I lose you. Quickly now, tell me what's going on with Maisy."

Mommy spoke urgently. "Maisy is in the hospital with RSV. She is not doing well, and they think her lungs, maybe the cells of her lungs, were not formed correctly. They need to have this information, but they can't take an image because she isn't stable enough to move. She goes into major distress if she is moved in the slightest. Do you have any information or images that would help from all those ultrasounds?" Mommy pleaded.

"Oh, I'm so sorry. No, I don't think I have anything that can—" and, just like that, the connection was lost. The phone call had lasted less than a minute. Mommy sobbed.

A day and a half later, the doctors decided they couldn't wait any longer and needed to move Maisy for the scan, despite the risks. Mommy and Daddy weren't allowed to go. An entourage bigger than Beyoncé's gathered around Maisy's bed. Mommy and Daddy gave kisses of good luck to their baby in her coma as she disappeared into an elevator, Mommy and Daddy left behind to pray.

The test showed her lung cells were not malformed. Thank God.

"Stormageddon" was what the obscene amount of snow that continued to dump unforgivingly from the sky was named. Any function that wasn't medically necessary in the hospital had been halted. In the early days of the blizzard, only one sandwich shop stayed open. Mommy could barely eat anyway, but she was afraid of her milk supply dropping, so she forced down a few bites of a turkey sub every now and then. Then the sandwich shop closed, too.

She then turned to the lobby vending machines. Mommy forced herself to have a handful of Fritos on occasion. It was so hard to eat. She was literally worried sick. All these idioms she had heard her entire life were now taking on a whole new meaning as they described the full impact of her feelings. There was the "worried sick" one. She was so worried about her baby girl that she felt sick constantly. She felt so sad, too sad to eat.

Her "heart was heavy." Mommy's heart ached. It felt so absolutely heavy hanging there in her chest. Mommy woke up like that. Before she opened her eyes, she felt her aching, heavy heart, and she felt fragile, incapable, and unable to support it much longer.

She and Maisy were both "hanging on by a thread"—like the situation when Mommy lost the phone call on the elevator before the stranger hugged her. There was no better way to explain it. She had been so close to losing Maisy at that moment, it seemed that the only thing holding Maisy to this dear earth was a small thread, so thin, like one of a silkworm's, dangling in the wind. Mommy felt like she, too, was only hanging on by a tiny, shredded thread. It was a thread that she was desperately holding on to, with all of her dwindling strength, the only thing connecting her to life and sanity. She, too, was dangling erratically in the wind, with only the hope of this thin fraying thread to anchor her, with the snow relentlessly falling down around them. Mommy couldn't last like this much longer.

The snow kept falling down.

Chapter 18

Green—Be Kind

". . . scenes so lovely must have been gazed upon by angels in their flight."

—Dr. David Livingstone,
upon seeing Victoria Falls, Zimbabwe

The stone had heated up, and, *swoosh*, Lark was back in the willow. Green was everywhere, even more vibrant here than by the green meadow next to the willow tree. It was an enveloping emerald that swirled into every shade of green imaginable, making everything around Lark feel alive. It was truly beautiful, but Lark was unable to appreciate it in this moment. Lark's heart was beating rapidly, and he screamed desperately out that he needed to get back. They needed him; Mommy needed him; Maisy needed him. He felt that maybe, since he knew that Maisy ultimately would live (hopefully, if that was still the case), his presence could help carry her through in some way.

It was like when Lark was watching a movie that he had already seen, but he was still completely wrapped up in the mystery of what would happen next, despite already knowing. It was always so frustrating if his parents turned it off at some critical point because it was time for Lark to go to bed or something, but he wanted to stick around and see the ending, even if he already knew ultimately what was going to happen.

"I need to get back, but I almost don't want to. It is so horrible. Especially being a part of Mommy and not knowing. I don't know if I can handle this, June."

"You can do it, Lark. You are stronger than you think," Pru's voice called down from what sounded like a mile above.

Lark glanced up and quickly smiled at the sound of her voice and her needed words of encouragement. It felt like ages since he had heard Pru's voice. He needed that connection in this moment here in the green realm. Lark started to climb quickly. He wanted, no, he *needed* to catch up to Pru.

She had finally paused and was waiting for him patiently. Breathless, he reached her.

"Hey stranger," Pru laughed with her toothless smile, and Lark, relieved, smiled back.

"Pru, how are you?" Lark exclaimed, exasperated. "I've been worried about you! Were you scared of the dark without my headlamp? I was so worried! Are you okay?"

"I'm okay, thanks for asking. And you look great. You and Echo look great together."

Lark smiled sheepishly and held up his arm to show off the intense swirling colors he had acquired during the merger.

Pru grinned back. "Try not to worry about me, Lark. It was a new experience, and yes, it was scary to me, too. As you know, I doubted the physical world in the dark when we first got in the willow. I didn't know what was there because I couldn't see it." Pru got a far-off look, and Lark could tell she was launching into one of her Pru-esque soliloquies. "I lost all of my confidence when my sight was taken away. I forgot we are supposed to be learning to see differently, to see with our hearts. That is the journey; that is the adventure. You and Echo reminded me of that. I have only ever seen the sunset/sunrise, Lark. I have never been in the darkness before. I'm not like you. I don't have another home to which I'm trying to return."

Lark suddenly felt a little bit sorry for Pru, for as pretty as the sunset/sunrise was in the outer-fort world, there was nothing quite so beautiful as home. A loving home encompasses a beauty that transcends the physical, and Lark knew that now.

Pru looked over at Lark and nodded with a knowing smile. "It's okay. Please don't feel sorry for me. I can almost feel what home feels like through you when you think about home, and yes, it is beautiful. Thank you for that, the gift of knowing 'home.' Thank you also for teaching me that the stars are always out, even when it is not night. That was so helpful to hear, you know, and how you said that we need to trust that they are there, and if we are patient, we will see them again soon when the light is right. I can imagine it. I imagine that's kind of what home feels like. Not just the house, but the people and the love and the feeling—you know, that comfort and familiarity that lets you be you. I bet you don't need to be physically home to feel that, do you? No, I imagine as long as you carry it with you, inside your heart, you are already home in some ways. Not completely, not physically, but metaphorically. So, I think I may already know what home is, now that I've met you."

Lark blushed at the sweet compliment, not in an embarrassed kind of way, just more of a touched kind of way. He and Pru had quite the connection.

"I've seen shooting stars in the sunset/sunrise," Pru continued. "Most people have to wait until darkness to see the stars. I imagine they must be beautiful, maybe more beautiful, when seeing them through darkness."

Lark let her words sink in, and he thought about his advice to Pru, taking it into his own heart where it was needed.

"Could you hear me calling out to you, Pru? I thought you couldn't hear me. Have you known I was there each time?" Lark inquired.

"Well, no, Lark. For a while there, I forgot again that I needed to listen with my heart. I only realized it when I reached the green; this is the heart realm, after all. There often is a message to find if we listen with our hearts that we cannot hear when listening with our ears. I think that is why I didn't hear you when you were calling out. I was so consumed with my own thoughts and my own fears that I couldn't. I forgot to connect again. Remember, I'm still a kid, too. I'm still learning," said Pru.

That's a whole lot of Pruisms, Lark thought.

Pru smirked. "Don't you forget them. You are teaching me as much as I am teaching you. Don't ever limit yourself."

Here she goes again, thought Lark with a smile, and she smiled back and continued on without pause.

"Don't give into the constraints of what others think you should be doing. Or, what you *think* others think you should be doing. Don't limit yourself. Their dreams may not be big enough for you. Even their wildest dreams may not be touching on what you are capable of, Lark. You have the power to change the world. We all do if we think and see and feel with our hearts and our souls."

"This is all so crazy. I mean, I am bopping around the universe, or some other universe or time or memories. I don't know. Do you know where I've been, or where I'm going?" Lark inquired hopefully. Pru shook her head. "It's hard, Pru. I don't know where I am anymore, or when I am, or even who I am," said Lark softly.

"Well, you are still you, and we are here in the green right now. That is all that matters. That is who you are, and this is when you are and where you are. The green realm, or chakra, is connected to the heart. Each level we are traveling through is a different energy source with a different lesson, combining to make us our true selves."

"Huh?" Lark asked ever so eloquently.

Pru smiled. "Well, chakras are energy centers found inside of each of us, but here, in the outer-fort world, *we* are inside of *them*. So, when you are traveling and experiencing your adventures, you are getting lessons on the different chakras as those moments relate to you and your loved ones. Perspectives change and lessons are learned. You can think of chakras as windows to the soul."

Lark looked at Pru, his confusion tangible.

"Um, okay . . . let me see . . . green is Anahata—"

"Ana-hu-huh?" Lark replied.

Pru paused and puzzled with a furrowed brow. Then her eyes quickly lit up. "No, okay, yes, I've got it. The green chakra is, as I said, Anahata. It is appreciation, attraction, acceptance, affection. It is authenticity. Blessed, balance, becoming, beautiful, breath."

Lark listened on, entranced, as he attempted to decipher the Pru puzzle.

Pru took a deep breath and alliterated on, "Here in the green it is cosmic, compassion, calmness, and connectedness. It is in found in doing, in deepness, and in the Divine. Empathy, energy, and essence of that Divine. Forgiveness, family, friendship, and feeling are here at the fourth chakra. And giggles." Pru let out her own giggle, and Lark smiled as he picked up on a pattern.

"Grace and generosity, giving and, yes, giggles, all here at the gateway between the physical and spiritual self. There is harmony, happiness, health, and the heart. That's what it is all about. It is the heart. The heart chakra is what surrounds us here in the green. Individuality, inner peace, yes, indeed! Joy and kindness. Laughter, loveliness, light, and love. Love. That is at the heart of it all. Feel the love and soak it up. Oh, yes, *Lark*. Let's add Lark."

Lark bobbed his head up and down in enthusiastic agreement, and Pru smiled her toothless smile and continued.

"It is miracles and manifestations and magnetism and magic. Nurturing. Openness and others and oneness. Power and peace." Pru paused for a moment or two, searching for the next words.

Lark started to giggle here amidst her rambling discourse, recognizing she was caught on the letter "Q." That was always one of the hardest to find when Lark's family was playing the game they played on road trips, where they had to find a word beginning with each letter of the alphabet, A to Z, out of the car window.

Pru's eyes lit up, and she continued on through her gapped smile. "It is quintessential. It is quiet contentment. Rhythm and resonating. Spirituality, sensuality, stillness, and serenity. It is found in a simple smile. Truth. True love and being true. It is understanding and vibrations. It is wonderful and warm and welcoming." She paused again.

Lark started to giggle again and so did Pru.

"Xylophones, Pru?" Lark suggested.

"Sure, xylophones will work and hmmm . . . yin, yang, Zen, and zippity doo-dah?"

They both laughed out loud. Once again Lark had that feeling. He had the feeling that in this moment, the green realm felt like where they belonged. An overwhelming feeling of love surrounded him, like a warm hug. He then felt a fluttering breeze and sensed June's presence, although they couldn't see her.

It is all that is green, that is fresh, that is new,
As the sun shines down, making sparkles on the dew.
Springtime buds burst forth from slumber in the dark earth.
It is here, once again, we can feel the rebirth.
We must give of ourselves and share our soul,
Look out for the greater good and mankind as a whole.
We must look out for others in this sweet life.
We must live a life of compassion and try not to cause strife.
We must take the strength from within and above,
For everything is connected by love.
It is through warmth and kindness that we connect with one another;
That is how we become sister and brother.

With that, *swoosh.*

Back to Africa. Lark glanced sideways and saw that Pru was with him this time, and he was so grateful for her company. Pru's eyes danced, and without saying a word or needing a word, they grabbed hands and together moved closer to Mommy as if this was all the most natural and normal thing ever. Lark was getting used to this roller coaster ride, and he was open to the lessons and the crazy ups and downs lying before him.

They were silent observers, here in the OT clinic, privy to Mommy's thoughts in the big hospital at the southern tip of Africa.

Mommy was working with a mother and her baby. The mother and baby had HIV. The baby girl also had severe brain damage. The baby was born with HIV, but the brain injury was new. It was the result of the interventions of her desperate mother who had visited the witch doctor in her village for help. This mother loved her daughter dearly. This respected elder, the witch doctor, recommended giving the baby poisonous cleaning fluids to cleanse the disease from her little body. The mother, in order to help her little love, followed the witch doctor's orders. Now her little baby had HIV and brain damage. The mother was distraught.

Mommy was in sad awe. Mommy could tell this mother loved her child very much, so much she was willing to try anything to help her get better. Now she sobbed with regret and remorse as she cuddled her stiff baby in her arms. Mommy was empathetic; she had already learned not to make assumptions. The mother had been gravely misinformed and thought she was doing what she needed to do in order to save her child. Mommy realized she needed to learn all she could here, not just about OT, but also about the cultural, social, and political environment in which she was now living. It was important to learn about all these factors to understand the individuals she was trying to help. Mommy worked with this mother on how to effectively care for her baby with HIV and her new diagnosis of brain injury and the challenges that came with that.

The more Mommy could learn, the more she would grow as both a therapist and a person. Mommy had already learned not to make assumptions or judgements, and she would try and carry that with her always. Lark had already added "don't make assumptions" to his list of important things he was learning. He would also try and carry all of these lessons with him always.

While working at the hospital, Mommy worked in the HIV outpatient pediatric clinic twice a week, although she would visit her patients daily, just to pop in and say hello. She also worked in the inpatient pediatric ward, the orthopedic ward, and the hand clinic. As part of the internship, she attended OT classes and went into the community visiting shanty towns and orphanages. She sang African lullabies to disabled babies in her arms on dirt floors of huts made of scrap metal. Mommy sipped tea out of chipped, stained teacups as she sat on shredded chairs and discussed therapeutic modalities between conversations about the political and societal challenges of South Africa. She listened, and she learned. Within these homes, it didn't matter to them that she was a young, white, American woman.

There was, of course, a flip side. Apartheid was still a fresh memory. Mommy saw racism directed from people of all races, black, white, mixed, or other, toward any race that differed from one's own. It was often subtle, but it was there, nonetheless.

Here in the tip of Africa, Mommy experienced racism because of the color of her own skin. It was a unique experience for a white, American woman. There were interactions with people of all colors, and there was total acceptance by some and racism by others. These experiences added to Mommy's ability to empathize with those faced with racism all over the world, those being treated poorly for something so superfluous as the color of one's skin. Mommy didn't pretend to know through personal experience the great injustices that racism had carved into both the past and present. It did instill a certain fear in her, though, a feeling of being threatened, and it impacted her. It opened her eyes a little bit wider.

Mommy had already learned in order to truly see herself, she needed to see herself in others. That was the lesson she learned in empathy back in the HIV clinic. If everyone could see themselves in others, to see that connectedness as a whole, she thought racism could end on the spot.

There was, however, still a long way to go. Apartheid had ended, but these things take time. Lark looked down at his own swirling colors and thought about skin color and what it meant and what it didn't mean. Lark's eyes were opened a bit wider as well.

Mommy had a diverse experience in Africa. In the city there were bombs, break-ins, car jackings, and mass shootings, all while she was there in the tip of Africa. In her travels, there were safaris with close calls with hippos and lions and elephants. Mommy went surfing with sharks and bungee jumping from bridges. She learned how to blow fire from her mouth and was tossed into raging rapids while white water rafting in rivers with crocodiles longer than their boat. She danced to drums amongst Africans with babies tied to their backs as they all laughed and sang next to a flaming fire into the wee hours of the night. Mommy spent significant time in trees and on the water and in the bush and in the jungle. She went to rugby games and cricket matches. She hiked mountains and explored caves. She rode on a motorcycle around the tip of the continent and drove a dirt bike through sugar cane fields in the middle of the country. She swam on top of waterfalls, peering down over the edge as the raging water thundered past. She stood on rocks at the bottom of these waterfalls, where the great mist of the falls created a rainforest for miles around. Dozens of rainbows could be seen from these rocks in "the smoke that thunders." She traveled down winding roads in the middle of nowhere as children with no shoes, and scraps for clothing, ran beside the car, laughing and waving and smiling as they called out for sweets. Mommy watched eclipses from mountainsides. She watched the sun rise, and she watched the sun set. She explored; she lived. There was joy, and there was sadness, and with each experience, Mommy lived, and she grew.

When Mommy was in the pediatric HIV clinic, she evaluated the babies' and children's development and then implemented the appropriate treatment interventions. She worked with these young children and their families on reaching the next developmental stage while finding joy and success in their current functioning stage.

There were some African mothers who, upon hearing that their children had HIV, became afraid to attach emotionally to their children. It was part of Mommy's job to teach them that quality of life was still important with these babies. Despite having only a small chance of growing up, they still deserved that chance, and it was important to make their time on earth as filled with love and experience as they were able.

In their villages, these mothers would often sit in a circle on the ground, babies in the middle on their backs, looking up at the sky as the mothers chatted around them. There were no toys with black and white geometric designs and bright colors that made crinkly sounds and stimulated them developmentally. The mothers, many of them young and also HIV positive, would also not stimulate these babies developmentally. When they weren't on the ground, they were tied to their mother's backs with towels or blankets. They were taken care of, but the development piece needed extra attention with these babies. They would not reach developmental milestones on their own as a healthy baby in a supportive and stimulating environment would do.

When these mothers and their babies came to the clinic, Mommy and her colleagues worked hard on development, trying to get these little babies, perhaps destined for a shorter life, to enjoy the time that they were here. Development happens with children through play and stimulation and interaction—through making a connection. South African mothers watched in amazement when their babies rolled over for the first time, when given stimulation to do so. They, too, would then actively engage in the therapy, working to recreate this "miracle" of the developmental milestone that seemed previously so out of their reach. Little accomplishments morphed into big accomplishments when those little things previously felt far-fetched. Near the Cape of Good Hope, these mothers finally found their own sliver of hope to hold on to. Some truly saw their babies for the first time. Connections were made. Even if the amount of time together is unknown, it is worth the effort if a connection can be made, a lesson learned, a smile exchanged, or a heart warmed.

Things were different here at the hospital in South Africa. It was different than any other clinical setting Mommy had worked thus far, with unique issues that would likely not be found in America. Dieticians had to watch out for mothers using rationed baby formula in their own tea rather than their babies' bottles. There were people who couldn't walk discharged without wheelchairs because there were none to give them. Children about to be discharged in the diabetic unit would steal candy, risking a diabetic coma for the opportunity to stay a bit longer in the hospital. The bleak hospital offered a more comforting shelter than the shanty towns to which they would be returning. Mommy interviewed many people about the home environment they would be returning to following their orthopedic surgery. Many of the patients lived without the luxury of running water or electricity in their homes. Many didn't have shoes for their feet.

Latex gloves were scarce, and situations that would usually warrant them at home had to be handled without. Without gloves, Mommy cuddled these sick babies with HIV. On an internship back home, gloves would be required when working with someone with an infectious disease like HIV. She would have been in big trouble for not using gloves and universal precautions. Mommy justified it to herself because there was no other option. Gloves weren't always available for her. You can't catch HIV from simple touch, touch without contact with bodily fluids. Mommy hugged and cuddled and connected with these HIV positive babies freely, without gloves. Perhaps this gloveless connection could help show others, who didn't understand the disease yet, that they, too, could do so.

Swoosh. Lark and Pru watched as people with post-surgery and pre-surgery hand injuries formed long lines in the hallway at the hand clinic. One by one, patients sat in front of a long table with hand surgeons behind it, making diagnoses and treatment plans from a surgical standpoint. Behind the doctors, the OTs stood and assessed the need for OT interventions such as splints and exercises to assist in healing. They escorted patients into another room, where they worked on these exercises and measured range of motion and measured for splints, and when they were all finished, the patients filed out with their damaged hands, shuffling back down the long hallway.

Many of the hand injuries were erratic lacerations from machete wounds, suffered in the middle of the night on the dark streets of Cape Town. America has guns. Africa has machetes. Mommy learned early on during her time in Cape Town that one must never come to a full stop at a red light after dusk. If you came to a full stop, the odds of getting car jacked were astronomical.

Mommy was in South Africa during the presidential election in the year 2000 when the race between George W. Bush and Al Gore was so close it demanded a recount. Mommy had not put in an absentee ballot. While in Africa, the impact that America and its president has on the rest of the world finally became apparent to Mommy. She had never realized that before. American politics cast a wide net with a ripple effect felt around the world. Mommy felt shame once again, this time for not having voted in the close election. American politics was a hot topic of conversation, and everyone wanted to know her thoughts on it, but she hadn't been very political before. Before coming to Africa, she thought that one vote wouldn't make a difference, so she hadn't bothered with the absentee ballot. She now knew that wasn't always the case. She had been taking her liberty for granted, and she was aware now that she must never do that again.

Mommy and her friend would stand behind the doctors in the hand clinic and chat between patients. Most of the doctors in the hand clinic had sun-bleached hair and tan faces. They would discuss their obligatory medical perspectives about their patients' hands, and then, the second the patient moved on, they would fall back into discussing what they really wanted to talk about, their plans for wind surfing and kiteboarding after work. Every one of them spent their free time riding in the constant ripping breeze off the coast.

Mommy's friend at the hand clinic was a young idealist and an excellent OT. She grew up on a private game park in Zimbabwe and was newly married. She told Mommy about her happy clappy church and her new husband. If she was ever caught in a daydream, she was doodling her husband's initials with a big heart around them as if carving it on a tree for all of eternity. Interjecting into the doctors talk of tides and wind, the friend would ask them if they were voting in the upcoming elections in Cape Town. They would shake their heads and tell her they weren't voting because if the person they wanted won, there would be more bombings all over town, and if the person they didn't want won, then there would be more bombings all over town, so it was a no-win situation.

The friend was at her wits end with their passive politics toward change, lamenting over how nothing would change if they didn't vote. Mommy thought about her own relatives in Zimbabwe. She remembered stories about ballot boxes floating down the Zambezi River in their so-called "democratic" elections. Mommy was privileged to know that her vote counted. It wouldn't be wasted floating down a river, and she knew now she would never squander it again. She had gained perspective.

Lark and Pru followed Mommy and her friend as they talked about politics and the need for change on their way to lunch. Mommy took it all in, learning, evolving. Lark and Pru soaked up these lessons as well. Mommy and her friend grabbed their lunches and joined the rest of the OTs already seated around the table. Someone dealt out cards, and they started their daily Uno game. They had modified the rules to make it speedier and crazier than usual. They always had to wait for a moment for a certain OT to finish unpacking her lunch. Born a princess in her village, she grew up sharing everything. Even if they didn't have much, they shared what they had. So, every day, even though she knew that people would pack their own lunches, she brought enough to feed everyone. Today, she pulled out an entire loaf of bread. She unpacked several pieces of fruit, avocado, cheese, and some sort of meat. She offered it to all, and most politely declined but truly appreciated the offer. Mommy had her first avocado ever with this African princess. Avocados were big in Africa, long before they started having their present "avocado moment" years later in America. Though this African princess had come to expect the declinations, she brought the food anyway. It was part of who she was.

After lunch, Mommy would again see patients. Mommy had one young patient that hadn't seen his parents in over a year while in the orthopedic ward. She had another patient whose parents lived seventeen hours away in a remote village. This little girl was wheelchair-bound now, with TB of the spine, and her parents couldn't be there to help her with this big life change. Her parents had only contacted doctors after she stopped walking and lost control over her bladder. Doctors were hard to come by in their remote village, so they had waited, hoping she would get better. She did not.

Mommy loved working with the various children at the hospital. She came up with fun activities for the kids in the orthopedic ward to get together, laugh, and socialize. These children were there for lengthy times, away from their loved ones. They spoke of how they were scared at night, lonely sometimes, bored, and sad. Mommy decided they'd benefit from group activities to boost morale. They went on field trips. They took their limited resources and made toys for other sick children in the villages to help with development and demonstrate how toys could be made out of common household goods.

Lark and Pru saw one of Mommy's favorite activities which took place in late October on Halloween. They cut holes out of large trash bags for their heads and arms, making the most of their limited resources. They used paper plates and string and made masks. They glued scraps of materials and string and yarn onto the trash bags and used crayons to color their masks. Mommy went through the wards full of her adult orthopedic patients stuck in bed and dropped off candy and treats for the kids for trick-or-treating later that day. Most of the kids and most of the adults hadn't heard of the American holiday of Halloween before. Mommy loved Halloween. This was going to be fun!

Mommy and the children gathered in the OT clinic later that afternoon and slid on their costumes of decorated trash bags and paper plate masks. Everyone was admiring each other's creations with smiles of delight when suddenly, one by one, the decorations started to fall to the floor, a bit of string here, a piece of felt there. The cheap glue was not strong enough to keep them adhered to the surface of the plastic trash bags. In a matter of seconds, they were all wearing plain trash bags with absolutely nothing left of the decorations. They looked at each other in disbelief, scraps of felt and string piled around their feet. Mommy braced herself for the tide of disappointment from the failed attempt of creating these make-shift Halloween costumes.

Beginning with only a muffled, muted sound, a noise soon rumbled throughout the OT clinic. It was a roar of laughter. It was the kind of laughter you get that brings salty tears streaming down your face and an inability to stand still in any dignified manner. They were still able to find joy in the situation. These children found the humor, the ridiculousness, the irony of the epic failure, and it led to more joy and laughter and glee than if everything had stayed glued on. When they finally composed themselves, they walked and crutched and wheeled out, wearing their plain trash bags and paper masks proudly and had their first Halloween.

Older patients with hip replacements lit up when they came by their beds. They "oohed" and "ahhed" over their wonderful costumes and happily plopped sweet treats into the kids' waiting pillowcases. It was one of the best Halloweens Mommy ever had. It was one of the best ones Lark ever had, too, and it was the first and best for Pru.

In the pediatric ward, there was a desk where all the nurses, called sisters, would gather. To the left of that desk was a metal crib, and in that crib lived a little girl named Viwe.

Viwe was three and a half years old, and she had AIDS. She had to be on constant oxygen, with tubes up her nose. She was behind on development and could not yet crawl nor stand nor speak.

Lark and Pru were a part of Mommy when she first met Viwe. Though she couldn't speak yet, Viwe communicated with her sauciness and sly smile. She would hold all at bay until trust was earned, a trust she would make them work hard for, for Viwe already knew trust was precious. Viwe's spirit could light up the room, but this little girl, so full of life, was very sick.

Viwe had been in the hospital for a long time. The doctors and sisters were always chatting to Viwe, although she was not yet able to answer back with words. The doctors and sisters gave Viwe great care with great love. Months before, Viwe's mom had left Viwe there, never to be seen again. Viwe had a six-year-old brother who had already died of AIDS, and Viwe's mother, who also had the disease, was unable to deal with the pain of losing another child in front of her eyes. Mommy was surprised when she heard Viwe had been left, but then again, she was not a mother yet, so she knew she didn't know. Mommy herself was not HIV positive; she hadn't lost a child; and she didn't have this hopeless situation eating away at her like this young mother did. Mommy did not judge Viwe's mother. She did not make assumptions. Instead, she empathized and came from a place of understanding and openness. It was from this place that Mommy opened her heart to this little girl needing a connection.

Mommy was up for the challenge. Viwe was weak, and it was harder for her to develop. Every day Mommy spent time with Viwe, and soon she began to see changes. Every day they worked hard under the disguise of play, and as they laughed and bonded in each passing moment, Viwe stole a little bit more of Mommy's heart.

Viwe needed this connection. Mommy also needed this connection. Lark and Pru could feel it through and through. Mommy and Viwe loved each other.

Swoosh. It was Mommy's last day of work at the hospital. She would be traveling around Africa in the months to come and, eventually, returning home. She went to the pediatric ward to see Viwe one last time before she left. Mommy entered the ward, but before she could even greet the sisters, Viwe let out a happy yelp and waved Mommy over to her crib.

"She's been waiting for you," the sisters all chirped.

Mommy strolled over to this sweet little girl with her warm, big brown eyes that held a twinkle of mischief at all times.

"Hi, my Viwe. How are you, my darling?" Mommy sang out as she approached the side of the crib to help her out.

Before Mommy could do so, Viwe held her hand up as if asking Mommy to give her a moment. She got a determined look on her face. She looked up at Mommy to make sure she had her full attention, and then, she grabbed the bars of her crib and pulled herself up so that she was standing. She glanced sideways, again making sure Mommy was watching, and then let both of her hands go from the side of the crib and stood tall, all by herself, smiling ear to ear. Viwe was as proud of herself as she could be, looking up at Mommy to share in this moment, this gift that she was both giving and receiving. Viwe had pulled herself up and was now standing by herself. It was a moment that felt bigger than any other moment Mommy had been privileged to witness.

Time stood still, and Mommy's heart burst with happiness. Viwe laughed and clapped and plopped down on her bottom. Mommy scooped her up, laughing as well. Viwe and Mommy hugged, and Mommy spun her around, singing her praise while the sisters cheered her on, each of them with tears in their eyes because it was simply magical. Lark and Pru felt the magic. They felt how great it was to make a difference in a child's life. It was a simple moment, but they also knew simplicity could be relative. They were sharing in a moment no one was sure Viwe would ever have.

Lark recognized Mommy's maternal instinct in full swing. This was that love for a child he had sensed earlier. The love for a child before having children of her own. Mommy loved Viwe. Yet her time at the hospital had come to an end. Mommy felt elation and sorrow in her heart all at once. That duality of emotions all in the same moment, just as Pru had described back when she and Lark first met. Lark was feeling it now, elation and sorrow as one.

When it was finally time for Mommy to leave Africa and head back home, she was still floating from her adventures. She had traveled extensively. She was heading home to people she missed and loved but was also leaving people she cared for deeply. Her heart was bursting with the experiences she had soaked up, the experiences she had lived, the growth she had made. She felt like the Grinch at the end of the Christmas special when his heart grows so much it busts right out of the little metal heart-measurer contraption. Then there was also the flip side. Mixed with the joy, there was despair, guilt, and confusion. These feelings were particularly churned up when she thought about Viwe.

Mommy gave serious thought to attempting to adopt this little girl. In the end, though, she decided against it. Logistical challenges aside, in many ways, Mommy felt like she was still a kid herself. She felt a bit hopeless when she thought about it. She vowed to send money over to the hospital, to the pediatric ward specifically, but Mommy, like Viwe's mommy, left Viwe behind in the hospital. Mommy's heart shattered a bit when she left South Africa as a piece of it was left behind. *Swoosh.*

Chapter 19

Angels

"Live each day as if it were your last, someday you'll most certainly be right."

—Steve Jobs

PRU WAS GONE, AND LARK WAS BACK AT THE PICU IN Baltimore. The days were blurring together for both Mommy and Lark. Mommy was talking to Gran on the phone down the hall from the PICU. Gran had moved into Mommy and Daddy's house for the time being, and her sister (Mommy's aunt and Maisy's great-aunt) had flown in to help. Auntie made her flight into town before all of the airports shut down. Gramps had left for a long business trip overseas when the snow started to fall. Who knew he'd be unable to fly home for weeks due to the relentless back-to-back storms that would ensue? Gran and Auntie set up camp, taking care of the three babies at home so Mommy and Daddy could be with Maisy. Gran and Auntie were two more angels on earth, helping carry them through this tough time.

A friend also sent her own babysitter to the house, giving up the help with her own young children, to help a bit with Maisy's three siblings. Even though she was a newer friend, a working mom with five young children of her own, she was willing to manage for a bit without the babysitter she relied on heavily. The babysitter arrived and pulled Play-Doh from her pocket, and Lark and Sophie gravitated to her as if she had known them forever. It gave Gran and Auntie a respite. Two more angels on earth, the friend and the babysitter, that swooped in so that Mommy and Daddy could have the extra help and the extra time to be where they were most needed. In between blizzards, people brought cooked food, groceries, shoveled their walk, prayed, helped with the children, and did anything they could. The support that flowed through the community was beyond amazing.

While talking on the phone a day or so after Maisy was intubated, Gran mentioned that they may want to think about getting Maisy baptized. Mommy got scared Gran was losing hope. Mommy felt if they baptized her here in the hospital, they were admitting that Maisy may not make it out of the hospital, and that was a thought she didn't like to entertain.

Mommy and Daddy met the Catholic priest the next morning. He greeted a couple of staff members and then came over to talk to Mommy and Daddy. He seemed almost amused that Gran had called him.

"Your mom wanted me to talk to you about baptizing your daughter."

Oh, Mommy didn't know she had done that. She didn't know Gran had called him.

The priest continued on, "I don't think it is necessary for us to do that now. Once she is baptized, that's it, she's baptized, and I'm sure you'd rather wait for a nice ceremony when she can wear a nice gown, with family and friends in your own church."

The sacrament of baptism was certainly something a Catholic would want to do before they left this sweet earth. Maisy was intubated and having a lot of trouble, but the priest didn't think it necessary right now. Mommy hoped that the priest knew something she didn't, and they agreed.

Maisy had a rough day, and the next day, the priest visited again.

"We need to baptize your daughter now," he said.

Mommy was caught off guard, but she didn't question why it was suddenly necessary now and not the day before. She wondered what had transpired behind the scenes. She didn't ask because she didn't want to know the answer.

Maisy continued to struggle, just as she had the day before and the day before that and so on, but if this was the day she needed to be baptized, so be it.

They gathered solemnly around Maisy's bed. It was obviously a different christening than it had been with Lark or Sophie. This was a baptism done in this moment because it had to be done in this moment, essentially acknowledging the fact that the next moment may not be available for sweet, darling little Maisy.

Hospitals and illness teach you a lot about living in the moment, with uncertain futures and tear-stained pasts that led you there in the first place. In a hospital, the good moments were cherished for what they were, a good moment captured within chaos. On the flip side, the bad moments dug deep, cutting deep into the soul, and time would stand still. However, after bad moments, the good moments, with their newfound perspective, would ascend higher and higher than even the best moments had before. They could be the simplest moments, but with perspective, they were appreciated for the magic they held. The simple moments *were now* the big moments. The fluttering of eyes opening after what felt like a hopelessly endless sleep. A finger being squeezed within the grasp of a tiny hand again. A plan for tomorrow. These were the powerful moments they were searching for now. Searching for synchronicity within the dichotomy of these simple moments. The tears streamed down Mommy's face as she looked down at their beautiful daughter, about to receive her first sacrament.

The priest pulled a round medal out of his pocket and explained that it was a firsthand relic from Blessed Father Seelos, a wonderful priest that was up for canonization. He coincidentally used to be the pastor at their church, St. Mary's Church, in Annapolis. Mommy recognized it immediately and told the priest that her mother also had a firsthand relic of Seelos. Mommy felt a connection.

The priest, being a bit of a "holier than thou" mind set, stated with authority, "Oh no, she doesn't have a firsthand relic like this."

Mommy was excited to see the familiar object and said, "Yes, I am pretty sure she does."

The priest shook his head and said no, he was pretty sure she didn't, in a bit of a patronizing tone. Mommy didn't say anything else because it didn't matter who was right or who was wrong. She was glad that he had it because she felt the connection. This connection went beyond the confines of this hospital unit and definitely beyond a small debate over who had what. Small coincidences can transform into a sign of hope or an answer to an unspoken question or prayer. Serendipity can bring clarity, or even a miraculous message, if one is willing to open up and receive this message. It requires the suspension of earthly logic for a moment and for one to see, hear, and feel with their heart and soul rather than with the typical visual, auditory, and tactile senses. What did matter was that Mommy and Daddy's baby girl was very sick and about to have an emergency baptism, and Mommy, at this moment, was also feeling a strong connection to her faith, to Blessed Seelos, to God, and to her daughter. A connection was made, and it was a sliver of hope that Mommy would not let the shade be drawn upon. Mommy knew they were not alone in this.

Mommy's dear friend, who would be Maisy's Godmother, had sent her a little bottle of holy water from Lourdes in France, a place known for great healing. Mommy had asked Daddy to bring it up when he was home gathering their things a few days ago. She asked the priest if he might also use that as part of the baptism, and he obliged.

Faith would have to carry them through this, for things had become too heavy to carry on their own. Mommy felt the presence of angels surrounding their daughter's bed. It was an almost tangible awareness that she felt to her core, and this also brought comfort. They knew the angels had been sent from the prayers of so many, and they were there to guard over their sweet little baby lying here in this hospital bed with her fate unknown. The priest blessed Maisy and said prayers with the relic, and then he wet her tiny head with this special holy water, washing away original sin and preparing her for her arrival at the gates of heaven, whenever that may be.

Maisy then received the second sacrament of her short life so far, the sacrament of the Anointing of the Sick. This sacrament brought comfort, courage, and peace to those gravely sick and in danger of losing their lives. It also had the power to forgive sins, not that Maisy had any sins in her short, sweet life, thus far.

The receiving of these two sacraments were not happy moments, but they were comforting, and they gave Mommy hope when she had initially feared they may take on the tone of giving up hope. Instead, however, the sacraments emphasized that they were not traveling this journey alone. Mommy kissed Maisy and told her baby girl that one day, Daddy would be walking her down the aisle on her wedding day for another sacrament, the sacrament of matrimony. It was important to look forward to the future and all the great things life would have in store for this scrappy, spirited girl. This too shall pass. They would be on the other side of it soon enough. They just didn't know what the other side looked like yet.

Mommy called Gran after the baptism and told her about the priest's relic of Blessed Father Seelos. Gran was elated about this connection and told Mommy that she was correct; it was exactly what she had, and she would send up the relic pin that she had of Blessed Father Seelos as soon as possible. Seelos had been the pastor at their church in Annapolis long before Mommy's time, long before Gran's time. He was on the path and process to become a saint. To become a saint, one of the requirements is to have at least two miracles believed to have been performed through the intercession of the person up for Sainthood.

Gran soon sent up the relic, and Mommy pinned it on Maisy's knitted pink hat because there was nothing else she could pin it on besides her diaper. The pin was the size and shape of a quarter and about a half of an inch thick. It had a gold metal encasement, and there was a round piece of glass on the top, allowing one to peer in, as if looking into a shadowbox. Inside lay the tiniest white relic: a small chip of a bone from the body of Blessed Father Seelos. It was now pinned next to Maisy, over a century later.

Mommy spoke to the doctor, and Lark was a part of her, listening.

"I don't understand. So, she has holes in her lungs, and the leaking air is gathering in her chest and causing her lungs to collapse. She has tubes going into her chest to let the air out and stop the pressure that is collapsing her sick lungs, but no real air is coming out of the tubes? What is stopping the air from coming out?"

The doctor, at a loss of words for the dangerous and declining situation, stated the truth: "We don't know."

Lark was watching Mommy and Daddy and Maisy. He was still in Mommy's thoughts and feelings but having his own as well.

Tucked away in the corner bed in the PICU, lucky bed number seven was where they lived. They read to Maisy; they sang her songs; they told her stories. They played music that comforted them and spoke to them and gave them hope, music which turned out to often be Bob Marley. They found reggae to be calming and comforting. Perhaps it was simply the daydream of being on an island somewhere, with crystal blue waters and white sand, that reggae conjured up. Perhaps it was the words or the melody. They sang those songs to Maisy and played those songs for her, as if sending the words up as a prayer.

Don't worry . . . everything is going to be alright. Mommy had always said the secret to parenthood, when things were crazy and children were crying and nothing else seemed to work, was to "put on Bob Marley and give 'em popsicles." It sounded simple, but she had learned it was important to keep it simple and not overthink things. When the craziness picked up steam, downshift and keep it simple. She found Bob Marley and popsicles could solve many of life's problems.

Maisy's lips were swollen and cracked as they surrounded the ventilator traveling into her little throat. Her chest went up and down, rhythmically pumped by machines, and there were tubes going in and tubes going out. Mommy bent over and started to sing "Three Little Birds" in Maisy's tiny, curved ear. Mommy loved the image of Maisy's three little siblings rising up to greet her soon, like in the words of the song. Mommy and Daddy turned the music up on their speaker, as they sought solace in the words of this powerful anthem. They would try not to worry about anything. They told themselves it was all indeed going to be alright as they offered their worry up as a sacrificial lamb. Next it was, "No Woman, No Cry," chanting a similar message, that everything would work out, it would be okay, it would be alright . . . over and over and over again. The words of these songs were sung to Maisy in a lullaby, bringing comfort and peace with the hidden hopes of luring her awake, rather than to sleep, as with a typical lullaby. Things would ultimately be alright. They just had to believe this to be true. Over and over again these songs echoed through the vast room of the PICU like a prayer. They played it for all to hear, to receive this message and gently rock their souls.

When they were waiting for results from some x-ray or test, or while Maisy was having a scary episode, time slowed to a screeching halt, as anxious seconds unforgivingly passed at the speed of a sloth. As if an oxymoron of time, the same situation, the same few seconds, could also hold the opposite effect, especially during the scary episodes. Sometimes it happened so fast, and there wasn't enough time. Time wove between the two extreme speeds, teasing them, taunting them within the same moment.

Maisy was only three and a half months, and that wasn't enough time. Mommy explained to the doctors that, though she was little, she was already a necessary part of their family, and they loved her madly. She told the doctors they had to help her get better: their family needed Maisy, and Maisy needed them, and not having Maisy was not an option. Mommy made sure that Maisy didn't lose her identity. The PICU was full of babies with diapers and tubes. She wanted to make sure the doctors knew how much she was loved and how much she was needed; she wasn't just another baby in diapers; she was Maisy.

It was happening again. People were running over to be at Maisy's bedside. Everyone was sprinting. The beeps from the machines indicated something was very wrong. Doctors and nurses worked tirelessly to slow things down. It was another big one, and they already had quite a few of those, but this was a bigger one. After the last one, Mommy wasn't sure if it was possible to have a bigger episode and still keep Maisy here on earth.

The doctor in charge, the most in-charge doctor in the whole PICU, happened to be working that shift, and he stood at the foot of Maisy's bed, rocking back and forth on his feet, arms folded over his chest as he firmly dealt out directions. He stood at the helm like the captain of a ship, quickly and authoritatively giving out orders, as if they needed to change course on a dime before the ship collided with the looming obstacle directly in its path. That is what it felt like; they were on a ship on an unchartered course with dark, rocky waters ahead.

Desperation. Yelling. Medical terms flying through the air like darts. Beeping.

"We can't get her back up."

"No—No . . . okay, got her—wait—NO!"

Things were not good. There was nothing Mommy could do but pray as the surrounding crowd worked feverishly on her baby. She needed to get out of the way but wanted to stay close to Maisy; she needed to stay close so Maisy would know she was there. She went up near the head of the bed, and Mommy put her hand on Maisy's little pink hat, and she prayed. She prayed in her heart and mind with all her might. She bargained with God, promising to go to church more if he would save Maisy. She pleaded with God to let her keep His gift to them, this precious gift of Maisy, and told God plainly that she wasn't ready to give her up.

While Mommy was praying, she felt the angels surrounding her again. She closed her eyes and felt the angels dancing above her head, above Maisy's head, and it gave Mommy peace, but she also feared she felt Maisy drifting away. With her hand on Maisy's head, Mommy instinctively reached out to touch the relic pinned to her hat.

Yelling. Beeping. Chaos. Mommy extended a finger and touched the relic as she was praying, but she immediately recoiled her finger from the glass covering it because the relic was burning hot. For a moment it felt as if she had been transported elsewhere. Lark had felt it, too. When her finger was on the relic, it was as if a warm blanket had been cast over the room. The loud noises of the machines and the yells from the people fighting for Maisy's life were silenced, and everything seemed still and calm. It felt serene.

Like a child with a finger to a hot stove, not learning her lesson the first time, Mommy couldn't help but to touch her finger to the scalding spot on the glass and hold her finger there again. Again, an ethereal shift in all senses and surroundings occurred. In the middle of the PICU, surrounded by total and utter chaos, Mommy felt an overwhelming sea of calm wash over her, and with it she knew everything was going to be okay. Cavernous, traveling thoughts, with the depth and knowledge of a lifetime and beyond, were contained within these seconds of time. They were only a few split seconds: that was all she could tolerate. Mommy's physical consciousness was still tied to this earth by the simple but profound awareness of the sensation from the heat in her finger.

Time literally stood still. Mommy felt as if she may have been given a small glimpse of what heaven might feel like. This time, a spiritual connection was made. There was a wisdom and a knowledge that suddenly just was, and probably always had been and always would be, but this wisdom was now within Mommy, and she knew. She knew everything was going to be okay in some shape or form. This message was received by Mommy with hesitation because *okay* was suddenly relative. Whether Maisy stayed with Mommy and Daddy or moved on to the realm of the afterlife, she was going to be *okay*. A different kind of hope and a different kind of comfort came from this realm. There was an acceptance of the loveliness of this space of which Mommy was given a glimpse. That being said, the connection to this earth also remained strong, and Mommy wasn't ready to turn Maisy back over to her true creator yet, not while Mommy was still on this earth. She couldn't help wondering if Maisy had seen it, too.

Mommy looked around her to check the reality of things, to see if she was in the same room that she had been in before. The noises from the machine, from the doctors and nurses working relentlessly on her baby daughter, returned to their chaotic, amplified state. It was the same as a second earlier, but she was no longer the same. She was shaking. Nothing had changed, and at the same time, everything had changed.

Due diligence and the need to explore what happened from a logical standpoint took over Mommy for a bit. Was it perhaps the lights over Maisy's bed that had made this relic so hot? Mommy explored the outside of the pin, the metal part that would have heated up if the lights caused the heat, but it was cool. The only hot part was above the relic. There seemed to be no logical explanation.

Mommy was finding many things within the walls of the hospital to be illogical and juxtaposed, like how time stood still as it slipped through her fingers at an alarming rate.

Then, for a third time, she placed her finger directly over the relic, and immediately she was transported again, as if in a vacuum or a black hole or maybe a white hole filled with light. The room had an underlying shimmer that made everything a bit fuzzy, like when Lark tried to touch the sunset/sunrise or when he and Echo had collided. She lifted her finger up again. She did not know how God worked, nobody did, but she did know right now there were forces beyond the doctors in this room and beyond this world, working on getting her daughter better.

Gran had put Maisy's name in prayer chains that were being said around the country, around the world. Thousands of people were praying for her that didn't even know her, not to mention all the friends and the family that did know Mommy and Daddy and Maisy. Mommy could feel the presence of these prayers surrounding her, holding them up. Perhaps Maisy might be okay if she left them, but even with her own strong faith, Mommy felt that she, herself, would not be okay. Mommy wanted Maisy here; her whole family needed Maisy to stay here with them. Mommy closed her eyes and prayed harder than she had ever prayed before.

This spiritual awakening that came with the burning relic was nothing short of a miracle. Mommy took it as a sign. Mommy would not give up hope, would not give up the fight, and she prayed Maisy would not either. More doctors were trying to get in by her bedside to help Maisy, and Mommy had to step aside. She moved near the foot of the bed, where Daddy was standing, and where the doctor in charge continued to rock back and forth on his feet, his finger to his lips, as if contemplating a fine piece of art, and he was, for Maisy was a masterpiece. She was their masterpiece.

Things were not going well.

"We are losing her!"

Mommy's heart lurched. Those four words surrounded Mommy's soul and hope and heart and started to strangle them in darkness.

Those words would haunt her in the moments, months, and years to come, but Mommy would not let all hope succumb to these four words without a fight, and Maisy was in the fight of her life. Maisy was in a fight for her life, again.

Lark wanted to escape, but he had no choice but to continue on in this moment. Mommy's heavy heart was pounding; there were salty tears that she tried to stuff back inside. She needed to be strong so her daughter could be strong and get through this. Medical terms. Dials adjusted. Nothing seemed to be helping.

"We are losing her!"

Those words ricocheted throughout Mommy, piercing her inside like a knife. Mommy and Daddy stood watching helplessly. Mommy felt her knees buckling and her head getting faint. She felt as if her soul might spill out all over the shiny hospital floor. She was folding over with devastating grief and fear, from the core of her essence, and the only thing holding her up was the strength of Daddy's hand.

So, this is what it feels like to lose your child. This unwelcome thought came barreling through, though Mommy tried to reject it. It came through anyway, and Mommy was forced to surrender to the possibility of the truth in this thought, and she braced herself. She thought about all those in the world who had lost a child before them, and she felt deep pain in her heart for their loss, too, for she was now aware of what it feels like to be losing your child. She felt surreal sorrow as her mind wandered in this excruciating thought. Mommy braced herself, held onto Daddy's hand, and watched helplessly as Maisy's grasp loosened on that thin, fraying thread as it blew wildly in this incessant gust of chaos.

Maisy was slipping away, and there was nothing that she, or anyone else, seemed to be able to do about it. There was nothing to do but pray. Mommy prayed and knew now, no matter what the outcome, that Maisy would, one way or another, be okay. She also knew that this too shall pass. This moment would pass.

It did. It passed, and Maisy, by the grace of God, did not pass. Mommy and Daddy, and now Lark, would never be the same.

Chapter 20

Blue—Speak the Truth, Be the Truth

"Not all who wander are lost."

—J.R.R. Tolkien

"YOU ARE CATCHING UP, SLOW POKE," PRU TEASED FROM above. Even in the blue, things were bright enough to see easily, and Pru no longer had any fear or hesitation about the dark. There was a bright light way in the distance, and Lark couldn't tell if the tree was open at the top, revealing the light from the sky, or if the last layer of colors ended in a bright white light. If they started in the dark and went through all the colors of the spectrum, it made sense to end in white. Was white the absence of color, or was it all colors combined? He had learned a bit about colors in art class, but he wasn't sure about this fact. He'd have to look it up in his *Book about Everything* later. He couldn't look it up right now because his hands were occupied climbing this ladder. Lark climbed up quickly as Pru paused on the ladder up above. When Lark finally reached her, June suddenly appeared, hovering next to them in the blue.

You are an individual; you are your-self, you-nique,
With your individuality, answers you will seek.
Seek your truth, speak your truth, loud and clear;
Be your authentic, wonder-full self, for all to see and hear.
You are a separate entity, connected to the whole,
Gain knowledge, gain wisdom, and free your soul.
Nurture your ideas and express them freely with pride;
Live that life of yours out loud and enjoy the ride.

Listen to others, but also listen to your own thought;
With the insight gained, this will not be in naught.
You are beauty-full, be-you-tiful; you are you,
Trust you, know you, you will know what to do.

June gave a wink and gestured for Lark to hop back on her back. Pru simply waved and flashed her toothless smile as she climbed on up toward shades of indigo.

Swoosh. Back in Africa again. Goodness, this was a wild ride Lark was on! He was alone this time, no Echo, no Pru. He was surrounded by people, Mommy being one of them. They were on a small plane of about twenty or thirty people, and Lark's aunt (Mommy's sister) and one of Mommy's best friends were on the plane, too. The propellers made a comforting buzzing sound as they flew over the wide-open landscape in the middle of nowhere.

"Buckle your seatbelts: we have to make an emergency landing," the captain's voice boomed over the speaker.

Worried glances were exchanged, and things were bumpy as the hurried descent began in a not so subtle way. "We hit a bird with one of our props. It's okay: we still have one prop, but we need to land. There is a game park down there; we are going to land just now."

In a few minutes, as promised, the plane swooped down on to a grassy field and bumped along erratically before coming to a full stop with a plane full of relieved cheers and tears. It was intense.

They disembarked and waited to hear what to do next. Mommy and her sister and her friend tried to make jokes to each other about the situation, to help themselves feel better. They decided to grab a cold beer to calm their nerves and cool their bodies down. The three of them clinked their bottles together purposefully as they fanned themselves in the middle of the bush on this hot day in December.

Lark hadn't been too worried. He knew they would be okay since Mommy hadn't met Daddy yet. Mommy didn't have that insight going into it, so she had been nervous.

After a while, the flight officials stated that they had fixed the plane, and they were ready to take off again. In some ways, it felt like they had been waiting a long time. In other ways, it had seemed like only a drop in the bucket of time. Were they really able to fix the plane efficiently in that amount of time? Time is relative. Mommy couldn't help wondering if it was going to fly and be safe.

Before she knew it, they were buckled in and bumping back down the grass "runway," taking flight. Again, there were cheers, and a few tears, and there they were, flying above the vast continent of Africa once again.

After they had reached their cruising altitude and the captain said they could unbuckle and get up if they needed to, Mommy started to relax. Soon after, another announcement came over the loudspeaker.

"Please get ready for your in-flight entertainment."

Mommy looked around, surprised, exploring the small plane for the small TVs she expected to drop down from some hidden compartment in the ceiling, most likely nestled cleverly between the oxygen masks and the lights and the little fans that you twist for cool air.

As she gazed up at the ceiling, she suddenly heard a loud sound. Alarmed, she looked toward the front of the cabin, and there, at the front of the plane, were five large men in matching outfits, shimmying down the narrow aisle with synchronized dance moves and lovely harmonized voices. It was the last thing in the world Mommy was expecting to see.

They sang the most beautiful African song with high energy and big white smiles. People clapped along in delight, and the last thing anyone was thinking about at that moment was a bird hitting the propeller. Next came a soulful rendition of "Silent Night." As the lead singer stood singing in front, the others hummed in a harmonized melody behind him. The lead singer had his eyes closed as he sang the words in such a beautiful voice and in such a beautiful way that it simply floated through the plane.

An elderly white woman in her upper seventies, perhaps eighties, had been in the lavatory in the back of the plane for the start of the entertainment. She was rather demure, with hair pinned back, a petite stature, and impeccably dressed. This elderly woman, a product of old Africa with its apartheid and white rulers and British influence, walked right up to him. With his eyes still closed and his soul lost in the words of his song, she grabbed his large dark hands in her small white hands with their thin skin, dotted with sun spots but filled with love. Surprised, his eyes opened quickly. She smiled at him, and he smiled at her, and they shared an immediate connection.

"Sleep in heavenly peeee—eeeaaaccceee . . ."

She joined him in the melody, and their voices and their hearts sang together as one. This young black man and this old white woman sang this song together, to each other, to everyone on the plane. In a way it was to all of Africa—the Africa of the past, and the Africa of the present, and, most importantly, the Africa of the future. It was beyond beautiful. When they finished, there were more cheers and more tears, and with this, there were connections made by all on that plane, thousands of feet in the sky. It was the best in-flight entertainment Mommy had ever seen. Lark hummed the songs in his head as he smiled to himself, thinking about how lucky he was to be a part of this unique experience.

Swoosh. Mommy returned to America after her time living in Africa and a few months of traveling. Time was hopping all over the place, but Lark, somehow, always knew where they were chronologically. Mommy was now working as an occupational therapist in a school for children with disabilities back in Annapolis. She had also met Daddy by this point, and they had fallen in love. They got married and bought their first home, and life was good.

Mommy's side of the family was going to have a family reunion in Cape Town that first Christmas after Mommy and Daddy were married. Thinking about her family all being in Cape Town over Christmas, where many people were in need, Mommy presented the idea of going to the hospital where she had worked to deliver presents to sick children on Christmas morning. Her family enthusiastically agreed.

Mommy contacted the hospital to ensure it would be okay. She then gave a presentation and started a fundraiser at the special needs school where she worked. The children at the school were very invested in raising money to help these children in South Africa, and so they did. However, before Mommy returned to Africa, she knew there was a question she needed to ask the hospital, though the answer may not be one that she wanted to hear.

Mommy contacted the head of the Pediatric Ward at the hospital in Cape Town via email. Viwe had stolen his heart, too. Mommy could tell. This doctor was, of course, sweet with all his pediatric patients, but there was a special bond between him and Viwe. It had been three years since Mommy had lived in Africa. Mommy knew he'd be able to update her on how Viwe was doing.

He responded quickly to Mommy's email. He told her that, thanks to money donated by caring people around the world, the hospital was able to buy new medicine to help slow down AIDS so that children with AIDS now had a chance at life. Unfortunately, Viwe started the medicine about one month too late. She was only the second child to try it in the hospital, but it wasn't in time. She had passed away of a chest infection in May 2002.

Mommy's heart stung as tears flowed from her eyes. The doctor said he thought of Viwe often, and although Viwe had passed away, things were looking up. AIDS was still a major problem, but now there was some hope.

Viwe was so sick when Mommy last saw her but so full of life. Mommy had tried to brace herself for the news, for the possibility of Viwe being gone, but she hoped it would be otherwise. She cried for the loss of Viwe's life. Mommy's mind wandered. Could she have somehow gotten those drugs to Viwe earlier? Maybe. Probably. That possibility would always weigh in as a heavy regret. Although Viwe had passed, Mommy would always have Viwe in her heart. This little girl taught Mommy the importance of living life to the fullest in the time one is given.

Once Mommy and her family were in Africa, they all went to a toy store and bought toys and baby supplies and wrapping paper and tape. Lark liked the experience of going to the toy store and picking out the toys and feeling the Christmas spirit that his family embodied with their connectedness. They sat around wrapping and chatting and laughing and singing. Someone bought Gramps a Santa suit, which consisted of a knee-length red robe and a Santa hat, all made of felt and fake fur. It was quite hot to wear on a steamy summer Christmas day in South Africa, but if Santa could do it, so could Gramps.

On Christmas morning, they stuffed their wrapped presents into their rental cars and drove around the winding streets until they arrived at the front of the hospital nestled on the slopes of Devil's Peak in Cape Town. Together, they unloaded the pile of presents onto the sidewalk and then parked their cars while others waited by the pile of presents and chatted in excitement. When they were finally all together again, the laughter and chatter came to a slow halt as all eyes fell upon the massive, suddenly daunting, pile of presents in front of them.

"How are we going to get them all up there?" someone asked innocently.

They glanced back and forth at each other, then to the extremely large building they needed to navigate, and then to the tower of brightly wrapped presents strewn all over the sidewalk.

Before another word was muttered, a car, parked a little farther down the sidewalk, pulled out, suddenly revealing a large rolling cart that had been hidden from view behind it.

"Look," Mommy pointed. "It's our sleigh."

They didn't ask a soul but ran over and grabbed it, quickly wheeling it over to the waiting presents. They laughed at their good luck and the uncanny coincidence as they worked, feverishly piling the presents up onto the sleigh.

Gramps wore the felt and fur Santa suit over his shorts and T-shirt, sweating away on this hot Christmas day as they worked together. A woman walked by, took one look at Gramps, and belted out, "Father Christmas, where's your pants?" in a strong Afrikaans accent as she breezed by them, not waiting for an answer.

"Ba-ha-ha!" they all laughed together, looking over at Gramps. With his shorts just above the bottom edge of the robe of the costume, it did look like he was missing his pants. Through tears of laughter, they connected even more as they happily continued their mission. They got all the presents piled up on the sleigh and wheeled the large cart into the hospital, through the long halls, up the elevator, and finally into the pediatric ward, singing Christmas carols and feeling every bit of the Christmas magic in Cape Town. When the family wheeled into the ward, the carols quickly subsided as they took in the sight. They'd known they would see sick babies and children but hadn't known how to mentally prepare. Empathetic tears filled their eyes. Curiosity and excitement filled the eyes of the patients well enough to open their eyes, but others were too sick or too weak. The family gave them and each other encouraging smiles, and they went to work delivering presents to these deserving children and their families.

Tears filled the eyes of many in that pediatric ward that day. There were tears of joy from children and parents receiving gifts as they exchanged smiles and hugs with this visiting family on Christmas morning. There were tears of joy from the family as they found profound joy in the act of giving. The family watched babies and children oooh and ahhh over their new toys. There were tears of joy watching these children's parents shed tears of joy watching their children shed tears of joy. There were tears of joy from the nurses, the sisters, as they felt the joy from these patients that they had cared for day in and day out. There were also sad tears, of course, because it is hard to see a sick child or to be a sick child, especially on Christmas. Lark shed all these tears, too, tears of joy and tears of sadness and tears because he was touched by it all. Lark's colorful tears streamed down his face right along with the rest of his family, even though they couldn't see him. He felt connected and thought they could feel him in some small way. *Swoosh.*

Chapter 21

True to You

"I saw the angel in the marble and carved until I set him free."

—Michelangelo

THEY WERE BACK HOME! HOME WAS A SIGHT FOR SORE eyes. Even though Lark knew he wasn't going to be able to stay long, he soaked up the familiar scene with appreciation and love, happy for the moment he was home again.

It looked exactly the same. Still observing the scene from an outsider's vantage point, he was able to hear Mommy's thoughts and feel her emotions. Lark knew that it was a few months before his tenth birthday, not long before he started his adventures. He could see himself here, an observer outside of himself. This Lark looked pretty much the same as he did now (minus the swirling, glittering colors). Mommy was glancing over at him. He could feel that she had been worrying about him. Lark felt the heartache. It was nothing like the worry he had shared with Mommy in the hospital, but there was a gnawing worry, nevertheless.

Mommy had gotten off the phone with the third boys' soccer coach to see if they had room for Lark on their team. Nobody had room. She was now realizing that people had signed their boys up, completing their teams, before they even registered. She had signed Lark up without requesting a specific coach and was just becoming privy to the ins and outs of the system. How was she just now finding this out? She had always just signed him up before, without giving it too much thought. Never had she thought, would he actually get a coach? Now, here they were, the soccer season already underway. Practices for Lark's sisters had already started, and when Mommy called the man in charge of the soccer league to check on Lark's team, she was told he wasn't assigned to a team and was now on a waiting list. There weren't as many kids playing rec soccer; many had moved on to club soccer by the time they were Lark's age, the ripe old age of nine. When Mommy expressed her concern and frustration that she wasn't notified Lark might not be assigned to a team, the man laughed and told her that he didn't care, and it wasn't his problem. She was livid.

Lark was able to step freely out of her thoughts for a second and ponder the scenario. He had played flag football that fall, coached by Daddy, and had loved it. He didn't realize how hard they tried to help him play soccer. He remembered being disappointed he wasn't going to play soccer, but at the same time, Mommy and Daddy got him extremely excited about playing flag football instead. He might not ever know how much he loved playing football if he had played soccer that year. Funny how things can sometimes work out differently, sometimes for the better, when you get a little time and perspective under your belt.

Swoosh. A month later, Mommy and Daddy asked Lark's assistant rec basketball coach if he thought Lark would have a spot on the team again this year. Sign-ups were opening up shortly. They had to work hard to find him a team last season. They wanted to ensure they weren't left scrambling to get Lark a place. Who would have thought this would be the situation with eight- and nine-year-old children's sports? Many of Lark's classmates had been on his basketball team last year. They had a great season; they were undefeated. Lark's favorite sport was basketball, and even though he was small and still developing his skills necessary to excel, he loved the game. He played with heart.

Lark sometimes needed encouragement to put himself out there. Lark had a fear of failure. He could resist trying things if he wasn't sure he'd be successful, and that made Mommy fear he might miss opportunities. Then there was the flip side of Lark. Sometimes he would jump right in. He was hard to figure out, and it was hard for Mommy to know how he was feeling, as Lark wasn't sharing his feelings with her as much these days. Mommy knew, if faced with a big challenge, there are three choices. One can run from it, or one can face it. There is also the third option of doing nothing, which is essentially still running from it, just with inaction versus action. If skiing were a metaphor for life, and you find yourself standing at the top of an impossible peak, looking down and wondering how on earth you are going to get to the bottom in one piece, there is really only one way to do it. When you start your descent into that challenge, you had better lean into it and face it straight on. If you don't, you will fail. It is as simple as that. Even if you fall a few times, as long as you get back up and keep trying, you are guaranteed to be better by the time you get to the bottom. You must push yourself to the edge to grow. Mommy's mind wandered from skiing to soccer to basketball and then back to Lark.

Lark was in her head right now, feeling this, realizing these thoughts. Mommy was trying to raise her boy into a man with confidence. He had been getting frustrated with Mommy lately, and he wasn't sure why. He now understood her perspective a bit more. Maybe he wouldn't get so aggravated when she encouraged him to take part in things. Lark didn't want to miss any great opportunities either.

Swoosh. Back in time again. He felt like he was in a pinball machine, bouncing around haphazardly. Mommy, upset about soccer, was walking down the stairs. Worrying about basketball. More worrying about this, Mommy? thought Lark. Lark as the observer was already feeling much better about things. He also, of course, had the insight of knowing it would work out for the best. Mommy knew it didn't matter in the big picture, but nevertheless, it would be nice if Lark were given the chance to play and have fun. Things were different in these times, in the world of sports. Would Lark, being a late bloomer, have the opportunity to play by the time he was ten, let alone in middle school or high school? Lark was still a bud in that analogy of a late bloomer. Children are like flowers. It is important to support these flowers, to hold them, but hold them loosely and not too tight, so that they are able to bloom as they are meant to bloom. They might surprise us. They may bloom into something more beautiful, more wonderful, than we could ever imagine.

As she descended the stairs, the sight of her son, Lark, the Lark she had been worrying about, stopped her in her tracks. He had turned the sectional couch into an amazing multi-room fort. He was sitting with his legs crossed, eyes closed, in one section of the couch in a cove of pillows, fingers in a meditative mudra position. He heard her on the stairs and opened his bright blue eyes, which immediately lit up when he saw her.

"Mommy, look at my fort! I'm in the meditation room right now. Look at all the rooms. I have a playroom. A nature room. A sensory room."

He was up now, pulling out all kinds of objects he had put in each one. Each room was decorated with scarves or beads or toys or books or items corresponding to the theme. He wasn't out practicing basketball shots or kicking a soccer ball. He was creating this magical, wonderful, imaginative fort instead, and honestly, it was truly amazing. He was not a kid that was "in the box," and Mommy suddenly felt so grateful for that. She almost felt a little guilty, as if she had been selling him short with her worries that were now melting away. Maybe Lark would never be great at basketball or soccer. Maybe he would. A lot remained to be seen. They had the highest hopes and dreams for Lark, but Mommy was suddenly aware that her hopes and dreams for him were that *he* would be able to accomplish his *own* hopes and dreams. Lark's dreams for Lark were what mattered.

Maybe Lark would do things beyond their wildest dreams. He was reaching for the stars, and it hit Mommy that any preconceived dreams she had for him needed to be put aside because if she held on loosely and let him bloom as he was meant to bloom, his dreams would go beyond the stars. She was blessed to be his mommy and to be along for the ride.

Swoosh. The assistant basketball coach got back to Mommy and Daddy a few days later. He said they had better find another team. He confided that the head coach was replacing Lark for someone new, someone taller. Ouch.

Lark hadn't known this at the time. He knew he was on a different basketball team this year. They actually beat his team from last year by about thirty points; the team that hadn't had "room" for him. Yes, sometimes plan B is the way to go. No experience is a wasted experience if you learn from it. Mommy had always told the kids of a great quote that she heard from Amy Purdy, a Paralympic medal winner, snowboarder, dancer, and double amputee: "You never know when your detours might become your destiny."

Lark had always had a hard time shifting mid-flight from his plan and his established ideas. He was now realizing the importance of being able to shift on occasion, for great things may lie around the corner, even if they weren't the expected things. *Swoosh.*

In the hospital there were all kinds of people, from all walks of life, thrown into a situation that none of them wanted to be in. But there they were anyway, and the one common denominator they had here in the PICU, connecting them all, was that they knew a sick child. When Mommy and Daddy first got to the PICU, there was a beautiful teenager in the bed next to Maisy. She had dark velvet skin, and her hair was up in a lavender silk cap. She had come in with a major asthma attack, but she was doing much better now. Her family surrounded her bed, hooting and hollering and having a grand old time, apparently not strangers to the PICU.

When she was discharged, a young child took her place in bed number six, next to Maisy. This poor child retched and cried and vomited for hours and hours.

He was then moved, and someone else came in. In and out, in and out, and all this time Maisy stayed there as days turned into weeks, not budging from bed number seven.

Baltimore city had come to a standstill. There had been three back-to-back snowstorms, each one bringing several feet of snow.

Despite the inclement weather, Mommy headed home because Gran said Gwynnie was not doing well. Mommy brought bags of her breast milk to Gwynnie, nursed her, and gave hugs and love to Lark and Sophie.

Then Mommy took Gwynnie to the doctor to make sure she did not end up next to Maisy in bed number six.

Mommy immediately felt a disconnect when the nurse practitioner did not recognize her from her second to last visit with Maisy. She was the same nurse practitioner that had sent them home the day before Maisy was admitted to the hospital. Mommy had been quite distraught, and Maisy was extremely worrisome and sick, and they had spent a lot of time nebulizing Maisy and checking her out. This nurse practitioner introduced herself to Mommy and smiled and told Mommy she looked familiar, wondering if they had met before. Mommy understood that she saw a lot of patients, but she needed a connection right now.

The nurse practitioner listened to Gwynnie and said Gwynnie was doing okay, but Mommy's mother's intuition was telling her differently. Gwynnie was having trouble breathing; she had a fever; she wasn't eating; and she was not herself. Mommy voiced her concern and asked about further investigation.

The nurse practitioner, in a defensive and unwilling tone, said, "Well, I guess if it would make you feel better, we could do a chest x-ray to confirm she doesn't have pneumonia. But I just listened to her, and I'm telling you now, she does not have pneumonia."

An hour later in the x-ray department, Mommy was told that Gwynnie did, in fact, have pneumonia. Mommy made a mental note to change pediatricians after they got through this ordeal. This practice was too big for what felt right to Mommy and their family; Mommy needed more of a connection, and she needed them to be somewhere where their voice would be heard.

Swoosh. Lark and Mommy were back in the hospital in Baltimore. Daddy was at home, checking in on the other kids and getting supplies, snow pants, jacket, boots, etc. to deal with the snow they were getting. The only bright side of being in the hospital, throughout all of this, was that their car had been in the garage, so they did not have to shovel it out like the rest of Maryland.

There were three friends visiting Mommy and Maisy in the PICU that day, one of whom was Mommy's friend whose sister-in-law worked in pediatrics at the hospital. The sister-in-law introduced herself and chatted with Mommy a bit as they all caught up with each other in the Ronald McDonald room over lukewarm cups of coffee. Mommy told her friends that the doctors weren't telling them much information, and the sister-in-law headed off, ensuring Mommy she would find out more.

She had her hand on the doorknob and was disappearing through the doorway when Mommy cried out, "Wait! I already know it's not good. If they think it is hopeless . . . um . . . if so, I don't want to hear it. I need to hold on to hope. I don't want to know."

The tears were back, and Mommy tried to choke them back, but she didn't need to hold them back because her friends had tears, too, even though they were all trying to be brave for each other. You can still be brave and cry. Sometimes it is braver to cry, and sometimes it can make a brave connection through showing tears and vulnerability.

The sister-in-law nodded her head slowly in understanding and off she went. When she returned, she spoke about a different ventilator they might try. She indicated the doctors were having a hard time figuring out what was going on with Maisy, but they were trying to find out. They were hoping she would soon turn a corner.

She then changed the subject. Mommy wanted more information, and then again, she didn't. She decided not to ask questions she didn't want to hear the answer to and thanked her for looking into things.

Months later, her friend told Mommy that her sister-in-law told her privately, when they were away from the hospital, to pray as hard as she could. She said that the PICU doctors told her Maisy was the sickest of the sick in that PICU, and they were extremely worried.

While the snow dumped relentlessly from the sky, some of Mommy and Daddy's friends pitched in for them to spend the night at a hotel a block away. The Ronald McDonald House that provided housing for parents with children in the hospital was full, and Mommy and Daddy didn't want to take the spot from anyone else since they had more support locally than many parents from out of town that needed the room.

There was nowhere for Mommy and Daddy to shower at the hospital. They had been getting dressed, brushing their teeth, and washing themselves off with a bit of water and soap from the sink in the communal bathroom down the hall. There was no food in the hospital for anyone but patients as everything was closed due to the snow. Next to Maisy's bed, they would catch a few winks at night until someone needed to check something or the hand holding their head up fell asleep. Then they woke with a start, going from one nightmare to another. One of the night shift nurses was strict about policy and did not allow them to fall asleep in their bedside chairs. If they accidentally drifted off, they were directed to leave. They would fight hard to keep their eyes open, to remain next to Maisy, but as soon as they nodded off, they were out. On occasion, they would trade off sleeping on a hard, grey couch in a post-op waiting room a few floors down that someone had mentioned to them, when it was free. They didn't ever like being two floors away, but their bodies started to shut down after a while. They were dirty zombies, living on Fritos and bad coffee from the Ronald McDonald parents' lounge in the yellow and white walls of the PICU.

Mommy and Daddy decided to take their friends up on the hotel offer and were sure the staff would probably appreciate it if Mommy and Daddy showered, too. They promised the nurse they'd be back early in the morning, and she promised she'd call if anything changed.

They exited the hospital to a total white out. The streets were empty. They had snow pants and boots, and they trudged along, one foot in front of the other, trying to push snow out of their way as they slowly plunged forward. Through the blizzard winds that sometimes blew them sideways, they trod through the waist-deep snow. The hotel was a couple of blocks away, but the walk was long and hard. As they were finding out with many things in life, distance can be relative.

They walked through the sliding doors of the hotel, leaving the insanity of the hospital and the snowstorm in their trail, and walked into a whole other level of insanity. The entire hospital staff must have been staying at this hotel; it was packed to capacity because nobody could go anywhere in the snow. They got their key, went upstairs to drop off their small bags, and decided to put the showers off a little longer while they grabbed food before the restaurants shut down for the night.

It turned out, only one restaurant in the hotel was open. Mommy and Daddy found a table, but when they went to order, the waitress informed them the kitchen had just closed. Daddy pleaded with the waitress to see if they might have some food, any food, that they could give them. The waitress said she would see what she could do and appeared back with a smile and a plate of French fries. These somewhat cold fries were beyond appreciated. Daddy ordered a beer and they sat there, eating delicious old fries and taking in the sights. There was loud music and dancing, and the scene looked lively and fun for those that were up and enjoying it.

A person came through the doorway behind them to also take in the sights. He lingered over their heads, looked around, and muttered "pharmacy people," shaking his head in disgust as he left. Mommy and Daddy got a kick out of that, whatever it meant. If they were pharmacy people, they looked like a fun crowd. It was funny how life carried on outside the walls of the hospital. Maisy was intubated a couple of blocks away, and these people were doing the Cupid Shuffle line dance and drinking shots, and it was all the same shared moment in time.

Mommy and Daddy took a good look around, trying to pay attention, just in case one of those people doing shots arrived for a shift in the PICU the next day. They had seen a PICU doctor at check-in, but she said she was heading up to her room, and after seeing this scene, they were glad she wasn't presently doing the Macarena with a shot of Jaeger Meister in her hand like many of the people in the room.

Mommy and Daddy finished their fries and headed up. They both took showers and then crawled into the inviting bed with clean sheets and uninterrupted quiet. Maisy made it through the night without the nurse calling them, and they were happy to go in the next morning feeling as refreshed as one can in these particular circumstances. They were learning to appreciate the little things, like a shower and a good night's sleep.

A couple of days later, their friends pitched in for another night in a hotel. The snow was even deeper. It was up past their waists now, and it was still dumping massive amounts from the sky. On this night, the nurse did call. Maisy had another episode. She was doing okay now. Suddenly she seemed far away. Mommy and Daddy put on their snow clothes and started the hike back to the hospital to check on their baby girl. Even though the air was cold, Mommy got hot from the energy exerted to get through the heavy snow. She tied her jacket around her waist, and step after step, one foot in front of another, they forged ahead.

When they arrived, Mommy realized her nice winter jacket was no longer tied around her waist. She thought she also had her wallet in the jacket pocket. She had a moment of feeling like she couldn't take it anymore. Mommy began to break down, not over the lost jacket or the lost wallet: they were the straw that broke the camel's back. She started to cry, and as she did, she plunged her hands in the pockets of her pants, and lo and behold, she found her wallet stuffed into them. Feeling silly and relieved and dramatic, she was now laughing behind the tears, or crying behind the laughs, emotions swirling in different colors all around. Mommy's emotions were very ADOS. She hoped someone who needed a jacket out in the streets of Baltimore that night might find hers and put it to good use.

The snow was relentless. It was like another world outside the hospital doors.

Mommy and Daddy were returning from getting food at the far end of the hospital. The sandwich shop was open that day, once again. There had been plenty of days when nothing was open, so they were happy to have this option. When they reached the unit, the doctor in charge was elated. They had found a blockage in Maisy's chest tube. It contained tissue, and that was getting in the way, so nothing could get through, and it was why her lungs continued to collapse and the chest tubes hadn't been working. Of course, Mommy and Daddy were happy to hear the news.

It also seemed so simple that it concerned Mommy and Daddy it hadn't been discovered before now. The doctors and nurses were supposed to be suctioning it regularly to prevent something like that from happening, so if they had been doing that properly, the blockage was baffling.

Nevertheless, it was a step in the right direction. It was Valentine's Day, and Maisy turned a corner in the days after that. What a gift! She had been intubated for over two weeks, relying on machines to do what her little body couldn't do.

Gran called to say that Gwynnie was doing much better. Mommy hoped that meant her identical twin might follow her lead.

Finally, after being on a ventilator for three long weeks, the doctors felt like Maisy could be taken off and attempt breathing on her own again.

The road to recovery was going to continue to be a long one with twists and turns. Maisy was still very sick and still in the PICU, but when the doctors said, "We are hoping," Mommy and Daddy could detect sincere hope behind the words, where before it seemed to be words without any solidarity to back them up.

The day came when Mommy got permission to hold her baby girl. She lifted her gently from the bed, so happy that her baby could feel her touch again and that Mommy could hold her and connect again in this way. Amongst multiple tubes going in and out and wires and needles and bandages, Mommy held Maisy close.

The doctors and the medical school students came by for their rounds. Upon seeing Mommy and Maisy curled up together in the papasan chair, they commented that it was a sight for sore eyes, many of them fighting back tears from their own sore eyes, as it had been a long journey for all of them.

Maisy had been on heavy narcotics up until this point. Withdrawal was a delicate road, especially with a child, and if it was done too quickly, her body would go into distress. She came out of her coma to pain and sickness and withdrawal. Maisy cried. She vomited. She was weak. She was exhausted. Mommy cried. She was weak. She was exhausted. Mommy said prayers that this would be the only time she would have to go through a drug withdrawal with anyone she loved. Her heart went out to any parent that had to go through this. With each new experience came a new empathetic awareness.

Gran called. It had been a couple of days since Maisy had been taken off the ventilator, but Gran was now calling to tell Mommy that their dog Coleman was sick. Coleman, being the big, wild, lovable, and crazy lab that he was, sometimes liked to eat things he wasn't supposed to eat. He ate random things like the zipper off a jacket and socks and stuffed animals. He usually destroyed dog toys within moments after he received them, leaving shredded stuffing or plastic bits that needed to be gathered and pitched. One time he ate a toy, but he didn't leave any remnants or clues behind. It was only when he started vomiting and they took him to the vet that they learned he had eaten something. That toy required surgery to be removed.

Coleman was getting sick repeatedly, and Mommy and Gran speculated he had eaten something he shouldn't have. They were worried he might need another surgery to remove some toy or sock or other inedible object. Gran was taking him to the emergency vet and would call Mommy back.

Time passed and the phone rang. Yup, they thought he had eaten something again and were going to perform emergency surgery on his stomach. Crazy Coleman. She would call back when he was through it.

A few minutes passed, and the phone rang again. It was Gran.

They had opened up his stomach to have a look, but they found no toy or sock or inedible object. What they did find was cancer. Cancer everywhere. According to the vet, with cancer like this, he only had a few days left. The vet wanted to know if they should close him up and let him wake up to post-surgery pain, combined with cancer pain, so that they could say goodbye and then put him down, or if they should put him down right now, while he was still sleeping peacefully from the anesthesia.

Shock. More tears. Mommy and Gran came to the conclusion that it was best to put him down right now.

He was running around and wagging his tail the last time Mommy had seen him, and just like that, he was gone. Mommy would not get the chance to say goodbye. She hung up the phone and sat there in the middle of the PICU, holding Maisy, crying hysterically. Doctors ran over to see what was wrong.

"My . . . dog . . . died," was all she could choke out.

They looked at her with mixed looks; some with confusion, some with relief, knowing it was not Maisy causing tears, and some with empathy, knowing how hard it is to lose a dog.

The next day they moved Maisy to the step-down unit. Another step in the right direction. Mommy was in their new room and had just gotten off the phone with Gran. Mommy was crying about Coleman. A nurse who looked like she was twelve came in to check on them. She had been the nurse working when Maisy was baptized. She looked at Mommy's tear-stained face, alarmed. Mommy explained that her dog had died, and the nurse cocked her head to one side, let out an insincere, "Aw—sorry!" and went about her business.

Mommy's heart hurt. She wanted the nurse to understand the validity of this hurting heart, in some weird way. Not that she needed it from an outside source, but she felt like the death of a great dog such as Coleman warranted more. Not everyone is a dog person, and there were a lot of sick babies around, but nevertheless, Mommy wanted more of a connection.

Mommy started to chat to the nurse about the PICU and how hard her job as a PICU nurse must be.

"Not really," she said. "I have faith like you, so I know if a baby dies here, they are going to heaven, so it makes it not too hard."

That was true and not true. Mommy realized this nurse didn't know. Heaven or not, it would be hell on earth to lose a child. Having a child is a love you don't know you are capable of until you experience it. Yes, faith helped carry them through this difficult time and probably would provide solace if, God forbid, Maisy didn't make it through, but it wouldn't take away the devastation of losing a child. It would, however, contribute to the ability to carry on afterward. The belief that one day you would meet again in heaven was probably the only thing that allowed parents that *had* lost their little loves to rise up each morning and continue on. How hard it must be for those who didn't have faith.

Mommy was tired and sad and felt like it needed to be admitted by this nurse that if a baby died on her shift, well, that would pretty much suck. Mommy wanted to create a connection because, if it came down to it and Maisy needed her help, Mommy needed to know the nurse would be all in, helping Maisy stay. Mommy already knew from chatting with this nurse the day Maisy was baptized that she didn't have kids of her own, and Mommy didn't bother to ask her if she had a dog. Mommy was pretty sure she already knew the answer to that question. The nurse was nice, but she was also young and naïve, and Mommy decided to leave it at that. You don't know until you know.

Once they were in the step-down unit, Daddy decided to head home for a bit to check on things and see the other three children. He couldn't believe the full fridge and the baskets of food and groceries delivered and cards and flowers—people desperate to help in any form. It was beautiful. It was a beautiful thing in a time of such darkness.

"Gwynnie woke up at 11:10, 3:45ish, and 5:20."

"Yup. Pretty much the same. 11:10, 3:44, and 5:20."

The next day . . . "10:50, 3:35, and 5:15."

"10:50, 3:30, and 5:15—almost exactly the same again. That is crazy."

A connection made. Well, a connection that was never really unmade.

This was a game that Mommy and Daddy continued to play once Maisy was out of her coma and through the worst of her withdrawal.

Her hospital stay was the first time she was away from her twin besides the extra time in the NICU. Before the hospital stay, they were on somewhat of a similar schedule with each other, but there had been no real schedule for either since they got sick. Maisy had been in a coma for three weeks. Mommy and Daddy continued to be amazed at the twin connection. The distance between Baltimore and Annapolis was irrelevant for Maisy and Gwynnie. Night after night, they would mimic each other, sensing when the other was awake and rising at the same time. It was uncanny. Mommy took it as a sign. It gave her even more hope.

Gwynnie had now fully turned the corner to shaking RSV and pneumonia out of her own little system, and Mommy felt like she would lead her twin to health with the powerful connection they had, of which physical distance didn't seem to matter. If Gwynnie was getting healthy, hopefully Maisy would, too. Lark watched, nodding in hopeful agreement.

A few days later, Mommy was in the Ronald McDonald lounge grabbing a quick coffee. The morning felt like it had a tangible hope in it. Maisy was going to get through this. This too shall pass.

She sipped her coffee slowly, taking in the comforting smell of the warm drink in her hands. She didn't even like coffee that much, but it was so good at this moment. A doctor from the pediatric ward strolled in and started up a conversation. Mommy told her this might be the best cup of coffee she has ever had. With Mommy's proclamation, the doctor started to laugh and then quickly apologized. She informed Mommy that the coffee in the lounge was notoriously some of the worst coffee out there; it was a bit of a joke in the pediatric unit. Mommy smiled and had another sip. Perspective. Her baby was getting better. Nope, it was still one of the best coffees she had ever had—maybe *the* best . . . and maybe just to her, but right now this coffee tasted simply fantastic. Apparently, coffee can be relative.

Finally, they were transferred out of the PICU and into the pediatric ward. Child Life brought some toys and things for stimulation in her crib. It was time to go beyond just survival and look at recovery. This was a great feeling, and they welcomed it with open arms. However, things were still very hard at this point. Maisy looked like she had been through battle, and nothing could be truer. Most of her veins had collapsed, so it was difficult to get an IV in her little body to deliver the needed medicine. She had IVs in her head and every other part of her body where they could find a vein. Each time a person had to draw blood, they thought they would be the one to find the mysterious eluding vein no one else could find. There was not much inventory to work with—almost none. Maisy was aware now, so to watch people poke into her over and over and over again, and to miss over and over and over again, and to have her scream and thrash and cry over and over and over again, felt like torture for both Maisy and Mommy. It was as if some crazed scientist were performing human torture on Mommy's little girl who had already been through enough. It really started to feel like torture. It was several times a day, every day, and nobody could ever find a vein. Lark felt this torture as he witnessed Maisy's tortured body and Mommy's tortured mind and heart.

Finally, someone recommended a nurse from the PICU. This nurse was the same nurse who wouldn't let them sleep in their chairs near Maisy's bed. He was the only one who could find a vein when others couldn't, and sure enough, he was able to get the IV into her little arm.

Maisy and Mommy were transferred over to the pediatric ward on a Thursday evening. It was a ceremonious crossing across the hall toward hope and health. Their first roommates in their new digs were a large woman wearing a hospital gown and her cute baby girl. The woman was big, black, loud, and bubbly.

"Whew, I just woke up. I've been asleep all day," she exclaimed excitedly.

She got up in her open-backed hospital gown that didn't quite fit around her, revealing some back rolls and no bra, then came over to Mommy and Maisy to introduce herself. Her baby had also had RSV. At first Mommy wasn't sure if they were both sick since the woman was wearing an undone hospital gown, but then she thought about the fact that they were in the pediatric ward and answered her own question. Mommy wasn't sure why she was wearing a hospital gown, but who knew, who cared? This wasn't a place for questioning fashion choices.

The woman went on to chat about her other kids and how one of her other daughters was born with all her organs on the opposite side than they should be, and she talked about the food in the hospital and the snow and a whole bunch of other things. They traded stories of their journeys here, and Mommy told her about her other children and a whole bunch of other things, and they talked about the snow some more.

Mommy and Maisy were exhausted. There was a bench/bed in the room for Mommy to lie down on in the horizontal position and sleep. Mommy eventually said she was tired and told her roomie she was going to try and feed Maisy and get some sleep. She drew the curtain and picked up sweet Maisy to feed her.

Maisy was learning how to eat again, and they had met often with a lactation consultant and a speech therapist to address this. They worked hard at it when she was first born in the NICU, and they would do it again.

They were up for the fight. As of now, it was not a smooth or easy thing for either Mommy or Maisy, but they were trying. Maisy was still weak. She couldn't hold her head up, a skill she had solidified long before she was sick; she had taken a big step back in her developmental milestones, but it was too early to say if any would be long lasting. They were hoping she'd catch back up. Right now, in this moment, Mommy was happy to have her sweet baby girl in her arms, holding her close. She wasn't worrying too much about the future. Mommy was enjoying the moment for what it was, and Lark was along with her, learning the beauty of doing that—and the *necessity* of doing that at times.

Mommy cuddled little Maisy and worked hard at getting her some milk.

"I'm going to watch TV. I slept all day, and I need to watch my shows," her roomie called out from the other side of the room.

"Okay, I'm going to try and get some sleep now. Good night." Mommy replied.

With that, Mommy placed Maisy back in her crib, and Mommy settled in for her first night in the hospital in a real pseudo-bed. It was heaven. It was heaven for a minute, and then the TV went on, and it was loud. It was full volume. Mommy, not wanting to seem unkind, put her pillow over her head and, being exhausted, hoped she'd eventually tune it out.

That did not happen. It was another sleepless night.

The roomie watched loud TV all night long, with her loud laughing and loud, ongoing self-commentary on her various shows. Maisy wasn't fazed. Mommy got up to feed Maisy a couple of times, and then Maisy fell back to sleep. Mommy did not go back to sleep because she never really slept. Mommy kindly requested the volume to go down once or twice in the middle of the night. Perhaps it was decreased by a notch or so, but if it was, she couldn't tell. Mommy did have some overemphasized rolls in bed, of which were partly required due to the need to adjust and reposition, but mostly contained a passive-aggressive message to her roommate. It didn't work. No wonder her roomie slept all day. She watched TV *all night long.*

In the morning, Mommy vowed to herself to request the volume to be turned way down that night, but it turned out not to be necessary. The nurses came in and told the roomie she and her baby were being discharged. They left by early afternoon.

Mommy and Maisy met their new roommates before dinner time. Another baby with RSV and another large mother, this one extremely tall as well as wide, with very pale skin and dark, frizzy hair—not to call another mother out on her bad hair day in the hospital. A good hair day would be stark contrast from the product-free, messy buns haphazardly thrown on top of most moms' heads without a second thought if their hair looked good because when you have a sick child, nothing else in the world, especially hair, matters.

This roomie had the physique and mannerisms one might expect from a linebacker. She was sweet and gentle, though, with her tiny baby. Mommy remembered seeing her and her baby come into the PICU two days earlier. Mommy knew they had been through a lot because any minute in the PICU is a lot, so her heart went out to them. This mother wasn't as chatty as the last roommate, and Mommy was fine with that. In the evening, the roommate said she was tired, and she was going to try and get some sleep, and Mommy was ecstatic about that—a roommate who slept during the night. They both put their babies to bed, said good night, all lights (and televisions) were turned off, and slumber was within Mommy's grasp.

"ZZZ-SNORT-HUMPH-ZZZZZ!"

Everything in the room vibrated. Mommy had never heard snoring like this . . . and never would she after. Her hope for sleep was slipping through her fingers.

"SNORT-HUMPH-ZZZZ!"

Never had she ever.

"ZZZZZZ-SNORT!"

Never. Ever.

Analogies of a chainsaw had nothing on this snore. This woman must have been exhausted to not be waking herself up with the noise. Mommy once again pulled a pillow over her head and tried to fall asleep. Sleep didn't happen.

About an hour and a half later, Mommy decided she couldn't take it anymore. She exited the room and headed down the long hallway toward the nurse's station near the end. As she exited the room, she realized the noise was in no way contained within the walls of their room. It reverberated and echoed down the corridor, following Mommy like a long shadow cast down the hallway. When Mommy came up to the nurse's station, before she could even say a word, they burst out laughing, unable to contain their giggles at the hilarity of the noise from their perspective. Mommy smiled knowingly and agreed, yes, it was unreal. She then let them know she hadn't really slept in a long time and was wondering if they had any earplugs or anything that might help her cause. They stopped laughing and understood her situation with empathetic glances, and they all felt a little guilty for laughing at the situation since it was at the expense of another exhausted mother, just like Mommy. Mommy had empathy for these nurses with such a tough and admirable job and for this exhausted mom who was sawing logs for all to hear, and amongst all this empathy, Mommy could appreciate them finding humor in the situation. They were here in the hospital, weathering tough situations together, and laughter was the best medicine after all.

Unfortunately, they did not have earplugs.

Mommy shuffled back down the hallway, defeated, and reentered the roaring room. She checked on Maisy who, still sick and on meds and pain killers, was sleeping soundly. Mommy got back into bed with a pillow stuffed over her head.

The nurses did come in with some orange earplugs they scored from audiology about thirty minutes later. They muffled the noise slightly, and Mommy was grateful for that. This hospital stint was helping her to appreciate the little things.

Chapter 22

Indigo—Enjoy the Moment

"Oh, give me patience when tiny hands
Tug at me with their small demands.
And give me gentle and smiling eyes;
Keep my lips from sharp replies.
And let not fatigue, confusion, or noise
Obscure *my vision* of life's fleeting joys,
So, when, years later, my house is still—
No bitter memories its rooms may fill."

—Anonymous

INDIGO. THEY WERE IN THE INDIGO SECTION. PRU WAS there with Lark, climbing quickly. Lark knew the colors of the rainbow. He was almost at the top. Deep blues and deep purples swirled together, forming an indigo that looked like twilight. The color that lingers all but a few seconds before night silently takes over. It was that color in the sky when the first star appears, but it is often gone before you can see the second star in the sky.

Even though indigo was a darker color, Lark didn't need his headlamp anymore. There was a light from above, from beyond. He wasn't sure if it was the sky, maybe a way out of the tree. He was in indigo now, though, and he needed to focus on that. The violet and the light would come if they were meant to, when the time was right.

June the Loon's voice flowed through from somewhere within the tree, but Lark couldn't see her right now. He could only feel that she was near.

"Lark, you are at the third eye; learn to see, and you will learn why."

Lark listened intently for the loon to recite her colorful verse for lessons of indigo.

For the first time you are seeing; for when you know, you know.
See with your heart, Lark. It will tell you where to go;
You now have insight; you know to look within;
It is through truly seeing yourself that your life will begin.
Protective layers and armor are replaced with authenticity;
In finding your true self, your soul will find synchronicity.
The balance of inner and outer, being in the now;
Rise up, it is time, and this journey is showing you how.

Pru startled Lark when she suddenly started talking as she climbed a few feet above him.

"Have you heard this story, Lark?" Pru inquired.

Lark shook his head side to side, and although Pru was above him and couldn't see him shaking his head "no," she already knew what he was thinking here inside the willow. Pru smiled at his quick answer before knowing what story she was going to tell. She smiled because they were in tune, connected, and Lark was understanding how things worked here in the outer-fort world.

Pru continued on. "A very religious man was once caught in rising floodwaters. He climbed onto the roof of his house and trusted God to rescue him. A neighbor came by in a canoe and said, 'The waters will soon be above your house. Hop in and we'll paddle to safety.'

"'No thanks,' replied the religious man. 'I've prayed to God, and I'm sure he will save me.'

"A short time later the police came by in a boat.

"'The waters will soon be above your house. Hop in and we'll take you to safety.'

"'No thanks,' replied the religious man. 'I've prayed to God, and I'm sure he will save me.'

"A little time later, a rescue helicopter hovered overhead, let down a rope ladder, and said, 'The waters will soon be above your house. Climb the ladder and we'll fly you to safety.'

"'No thanks,' replied the religious man. 'I've prayed to God, and I'm sure he will save me.'

"All this time the floodwaters continued to rise until soon they reached above the roof, and the religious man drowned. When he arrived at heaven, he demanded to speak with God.

"Ushered in front of God, he said, 'Lord, why am I here in heaven? I prayed for you to save me; I trusted you to save me from that flood.'

"'Yes, you did my child,' replied the Lord. 'And I sent you a canoe, a boat, and a helicopter. But you never got in.'"

Lark looked at Pru for a minute and let out a giggle at the irony of the story or joke or whatever it was, and then—*swoosh.*

It was the next day, and Lark was still a part of her. Mommy was heading home to Annapolis for a bit. Before she left, the nurses had come into the room to try and draw blood again, and Mommy and Maisy endured another miserable experience. Mommy felt her heart in her throat as she held Maisy's little hands, and Maisy's big brown eyes looked pleadingly up at her, crying and writhing about, begging her to stop, questioning why Mommy was letting this happen over and over and over again. The IV in her right arm was looking irritated, and the nurse agreed they needed to take that out. Her shift was ending, but the next nurse needed to do it. She would make a note of it and mention it to her verbally, too.

Mommy hadn't left the hospital in a long time, and she was excited to be going home to Annapolis to see the other kids. Daddy had to do a little bit of work. He hadn't been to work since that first big incident, but now that they were out of the PICU, he was in his office a few blocks away. Daddy's mom, "La-la," was coming to spend the day with Maisy.

La-la arrived bright and early. Mommy gave directions to La-la of how things worked and emphasized the IV needed to be changed.

Mommy went home. She helped build a snowman. She cuddled and read and sang to Lark and Sophie and Gwynnie and tried to take steps toward normalcy. While she was there, more food arrived from friends, and the support brought tears to her eyes. She was so humbled by the beauty of it all, the beauty that rises from the bleak, light from the darkness.

Gran and Auntie were holding down the fort the best they could, and Mommy was beyond appreciative. She laughed with her children and felt real joy, an emotion that had eluded her the past month. She had a good day. Things were looking up.

She drove back to Baltimore in the afternoon, still smiling from the time at home. When she got back up there, La-la and Maisy were happy to see her, and she was happy to see them.

Then Mommy noticed Maisy's arm. What had been an irritated IV when she left was now swollen, reddish, and purplish, with hints of yellow around the IV.

"They didn't change the IV?" Mommy asked in a panic.

La-la had forgotten about it, and the staff, whose responsibility it was to tend to the IV, hadn't followed through.

Mommy felt guilty for leaving and kicked herself as the beauty and importance of her time at home began to fog. It seemed if she ever left Maisy's bedside, things went wrong. It was so important to advocate for those who don't have the voice to do it themselves.

La-la left, and Mommy thanked her sincerely for the gift of time with her other littles while also having the gift of knowing Maisy would still have a loved one by her bedside in Baltimore. Mommy was frustrated with the staff about the neglect of the IV, and as soon as La-la departed, she demanded they come in and take a look. Their shocked initial expression upon viewing the IV was telling as they tried to downplay their mistake. They took the IV out and, poke, poke, poke, tried to find somewhere else to stick in a new one. Again, after trying for forty-five minutes, they called in the master from the PICU. He was able to find a vein in her forehead and taped it down. Her little arm looked like someone had given her an Indian burn, resulting in a painful tie-dye of reds, blues, and purples. Lark, the observer, wondered what exactly an Indian burn was as Mommy's mind contemplated the political correctness of terms like Indian burn, whether kids even do that nowadays, and why on earth did they used to do it to each other when she was young? Lark looked down at his arm of beautiful, swirling colors and back at his baby sister's arm full of unwanted, painfully stained colors. Tears streamed simultaneously out of Mommy's and Lark's sad eyes.

Daddy arrived for the night shift, and Mommy handed over some more orange earplugs and headed back to Annapolis so she could be there when her other three little ones got up in the morning. She was finally going to sleep in her own bed!

An hour after she arrived home, Daddy called, and again she drove north to the hospital instead.

Maisy had a high fever. She was vomiting and miserable. When Mommy arrived, the doctor was already talking to Daddy. She was a Muslim woman with beautiful green eyes and hair covered by a silky black scarf. She told Mommy and Daddy that Maisy had contracted a staph infection, and now she had meningitis, and the fluids around her brain and spinal cord were infected. Her blood was infected. Possible brain damage. Possible death. The doctor told them she was one hundred percent sure that was what she had, based on the symptoms alone, and she wanted to prepare Mommy and Daddy for the road ahead. They needed to do a spinal tap to confirm what the doctor already knew.

Maisy was only five months old, and this would be her second spinal tap. They went into a well-lit room, and there was the doctor in charge of the pediatric ward and the interns and residents that the doctor in charge was in charge of, and there was Mommy and Daddy, all surrounding Maisy on a sterile bed. Mommy noticed the Muslim doctor standing with the interns in the crowd. The attending doctor went on to explain the procedure, and Mommy sensed them all salivating under their masks at the opportunity that lay ahead of them, the chance to do a spinal tap on this helpless, little body. After the description of the procedure, the doctor asked the crowd who would be interested in doing it, and all hands went enthusiastically up.

Mommy's hand also went up, not to volunteer, but to interject. All eyes turned to her. Mommy's body and voice shook, both from fear of the dire situation Maisy was in, with meningitis looming over their heads, and because she knew they weren't going to like what she had to say.

"I also have a question. Who here has ever done a spinal tap?" Mommy asked.

They all gave her a confused look, wondering if it was okay to answer the question presented by someone other than the doctor in charge.

"I am her mother, and I want to know who, out of all of you, has ever done a spinal tap?"

The crowd's hands, still hovering from the previous question, slowly went down, and only two people were left raising their hands, one of whom was the doctor in charge.

Mommy turned to the doctor. "How many have you done before?"

"I've done three."

Mommy turned to the other person raising their hand.

"How many have you done?" Mommy asked.

"One," they answered, casting their eyes to the floor.

Mommy turned to the crowd.

"I know this is a teaching hospital, and I know you need to get practice and experience, and I understand that you would want the opportunity to perform a spinal tap. She—no, *we*—can't handle one more prick or poke that doesn't do what it is supposed to do. I can't take it anymore. Maisy can't take it anymore. I am watching her get tortured day in and day out. We have been here over a month, and she is still sick, but now with something *new* added to the mix. So, I'm sorry, but you—" she turned toward the doctor in charge, "are the only person we are going to let touch our daughter. You are the only person we give permission to do this spinal tap."

Silence and disappointment overtook their eyes, and underneath masks there were frowns on the faces of the salivating residents who were not going to get the chance to perform their first spinal tap today.

Mommy's eyes swept over the crowd. A couple of the interns nodded in silent acceptance and empathetic understanding. It was hard to tell, but Mommy bet those were the ones who had been there for some of Maisy's torture up to this point.

The doctor in charge started to say something but then thought better of it. They had no time to waste. She needed to perform the spinal tap to confirm the *one hundred percent chance* of meningitis diagnosis from earlier in the evening.

That diagnosis was one hundred percent incorrect. Maisy did not have meningitis. She was sick and septic, with a bad staph infection that had spread to her blood. Mommy was no doctor, but she was pretty sure they weren't supposed to throw out one hundred percent diagnoses until they were one hundred percent sure they were correct. Before that, the wording should contain words like "possibly" or even "probably," but the "definitelys" and "one hundred percents" needed to be saved for things that were without a doubt definite. An intern also probably shouldn't have been the one throwing out anything definite yet.

Mommy's trust in the system waned a bit more. She was relieved it wasn't meningitis, but she was left with doubt. A gnawing doubt in the road to this moment and what the future held.

Lark felt this weight on her, and he wanted to scream that it would all work out. Lark was learning, though, that doubt can lead to the detour that can determine your destiny, so he would have to trust the process. It was not like she would have heard him if he screamed out anyway, but he accepted he was here for the lesson in the experience and continued to watch and learn.

Back in the PICU side, they were in defeated isolation. The infectious disease doctor and her team came in to describe the various types of staph infections to Mommy and Daddy. This was Maisy's second staph infection to cause her to go septic in her short five months of life. The IV site got infected, and now the infection was in her bloodstream. This was another life-threatening situation. The infectious disease doctor suspected in might be MRSA. The doctor and her team had charts and diagrams and handouts to explain Methicillin-resistant Staphylococcus aureus (MRSA) and how it often eluded doctors, popping up anywhere in her body, not just near the infected IV site. MRSA is also very resistant to antibiotics. If it was MRSA, it would not be good.

The tests came back. It was not MRSA. It was still a dangerous situation, and she still had a staph infection and was still septic, but it could be worse: it could be MRSA. So, this was good news, relatively speaking. Of course, if Maisy lost her life to it, it would be irrelevant as to which type of staph infection she had, but they were hopeful antibiotics could help her.

Maisy continued to have a high fever and continued to get sick and continued to feel miserable. The infectious disease doctor also wanted to start looking at Maisy's immune system because it was not common for a little one to have two major staph infections and this horrible, atypical case of RSV. Exploring her immune system would be a process that would be done over the course of several months ahead. One step at a time.

Maisy needed to get a peripherally inserted central catheter (PICC or PIC line). This would be used for long-term intravenous antibiotics, medications, and blood draws. Maisy was going to be on meds for a long time. The IV on her head was getting irritated, and they needed to call in the expert from the PICU again. This time, the only vein he could find was in the tip of her big toe. Every other one of them had collapsed. He emphasized the importance of that IV. That was the last frontier. There were no other angles. Maisy simply did not have another vein to torture, and if that came out before the PIC line went in, Maisy wouldn't be able to get the medicine she needed.

With this needle in her toe, Maisy was transferred back over to the step-down unit and then, shortly after, to the pediatric ward, the ward where Maisy contracted the infection from the neglected IV in the first place. Mommy, and consequently Lark, was feeling scared and distraught.

Back in the pediatric ward, they had different roommates once again. It was the young couple from the PICU and their baby, Jason. The young grandmother was also in the room as a constant fixture. They kept to themselves and drew the curtain, although it didn't quite go all the way across. Some privacy was fine with Mommy. Maisy's fever was still high, and she was very fussy, sick, and miserable.

Curtains weren't soundproof, unfortunately. The first thing Mommy heard was the daughter, the young mother, relentlessly yelling at her mother, the grandmother, who, from what Mommy could hear, was just trying to be supportive. Not that Mommy wanted to be listening to this exchange, but it was happening just beyond the curtain, and nobody was trying to speak quietly. Many explicit words were used over and over, directed at the distraught grandmother. Mommy's heart went out to her. Maisy was fussy and vomiting, so she tried to focus on Maisy and block out what was happening behind the curtain. Mommy picked up on more foul language. This time it was a little quieter but still plainly audible, now complaining about Mommy and Maisy from across the curtain. Mommy looked in the direction of the hurtful words and saw the couple glaring through the partition in the curtain as Mommy was trying to discretely nurse Maisy under a blanket. They mumbled and grumbled words like "disgusting" about breastfeeding and complaints about that "damn vomiting baby girl."

Then baby Jason made the slightest little whimper. "Shut the f*** up, Jason!" the young mother screamed at the top of her lungs.

That was it. Mommy couldn't take it anymore. This was her breaking point. She placed Maisy in her crib and spilled out of the room, shaking, into the hallway. It was late at night. She approached the nurse's station. They looked at her, concerned. She was crumbling, unraveling right there in front of them. Jason had been sick, too. He had also been baptized in the PICU; he had also been fighting for his life.

Mommy asked the nurses if there was anywhere else that she and Maisy might be able to move to, and they asked her what was going on. She couldn't keep it inside. She told them about Jason and what the parents had said to him. She didn't want to share a room with those people anymore. Their baby was sick, and they didn't seem to care. Mommy's baby was sick, and she needed to care for her. She couldn't be around people who didn't care.

She wanted the nurses to know for her own sake, for Maisy's sake, and most of all, for Jason's sake. If they were verbally abusive now, while their son was a newborn, God knew what the future held for that little guy. Perhaps this would be a catalyst for some sort of parenting intervention, and the staff could enlighten these young parents on what and what not to do. Maybe a professional counselor could intervene before it was too late. Regardless, Mommy couldn't stay in that toxic environment any longer.

The nurses jumped into action. They had one tiny room that had recently opened up. They insisted they move Maisy and Mommy right that minute. It was late in the evening. Mommy said she could make it to the morning.

Perhaps recognizing that Mommy was a woman teetering on the edge, the nurses insisted, "No, we are moving you there, right now."

They moved them immediately, down the hall into a tiny room which resembled a glorified closet. It had enough room for a crib for Maisy and a window seat for Mommy to sleep on. The room had a small table with a TV on top of it, and that was about it. It may as well have been a suite at the Ritz, it was so appreciated and cherished in this moment. Perspective. Relativity.

They would have no more roommates at this hospital. Lark continued to be an observer for all of this and quietly soaked in each experience. Lark appreciated his parents all the more as he witnessed some of these different parenting styles at the hospital.

Maisy needed the PIC line put in ASAP, and they met the woman that would be doing it the next day after they changed rooms. She did the necessary pre-procedure assessments. She would be able to put the PIC line in tomorrow.

Mommy had a bad feeling. The woman was not warm and fuzzy, but it was beyond that. Mommy had lost a bit of trust in the hospital, but it was beyond that, too. She got a dark, unspoken, sinking feeling as this woman worked with Maisy. Mommy started to dismiss it as paranoia after all that had happened, but it wouldn't let itself be shaken and Mommy, in turn, was very shaken.

It turned out, one of Mommy's best friends had a baby shower in Baltimore that day. Maisy wasn't getting sick anymore and appeared to be feeling slightly better. Mommy decided she would pop into the shower. It was a nursery rhyme theme and dressing up was encouraged. With her limited resources, Mommy took some lipstick and made a fake hickey on her neck. She borrowed some scissors and cut the body off a turtleneck, leaving just the neck. She took the stethoscope that one of the doctors had given her to bring home for Sophie and Lark to have as a toy. Hickey, dickie, and the stethoscope made doc. Hickory, dickory, dock conjured up with limited resources and a little ingenuity. Although it certainly lacked class, it would be good for a laugh, and Mommy could use all of the smiles she could get.

Maisy would be on her own for a bit with the doctors and nurses checking in on her while Mommy ducked out to go to the shower twenty minutes away. Maisy was sleeping when Mommy left, and Mommy turned off the lights, and the TV was off, and it all seemed very peaceful.

Mommy would be at the shower for an hour or two and was looking forward to some friendly faces and a small break. The expectant mother had visited Mommy and Maisy in the hospital a couple of times. She was one of Mommy's best friends. It wasn't easy to visit them while very pregnant through several feet of snow and to spend time in an environment so overcome with illness and grief. The PICU was a scary environment full of sick children, and her friend, pregnant for the first time, had come to sit with them and spend time with them and support them. Mommy wanted to be there for her on her special day.

The nurses had promised to check in on Maisy often. Mommy walked out of the hospital, and it all felt surreal—the way life happens, and continues to happen, outside of the hospital walls. Even when someone's life might suddenly not be happening any more inside those walls, life goes on outside. It was also a weird feeling leaving her baby in the hospital to go to a baby shower, to go to a party, but Mommy did feel like it was the right thing to do right now. She would go and support her friend.

While Mommy drove up the highway, her mind wandered and wound around back to the weird and scary feeling she had when meeting with the woman about the PIC line. She started to contemplate the events leading up until now. When Maisy was sick back in Annapolis, Mommy and Daddy were given the choice between a few hospitals, and one of them was Johns Hopkins, which was a bigger name, but wasn't as close to Daddy's office. At the time, they were told that Maisy would be fine, and they were not to worry much and wouldn't be in Baltimore long.

Over a month later, Mommy was questioning their decision to come to the hospital they were in. She couldn't help wondering if things would have been different if they had chosen Hopkins instead. It was a pointless thought, but she was wondering and wandering there, nevertheless. Maybe nothing would have been different elsewhere, or maybe everything would have been different. She did have a feeling Maisy wouldn't be septic right now. The hospital had lost her trust, and Mommy was starting to doubt things. Her thoughts wandered back to all the incidents that had brought them to this point, and she was left pondering the PIC line procedure scheduled for tomorrow. Mommy shivered at the thought of it; that bad, sinking feeling was still there inside. She didn't have to try hard to listen to her mother's intuition, for it was speaking to her loudly. Lark heard it, too.

Sometimes it is good to step away from a situation and get some perspective for a moment. As Mommy drove up the winding highway, her mind was winding through many thoughts about the experience in the hospital over the past month. She dissected decisions and different events of the past, present, and future. The sinking feeling, that feeling that she had when she thought about the PIC line insertion, held steadfast. It was intuition screaming at her, and she had no choice but to listen.

The thought hit her like a ton of bricks. They should move Maisy to Hopkins.

This realization poured in, crystal clear, as if someone was saying it to her from the passenger seat at a very audible level, and she had no choice but to listen. Hopkins—they needed to transfer her to Hopkins. As this thought crashed in, she wound around the next bend of the highway, and there, right in front of her, was a tall billboard with the words "Come to Johns Hopkins" printed in large letters. Mommy got goosebumps. Was that a sign meant for her? There was no debating it was a sign; it was a huge billboard on Highway 83. The question was whether it was a sign with significance for her. Was she meant to see it at that exact moment she was having that exact thought? It was hard to dismiss it as having no meaning. It was certainly serendipitous.

She continued to drive north, contemplating choices, her mind winding through her thoughts, as her car was winding through the streets, and then before she knew it, she had arrived at the home of the hostess of the shower.

Everyone was excited for the mom-to-be, and it was a lovely shower. Many of the women asked Mommy how Maisy was doing and inquired about life with infant twins and life with four children, and they talked about the food at the shower and the lovely home of the hostess and the weather and snow and how the expectant mom was glowing and other chit chat that one might find at a baby shower.

The mom-to-be had been at the same hospital where Maisy was now, a couple of years prior, to have a benign brain tumor removed. It was scary. Mommy had visited her in the hospital after that surgery and, luckily, the surgery had gone well. Five weeks after the surgery, her head suddenly swelled up so much that her ear was facing forward. She went back into the hospital, and sure enough, she had an infection that she had picked up back when she was in the hospital. She was admitted, and they were able to treat the infection. She was eventually discharged, healthy but a bit shaken.

She asked Mommy about Maisy and her infection and how things were going. It turned out that she had the same infectious disease doctor that Maisy was seeing. She told Mommy she was one of the doctors at the hospital with whom the friend had been very impressed. Mommy was glad to hear that; a connection was made.

The next conversation Mommy had was with her friend's mother, the soon-to-be grandmother. She had heard about Maisy and was wondering how she was and where she was—which hospital. Mommy told her, and as if it was a knee-jerk reaction that couldn't be avoided, "I hate that hospital," slipped out of the mom's mouth. She backtracked for a moment with some sort of apology for her opinion, but Mommy wanted to hear her honest thoughts. She talked about the infection her daughter, Mommy's friend, contracted and how she held the hospital accountable. They were both mothers, feeling helpless, who were forced to watch their daughters suffer at the hands of some daunting infection that had nothing to do with the reason they had come to the hospital in the first place.

Mommy wholeheartedly understood her reaction. Both had contracted infections in the place that was supposed to be making them better. Since then, her friend's mom had heard many others tell similar stories. There were too many similar stories, and she didn't trust that hospital anymore. Mommy told her she was losing trust, too, and shared the sinking feeling she had about the upcoming procedure. Mommy told her about the thought of transferring to Hopkins, if that was even a possibility, and her friend's mom encouraged her to listen to her intuition if it was trying to tell her something.

Infection is certainly a risk at any hospital. Was Mommy overreacting? The PIC line was one of the more routine things Maisy was facing on this journey, but it was still very invasive and obviously had risks. The idea of a line going through her little veins, up next to her heart, was a big deal right now. Mommy's head was reeling by the time she headed back down the winding highway. She turned on the radio to distract her from her thoughts, and the first thing she heard was a commercial for Johns Hopkins Hospital on the radio: "Come to Hopkins."

This was too much of a coincidence. Mommy parked in the hospital garage and headed up to the pediatric ward.

When she arrived, she ran into the nurse that had been checking in on Maisy. The nurse had peeked in a number of times but hadn't stayed in the room since Maisy had been fast asleep the entire time Mommy was gone. Mommy felt relieved and glad Maisy had a good nap. Maisy hadn't known she was gone, and this helped alleviate any mom-guilt she had been feeling. Mommy entered the room quietly, so as not to wake her sleeping baby.

The room wasn't completely quiet, though. The TV was on, even though Mommy knew she had it off when she left. This struck her as strange since the nurse had told her she had peeked in the room and not spent time in there. Mommy glanced up to yet another commercial for Johns Hopkins playing on the TV with the message, "Come to Hopkins" reverberating through the room.

That was it. Intuition was pleading, and Mommy was listening. Her mind was made up, and she knew what they had to do. Lark couldn't help but think back to Pru's story about the man and the flood who passed on all of the lifelines offered. Mommy was going to make a different ending to Maisy's story.

Mommy sat down with the hospital's patient advocate.

"I'd like to have Maisy transferred to Hopkins to get the PIC line and finish our stay in Baltimore there."

The advocate, shaking her head, declined the request.

"You can't move to another hospital of the same level of care. It has never been done before; it can't be done."

Mommy wasn't going to take that for an answer; there was a first time for everything. "We have been here over a month, and my daughter is not better. I have such a strong feeling—it is mother's intuition, beyond words, beyond this world—that we should *not* have the PIC line done here. She got this horrible infection here, which is the whole reason she needs the PIC line in the first place."

The woman looked at her solemnly, still shaking her head back and forth.

Mommy continued, "The definition of insanity is doing the same thing over and over again and expecting different results. I need to change something." Tears stung Mommy's eyes. She didn't want to cry. She wanted to be strong. "If we do stay here, we're going to lose her. I know it. We have almost lost her so many times. I can't lose her now, and if we stay, somehow, I know we will, and I can't stand by and let that happen."

The woman looked at her curiously.

"Are you a mom?" Mommy asked with sincerity.

The woman's curious expression morphed into surprise, which quickly melted into a far-off look, undeniably full of her own memories and thoughts. She drifted away for a second or two and then slowly nodded her head up and down, a hint of tears hiding behind those far-off eyes.

"Well, then you know. When you know, you know, and I know we can't stay here. Just because it *hasn't* been done before doesn't mean it *can't* be done. There is a first time for everything. We are going to make this happen. Will you help? Please, will you help me? Will you help us—help Maisy?"

Mommy's tears had finally escaped and were now streaming down her face and the advocate looked back at Mommy with understanding in her eyes. A connection had been made. The advocate's mannerisms softened, and there was complete understanding and total compassion as a tear of her own, a tear of connectivity and solidarity, escaped, plunging down her cheek before she had a chance to stop it. The advocate said she understood what Mommy was saying, and she agreed to help Mommy in this request. She got right to work making phone calls.

Mommy's family also had connections at Hopkins, and phone calls were made from her end, too. Gramps had a friend that used to be in charge of the pediatric ward. He was retired now, but Gramps put a call in to him, in case he had some pull. A woman high in the hierarchy at Hopkins had helped them over the years with Mommy's niece. Her niece went to Hopkins periodically for therapy at its renowned Kennedy Krieger Institute. This woman was contacted by Mommy's sister with the request for the transfer. In addition, the patient advocate was hard at work, making many phone calls after her heartfelt chat with Mommy. Hopkins would be bombarded with this unprecedented request.

Time was, once again, of the essence. Maisy's IV in her big toe wouldn't last much longer, and this procedure needed to happen soon. After one and a half nights in their tiny private room, they loaded Maisy into an ambulance and transferred her to Hopkins.

Lark took note. Just because something hasn't been done, doesn't mean it can't be done. He added that to his lessons learned on his amazing adventures.

It was quite the process to get admitted once there, but Mommy knew in her heart it would be worth it. Maisy had a reaction in the waiting room to the meds Hopkins administered upon their arrival, quickly turning bright red with a sudden spreading rash. Mommy noticed it was happening, spoke up, and they were on it, working on her, and the problem was quickly fixed.

It was scary though, and doubt crept in regarding this decision for the transfer. Had she made the right decision? This lasted but a moment, and then it was dismissed by Mommy with authority. There was an unspoken knowing that they were right where they needed to be.

After much paperwork and much waiting, they were finally directed to the pediatric ward and to a bed at the end of a large room with eight other beds, all full of sick children. So much for their little private room they had finally secured at the other hospital. Mommy didn't care at this point; she was so relieved to be here. They were leaving the nightmare of the past month behind them and heading toward a fresh start and toward what really felt like recovery for the first time in a long time.

Mommy and Daddy knew in their hearts it was the right move. The doctors and their residents doing the rounds at Hopkins had a different approach than the other hospital. The PICU at the other hospital had seemed efficient, for the most part, and they had certainly saved Maisy's life on more than one occasion, although they had some bumps along the road that were perhaps questionable. Yet, once they had crossed the hall to the pediatric ward at the other hospital, things seemed sub-par, and Maisy had suffered. This pediatric ward at Hopkins was beyond thorough.

Mommy and Maisy were in the bed at the far end of the large hospital room. The room was full of children of all ages and all different ailments. There were many doctors checking in on them, and their efficiency and proficiency were palpable. It was reassuring.

Within the first hour of settling in, a doctor came by to talk to a couple and their little boy in the bed right next to Mommy and Maisy. The curtain was already slightly drawn around the boy's bed, and the doctor pulled it completely shut behind him.

Maisy was napping as Mommy tried not to hear the conversation next to her, but in a hospital, even with a thin little curtain separating them, it was impossible not to. The doctor was talking to this family, these parents and their darling little boy, about cancer. Sobs and questions and sadness emanated from the curtain next door. It was obviously a brand-new diagnosis, and there were many questions and much uncertainty. Tears streamed down Mommy's face, too. She felt sad for this family, starting out on their own journey of battling a life-threatening illness with their innocent little child. Mommy had such an understanding now of what it felt like to have futures threatened with unwanted unknowns. At the same time, Mommy was grateful for the awareness that Maisy was now on the road to recovery, and she was empathetic to this family starting their long, hard journey ahead.

Time really was relative here. Mommy felt like it had been a long time since they first entered the hospital on that snowy night over a month earlier. The family next to her was in for a much longer journey ahead, and it would need to be quite the fight. Perspective. More perspective. Deeper perspective.

Mommy, catching her wandering mind, felt like she should try and give them some sort of privacy, beyond a drawn curtain. She scooped up her baby girl from her nap, and Mommy, with her new perspective gained, exited the room to find two silly clowns doing tricks, juggling, and telling jokes to entertain the patients. Maisy was a little young to be fully enthralled, but it was a welcomed distraction. If nothing else, Lark, as an observer, enjoyed their show.

The PIC line was inserted successfully, and after a week at Hopkins, they were transferred back to the hospital in Annapolis and spent another week there. Lark saw his three-year-old self visit Maisy in the hospital in Annapolis. Mommy had brought only Lark to see Maisy. He had been asking about her, and he was also more aware since he was a little bit older. He sang Maisy songs. He jumped on furniture. He lightened the mood.

Lark got a kick out of how small, how funny, how cute his three-year-old self was. Lark was washed over by a sea of self-love and awareness. He felt good about himself. It was like watching an old movie of himself and his Mommy and his sister, and the movie was simply full of love. It was a deep love, one of appreciation and understanding and gratitude. It was a love that laughed in spite of itself and soaked all in its path.

Lark felt good about Maisy's situation right now and could tell that Mommy did, too. Maisy was still weak and battered and not the same as she was before the hospital, but none of them were, and never again would they be, and that was a blessing in disguise. Lark hoped he wouldn't travel back to when Maisy was so sick anymore. He wanted to be in the present, or perhaps looking forward to the future, when he may be out of the tree, out of the outer-fort world, and really be home. These experiences were ones that he wished he didn't necessarily have to have while at the same time, especially knowing that in the end Maisy was okay, he was grateful for these invaluable lessons. We are never the same as we are before; change is inevitable, and it shapes us and molds us. That is its very essence. His ten-year-old self recognized that.

These experiences would shift everything after. The lowest of lows help one gain the highest of highs. Lark simply felt more now. Lark was capable of a greater love due to this great sorrow with which he had danced. It helped him feel deeply, and for that, he was grateful. He realized that even when you love someone with all of your heart and all of your soul, you can still expand this love further. With new awareness new dimensions may be added. Love is limitless. Lark was aware now. He felt love to his core.

Finally, the day came when they were able to go home from the hospital. It was late March, and the day sang of spring and new beginnings. It was a sharp contrast to the cold, bleak January day when they first arrived.

When it was time to bring Maisy home, Mommy brought Gwynnie to the hospital with her for a little reunion. She took Gwynnie out of her car seat and placed her on the bed next to Maisy. Gwynnie rolled over toward her twin, and her eyes lit up as a smile of love and recognition and joy took over her chubby cheeks. For the first time in over six weeks, the twins were finally back together. Gwynnie reached her pudgy hand up and touched her twin's battered cheek. She stared at her adoringly, cooing and smiling. Maisy had lost the ability to roll over or turn her head, but she glanced sideways at her twin, and she, too, smiled a knowing smile. *She glanced sideways.* Lark must remember to glance sideways, to make that connection. The twins' reunion reignited an important connection. It was not that the connection was ever lost, of course, but there was a physical distance between them while Maisy was in the hospital, even if their emotional and spiritual connection held steadfast. Mommy shuddered to think there had almost been the distance of heaven and earth between these twins. But there wasn't. They were together, and it would be necessary to let go of the "almosts" and "what ifs" that had been presented because, yes, they almost lost her, but they didn't. Maisy was here. Maisy was here to stay. Heaven can be found on earth if one looked at it the right way.

The family made signs and decorated the house and baked a cake. They sang and dressed everybody up in green as they celebrated Maisy's homecoming on St. Patrick's Day. It had been exactly one year to the day since Mommy and Daddy had first learned they were having twins. What a year. What a ride. What a blessing.

Maisy continued to see the immunologist from the hospital, and six months later, after more endless poking and prodding and needles and worry and waiting, they decided that her immune system was okay. Mommy breastfed her up until that point, wanting the healing powers of breast milk to be in her system, in case her immune system needed extra help.

Swoosh, swoosh, swoosh. Time was moving quickly now, and Lark was trying to keep up. Maisy had to see a physical therapist for the next year and a half, then a developmental therapist for a year, then a speech therapist for years to come, but she was going to be okay. She was going to be okay here on this earth and so was Mommy and so was Lark. *Swoosh.*

Chapter 23

Violet—Wisdom & an Attitude of Gratitude

"I went to the woods because I wished to live deliberately, to front only the essential facts of life, and see if I could not learn what it had to teach, and not, when I came to die, discover that I had not lived. I did not wish to live what was not life, living is so dear; nor did I wish to practice resignation, unless it was quite necessary. I wanted to live deep and suck out all the marrow of life, to live so sturdily and Spartan-like as to put to rout all that was not life, to cut a broad swath and shave close, to drive life into a corner, and reduce it to its lowest terms, and, if it proved to be mean, why then to get the whole and genuine meanness of it, and publish its meanness to the world; or if it were sublime, to know it by experience, and be able to give a true account of it in my next excursion."

—Henry David Thoreau

June the Loon was floating next to Lark as he climbed up the ladder inside of the willow on a sea of violet. "From the low depths of sorrow emerged the greatest of love, And this is how he danced beyond the stars above."

Lark waited for the next line—the ongoing, ascending poetic advice in the violet realm—as he ascended through chakra-like levels and lessons on his path beyond the stars. June smiled at Lark, and he realized this was all she was going to say for now. He smiled back and slowly and deliberately continued to climb, contemplating the loon's poetic thought within this violet realm.

Lark had made it to the violet. It was the very tippy top of the tree, and past the violet was light. The light was too bright to look at, so it was impossible to tell if it was the next level, the next realm, or the outside, an exit out of the tree. Lark supposed he would only know when he got there. He had learned to enjoy and appreciate where he was now rather than focusing so much on where he was going and missing the moment that he was in presently. That was a big lesson that he had gained and integrated.

He felt peaceful as he continued to climb, one foot above the other, hand over hand, up the ladder. Things felt so different here in the violet realm. It was like everything was settling into his bones. Everything he had seen, everything he might see in the future, felt as it should, as it was meant to be. He felt Wise, just as Gramps had said he was, but then again, still just ten.

Pru was here in the violet with him. She was ahead of him again, and when he spotted her, Lark tried to climb as quickly as he could to catch up. He didn't know what came after violet, and he wanted to be sure to connect with Pru before they were out of the violet and into the unknown. Although, it was all the unknown beyond the moment he was in. Lark was feeling Wise and insightful indeed, and he had a true appreciation for himself and his amazing adventures.

"Pru!"

No answer. He climbed faster. He yelled louder.

"Pruuuu!"

She paused for a moment, and then she finally looked down. She hadn't paused much, or looked down much, since they started this journey. Wasn't she the one that had told Lark to be sure to glance sideways, or in this case, down, to make those connections?

"I always know where you are. I always have; I always will." She smiled her toothless smile from above.

"Huh?" inquired Lark in anything but a poetic manner.

Pru was reading his thoughts. She stopped climbing, and Lark hastily ascended, trying to catch up.

"I'm like Echo. I am Pru, but I am also you. I am part of the true you," she said, softly this time.

Lark couldn't tell if she said it with her mind or with spoken words. Lark realized he wasn't delineating between the two anymore.

"Right, Lark. That's why I didn't need to look back, didn't need to see you in the black. I always knew you'd be okay; I always knew you'd find your way," she said, still smiling.

Lark smiled back at her.

"Why are you rhyming like that, Pru? You sound like June the Loon."

Pru nodded quickly. "You are right. Because June is also a part of you, a part of me . . ."

Then it was June's traveling whisper, the Loon that sent goosebumps to the soul.

Violet, the crown,
Transcendental wisdom,
Connectedness,
The swirls of colors, of people, of everything.
It is spirit, it is body, it is peace.
There is meaning, there is hope, there is everything.
There is love.

There was serene silence as these three creatures looked at one another with shades of purple reflected in their eyes, again contemplating these words of the Loon that floated around them in this violet vortex.

"June?"

"Yes, Lark?"

"That was deep and beautiful and poetic and all, but well, why aren't you rhyming anymore?" Lark asked with an inquisitive yet sincere smile. "And why is Pru suddenly rhyming? What is going on here?" He glanced back and forth at his two companions.

"It is time, and I didn't feel like a rhyme," June said with a wink.

Swoosh. Mommy is having trouble. She is in her room. Is she sick? No, but she seems sick. Lark dives in, this time almost able to will it, as he dives into her emotions to investigate, to explore.

The room around him is still light, but inside Mommy feels dark right now. She feels empty. Sorrow fills her completely. Lark wanted to dive out of her emotions; he doesn't like them. He didn't know his mother could ever feel like this. It was sorrow without hope.

"Stay."

It was June's voice. Lark looked for June but did not see her. He had endured many unpleasant feelings up until now. He had endured, and he had learned, so he would stay if June wanted him to stay. It was part of the adventures. The amazing, but hard, adventures.

Lark stayed in her thoughts. Inside of Mommy felt like a dark and empty room. A room in which a shade had been drawn that she couldn't pull up to let the light in, no matter how much she wanted to. She felt sad. She felt alone. She felt nothing, felt that she was nothing. She felt deep sorrow. It was too much. It was not anything, and it was everything. She was empty. She was nothing.

Swoosh. Lark traveled back in time, before the darkness he witnessed, but it was well after when Maisy was better. Where had that horrible darkness come from? It made his soul shiver. Mommy had perspective now; Lark had perspective, and the darkness was coming from a time after they had gained this perspective. Although, he supposed, we are always gaining perspective, in one way or another. Lark needed to see if there was a way to help Mommy.

He was watching total and complete chaos; he felt it from Mommy's mind, watching it with his own eyes, and he was causing it, along with his three sisters, total and complete chaos, and Mommy was feeling overwhelmed. Four children were crying. Every one of them, over everything, over nothing. They were loud and jumping up and down and on each other and then laughing and crying and yelling and throwing, and it was an average snippet of any given moment in their lives.

Am I doing okay? What does okay even mean? I'm in over my head. Are they going to be okay? Twins are hard. Four babies, I have four babies. We can't afford it. He is working so much. He thinks we can't do it. Sometimes I think I can't do it. It's too much. This is insane. Life is so crazy. When Maisy was sick, if she didn't make it... We are lucky to have the chaos. I can do it. It's not too hard. Don't think it, don't say it. I almost had one less. I am lucky, but every one of them is crying right now, and Maisy especially seems to cry at everything. Maybe she isn't okay. Did I take on too much? Can I give them all that they need? Her mind wandered and wound, and the more it raced in circles, the more tangled these thoughts became.

This was before the big darkness, the one where Mommy couldn't get out of bed. Mommy was wondering if she needed something like Prozac. She felt she had been wrestling with postpartum depression ever since the twins were born. When she mentioned it, everyone responded that she had been through a lot, and it was understandable to feel down. Everyone told her what she felt was normal.

She didn't feel normal. It was true: the pregnancy was hard and scary. The C-section and the NICU experience left her feeling removed and alone in some ways. The RSV battle took its toll emotionally, but at the same time, she gained information about the fragility of life. The many months of torturous tests to determine whether Maisy's immune system was compromised had also been hard. More pain and more fear of unknown results and unknown situations. But Maisy was okay. Mommy should be okay.

Mommy was not okay. She couldn't handle her life right now. The simple things seemed too much. This was the life she signed up for, but right now it felt like too much. Mommy was aware now, so why was she feeling so blue? It didn't make sense.

She googled therapists. She read about a few. On one wellness sight, there was a link for therapists and a link for chiropractors. Her mind wandered, as it had a tendency to do, and Mommy suddenly took note that her back hurt. She historically had a bad back, but she is now profoundly aware that her back *really* hurts and has been for a while. She had been dismissing the pain as she honestly didn't have time for it. Maybe that was why she felt blue? Back injuries were exhausting. Pain was exhausting. It affected everything she did. Maybe she would feel better if her back felt better. She detoured from her search for therapists and Prozac and found a holistic chiropractor related to neither of those. She read about the chiropractor. She had never gone to a chiropractor, even with all her years of back pain.

Mommy continued to detour, as she often did. She searched the rest of the providers at the practice and read about the various services they had to offer. Then she read about something called "reiki." It sounded like it might be helpful. Mommy decided to try the healing energy of reiki first before she ventured into the pharmaceutical world of Prozac or therapy or chiropractors. ADOS, detours, and destiny lead her to reiki.

Reiki is a healing technique that channels energy to promote healing where it is needed. Mommy had never had reiki before, and she didn't know even really what it was, but at this point, she figured she had nothing to lose. Whatever she was doing right now wasn't working, and she knew that much, so it seemed like a good time to try something new. You never know until you try, and then, of course, when you know, you know.

Mommy walked in for her reiki appointment with a forced smile on her face and chirped out a cheerful "hello" to the woman who would be doing the session. Mommy had never laid eyes upon this woman, who gave her a quick, worried look.

"Oh, my goodness," the woman gasped. "What is going on? Come here. You are unraveling."

Mommy's forced smile quickly vanished. This complete stranger looked right into Mommy's eyes and then hugged Mommy, and just like that, she no longer felt like a complete stranger. It was a big, strong hug, like the one from the woman on the elevator in the hospital, and out of nowhere, Mommy folded over, crumbling into grief, shaking as she sobbed into this comforting shoulder being offered up for support.

"I am . . . I am unraveling."

A connection was made.

The woman ushered Mommy over to lie down on the table for her reiki session. The woman explained that she would work on Mommy's chakras, her energy centers. Mommy didn't know much about that either, but she knew her energy needed help. The woman also explained that when Mommy's energy centers were opened again, she would notice more things around her: answers to questions, clarity, or increased awareness could follow a reiki session. Remaining open and aware was key.

Mommy nodded her head and closed her eyes. Everything felt calm. She lay there, and then the positive and healing energy of reiki came through, leaving Mommy's distraught nest of thought untangled and clear.

Mommy got up off the table, and she still didn't know what exactly happened. She knew the woman did some invisible voo-doo-esque energy work called reiki, and afterward there was no denying that Mommy felt better. She felt like the weight of the world was on her shoulders when she walked into that room, and when she walked out an hour later, she felt like it had been lifted. It was beyond words. She didn't know why she had been in a dark place in her heart, and she didn't know what had changed in the past hour, but something had. Everything had, even though nothing had except her energy and her new perspective.

Mommy walked outside. The sun was out, and the sky was blue. She got in the car, and Bob Marley happened to come on the radio, singing soulfully at the top of his lungs. It seemed serendipitous. Mommy smiled, rolled down her windows, and joined in singing soulfully, albeit out of key, at the top of her lungs.

On the drive home, an awareness, a sudden realization, came pouring in.

It was that thought when things at home seemed out of control. It was that thought, and the guilt that came with it. The thought that she almost had one less. She scarcely let her mind go there on a conscious level. That was why she had never been able to think about it rationally. She had never given herself permission to acknowledge these fragmented thoughts, these battle wounds from the time when Maisy was sick. Somehow, Mommy convinced herself that she shouldn't *ever* feel overwhelmed because she was lucky to still have four kids and not three. Mommy had been thinking it but not acknowledging it. In the car on the drive home, that thought was acknowledged. Those feelings were finally acknowledged.

When the thought was brought to the forefront at the conscious level, Mommy was able to explore it rationally. Of course, she was allowed to feel overwhelmed at times; that was to be expected. If she was overwhelmed, it was okay to admit that to herself and others. She acknowledged the absurdity of thinking she should never feel overwhelmed. She could accept her life, without dwelling on the "almost" and "what if."

With that recognition came this realization. She could embrace her crazy, wonderful life in all its tangled, imperfect, absurd loveliness. She was able to take the tangled scribbles of her messy mind and not worry so much about coloring neatly within the lines. Things could be magical, messy, chaotic, and beautiful all in the same moment. It was the moment she was in, and she was going to live it fully in the best way she knew how.

Reiki helped make things clear. She had been holding on to fears from the past. She had perspective, but with that she was holding on to the fear piece versus the flip side, the positive side, that they had, *in fact*, made it through. She needed to work on letting the fear go. That was why she had been unraveling.

All of this came pouring into Mommy's thoughts and soul as Bob Marley in his brilliance belted out the powerful reminder once again that she needed to hear, needed to trust, needed to believe. The message that everything would be alright.

Mommy went back to her happy place. She spilled out of the car after that reiki session and walked into the same chaos she had left before the appointment. It was the same chaos that was too much for her to handle an hour ago, and now she dove into it, loving every second of it, in full acceptance, full acknowledgement, full love. She was rolling on the floor with four blonde maniacs, all laughing, and it was joy. Pure joy.

Once again, she had changed. Nothing was different, and yet it was. Everything had shifted.

Mommy got pregnant shortly after the reiki session. It was a big surprise, but a surprise with a deep perspective of how precious life was, and what a gift a child was, and she knew they could handle it. Her heart was open, and it apparently was making room for another love in her life.

Things usually have a way of working out for us. Mommy was presently thinking this thought. Lark followed along on her train of thought, and he was privy to her strong internal feeling that this statement was true to Mommy and Daddy. They believed it wholeheartedly. Mommy's mind was wandering, and Lark was once again there to hear it.

We will have those moments when the stuff hits the fan, and things seem to be whirling around out of control, but when it is all said and done, and the dust eventually settles, we are always doing just fine. It is empowering. Does it work out because we believe it will? Is it an ability to see the bright side in a situation? Perhaps a little of both.

People are funny. If things in a person's life suddenly take a tragic toll, the human tendency is more inclined to grasp on to the things in a situation that didn't go wrong rather than focusing on all that went wrong. We often embrace that we are lucky; that it could have been worse. That bright side, or counting blessings, is easier to grasp on to than the alternative.

Mommy was presently feeling lucky for the ability to recognize luckiness in both good and hard situations. She could usually find the bright side, the silver lining, the glass half-full. The power of positive thinking can work wonders. Luck can be relative.

After the Christmas in Cape Town, Mommy and Daddy wanted to do more traveling while in Africa. They had gone to Mexico for their honeymoon six months earlier, and they had saved up for what they considered the second part of their honeymoon, the part where they would travel within Africa together. This was Daddy's first time in Africa, and it would be a shame if he didn't get to explore some of the wilder parts of the continent and, hopefully, see a wild animal or two while they were at it.

They traveled with their brother-in-law and Mommy's sister for the first part of their excursion. Together, the four of them had wonderful and wild adventures in both Zimbabwe and Zambia. Then it was time to carve out some time with just Mommy and Daddy in a tented safari camp near Kruger National Park in South Africa. They were having so much fun that they looked into extending their trip a bit longer. They were willing to take the financial splurge on the additional experience, but unfortunately, all flights were booked solid for the next week and a half as it was the holidays. They didn't have that much time off from work to consider a stay that would involve another week and half, but a few days would have been nice. They would have to return as scheduled, which they were sad about. It would be back to reality but first, their safari!

They flew into Johannesburg and rented a car, and off they went toward the park. The safari would be expensive, so they had only two nights at the park but were hoping to make the most of it.

They arrived in the early afternoon and were shown their tent and had a safari booked for later that day, early the next morning, and the next evening. Soon they were bumping through the bush on the back of a land rover in search of animals. They saw none of the big five (elephant, rhino, lion, buffalo, and leopard) and no animals up close. They had fun, enjoyed sunset and the sights, but were slightly let down that they hadn't seen more. It was one of those things there's no control over. This is partly what makes it so fun when one does spot animals on safari. If it was guaranteed, some of the adventure would be lost.

That evening they returned to a gourmet meal, and they met a bunch of lively and fun Germans. The wine flowed, and they had a grand old time in to the night. The next morning, they were awakened around dawn with tea and scones and were soon back on the land rover, bouncing around again but this time with a bit of a hangover. That eventually melted away as there is no time for a hangover when on such a special experience like a safari, but again, the animals were not coming out. There were some of the more plentiful animals seen, and some interesting birds, but nothing that seemed extra special. Safaris are a bit harder around Christmas, in the dead of summer, when the bush has grown tall and there are more spots for the game to hide.

Finally, it was time to return to camp, and although, again, it was a nice experience, the animals were definitely lacking.

The last safari, that evening, was more of the same. They did spot a rhinoceros in the distance, but even with binoculars, it was quite hard to see. It was Daddy's first safari experience, and it was a bit of a flop. Mommy couldn't help wondering if the animal population had dropped dramatically due to something like poaching or droughts or whatever else might impact it. It was dramatically different from any other safari she had been on, even from three years ago, when she had many successful safaris with every animal imaginable.

That night they had a delicious and low-key dinner and swam and enjoyed their time together on their last night of their trip to Africa. It was a special experience, even if the wildlife was lacking.

Alas, it was time to pack up and return to the USA. They woke up leisurely the next morning and packed their bags and hopped in the rental car to start the long drive back to Johannesburg to catch their flight home late in the afternoon. It would be hard to leave this magical continent.

They headed off toward the gate of the park. However, a couple of miles from the exit, a towering angry elephant had another plan for them. It was a large male, and he stood right in the middle of the road with no plans of moving. There was no room on either side to go around. He periodically charged the car, trumpeting, legs lifting off the ground, swinging his head side to side with a definite "not gonna happen" directed at Mommy and Daddy. A park ranger was there to try and help, but he, too, eventually admitted to Mommy and Daddy that they weren't going to be leaving the park any time soon. With a flight to catch and hours of driving ahead, they were on a strict timeline. The ranger told them there was one more exit, but it was through the middle of the park, and roads weren't marked, and it would be difficult for Mommy and Daddy to find.

They had no choice. The ranger handed them a map, consisting of a couple of lines drawn in faint pencil, and wished them luck. This was all pre-cell phones, pre-GPS, so luck was needed, for sure.

Daddy backed their car up until they were able to turn around, and off they went on a self-led safari in search of an exit this time instead of animals. What they didn't find was the exit. What they did find this time, though, was the animals. It was truly unbelievable. Every twist and turn they took led them to a new sea of animals. Wild game surrounded them everywhere. They drove with a gigantic herd of buffalo and wildebeests through a wide-open field. A large family of giraffes surrounded them curiously. A lion walked across the road in front of them. Mommy spotted a leopard in a tree. Happy elephants waved their trunks as Mommy and Daddy drove by, putting the worry of being both lost and late aside, for now, as they bumped down the road ahead. They were unsure of exactly where the road was going but felt like it was taking them where they were supposed to be. It was as if God had said, "Cue the animals," and out they spilled, surrounding them in a showstopping safari just for them. It was divine animal intervention. It was the best safari Mommy had ever been on in her life. For Daddy, it was the same, obviously.

After a long time driving, and loving every moment of this experience, they finally found the gate. It would be a close call for their flight, if they made it at all, but if they drove extremely fast, they might have a chance.

As they sped down the road, within twenty minutes of leaving the gate, two dark men with dark brown, bloodshot eyes in army green outfits holding machine guns stepped into the middle of the road. Pointing their guns directly at Mommy and Daddy's car, they signaled for them to pull over.

The possibilities of what might happen next in this moment were endless. Mommy and Daddy had no idea if they were army men, cops, vigilantes, or militia. Their English was poor, and Mommy and Daddy showed their Maryland driver's licenses and passports and tried to explain where they were coming from and where they were going and did a bit of charades to indicate they were trying to catch an airplane. They tried to emphasize the urgency in the situation, but these men with guns didn't seem rushed. Finally, after a very long time, the men with their machine guns pointed them at Mommy and Daddy once again and waved them onward. They couldn't be bothered with the hassle of dealing with weird foreigners, and for that Mommy and Daddy were truly thankful.

Unfortunately, by this point, there was no way they would ever arrive in Jo'burg in time to catch their flight. They knew there were no other flights back to the USA for quite some time, but at this point they had no choice but to remain calm. It was one of those situations out of their control. They started back down the road on the five-hour drive to miss their flight that would be leaving in three hours.

As they continued along, Mommy yelled, "Stop!" Daddy came to a screeching stop in the middle of the remote highway in the middle of nowhere.

"What? What is it? What's wrong?" he asked in shock.

"I think I saw a tiny sign on the side of the road with a picture of an airplane," Mommy replied hopefully.

"I mean, we are in the middle of nowhere," was all Daddy said.

"I know. Can we turn around and look? At this point, there's no way we're making our flight, so what's a couple of minutes to go check?" Mommy said.

"Okay, it's worth a shot," Daddy stated. He pulled a quick U-turn right in the middle of the highway. Luckily no men with machine guns were watching this traffic violation.

Sure enough, when they headed back just a bit, on the side of the road was a little wooden sign with a picture of an airplane next to a hidden road leading into the bushes. They decided to head down the road and see where it took them. Much to their surprise, here in the middle of the bush, in the middle of "nowhere," was a hidden, little airport. It had a little section with rental cars, a couple of planes, and a little terminal. Mommy and Daddy pulled right up front and ran for the desk, where two employees looked at them questioningly.

"Do you have any flights to Jo'burg?" Mommy and Daddy yelled in desperation.

The employees looked them up and down, not sure if they wanted to answer.

"It just so happens, there is one flight to Jo'burg, but it's about to leave. It is already on the runway."

"Please, are there any seats available? We must get to Jo'burg today. Please," Mommy pleaded.

Checking her large computer, the airline worker's face lit up. "Yes, mum, there are two seats left. But it's leaving in less than ten minutes. I'm sorry, I don't know if you can make it."

"We will take those tickets," Mommy and Daddy both replied in unison once again.

What happened next was a little blurry. Daddy ran to the rental car station and tossed them the keys. Mommy stood at the counter getting their boarding passes. In a couple of minutes, they had their bags and their newly issued tickets, and they ran out to the runway. The propellers were already spinning, but the ladder staircase was still there next to an open door. Mommy and Daddy clambered onto the small plane, which was full of passengers looking shocked at these two late and hectic additions. Within the next minute, Mommy and Daddy were laughing hysterically, buckled up and taking off into the sky toward Johannesburg.

Yeah, things usually have a way of working out for us.

Chapter 24

Moments in Time

> "Hardships often prepare ordinary people for an extraordinary destiny."
>
> —C. S. Lewis

SWOOSH. LARK HAD THOUGHT, HAD HOPED, HE'D BE heading home since he was in the last color, but there was more traveling to do, more for him to see, apparently. Lark was ready to see his family again, and for them to see him. He started to feel a bit sad, a bit lonely, and homesick after being in the outer-fort world for so long. He put his hand in his pocket to touch his lucky stone to make sure it was safe. He thought about when Gramps gave him the stone. Had Gramps done these kinds of travels, too? Gramps got the stone when he was also ten. Lark wondered if he, himself, was still ten. The concept of time was irrelevant here. His tenth birthday felt like forever ago. Lark bet that Gramps had adventures like this when he was ten, too, but he had obviously returned from his adventures. Lark would probably, hopefully, return, too—one day. Probably . . . possibly . . . hopefully. Gramps had grown up to meet Gran, and together, they had Mommy and her siblings. Gramps hadn't been gone forever. Hopefully Lark wouldn't be gone forever either.

Lark caught his wandering thoughts and redirected himself. Where was he now? When was he? Back as part of Mommy again, as he was beginning to expect. It was the future, though. Not the future from after Lark was ten, so it was still the past, but it was the future from when Maisy was sick. It was also the future after

Mommy's reiki session. Lark recognized the surroundings of their local rec center. Mommy was there with her girls. Sophie was four, the twins had just turned three, and baby Bliss was a cooing infant. Then, just like that, Lark was not an observer but fully part of Mommy's perspective.

Sophie, Gwynnie, and Maisy were all in the same ballet and tap class in the basement of the recreation center. In the hallway was a polished concrete floor and big windows for mommies and daddies to sneak a peek into the class to see their little pink lovelies doing pliés and twirls. Ballet, at that age, was all wedgies and pot bellies and feeling oh, so beautiful. There is something so divinely sweet about the uninhibited dancing of a child. They are wild, and they are themselves, and they don't care who sees. If only the child could, somehow, harness this freedom and hold it in their heart forever, before someone tells them to be otherwise.

Mommy had been feeding Bliss when suddenly they were surrounded by a swarm of pink tutus flooding out the door. It was time to change from ballet slippers to tap shoes. The girls exited the room in a frenzy to find Mommy, who quickly put Bliss back into her car seat and dug in her bag to find the three pairs of tap shoes. The changing of the shoes was quite hectic; the changing of the guards at Buckingham Palace had nothing on the changing of the shoes at the Annapolis Rec Center, and Mommy felt pressure to execute it all in an organized and timely manner. Even with the best of Mommy's intentions, it was always the opposite of organized or timely, especially with three pairs of feet to address. Mommy was tying one of Gwynnie's tap shoes and asking the other two girls to gather their ballet slippers that they had thrown haphazardly all over the floor, lost in a sea of all of the other pink slippers tossed aside from all of the other little ballerinas. Mommy asked her girls not to run, and Bliss started to fuss as Mommy tried squeezing Gwynnie's pudgy, little foot into her shiny, black tap shoe. Sophie was holding her tap shoes over her head, clicking the heels together, waiting for her turn, and Maisy, still over by the windows with slippers cast aside, squealed out a loud, "Mommy!"

Suddenly a pink bundle launched up in the air, pink-stockinged feet flying up, and Maisy's little head plummeted down on to the slippery floor. Her head hit the concrete with a sound that would haunt Mommy for a long time—with a skull-crushing thud.

There was the echoing thud of Maisy's head hitting concrete, and then Maisy began to shake. Maisy started having a seizure three seconds after she yelled "Mommy," two seconds after her stocking feet slipped into the air, one second after her head went thud on the hard, shiny, concrete floor. Mommy's heart stopped for one second, fear and sorrow washed over her within two seconds, and within three seconds Mommy feared her darling baby girl had acquired a traumatic brain injury. She used to work with people with traumatic brain injuries; she knew the devastation. She knew life could change in three seconds. She also had a friend from high school who sustained a traumatic brain injury just like this. He fainted, and he hit the floor. His head hit concrete just like Maisy's did, and he was no longer himself. It could change everything. It could take people away. Even if, by the grace of God, one remained on earth after a brain injury, they could still essentially be taken away.

Maisy was unresponsive but breathing. She shook, seizing violently and relentlessly. An employee at the rec center called 911 and tried to give words of encouragement while they waited for an ambulance. Sophie and Gwynnie and the crowd of other ballet moms stood by, scared and confused. They joined Mommy in shedding tears—little ballerinas, little ballerina mommas, all crying as Mommy repeated the *Hail Mary* and other prayers in between desperate pleading.

"No, not her, not Maisy, not now."

Mommy, trying to revive her daughter, pleaded with God out loud with desperate, racing thoughts.

"Please, no, not Maisy. We already made it through. She already made it. Don't take her now. Hail Mary, full of grace . . . Help us! How long has it been?"

Maisy continued to shake.

"Oh, my sweet, dear Maisy. You are going to be okay . . . you have to be okay. Open your eyes. It's Mommy. I am here. Mommy is here. Please God, help her, help . . ."

She felt helpless. Things felt hopeless. Lark felt all of this with her, and it was scary.

The ambulance arrived. It felt like an eternity since it was called, but Mommy knew all too well that time was relative in situations like this.

"We can't fly her there. The helicopter is grounded due to wind. We're taking her to Hopkins, and we'll get her there as fast as we can."

The EMTs were efficient. They were on it. Within minutes, they were zooming up the highway. Once again there was no helicopter available, wind this time instead of snow, but this time the siren was blaring loudly as they barreled up the highway. Mommy left her other three daughters there with a friend of hers, in the basement in a blur. Maisy continued to shake. Maisy would not respond to questions, to anything. Mommy made desperate phone calls to Daddy and a couple of other family members from the back of the blaring ambulance in full hysterics, giving a short synopsis of what had happened and pleading for prayers.

Maisy opened her eyes briefly. Mommy's heart started to leap, but they quickly fluttered shut again, and Mommy's heart sank. Eventually, the shaking calmed down. It continued but was less extreme. Maisy was still unconscious. They sped through Baltimore as the EMT staff worked fervently. Lark felt Mommy's fear, and he was unsure of what would happen next.

Soon they pulled into Hopkins and unloaded Maisy from the back of the ambulance. They had her head and body strapped down in traction to a long board. Maisy opened her eyes and kept them open with a blank stare. She did not speak.

"Maisy, sweet girl, it's Mommy . . ."

Maisy stared blankly up at the sky.

"We need to give her a CAT scan immediately," someone in a white coat was saying to Mommy. Staff yelled medical terms to each other as Mommy and Maisy exited the ambulance and wheeled down the long, strange hallway.

They entered the starkly white CAT scan room with its bright lights and a crowd of doctors waiting to spring into action. They pulled out glistening silver scissors and methodically cut off Maisy's pink leotard, and they cut off her puffy, pink tutu, chopping through the layers of pink tulle as if they were slicing through a piece of brie . . . cut, cut, cut, and then her tights . . . all removed within seconds with silver, sharp scissors. Maisy lay there in traction, silent, but with her brown eyes wide open now, still staring blankly, as all other eyes stared at her intently, her pink ballerina outfit scattered in shreds at their feet.

Question after question, Maisy lay there silent, slowly opening and closing her eyes. "Sweetheart, what is your name?"

Silence.

"Who is this?" They pointed to Mommy.

Silence.

"Tell us, what is your name?"

Silence.

The doctors tried to give Mommy reassuring looks, but Mommy knew those looks, and she could see the worry behind those eyes.

They looked back at Maisy. "What is your name?"

Silence can seem like an eternity when you are waiting for it to end, but then—

"Maisy Jane," Maisy suddenly proclaimed loudly, glancing sideways toward Mommy and managing a weak smile.

Strong smiles overtook the room. The sparkle in her eye returned in that instant as a small roar of pleased comments erupted across the room.

The doctor gleefully screamed back, "Yes, that's right, you are Maisy! Maisy Jane?" he said, turning to Mommy to ensure Maisy was correct.

Mommy, with a huge smile of relief, looked down adoringly at her little girl and said, "Yes, Maisy Jane—Jane, that's her middle name. I've never actually heard her say it. I didn't know she knew her middle name, to tell you the truth." She gave a little laugh as tears streamed down her face; tears with remnants of sorrow and fear were being washed away by new tears swirling with colors of joy and relief. Mommy laughed, and the doctors laughed, and Maisy again mustered a small smile.

Hearing her daughter say "Maisy Jane," well, those were two of the sweetest words she had ever heard spoken. She kissed her little girl and thanked God. Prayers had worked once again.

Lark had slipped into just watching now, with his own separate thoughts. Lark remembered this story. He had been at kindergarten. He remembered Gramps had picked him up from school that day. Maisy later had a fever while in the hospital. They didn't know if she had a fever which caused the seizure, making her fall and hit her head, or if she fell and hit her head which caused a seizure, then the fever appeared. The CAT scan showed a bad concussion, but ultimately Maisy would be okay. Okay. Another word that Mommy and Lark now knew was relative.

Maisy was okay, but Mommy, again, did not feel okay. She was haunted deeply by this seizure experience. It shook her to her soul. She felt fragile and raw afterward. Why did they have to go through that—especially Maisy, poor thing. Hadn't she endured enough?

Mommy started to unravel a bit again. She was on her way to getting tangled, but this time she wouldn't let herself get there. Forced to revisit a situation in which Maisy's life was in question again, Mommy was given the gift of another realization. The gift of clarity came flooding in with such a surge that Mommy was finally forced to listen to her true feelings that had been floating deep inside and had now suddenly risen, floating to the surface.

Mommy was getting in the way of herself. She realized she was still wearing the heavy armor she had donned for that fight a few years ago when Maisy was sick as a baby. In still unknowingly donning this armor, she perhaps sought some self-preservation, but she also was not allowing herself to feel as she should, protecting herself from her own thoughts and fears within.

She had to show the world and her husband and her children that she was strong and could handle all that came her way. She had to wear this armor and prove it to herself, but the armor was getting in Mommy's way. Mommy was getting in Mommy's way.

This situation with the seizure had catapulted her right back into those raw moments in the PICU in Baltimore. The moments where she felt herself spilling in grief on to the floor. Mommy was still dangling in the wind by that thin, fraying thread.

A profound awareness came pouring in as if someone had lifted a shroud of darkness to reveal a bright light containing the hidden truth. Mommy hadn't truly let go of a deep fear left over from that time. She hadn't let go of it because she hadn't acknowledged it, perhaps afraid that acknowledging it would somehow give it power or validity.

It was the rest of the reiki message. She had unknowingly stopped it short before, but with this experience, she was forced to look it square in the eyes and make a decision on how to proceed.

I feel like Maisy is on borrowed time, like God is trying to get her, trying to take her from us, like we cheated heaven in some way with those prayers. I feel like maybe we changed Maisy's fate from going to heaven already. Maybe those prayers did change her fate . . . but Maisy wouldn't be here if she wasn't meant to be here.

Mommy let those thoughts sink in, and Lark felt it, too. She gave herself permission to recognize her truth.

Every time I feel overwhelmed—and I have five little kids; I'm allowed to feel overwhelmed—but I still feel guilty, like God's going to hear my thought of feeling overwhelmed for that moment, think he gave us more kids than we can handle, and then he might try and take her away from us. Mommy shook her head, deep in thought. She shook her head no.

Oh my God, I didn't realize I was . . . no. No. That's NOT how it works.

Tears streamed down Mommy's face.

"Maisy is *not* on borrowed time. God is *kind.* He isn't trying to *get* her, to *take* her. She is meant to be right where she is right now. She is supposed to be right here—with us," Mommy said out loud, to herself, to the universe, with authority.

It was an "aha" moment. This was the true source of darkness, that unraveling feeling, she felt before she got reiki. This was the *whole* truth revealed, and she wouldn't have realized it if they hadn't gone through this recent, awful event. It was a thought that had lingered, festering, in her soul, that she had buried in her heart. Mommy was now aware of the source of this bleakness and sadness that had been underlying her being in subtle ways and sometimes not-so-subtle ways. She acknowledged it. She shared it. With that, the bad feelings got smaller and smaller until they all but disappeared.

Mommy and her little observer, Lark, were learning that you need to let those you love in on your moments, just as those moments are, good or bad, for those people will help carry you through. Those you love will hold you up in joy and celebration during the good moments in life, and they will hold you up and give you strength and support during the bad moments.

Mommy was now feeling a higher high and a higher understanding and a higher appreciation for the gifts in her life. She had danced with sorrow, and she had survived. She was now able to soar through the sky, reaching for the stars with joy, and the possibilities were endless. Lark felt her heart soar. He felt her heart sing. He was glad he stuck around to feel the darkness earlier because, without that, they wouldn't be soaring with total and complete happiness as they were now.

Parenthood—not for the faint of heart. This thought echoed through Mommy's head once again. Lark fully grasped what she was thinking now while also realizing that this was not the thought that your typical ten-year-old would usually be able to understand. Then again, he was Wise now. He was Wise enough to know that there was still much to learn and still much to know because he was only ten. He would remember to glance sideways. He would also remember the lesson of glancing within, and this would allow his heart to soar as he reached for the stars, too. *Swoosh.*

Geez. They were back to the time of the PICU. Two scheduled vasectomies. Two canceled vasectomies. Daddy had one scheduled for the week Maisy got sick. They had four babies, after all. He canceled it and rescheduled for a month later. Maisy was still sick in the hospital a month later. He canceled that one, too. They didn't know the time frame of when things would be better, so for now, he did not reschedule a third vasectomy. There were too many things up in the air to even think about doing it at this point in time. Mommy couldn't think about taking away the ability to have a baby at this time.

What if we had lost her? Mommy shuddered at the thought.

We didn't. Don't even think about it.

Mommy needed to shake the "what ifs" because Maisy was coming out on the other side. It wasn't a good idea to dwell too long in the land of "what ifs." It was necessary to acknowledge them, to process them, to come to peace with them, and then to move on. Feel those feelings, let them wash over you fully, and then let them go. The fear of losing a child, when children are such a gift, coupled with the idea of taking away the ability to have children with a vasectomy, was too much to contemplate back in those critical moments. Maisy's immune system was still in question as well. Things were too raw. So, Daddy waited before scheduling one for the third time.

Maisy's immune system was finally given the clear. It was time to find their new normal, if normal was even a real thing. Normal can certainly be relative. Life was beyond busy. There were ups and downs, but mostly life was good. When Mommy hit that point where she felt like she was having more downs than ups, she stumbled across reiki. With her reiki-assisted revelation, her reset button was then pushed, and happy chaos ensued once again. Mommy was able to embrace her happy chaos in all its splendor. She embraced life and its beautiful, messy loveliness. Mommy felt truly happy to her core.

Soon after her reiki reset revelation, they found out Mommy was pregnant. There was, of course, shock at first. Shock and then simply pure joy. At this point the twins were almost two years old. Five kiddos. They were going to have *five* children. It wasn't the plan, but they were always loosey-goosey when it came to plans, so Mommy didn't mind veering from a plan. She was sure they could handle it. She knew it was how it was meant to be. Daddy needed a little convincing that they could handle it, but he was eventually on board with the pure joy and excitement, too, even if the "handling it" part was a little up in the air for him. This detour was leading them on the right path; they were sure of that. Different plans can sometimes be a gift, if given the chance. For instance, they hadn't planned on twins, but the egg split, and then they had four kids and wouldn't have it any other way. Now they were going to have another! Mommy's perspective had been fuzzy for a bit, but everything was clear again. With this new low she had experienced, back when she was unraveling, came a new high, and this felt so right. Maybe it had all been leading to this moment. They were open to it, and so it came.

Swoosh. Mommy was flying back from Denver. Daddy had a work trip in Colorado, and Mommy had flown out to join him. They told one coworker and his wife on the trip about the baby because they were good friends. It was still before the three-month mark, so they kept the pregnancy under wraps from the rest of the people on the trip. Right before they left for Colorado, they told Mommy's family. They also shared the news with a few select friends because it was exciting, and it was nuts, and they couldn't contain it. They were going to have *five* children. Lark was watching this and realized it must be Bliss. He was so glad, contemplating things, that this was the way it worked out. Bliss was awesome, and he adored his little sister and couldn't imagine life without her. He didn't know she wasn't planned. He was so glad she came anyway. He dove into Mommy's head and thoughts.

She was reading a book on Buddhism for mothers, even though she was Roman Catholic. There was a part where the mother, the author of the book, was traveling and away from her children for three weeks exploring her family heritage with her husband in Poland. She was touring Auschwitz. As she walked through this horrific concentration camp from this horrific time in history, they came upon a room filled with eyeglasses, piled up to the ceiling. They walked farther, and there was another room filled with shoes. The whole room was full of little shoes that belonged to little children killed in the gas chambers at this horrific concentration camp.

As she stared at this mountain of little shoes, suddenly this author, this mother, right at that moment decided she no longer wanted to be on this trip, even though they had many lovely plans in Poland, beyond Auschwitz. She didn't want to be away from her children for one more extra second because she was suddenly so profoundly aware that these children who used to wear those little shoes would have done anything to have still been with their mothers at the time, and their mothers would have done anything to be with their children, and that was all robbed from them in a matter of seconds. They didn't have a choice.

She did have the choice. She could be with her children right now. She had that choice, that option, so she changed her trip and flew home early the next morning. She was profoundly aware.

Mommy was reading this anecdote and thanked goodness she was reading it on her way home to her children, rather than on her way out to Colorado. She couldn't wait to scoop them all up and give them kisses. It had only been a long weekend, but she had missed them all very much. She enjoyed the special time with Daddy, but now that they were on their way home, she was ready to see her little tribe. Trips were usually like that. She was able to fully enjoy the experience of a vacation and being away, but when it came time to leave, the day they were going home, she got anxious to return home.

Mommy had gone for a sonogram before she flew to Colorado. Daddy had already been out west for a couple of days before that. The sonogram had actually been a bit of a scary situation. Her doctor thought something might be wrong with her baby, and the archaic ultrasound machine her regular OB/GYN had in her office didn't give an efficient reading. She sent her for a more thorough sonogram with better equipment in another part of the hospital to see what was going on. Her doctor said she wanted to make sure everything was okay, but Mommy could tell she seemed concerned.

So, Mommy went for a more thorough sonogram. The baby's heart was beating strong. Everything looked fine. The moments leading up to that, though, were scary. Mommy was too aware that things sometimes go in a very different direction than anticipated in life. There was always a certain degree of finger-crossing inherent with sonograms. Her first sonogram with Lark, almost five years earlier, had been filled with blissful ignorance. She knew more now. She wished she could go back to blissful ignorance in some ways, but in some ways, with this awareness came a greater appreciation. She knew to her core children were a gift, and she was going to try and enjoy the miracle of pregnancy. She trusted things would be okay. They had already started talking about names. Five children. Unreal. The sonogram looked great.

Mommy had tucked the sonogram pictures into the book she was reading to show them to Daddy when she got to Colorado. On the plane ride home, she used the strip of pictures as a book marker, the cutest bookmark ever, which made her smile whenever she opened and closed the pages. She slept a bit. She watched part of a movie. She and Daddy chatted.

Finally, they arrived in Baltimore. They couldn't wait to get home and see their four children.

When they did get home, Mommy realized she had left the book on the plane. *Swoosh.*

Mommy and Daddy were lying in a field, looking up at the stars. They were in the country, at the farm. Lark knew they were traveling backward in time from the moment he was in, on the plane, and they had just learned that Mommy was pregnant. They had a family farm, and it was one of the best places in the northern hemisphere to see shooting stars. Mommy and Daddy lay on their backs in a field, talking about life, talking about the baby, and the whole time Mommy was also looking for shooting stars. Mommy wanted to make a wish. She felt nervous about the baby. She wanted to make a wish that everything would be okay, and she anxiously scanned the vast sky. She almost always saw a shooting star at the farm. Suddenly a shooting star erupted across the sky. Mommy pointed up and quickly made her wish. *I want this baby to be okay.*

The thought shot from her mind, and as soon as it did, the star stopped. It fizzled. She had honestly never seen anything like it.

The star stopped before it got started. Midflight, it fell out of the sky as soon as she made her wish. She tried to dismiss the eerie nature of this burnt-out, falling star. *Swoosh.*

Daddy was on the phone with the airline. Yes, they had the book. Yes, the sonogram pictures were in there. They were putting it aside. This same woman would be at lost and found when Daddy came by after work to get it. She was setting it aside, right now.

Daddy went to the airport to get the book after work. It was gone. Someone had taken it from where the woman put it. So strange. She was sorry, but she couldn't find it. It was lost again.

That was a Sunday. Monday, Mommy did the elliptical machine at the gym. She worked out longer than she intended to. She had been told to take it easy by her doctor, so she felt a bit guilty and worried but resolved to be more careful next time. Monday, Sophie was horsing around and crashed into Mommy's tummy. Hard. Monday, Mommy felt like she was a little swollen from flying. Monday, Mommy went to the bathroom and saw something a little red, a little pink, in the toilet bowl. She had spotting with other pregnancies. It could be harmless spotting, but it didn't feel like harmless spotting. Her mind tried to tell her it was harmless, to comfort her, but her heart told her a different message. Monday, Mommy miscarried the baby, but she didn't know it, not for sure. She feared it, and maybe somewhere inside she knew, but she didn't want to know.

Monday, Mommy called the doctor. The doctor didn't get back to her. She called again on Tuesday. And Wednesday. Finally, the doctor gave her an apologetic call and let her know she reprimanded the staff for not getting her the message sooner. Mommy went in for another thorough sonogram on Thursday. She knew now. Mommy had miscarried the baby. Had she done something wrong? How could this have happened?

Mommy was alone when she went for the sonogram, the sonogram where she found out she had miscarried. She wanted to believe the sonogram was something she could do alone, as usual. Daddy was at work, and he was trying to figure out a way to pay for five kids, and the last pregnancy with the twins, she had three sonograms a week, and Daddy couldn't be there for each one, so here she was alone. Mommy lay there on the table feeling devastated as she stared at her lifeless sonogram.

Lark was there, from the outer-fort world, but Mommy didn't know that. He never knew she lost a baby. When she had entered the room, the tech, recognizing her from the last sonogram a week earlier, joked how this baby was keeping Mommy on her toes. Mommy smiled in agreement and looked down at her belly hopefully, this belly that was already growing to accommodate this new soul. The tech started the sonogram and then . . . silence . . . and then, with a worried glance and more searching, she said, "I'm sorry."

Mommy's heart skipped a beat. It skipped a beat, and then it shattered. The tech was talking, but Mommy barely heard her. The tech told Mommy there was no more heartbeat . . . no more baby, no more hope . . . the baby died on Monday.

Devastation. Feeling so alone, Mommy lay on the table, this table where she had listened to her beautiful baby's heartbeat a week earlier. She had heard that heartbeat a week ago and knew in every part of her being that she wanted this baby. Mommy and Daddy had been shocked at first when they found out she was pregnant. They had taken precautions not to get pregnant again, but somehow this baby had decided it was coming anyway. It was not plan A. It was not even plan B. It became the new plan B, and the new plan B was beautiful.

Darkness returned. Bleak. Alone. Sad beyond sad . . . sinking into a hole that was closing in on her . . . the shade was drawn. Lark recognized that darkness. This was the first darkness he had visited. The big darkness when Mommy was in bed. *Swoosh.*

It was the day of Mommy's D&C, a medical procedure necessary after a miscarriage. Mommy had to go for a week with her lifeless baby inside of her before they could get her in for the procedure. She had seen her specialist, to confirm the hopelessness of the situation with someone she knew and trusted so much, and he confirmed what she already knew. She had to hear it from him before this invasive procedure. Lark watched from the outer-fort world. Mommy wrote a letter with tears streaming down her face . . .

To my dearest, sweetest, little baby,

I know that you are in heaven now—a little angel looking down on me as I write this letter to you. I imagine Mary, our blessed Mother, is singing you lullabies as Jesus rocks you gently in his arms. I know we will be together one day and am so excited that someday we will all be together again. You would have loved—or you probably already do—your big brother and sisters—they would have really loved you. I guess that is one of the hardest things—the loss of what could have been. The fun you would have had in this lively family and the chance to meet you and love you and watch you grow and blossom here on this earth with us. I have to wonder if I could have changed anything, but I am trying to let go of any guilt of if I did anything wrong. If I did, I am so sorry, and truly I didn't know. If I had known better, I would have done better. As you probably know, you were a huge surprise. I hope you know any thoughts of shock, fear, or doubt were never over whether we loved you or wanted you. We loved you before you were even conceived. We loved you every precious moment you were inside of me, and we will love you forever more. With my first sonogram, when they weren't sure if something was wrong, I got to see your little heartbeat and your sweet, little self and have honestly never been so sure of something in my life. I loved/love you and wanted/want you more than anything. This journey has been extremely painful—a roller-coaster of emotions that has left me very raw. I guess I had a feeling—that shooting star that fizzled out so quickly, the lost sonogram pictures . . . little signs that perhaps pointed to this, no matter how much I tried to put it out of my head.

I don't regret going through this experience. You gave us so much joy in the six weeks that we knew about you, and you were alive—inside of me, part of me. Although today will end the time that you are inside of me physically, you will always be a part of me. You will remain in my heart, thoughts, and soul always. I can't help but think of a beautiful butterfly who only lives six to eight weeks. What beauty and joy a little butterfly can bring. You are my butterfly.

It was interesting. As I was sobbing this morning, I went to hang a rosary on my statue of Mary, and there, reaching out of a vase next to the statue, was an orange butterfly. It was a decoration I had haphazardly stuck in the vase months before and hadn't noticed since. This butterfly was serendipitously resting on Mary, and a blank note with "Thank you" printed on the front was leaning up against her as well. I hadn't put that note there, but there it was. Thank you, my darling. Thank you for touching my life in a way it has never been touched before. Thank you for sharing your little soul with us. I am still so sad I won't ever get to see you grow up, and it is hard as I look at your brother and sisters and know how blessed I am, but it also clarifies what could have been. It makes what was the wonder of your life for those seven weeks and five days so tangible—the wonder of what was and what could have been. I do find peace in knowing you are with God and all those loved ones that have gone before us.

We have had a brush with death before, with your big sister Maisy, and the experience changed us forever. We look at everything differently now. I am glad—so glad—she was able to stay here with us and am not sure why you were not. I know God has a plan. I have grown from this experience and hopefully will find happiness again. It has given me a true understanding of all those that have been through this before, and it is not easy. I am aware now. I hope you will help guide us, my darling angel baby. You have opened our hearts and minds to five children on this earth, and that path is one that has been shown to us thanks to you. I trust in God and that He will lead us to what is meant to be. We love you, our sweet, little angel baby. We love you, we love you, we love you—now and always.

Thank you for sharing your short life with us and letting me be your mommy; no matter how brief, it was wonderful. I will see you in heaven one day and can't wait until I can sing you lullabies and rock you in my arms and kiss you and hug you in person.

Until then, please know that you are loved, and you are missed. I will think of you and pray to you often, my little love. My sweet, sweet, little love. Thank you.

XOXOXOXOXOXOXO & love always,

Mommy

P.S.: I am going to name you Prudence. If you were a girl, that is what I wanted to name you, and somehow, deep in my soul, I already know you are my Pru. Your middle name is Viwe. It is a Xhosa name meaning, "one who is heard." I knew a little girl named Viwe who stole my heart. She is up there with you in heaven, and I hope you can find each other, my sweet Prudence Viwe.

Chapter 25

Light

"Nothing can dim the light that shines from within."

—Maya Angelou

SWOOSH. LARK WAS ALMOST UP TO THE LIGHT. HE HAD swooshed back to the tree. He never knew Mommy had a miscarriage. He didn't know exactly what a miscarriage was, but then again, he did because he knew things now. Pru? Was Pru his sister? She must be. He had another sister. He couldn't believe it. She had red, curly hair. Where did that come from? How was this all possible? And then, he stopped. He stopped trying to figure it all out. He stopped questioning it. He had learned on his amazing adventures that there were times to accept things as they were. Pru was his sister. Perhaps Viwe was a part of her in some way. Perhaps they both were a part of Lark.

Pru was there, watching and listening to his tangential thought process. She was sitting on a rung of the ladder above, swinging her legs, looking quizzically down at Lark with that infamous, toothless smile.

"Pru, I didn't know," Lark said through colorful, salty tears. He climbed up the ladder and gave her a hug with his free arm. Pru let go and hugged him hard with both arms, and she also cried colorful, salty tears.

"When you know, you know," said Pru with a wink.

"Pruisms," said Lark, and they both let out sincere laughs of pure joy. Lark realized Pru's laugh sounded like Bliss's laugh.

"You are my sister," said Lark gleefully, stating what they both now knew to be true but wanting to say it out loud.

"Larkisms," she stated back, and again they laughed, and Lark saw the twinkle in her eye, and a deeper connection was made, and Lark realized her green eyes were the exact same color as Bliss's eyes.

Lark enjoyed this moment simply and truly for what it was: he had found his sister Pru, and he hadn't known he had ever had her, let alone that he had lost her. He suddenly got very emotional, reflecting back on all that led him to this point.

"Pru, if you know so much about how I feel, and I'm sure I know what you are thinking . . . how come I didn't figure this out until right now? Did you know this whole time? I mean, I keep traveling to these super scary or deep moments. I don't know if it'll work out the same way things did before I left. I mean, will Maisy be there when I get home . . . and Sophie and Gwynnie and Bliss? Now that I know you're my sister, I don't want to leave you, but I also desperately want to go home. We are almost to the light. Can you come with me? I'm ready to be home, but I don't want to lose you again, either."

Pru nodded knowingly, and Lark continued on.

"I feel like I'm too painfully aware of how fleeting life can be. It almost makes me too terrified to move on. Almost too terrified to live it. Even when you think you are through the rough parts, life deals you more. Life is so . . . fleeting." Lark definitely did not feel like a typical ten-year-old anymore as he babbled these Larkisms to his newfound sister.

Pru kept smiling, swinging her legs, but she seemed lost in her own thoughts. Lark felt Wise beyond his years, and this awareness, in and of itself, was exhausting.

"Lark, my boy, this is the deal," Pru said, sounding a great deal older, even though she wasn't . . . or maybe she was . . . who knew at this point? "You are feeling exactly like Mommy felt after her miscarriage. She had an ongoing list of the bad stuff that kept happening. She was trying to learn the lesson but kept getting in her own way. It was only when she recognized the 'fleeting' factor that she really got it. You are on earth for a finite time, so what are you going to do with that time? It's up to you."

Lark listened intently and realized Pru was right; some of his feelings were ones he had picked up while being a part of Mommy's thoughts, back when she was feeling dark. She hadn't stayed dark, though. Mommy was the opposite of dark.

"We showed you these parts of your amazing adventures for that very reason. Life *is* fleeting. Moments fleet, but if we stop for a second and let these moments touch our soul, they can last a lifetime, fleeting or not. Fleeting is relative. Moments well-lived, lived to the fullest, can carry you into the moonlight hours of your one magical, magnificent life. There are moments you can bring back and hold on to for a bit longer if needed. A moment well-lived may be essentially lived all over again through a memory when we need a lift or a smile or a distraction. Or maybe it was a memory of something hard, but you remember that you prevailed, that you made it through, and in that you find strength to make it through again. It is important to live in the present and not dwell in the past, but there are lessons in moments and memories. Hold on to the lessons. You must weave them in carefully and consciously, for they are the precious fabric of your life."

Lark felt something shifting inside of him. Pru's words resonated with him. This was a lot for a ten-year-old to grasp, but he was Wise, and he was weaving this into his very being.

"When you know, you know." Pru smiled and looked sideways, and there was June the Loon floating next to them, hovering within the willow tree mid-flight beneath the light.

June the Loon now chimed in. "Yes, Pru, that is all so true. Well, Lark . . . I'm not going to try and rhyme right now. Sometimes I shall, sometimes I shan't, sometimes I can, sometimes I can't . . . but this is what we know. You may not realize it now, but when you are older, when you are something like ninety-nine-years-old, you are going to look back and wonder where it all went, and I promise you, you will be in awe of how fast it went. Life *is* fleeting. This is true. That is why we need to live it to the fullest . . . because we can.

Lark, what would you do if you knew it was your last day on earth . . . and what, my boy, are you waiting for?"

Lark thought about this for a moment as he glanced back and forth between Pru and June.

"Your mom learned this lesson after her darkness. She learned it after she miscarried Pru. Within that loss, through that loss, she found life and light and truth and ultimately herself. It was a choice, though. Mommy could have made the choice to lose herself in sadness and hopelessness. She was there for a moment, but she did not dwell. Instead, she chose to live her life to the fullest. Bliss wouldn't have happened if she hadn't made that choice. That is how she found Bliss, and that is how bliss found her. That is why we have shown you that moment, those feelings, so you can learn it *now,* when you have so much life ahead of you. You can focus on the good, or you can focus on the bad. You choose. The cup is half empty, or it is half full, but it's all the same cup. Whichever way you decide to look at it will be how you see it and often how others see it, too. Remember, positivity is contagious, as is negativity. You will get back what you put out there. This is true in energy, in work, in love, in kindness. Choose wisely and choose positivity. Even in the dark moments, try and find the light. Don't stop searching for the bright side, the silver lining. Search for the light. *Be* the light, Lark."

Lark was understanding it all on a deeper level now. His fear of "fleeting" was dissipating. June was saying this awareness was a gift, rather than an obstacle. Obstacles often lead to detours, and Lark had already learned how detours can be a good thing, even a better thing. Lark was finding the silver lining within June's wise words. June, understanding his thoughts, winked at Lark and continued speaking.

"It is important to not discriminate when contemplating meaningful moments. You are right about this awareness being a gift. We open our eyes each day, and that is a privilege, a gift. Not everyone gets that gift. Some people would have given anything for one more day, for themselves, for a loved one. One more sunrise. One more sunset. One more chance to say, 'I love you.' One more birthday. One more ice cream cone. One more chance to hear their child's laugh or feel their hug or see their smile. One more chance to *be* that child to laugh, to hug, to smile. We have given you this gift with your amazing adventures. You have learned many lessons. The greatest gift of all is that you are going to take these lessons with you, as part of you. You get this perspective and insight that most people only get from growing up. Most people only truly appreciate the highs in life when they have also experienced some lows. You will be aware now. You will be Wise. Of course, you are still young, and there are many more lessons to experience and experiences to live."

Lark tried to make sense of it all. He was listening to every word, but he was still slightly confused. June smiled her knowing smile.

"When you were born, Lark, it was one of the happiest days of your parents' lives. Around that same time, they had friends whose baby only lived for a day and a half. This couple mourned. Eventually, after a long road of miscarriages and pain, this couple had another baby, and that baby was healthy and beautiful and fine. That was one of the happiest days of their lives. When you were born, Mommy and Daddy were as happy as they could be . . . but, when their friends had this healthy second baby, a baby that they would raise with them here on this earth, after losing their first baby, these friends were possibly a smidge happier than your Mommy and Daddy because they knew the flip side. Their sadder sad allowed a happier happy. Do you understand? Feelings are not finite. You may think you are feeling the deepest feeling you can ever feel, and then something can happen and somehow that feeling can grow even deeper . . . the colors of those feelings keep getting brighter and brighter and brighter."

Lark was soaking it in, but it was still a bit confusing.

"It is all relative. People in Los Angeles, California, are probably not as happy when they walk out to a sunny, warm day in November as people in a typically rainy place, say, Ireland. Both are beautiful places, but someone in Ireland may appreciate that warm, sunny November day a smidge more. People in Los Angeles probably don't get to see many rainbows, though. Sometimes there is something so beautiful about dancing in the rain, getting soaked to the soul, especially if you know that this too shall pass, and some time, someday the sun will shine again. Simply dancing in the rain can make you feel alive. Look at the beaches in places like Ireland. Never have you ever seen a beach spotted with more people, so pale their skin is almost transparent, when the sun is mostly submerged behind clouds and a slight rain misting the air. But they are all over the beach because maybe it is August, and it is a school holiday, and the sun might come out for a minute or two, and so they are there to not miss it, if the sun does decide to shine. All different perspectives. So, Lark, you are going back home, feeling a little deeper. You have experienced these things through Mommy and have learned so many important lessons.

"Of course, there is always more to learn. You need empathy to get the lessons. There are people going through life-changing moments all around you, and the lessons will be there if you are willing to be open to them and make those connections. You will know things and have perspective, but you have the amazing gift of still being able to see everything through a child's eyes, through a child's curiosity and innocence, while maintaining trust and hope. *That* is the true gift."

Pru clapped in glee at June's words, and Lark sat there, trying to process it all. This was a lot to take in for a ten-year-old, even if he was a *Wise* ten-year-old.

"Curiosity, innocence, trust, and hope sometimes get sacrificed by grown-ups in pursuit of knowledge, Lark. You'll see one day, when you, too, are a grown up, how other grown-ups might lose these important qualities. It is simply a shame. There is so much to learn. So much to learn during your whole life. It doesn't stop after childhood, as long as you can hold on to those qualities. The world *wants* us to be happy. We don't necessarily have to experience the lowest lows ourselves to feel the highest highs. If we are filled with deep empathy, and remember to glance sideways and glance within, we will feel ever so deeply."

Lark smiled as he glanced sideways over at this Wise, floating loon, barely taking a breath as she imparted her deep thoughts and words on little Lark on the ladder.

June continued on, "If an adult wants to truly notice the world around them, they must walk hand-in-hand with a child. Feathers and sea glass and shiny pennies will not be missed nor overlooked while walking with a child. Within these discovered treasures is a reminder of the sweet simplicity of life that sometimes gets hazy and cluttered as life speeds up. Grown-ups sometimes get so distracted. They lose sight of what is important and forget to pay attention to the little things. Remember, the little things can sometimes be the *big* things, depending on how you see them. Some grown-ups forget to glance sideways or glance down or up or notice the world all around. You don't want to look back on life one day and realize you've missed the point. Don't let moments pass you by. You have one life. Live it out loud. Hold on to that gift of a child's perspective, even when your hair turns grey and you have grandchildren clamoring to get on your knee, *especially* then. It is still a choice. You can keep this perspective if you choose to, as if you are seeing everything for the first time. The great thing about becoming a parent is that you get a chance to remind yourself of these lessons through your own children . . . and then again through grandchildren. Children are often the greatest teachers. They enter their parents' world, and in an instant everything changes. Being a parent is hard, but you'll see. You wouldn't change it for the world. Every hope, wish, and dream in life is held within the moment you first hold your own child. A connection is made. Love is everything, and you feel it in your soul.

"You have learned that the greatest moments aren't always the easiest moments. Often the greatest moments are found when you are pushed to the edge. Lean into those moments and get the lesson. Connect with others and connect with your one, true, authentic self. Don't try and grow up too fast. Slow down and notice things. Do you see? Do you understand? Innocence is often lost while perspective is gained. Not with you. You will keep it. You get the gift of perspective without losing curiosity, innocence, hope, or love.

You will remain wild and free all of your days, and you will find the magic in the perfectly imperfect world that surrounds you. You will cherish the magic of your perfectly imperfect self."

June the Loon smiled after this long testimony, and she gave that familiar wink. Pru looked over at Lark and smiled her toothless smile.

June's words floated around him and into him, and he knew, even if he didn't understand every little bit, that one day he would. He was wise enough to know that was all that was needed. He did feel better. He felt great, better than he ever had before.

"Lark, do you have anything you want to ask before you take on your new task?" asked June.

Lark had a million things to ask, but he had no idea where to start.

"Now, what about Bliss?" asked Lark. "Did she come right after you, Pru?"

Pru nodded her head and answered softly, "Yes, Lark, Daddy didn't know if they should try and have another child. Mommy was so sad after losing me. Daddy didn't want to see her go through that ever again. He thought they shouldn't push their luck. For Mommy, the loss of the *hope* of another child to raise, when she knew in her heart that it was meant to be, seemed too much to bear. Loss of hope. That was that feeling of darkness. However, a little hope still lingered buried in her heart. She had learned to not give up on hope when Maisy was sick, so there was still a sliver of hope inside that darkness. Bliss found that sliver and held on. Mommy knew there was another soul meant to join your family on earth, and her heart was open to that, so Bliss slipped into your lives—another complete surprise shortly after I left. Prayers were answered. Bliss was simply meant to be bliss for all of you."

Lark smiled, aware now and privy to all this new insight with his new perspective and Wise-ness.

"Pru, you said you were a part of me . . . like Echo . . . is that right?"

"Yes, I am your Pru. I am your sister. I am your True. I am your Wise self, your self that knows. Boy, girl; yin, yang; black, white; it is all swirling colors. We all have different sides to us. I am a part of each of you in my family, even if I am not physically with you on earth. I love you. I always have, and I always will. I can be with you always. I will soon have wings. We can all fly if we let our imaginations and memories collide. We are fluid. We take a part of everyone we meet with us, and we can be whatever we want. Just like Gramps and Gran manifested into a Loon named June."

Lark looked quickly sideways at the large Loon floating next to them. "June the Loon is Gramps . . . and Gran?" he whispered softly, examining June with surprise, letting the truth seep in.

"It is true. Listen to Pru," said June with her beak beaming in a huge smile now, and that infamous wink that Lark suddenly placed as the same as his dear old Gramps—and that smile, that smile that had been vaguely familiar from a memory of someone he once knew so well, that smile that he now realized was Gran's smile, although he wasn't used to seeing it on the beak of a bird.

"I don't . . . wait, so you are Gramps and my Gran? Oh, Gran!" Lark looked at the loon in awe, and she motioned him over. He threw his arms around June's neck and nestled in her feathers, never wanting to let go.

"I love you, sweet Lark. My dearest, sweetest little boy."

Lark gazed up at her lovingly, in complete awe and admiration.

"We are all swirling colors, mixing with each other here, forming new colors, leaving sparkling stardust in our path and trying our best," said June. "We will always be here, but we will also be a part of you, just as Pru was saying. Everyone you love is a part of you. That is why you have done much of this journey through Mommy's perspective. She loves you dearly. She wants the best for you. You haven't been appreciating her very much. She is Wise, too. She has also been on adventures. To be Wise, you must realize you still have much to learn and be open to learning for your whole life. Always be open to learning new things about yourself and the world around you. You have many more adventures ahead. You will travel to places all over the world. We had to show you some of the harder stuff first so you could feel deeper, so you'd be ready to see the other adventures that lie ahead and truly appreciate the miracle of each and every joy. Plus, you now know some of the happiest times don't need to be life-changing, monumental occasions, as you may have thought before your adventures. You now know how to soak up a sunset, to enjoy being with those you love. You can find happiness in something as simple as finding sea glass or seeing a baby smile. Every day will offer you the gift of beauty. It's all in how you view it. You have learned to choose adventure, be courageous, have an attitude of gratitude, and follow it up with action. Recognize joy. Recognize feelings. Show feelings. Share feelings. Be kind. You must make decisions sometimes. Sometimes plan B works out just fine. These are some of the things. We have many more travels ahead."

"But I think I am ready to go home now . . . can I do more adventures on another day, perhaps? June . . . I mean, Gran . . . and Gramps . . . Pru—I understand, I really do. Now, can you help me get home?" Lark pleaded.

Pru smiled that toothless smile. "You have always been able to go home. You have the lucky stone."

Lark reached deep down into his pocket and found the stone. It was already heating up again.

"How do I know it won't take me back to some other memory from the past? I felt like I was getting good at controlling whether I was jumping into emotions, or watching a scenario, but I still have no control over where I end up."

"You have always had that ability, too, Lark," said Pru. "Look in your backpack."

Lark took his backpack off. He reached in, and the first thing he felt was his headlamp. Next, he pulled out his nerf gun. He pulled out a half-full bottle of grape soda. He pulled out two Zotz candies and instinctively offered one to Pru, as he had wanted to do earlier, and she enthusiastically took it and popped it into her mouth with a smirk. Lark also pulled out his book—his *Book about Everything.* Holding the backpack's contents, he looked up at June and Pru, confused, once again.

"Just look, look in the book," chimed June.

Lark hesitantly cracked the book open to the table of contents. The first chapter was titled, "How to Return Home from the Outer-Fort World of the Never-Ending Sunset/Sunrise and the Hollow Willow Tree." This was to be found on page three. Lark looked up at Pru and June and eagerly turned the page.

On page three, it read, "Please turn to page 22 and read." So, Lark did just that . . .

SEEING THROUGH THE SNOW

A story about love for dear, little Maisy

Once upon a time,
In a little town near the bay,
Lived a guy and girl
Who got married one day.
They lived in a small house
At the end of a street,
Living a life full of love
And everything sweet.
They shared their home with three dogs,
Digger, Coleman, and Finn,
Three loveable labs.
And so, the story will begin . . .
Now the guy and the girl,
With their dogs, had a full life;
The girl loved her husband,
And he loved his wife.
Their hearts were so full,
This thing they had was so strong,
It burst into four shooting stars, and
Gwynnie, Maisy, Sophie, and Lark came along.
The house overflowed with love,
Each family member unique.
It's impossible to capture it all,
But we'll give you a small peek . . .

Lark was their little boy,
A gentle spirit sent from above;
He was funny and smart,
A kind and wonderful little love.
Sophie was pure joy . . .
With some sass thrown in,
With a mop of blonde hair, big eyes,
And the most contagious grin.
Maisy was sweet and scrappy.
Her smile brightened the room.
She was only a few months old,
But her personality was already in full bloom.
Gwynnie was her twin.
She was pudgy and sweet;
Gwynnie was always happy,
From her head to her feet.
That was part of the family,
But don't forget their dogs so dear.
They had three loves with fur in their life.
We'll tell you about them here . . .
Digger was a yellow lab,
With endless energy, barks, and chase.
He loved fetching tennis balls,
And he had such a cute face.
Finn was a black lab
With a heart of pure gold.
Finn was all about the love,
A faithful boy that did as he was told.
Coleman was the color of rich caramel.
He brought the family so much joy.
The family nicknamed him "Nana"
As he watched over the girls and the boy.
The house was filled with laughter
And smiles and much fun,

With the light of their pets
And their daughters and son.
Life was often pretty busy.
Sometimes they forgot to slow down.
They were busy with the hustle and bustle
When the snow began to fall on their town.
Now, when the snow started to fall,
There was a change in the air;
Challenges lay ahead,
And only God knew how they'd fare.
The babies fell ill,
And after many a sleepless night,
Little Maisy was hospitalized;
What lay ahead was quite a fight.
In the snow-covered streets,
In an ambulance they rode,
North to the PICU in Baltimore,
"To be on the safe side," they were told.
But she had more and more trouble,
And all were riddled with fear.
They wanted her home;
They all wanted her near.
Her little twin was also sick,
Although she didn't have to go.
Gwynnie was home in their crib.
All were surrounded by snow.
There are no real words to describe it,
Although one may have tried.
They all felt so helpless
As they hoped, prayed, and cried.
In the hospital, a minute could last a lifetime,
Yet the days all seemed to blur into one;
Time is all relative
When things unravel toward undone.

Idioms such as "a heavy heart"
Came to mean something real;
"Hanging on by a thread"
Was how they truly did feel.
They almost lost their little Maisy:
The doctors couldn't figure it out.
There were many scary episodes.
Everyone's faces showing their doubt.
But in the quiet still, if one could find it,
Amongst the beeps of the machines and the cries,
Her parents could feel it
If they just closed their eyes . . .
Keeping watch over their baby,
Angels dancing above her head;
The prayers from many being answered
As Maisy quietly lay in her bed.
The support from endless people,
All helping in their own way,
With their prayers, hopes, and wishes,
The family humbled by such love each day.
But Maisy was still so sick.
As the snow continued to fall,
The hospital seemed bleak
As heaven continued to call . . .
God was calling an angel home:
He needed another soul.
It was time to leave this earth . . .
Yet, it was another who took on that role . . .
It was with a gallant wag of his tail,
When God called out for this need,
That their beloved Coleman said "I'll go.
Maisy, you stay. I want to do you this deed."
And with that their sweet, sweet Coleman,
With a heart as big as his head,

Lay his body down to rest,
His body never again leaving that bed.
But his soul, oh, his soul, it was so true and so bright
That poor baby Maisy
Finally started seeing the light.
For there was another angel now in heaven,
And he had an important task to do.
His darling little baby Maisy
Was going to get life anew.
The family missed Coleman terribly.
Many tears were shed remembering their lab love,
But with a wagging tail and angel wings,
Coleman watched over Maisy from above.
The snow started to melt.
The ice began to disappear.
Maisy finally smiled again . . .
She would stay with them here.
The family learned so much from that time:
They learned the depth of true love;
They learned about miracles;
They learned of the power from up above.
They learned of the magic of support from others;
They learned about giving and receiving in life;
They learned that life has many uncertainties;
They learned a lot—that husband and wife.
They know that as you read this story,
There are hospitals filled with both the old and the young.
Perhaps this family had to go through this pain
To truly hear the song of life being sung.
For they will now take in the moments;
They will hold all they love extra tight;
They now know what is important;
And they will always keep this in sight.
They also know that angels surround them.
They find peace, knowing Coleman is near.

They will all live life to the fullest
And hold life's blessings—oh, so dear.

Lark, read this story to your sisters when you get home. You will still find it here on page 22.

Now please turn to page 42.

As if it was one of those old Choose Your Own Adventure books of Mommy's that Lark liked to read, Lark quickly flipped pages in a frenzy until he found page 42.

A story about love for our dear, little Lark.

"Lark is a piece of art. He is a unique blend of colors—vibrant colors of curiosity, wit, and exuberance. He finds joy in life's simple twists of fate as he paints his soul with each new experience, determined to find the beauty within each new day. He is a wonderful combination of both realist and dreamer, with a good head on his shoulders, but he is not afraid to, at times, cross his fingers and take a leap of faith into adventure and the unknown. Lark has a motto: choose adventure. No matter what you do, choose adventure. Oh, that and be kind, of course. Yes, choose adventure and be kind. Those are two of the most important things Lark learned on his amazing adventures. He will simply never be the same.

"Experiences can catapult time into lightening-speed, or they can bring it to a screeching halt, depending on the nature of the moment. Time is relative. That was a big concept for little Lark at first. When something feels bad or scary, a split second of time can feel like it lasts forever. On that same note, the fun moments can fly by so quickly if we aren't careful, slipping through our fingers as we desperately try and grasp at them to hold on. Other times, we are almost oblivious to these wonderful, fleeting moments until they are over, until they fleet. Then we have to try and pull in the moments after the fact, the details all fuzzy and tangled, the feelings being something familiar, but faded.

"No, it is much better to recognize them as they are happening. We shouldn't try and cling on in desperation, but if we can take a moment to recognize them for what they are, with a little luck we can catch one—or, if we are really lucky, they will catch us. Then we can soak them in and hold them close and truly feel them. It is like chasing a butterfly. A butterfly will almost always elude you if you are chasing after it, but sometimes, if you sit quietly, it may find you and rest gently upon you. That is how those happy moments are best captured. We need to let them happen and, most importantly, recognize they are happening.

"We need to be a witness to the miracle of that happy moment and give it the awe it deserves. This allows us to live our life to the fullest, embracing every precious moment with strength, grace, and enthusiasm. Lark, you learned how to do that by the time you were ten years old and a day. You are now able to catch the joy of the moment, sprinkling it all around you so one can't help but get soaked by each little drop—a mist of love and life that catches the light and makes up this colorful spectrum that constantly surrounds you. These swirling colors that you so graciously share with all that know you.

"Happy moments happen every day. It isn't just tenth birthdays and winning championship games and weddings and births and summiting mountains. It is pausing to recognize the hope in a sliver of blue sky with splintered sunlight, trying to shine an escape after a week of rain and grey. It is that moment when you are in line in the grocery store, and the stranger's baby sitting in the cart in front of you peeks back with his big brown eyes and his unabashed, never-ending gaze, and his face suddenly bursts into a huge gummy smile just for you, unbeknownst to his distracted mom as she piles diapers and baby food onto the conveyer belt. It is knowing the answer in math class. It is when your mom says you can have leftover birthday cake for breakfast the morning after your birthday. It is when your grandson reaches up to hold your hand because you are there and he is there and your hand is there, and it is the natural thing to do, naturally. It is love. It is a moment in time, and it warrants recognition. Soak them in and hold on. Hold on to as many as you can. You won't run out of space. Love isn't limited to some finite amount. It doesn't become less, or get divided, when more people come into your life to love; it multiplies, grows.

"On the flip side, there are hard moments. Don't let them stop you in your tracks. Your life may seem a tangential tangle at times, but its tangled twists will somehow come together into a purposeful nest of thoughts and ideas and purpose if you handle them with care. Look for the lesson, and if you can find it, you will find that every experience is a gift; glance sideways and within, sweet Lark. The journey *is* the destination.

"Adventure doesn't always seem like a choice. Sometimes adventure seems too daunting, too big, or too unknown. Some things are not in our control, some things are scary, but there is always a choice. It is okay to be scared. Courage isn't the absence of being scared; it is being scared and forging ahead in spite of it. When you feel so scared, more terrified than you have ever been in your entire life, and you aren't feeling very brave at all, those are your most courageous moments: knees shaking, heart racing, and all. That is exactly the point when you grow closer toward who you are supposed to be, but you need to take it to the edge to do so.

"The choice lies within one's heart, no matter how heavy or how light or how scared it may be. It lies within the attitude we have toward a given experience. The choice lies in choosing to tackle each unknown as an adventure, as a lesson to be learned. There are no wasted experiences if you learn something, even if the lesson is simply that you never, ever, want to do that again. Feel, Lark, simply feel. You haven't always known the importance of feeling and of sharing those feelings, but now you know.

"Lark, you are a piece of art—a masterpiece—and when you are finally able to recognize that, it changes everything."

Now please return to page 3.

Lark quickly flipped back to page three but found that the page was completely different from when he had left page three a couple of minutes earlier. He was so used to craziness at this point, though, that nothing fazed him.

If one wishes to return home from the outer-fort world of the never-ending sunset/sunrise and the hollow willow tree, one will need a rather large loon, a Zotz, a glow-in-the-dark nerf gun, some grape soda, and amazing adventures behind and ahead.

1) Board the back of the Loon, taking care to place oneself in the middle of his/her back, between the wings.

2) Place Zotz inside the grape soda and shake.

3) Have Loon drink the Zotz/Soda combination.

4) Hold on tight as loon propels forward at a great speed.

5) When passing a star that reminds you of a twinkle you have seen before, shoot a glow-in-the-dark nerf dart from the nerf gun at this target.

6) Wait and see what happens.

7) Close the book now and do not read one more word. Now. I mean it, Lark.

Lark closed the book and looked at Pru with colorful tears in his eyes.

"What are you going to do, Pru?" asked Lark, wanting to make the moment last a few seconds longer because goodbyes can be so hard.

"Don't worry, Lark, I will see you again before you know it. Your adventures have just begun, and I will join you for more because—don't ever forget—I am always with you if you look in your heart. Don't forget all your lessons. I'm going to climb up to the top of this ladder and see what is in that light. I have a feeling I may get my own wings, and maybe I can take you flying and floating next time. I also want to meet Coleman and Viwe, and of course, Gran will be up there, separate from June, separate from Gramps. There are others I would like to meet, too. Others that have reached the top before me. I heard they have been waiting for me, but first I had to wait for you. Now I know you, and you know me, so now I can go, but we will meet again. I promise you that."

With that, she blew Lark a kiss, smiled her toothless smile, and climbed up into the bright light. Lark tried to watch her go, but it was too bright, and his blue eyes couldn't look toward it any longer. So instead, Lark looked sideways. He looked over at June the Loon.

"Why a loon named June?" Lark inquired with a sly, crooked smile.

"Why not, Lark? why not?" June the Loon replied with a wink and a twinkle in his/her eye.

"Why not is right," replied Lark. "I know I'll see you soon, Gramps. But Gran, when will I see you again? I feel like I just found you. Even though we've been together, I didn't know it . . . should I stay longer? May I stay a tiny bit longer?"

"As Pru said, there are more adventures to come. Your whole, beautiful, wonderful life lies ahead, but don't you worry, my dear, I will always be with you. You carry me in your heart, my darling little love."

Lark nodded in a respectful understanding at his grandparents. Lark reflected on the fact that Gramps and Gran were together again, manifested in this crazy loon named June, and mustered up a small smile.

"Yes, we are an absurd bird," June said with a wink as she took in Lark's thoughts. "No need to stay here. You are needed back home, my dear. And don't worry, even though you've been away, you are still only ten years old . . . and a day."

Lark felt the stone in his pocket heating up. With tears in his eyes, Lark let out a deep breath and began following the directions from the book. He was excited and sad and nervous all at once; those mixed feelings Pru had told him about back when he first met her in the outer-fort world of the sunset/sunrise. Those mixed feelings Gramps had talked about when that tear had escaped at Lark's birthday party. Lark thought back to those moments that seemed so long ago and found slight amusement in his new understanding of time and what that actually meant, or didn't mean, and how many moments, thoughts, feelings can coexist in one.

June cleared her throat, and Lark's ADOS mind snapped back from his philosophical journey down memory lane. He looked up at her and couldn't help but laugh. Lark laughed at it all, this adventure in its magnificent ridiculousness and glory.

Lark climbed up on June's back and proceeded to make the Zotz and soda combination. Giving it a bit of a shake, Lark held it up to her waiting beak. Lark wrapped his arms tightly around her neck before she swallowed it with one gulp.

In an instant, they were no longer in the willow as June shot through the sky, her wings tucked back tightly, through the sunset/sunrise. Lark was holding on for dear life, dangling like a kite in the wind from her black, shiny neck.

Suddenly a single twinkling star appeared in the twilight, and everything took on shades of violet except this star with the familiar twinkle. Lark grasped on with his legs around June's neck and let go of one of his hands. He quickly took the nerf gun into his little hands, aimed it at this solitary star, and shot his glow-in-the-dark nerf dart right at it. The dart cast a sparkling trail of stardust behind it that suddenly pulled Lark with it, as if he was attached to a harpoon flying through the sky. He was no longer on June's back, and he knew he was no longer supposed to be.

He didn't close his eyes this time. He looked at the beauty all around him. He soaked it up. He soaked it all up

"Lark, honey."

Mommy was outside of the fort. Confused, he awoke with a drowsy start, exploring his surroundings. Was it happening again? Was he traveling? No. This was different.

"Lark, darling, why don't you get up? It's after midnight. You fell asleep in your fort. Come on, sweetie, I'll help you to bed. You were so tired from your busy day; I didn't have the heart to wake you, but I think you better get in your own bed now. Come, my boy, you are ten years old and a day now."

Had it been a dream? Lark got up drowsily from his fort. He put his hand deep in his pocket to feel the lucky stone. It was smooth and safe but cool to the touch. Mommy smiled down at him as she held his hand.

His hand which still had the faintest shimmer of colors to it, if one knew to look for it.

"Wow. Ten years old and a day. I can't believe it! So grown up. But you know, Lark, quite the adventure still lies ahead," she said with a knowing smile.

Lark looked up at her lovingly. He no longer felt the need to delineate between reality and dreaming. Lark understood that sometimes the line may be blurred, and sometimes that is okay, perhaps even preferable.

"Come, let's get you into bed, and when you wake up, you can have birthday cake for breakfast. How does that sound?"

Lark gave her a tired smile and a big, long hug.

This was a connection that was always there and always would be, no matter where they were. Mommy led Lark down the long hallway. He shuffled past the cracked door of the twins' room as he drowsily made out the images of them, both sleeping soundly in their beds. Lark leaned into his mother for support and for comfort and for a continued connection as they shuffled toward his room. He passed by Bliss's room, then Sophie's, and across the hall, he opened his own cracked door to find Finn curled up, sleeping at the foot of his bed.

"I love you, Lark. Now into bed, sweet boy."

Lark crawled into bed, and Mommy tucked him in as his eyes drowsily closed. Lark was beyond appreciative to finally be in his own bed after what felt like a very long time.

"I love you, too, Mommy."

Lark was happy to be home, happy to be ten years old and a day. He would choose adventure when the opportunity arose, but for now, Lark was happy to be right here in this perfect moment.

"Oh, and thanks, Mommy. Birthday cake for breakfast sounds great."

Acknowledgements

I'D LIKE TO EXPRESS DEEP GRATITUDE FOR THE STAFF AT WiDo Publishing for taking a look at this manuscript and accepting it and supporting it along the way. With me being new to the publishing world, I'm sure it was no small task guiding me through this process, so thank you for helping my story take form. Thank you especially to my editor, MaryAnne Hafen, for accompanying me on the long road to get here. I really appreciate all your help and advice and input. In addition, I would like to thank Karen Gowen at WiDo for helping me through to the end. Your kindness, guidance, and patience have been invaluable.

My mom has always believed in me and who I am and what I can do, and that is a blessing for which I am eternally grateful. Thanks, Mom, for your support in all of this, and everything really, in every way. I couldn't have done this without you. Thank you, Dad, for your support in helping me become the person I am today. It was my parents who first taught me about love. Thank you for that gift, as that is the essence that guides it all. As a result, in addition to my parents, I also have the most amazing family and friends. As not to run on too long, here is a big blanket "thank you" to you all, especially my siblings, Aunt Tommy, Randy Champagne (aka RMC girls), all of my Annapolis tribe and my sweet pup McNasby (even though she can't read this). Thank you also to my special angels up above.

Last and not least, my dearest Kelby, for all of your patience and support on this journey, I will simply say thank you and I love you—madly and forever. Thank you to my children for the gift of the ever so magical adventure of parenthood, and to each of you, thank you for just being you. I love you with all of my heart Kelby, Grady, Tilly Bloom, Eliza, Magnolia, and Waverly. You have taught me what really matters. You have shown me the magic of the moment, both the big and the small, and how they equally deserve our wonder and awe. Thank you for your unconditional love and light.

About the Author

RHIANNON GELSTON HAS ALWAYS LOVED LITERATURE and the wonderful places one may explore through reading. She has a BA in English and also earned a MS in occupational therapy with a pediatric focus. Her graduate degree took her over to Cape Town, South Africa where she spent several months completing her studies and traveling around Africa. Upon returning, she started her career in occupation therapy and shortly after met her husband, Kelby.

She likes to lose herself in all things creative and enjoys writing, painting, live music, traveling, sports, being outdoors, exploring, playing, spirituality, and energy work.

Rhiannon lives in Annapolis, Maryland, with her husband, their five lovely and lively children, and their black lab, McNasby. They enjoy time with family and friends in, on, and around the Chesapeake Bay.

CPSIA information can be obtained
at www.ICGtesting.com
Printed in the USA
BVHW071504251120
594058BV00001B/38